*That you may proclaim the wonders of him
who called you out of darkness into his marvelous light*
1 Peter 2:9

The Disciple's Wife

The Disciple's Wife

Chapter 1

Sarah's husband slumped over his fishing net, mending holes in something made of holes. From across the beach, she watched the sunlight dance through his hair but knew it did little to brighten his world. Around him, men of all ages scrubbed the hulls of boats and stretched nets on rocks, finishing one day's work in preparation for another. Laughter and teasing filled the air, along with the familiar reassurance that tomorrow's catch would be better.

Simon once laughed and teased like the younger men, before the weight and worry of family wore him down. At least they had a house, even if it wasn't as nice as what the neighbors had. And they ate well-enough, as her roundness attested, but she had expected more. Exactly what, she didn't know. But more.

An unfamiliar man walked along the shore road, and the casualness of his step caught her eye. No hint of weariness, no sense of urgency. He didn't look out at the water in search of peace as she so often did. Instead he looked at every man he passed and greeted each with a smile and words she couldn't hear. Although no one smiled back or did more than nod in his direction, he didn't seem hurt or offended but passed by with a quiet confidence.

The sea wind blew his hair across his forehead as he turned toward the beach. Simon's brother waved to him and said something to Simon, who didn't look up from his net even as Andrew left their boat and walked over to the man. They stood in the bright sunlight, talking a few moments, Andrew becoming more animated while the stranger seemed to grow quieter.

Sarah studied the man, trying to imagine where he'd come from, what business he could possibly have in Capernaum.

The stranger listened as Andrew chatted but looked beyond him to Simon. After a few minutes, he walked over to where her husband sat. Still Simon didn't look up, intent on finishing his work, letting his schedule dictate his existence as if sticking to a routine gave him some kind of control over life.

The man stood beside him in silence for several minutes before Simon finally gave up and glanced at him. Moments later, he set down his net and walked with Andrew and the man toward Zebedee's sons.

The older of her neighbor's two boys, James, ignored them and kept working, hammering a nail into a loose plank, but John jumped off the boat and ran to the man, greeting him as if he were his best friend.

How could he know someone so well when she'd never seen him before?

They talked a few minutes, then walked back across the sand to where his brother worked. Sarah understood the wariness in James' face as he looked up from the nail, brushed short ebony curls out of his eyes, and watched them approach.

John's eagerness didn't surprise her. With the zeal of youth, he embraced friendships readily, but not James. Always guarded in his relationships, he seldom let anyone into his life. Despite his good looks, it was no wonder he wasn't married.

The stranger said something to James, and she waited for his response. Would he explode and tell them all to leave him alone so he could get back to his work, or would he just ignore him? To her surprise, he straightened up, dropped his hammer, and followed John and the man, Simon and Andrew down the beach, away from their boats, their nets, and her house. The small group disappeared around a bend along the shore, abandoning everything to the waves.

Next door, Zebedee's wife, Salome, stepped out of her courtyard and stood in the dust, watching them leave, her wiry gray hair struggling to stay contained within her headdress, her thick frame planted firm and steady in the sand. "Where are they off to?"

"I don't know," Sarah said. "Simon didn't say anything to me."

"That man's trouble."

"Why do you say that?"

"John's been talking about him non-stop for the last two days. And I heard from some women at the market that he caused a real commotion at the synagogue in Nazareth."

"What happened?"

Salome leveled her gaze squarely at Sarah. "He read from Isaiah, the part about *the Spirit of the Lord is upon me.*"

Sarah looked at her with no reaction.

"You know, *God anointed me to preach good news to the poor, release the captives, give sight to the blind, free the oppressed.*"

Still getting no response, she said, "You don't know it? Don't you listen when the men are talking?"

"I know the Prophets, Salome, I just don't understand why that would cause trouble in Nazareth."

"Because after he read it, he handed off the scroll and proclaimed that the prophecy had been fulfilled."

"Fulfilled how?" Sarah said.

"By him. He said it was fulfilled right then and there. He was the fulfillment."

"What did they do?"

"They ran him out of town, that's what they did. They wanted to throw him off a cliff, but he managed to get away. And now, he shows up here."

3

Sarah looked again at the twist of shoreline where she had last seen her husband, and an uneasy fear stirred within her heart.

***

After cleaning the last remnants of dinner from the heavy clay pot, Sarah set it on the hearth. Shadows from a lantern flickered around the room, illuminating the worn wooden stools and tables and the hewn stone openings that served as windows.

She lit a torch, then carried it out into the dusky courtyard. The soft glow seemed to shut out the rest of the world, leaving her in a place where the only things that existed were the things she could see. The smallness of that world felt manageable and safe.

This was usually her favorite time of day. She and Simon would often slip down to the shore and sit together, watching the water reach across and drag the sands back to its depths. But this evening, Simon was nowhere to be found. The last she'd seen of him was midday, when he'd gone off with that man.

She looked down the road in search of any silhouette that might be her husband. Seeing nothing, she left the courtyard, went alone to the beach, stuck the torch into the sand, and sat.

The last blush of dusk's reflection rippled on the sea as the air calmed with the sounds of night. Distant conversations disappeared behind neighbors' closing doors, replaced by the soothing song of crickets.

Approaching footsteps caught her ear. She peered into the grayness to see Simon making his way toward her and wrestled with whether she should be angry or relieved.

She opted for apathetic.

"You're back," she said, turning her attention out again to the water.

"I am indeed."

"Where did you go?"

"With a friend of Andrew's, a man named Jesus."

"How does he know him?" she asked. Newcomers were rare in Capernaum. Most just passed through on their way to somewhere else.

"John the Baptist."

Sarah bristled at the name. Andrew and John spent as much time as they could with the man. Andrew tried to tell her about him, but what little she listened to seemed bizarre. She'd told Simon he needed to talk to his brother, steer him away from the Baptist and his followers, but Simon had insisted Andrew needed to search. He was hungry for truth, looking for purpose, for meaning. If he didn't search when he was young, when would he get the chance? Her husband's words had drifted off into what seemed like sorrow. Maybe even regret.

"They said the Baptist was in awe of the guy," Simon said, as he dropped onto the sand beside her. "Called him the Lamb of God."

She turned from watching the waves lap at the shore. "You don't think that's a little odd?"

"Well, the Baptist is a bit odd anyway, Sarah, but he's the last person I know who would hold up another person as some kind of prophet or something."

"You're saying this guy's a prophet?"

"I'm not saying anything."

"Then, why did you disappear with him all day?"

"We were talking, and the next thing I knew, we started walking."

"To where?"

"Just up into the mountains where we talked. Well, he talked. We listened."

Sarah looked back out at the darkening waters. "What did he talk about?"

5

"Mostly the law. But everything he said seemed to shed new light on it, bring it alive, give it meaning." As her husband's voice rose with enthusiasm, the fear that had clutched at Sarah's heart earlier in the day tightened its grip.

"Salome says they ran him out of Nazareth, you know," she said quietly.

"I heard. And I can imagine why. He's radical." Simon grew still a moment, then said, "But radical isn't necessarily wrong. I didn't hear anything that would make me run him out of town. Everything I heard him say makes me want to know him better."

The last hint of dusk vanished, and darkness enveloped them as a chill blew in off the sea.

Chapter 2

The sun hadn't yet risen over the horizon. Sarah nudged Simon awake, then began her day. The water she'd splashed on her face had done nothing to invigorate her. Groggy, she stepped out into the cool courtyard, poured wheat into the stone mortar, and began to grind the grains for her family's daily bread. As she worked, the sea air mingled with the earthy aroma of the freshly ground grain, and she relaxed in the fragrance of a new day. The light of her lantern flickered, no more than a spark in the vast darkness that enveloped her, a darkness so still even the waves rippled to the sand in silence.

Simon stepped out and stood by the courtyard wall, eating some of yesterday's bread. He gazed at the fading stars until only the morning star remained, then pulled some dried figs out of his sack, kissed Sarah, and headed off to his boat. A few minutes later, his brother hurried out of the house across the courtyard to join him, smiling in quiet greeting to Sarah.

The softest touch of dawn lit the sky as she watched the shadowy figures of other men leave their homes and walk across the road toward the shore. Even in the dim light, she could see her husband struggle under the weight of the nets he tossed into his boat. He wearily climbed in, a sharp contrast to the vigor of Andrew, who shoved the boat into the water and jumped on board.

As a rooster crowed, the goats bleated their reminder that it was milking time. A step-drag sound behind her warned that her mother was approaching, and she knew the day had begun.

"He's getting old," Leilah said.

"Simon's not old, Mother. He and Andrew catch as much fish as any man out there, you know that. He works hard to give you a good life."

"He does what he can, I guess."

"I'm going into town later," Sarah said, changing the subject. "We're low on barley. Do you want to come?"

Leilah sat on the bench beside the courtyard wall, vines hanging low above her head. "No, you go. Don't worry about me. I'll stay here with the children."

Sarah took in the gray pallor of her mother's sun-aged face and the stoop in her thin frame. "You don't want to get out a little?"

"Why, Sarah?" her mother said. "I've been in town thousands of times. Same people, same shops. Nothing new. It's just another day."

***

The marketplace hummed with commerce. Women bargained with fruit vendors, and merchants dangled enticing wares in front of those who passed. Sarah filled her basket with fruit, beans, and barley, then stopped to admire the stitching on a pair of sandals at a nearby booth.

She wanted to ask the man how soon he could make a pair for Simon but couldn't attract his attention. He leaned on a shelf at the back of the booth, engrossed in conversation with a man she recognized as one of James' friends, a slightly younger, slightly shorter, slightly stouter man named Philip. Outgoing, exuberant, he couldn't be more different from James in temperament.

She shuffled a little to the side, hoping to catch the merchant's eye, to no avail. Then she coughed, still without result.

Sighing, she started to walk away when she noticed Jesus coming down the road toward her. His stride was that of a man with a purpose, and Sarah froze, wondering why he would have any reason to approach her.

Before she could turn away, he walked past her, slowed his pace, and looked steadily at Philip, who glanced his way with no interest or recognition.

Then Jesus said, "Follow me."

Without hesitation, without a word to the sandal seller, Philip fell into step beside Jesus and followed him through the market. Sarah looked around. No one else seemed to notice or think anything odd had just happened. Even the sandal maker started tooling a piece of leather as if Philip's sudden, rude departure were perfectly normal.

She forgot about Simon's sandals and hurried to keep pace with the two as they made their way past bartering men and women. Children nearly tripped her as they shot out from behind booths and ran across the road.

Just as she caught up to them, Philip disappeared into a shop. Sarah turned to a stall filled with dyed rugs and pretended to care which better suited her. Out of the corner of her eye, she watched Jesus.

Even though he stood surrounded by wares, he didn't seem to notice anything anyone sold. He seemed only to notice the sellers and the buyers as he watched people busily trying to fill all their needs.

A few minutes later, Philip reappeared at the door. A man still inside said, "Can anything good come out of Nazareth."

Sarah glanced at Jesus and saw a smile cross his face.

She recognized the voice. Nathaniel, a kind man, a prayerful man. One of the few people Simon trusted without question. His name seemed to come up every Sabbath when Simon shared the synagogue discussions with her.

"Come and see," Philip said, as he walked out to the road, excitement dancing in his words.

Nathaniel stepped into the sunlight, his red hair tucked behind one ear, doubt darkening his eyes.

Jesus greeted him. "Behold, an Israelite indeed. An honest, straightforward man."

Nathaniel stepped back into the doorway and stood, his arms folded across his chest, his only available barricade in the moment. He looked to Philip as if unsure whether to stay or go back into the shop.

Then he glanced sideways at Jesus. "You don't know me," he said, "You don't know anything about me." And he turned to go inside.

"Before Philip ever went to get you," Jesus said, "when you were under the fig tree, I saw you."

Nathaniel stopped. He looked over his shoulder at Jesus, then slowly turned to face him. "Rabbi, you truly are the son of God. The king of Israel."

Sarah stared at Nathaniel in disbelief. Son of God? King of Israel? What brought that on?

Jesus smiled and said, "You believe this just because I said I saw you under the fig tree?" He moved closer to Nathaniel. "You will see far greater things than that. Truly, truly I tell you, you will see heaven opened up, and the angels of God ascending and descending upon the Son of Man."

He put an arm around Nathaniel's shoulders, and the three men walked off, leaving Sarah alone in the middle of the crowded marketplace, sorting out words that made no sense.

A child bumped into her, knocking the bag of barley out of her basket. She stooped to pick it up, then headed back to her house.

As she rounded the bend, she saw Simon slip his fishing knife into the leather scabbard that always hung at his waist. He tossed a net over a rock and walked across the stone-strewn beach, his shoulders stooped, his gaze locked on the ground as if measuring the steps he needed to get home.

She rushed to her husband's side. "You'll never believe what happened today."

"What?"

10

"I saw that Jesus in town."

The weariness left his face as he gave her his full attention.

"You know Philip and Nathaniel?" she said.

Simon nodded and took the heavy basket from her arms.

"Well, first, I saw Jesus walking down the road. Then he noticed Philip, and said, 'Follow me,' and Philip just walked away from what he was doing and followed him."

She waited for a response. Getting none, she said, "Then Philip went into Nathaniel's shop and brought him out to meet Jesus. Jesus took one look at him, and said, 'You're an honest, straightforward man' like he's known him his whole life."

She paused and waited again for a reaction.

"So, what did Nathaniel say?" Simon asked.

"He wasn't impressed, believe me. He looked like he wanted to get as far away from Jesus as he could. But Philip's standing there, smiling and nodding. So, Nathaniel said, 'You don't even know me.' And Jesus said something about seeing him under a fig tree."

Simon stopped walking.

"I know, strange, right?" Sarah said. "I can't imagine what he was talking about, and, by the way, I saw some sandals I think you'll like. Anyway, Nathaniel spun around like he's shocked or something, and said to Jesus, 'You are the son of God and the king of Israel.' Can you believe it? I mean, king of Israel is bizarre enough and not the kind of thing you want to shout out in the middle of the marketplace, but son of God? Not a son of God, but the son of God. And he said it with this kind of awe in his voice, like he meant it. I thought you said Nathaniel was a good, faithful man."

"He is," Simon said, looking down the road toward home, and not at her.

"Well, explain that, then."

"What can I say, Sarah?" He hesitated while she waited for more of a response. "Nathaniel once told me that he had some

11

kind of experience of God years ago, when he was sitting under a fig tree, praying."

"What kind of experience?"

"I don't know. You don't ask somebody something personal like that. But it was powerful enough that I could tell it still resonated with him."

"So someone must have told Jesus that," Sarah said.

"I had the feeling Nathaniel didn't run around sharing it with everyone."

"Maybe it was just a lucky guess then, but even so, why would Nathaniel call him the son of God? Why would he call anyone that?"

Simon looked steadily into his wife's eyes. She could tell he was weighing his words and whether she was the one to share them with.

"Andrew told me the Baptist said when he baptized Jesus, a dove came out of the sky and rested on his shoulder."

"So? We've got birds flying around all over the place."

"That's not all," Simon said. "Then the Baptist heard a voice say, 'This is my beloved son.'"

"A voice?"

"A voice."

"Who's voice?"

Her husband took a deep breath, then said, "God's."

Sarah threw her hands up in the air. "Well, of, course. God's voice. Come on, Simon, you don't believe that nonsense, do you?"

Simon looked off to the sea. Then he resumed walking down the road, leaving Sarah and her unanswered question behind.

Chapter 3

A screech shot through the courtyard, and Sarah looked out the window in time to see her son, Micah, chase Abigail with a lizard. Little Hannah drew in the dust with a stick, alone in her own world, ignoring the commotion around her.

Inside, a plate clattered as Leilah dropped it onto the table.

"I can do that, if you're still not feeling well, Mother," Sarah said.

"I'm fine. Don't worry about me."

Sarah watched the trembling hands move the cups into place. "Maybe you should stay home today."

"And miss the wedding? Not on your life. I'm not that old. I can make it the short distance into Cana."

Simon walked into the room with a smile so relaxed, he looked like a boy. "Big day today."

"You're not a fan of weddings," Sarah said.

"Depends on the crowd."

"You sure weren't looking forward to this one."

"That's before I found out Jesus will be there."

Her anticipation of a pleasant family outing evaporated at the mention of the name, a name that seemed to be in the midst of every sentence Simon uttered lately. When he'd been home. When he wasn't sitting on a rock at the shore listening to the man talk or wandering off with him for hours on end.

"You're kidding, Simon. I'd hoped we could just enjoy the day together."

"I'd rather spend some time with him."

The response stunned her. Simon walked out the door without even noticing.

Maybe it was time to get to know this man herself.

13

***

Music, laughter, and the scent of honeysuckle filled the air as the bride and groom made their way through the gathering, greeting everyone and looking with love into one another's eyes. Sarah remembered her own wedding and the promise the day had held. Then she looked across to Simon walking through the crowd toward where she stood, bringing with him the man he couldn't stop talking about, the man suddenly more important to her husband than she was.

"Sarah, this is Jesus."

She glanced grudgingly into deep eyes that gazed at her with intent, an unsettling look that seemed to see into her very heart.

Before she could acknowledge him, a petite older woman with soft features reminiscent of his calmly took his arm, and said, "Jesus, they've run out of wine."

Sarah looked at the woman, stunned. Run out of wine? How could anyone run out of wine at a wedding? What kind of planning had they done? If they couldn't afford something so lavish, they should have made it a smaller event. Half of these people didn't need to be here anyway.

Jesus looked into the woman's gentle face, and said, "How does that concern me?"

That's right, Sarah thought, studying the woman's peaceful, confident demeanor. What was he supposed to do about it, run down to the marketplace or magically manifest wine out of thin air?

When the woman didn't answer, he said to her, "My hour hasn't yet come."

Sarah turned from studying the woman to gaze at Jesus. What a strange thing to say. His hour for what? She looked at Simon, who seemed to think this was a normal conversation.

Then the woman turned to the wine servers, and said, "Do whatever he tells you."

14

Some kind of interior struggle passed over Jesus' face as he seemed to wrestle with a choice. He walked over to the servers and nodded toward the large clay vessels lined up along the wall near the entry to the courtyard. "Fill those jugs with water."

The servers looked confused and glanced at the woman, who nodded quietly to them. "Do whatever he tells you."

In a sort of relay, they drew water from the nearby well, then passed the bucket along from server to server, until the last one poured it into a vessel. Jesus stood by, gazing into each jar as it filled. Sarah watched, knowing everyone was going to be furious when these servers started pouring ladles of water into their cups. Putting it in these vessels wasn't going to make it taste any better.

It really was a shame. The day had gone so well until now. But this is the kind of thing people never forget. At every wedding for decades to come, this is the story everyone will share with laughter and derision. She looked at the couple standing in the midst of a crowd, chatting and smiling, oblivious to the disaster taking place at that very moment.

When the jugs were nearly filled, Sarah glanced across the room to see the steward shove people aside as he made his way over to them.

Jesus saw the harried man approach and told the servers, "Take some to him."

As he drew nearer, the steward said, "Why aren't you serving the wine? Everyone's cup is empty. They're all waiting. Is something wrong with it?"

He yanked the dipper from the server's hand. After tasting it, he looked with surprise at the servers, then turned to the crowd and called the bridegroom over to him.

"What's going on here?" he said to the puzzled-looking young man. "People always serve the good wine first, then, after everyone's had so much to drink they don't care what they get, they serve the lesser wine. But not you. You've kept the good wine for last."

One of the servers dipped into a nearby vessel and started to pour something into her cup, but Sarah stopped him. "I don't want water."

He raised his eyebrows, expressing the incredulity she would soon feel, and proceeded to pour sparkling deep red wine into her cup. She sipped it, and a pungent velvet fruitiness warmed her throat and flowed like soothing fire through her entire being.

A murmur rose up from the guests as word got out about the wine. Sarah listened as her mother engaged in excited conversation with the women around them.

"He's my son-in-law's best friend, you know. I've only just met him this morning, but he's so nice and friendly, and," she added with a sidewise glance, " he's single, too."

Chapter 4

A sweltering breeze blew in through the window and hung heavy in the room. Leilah lay on her cushion, unable to stand.

Sarah dabbed at her mother's forehead with a damp cloth, and said, "Have some broth. Just a little."

Her mother weakly waved her hand. "I just want to sleep. The wedding seems to have taken it out of me."

"But you have to eat something. You haven't had a bite since yesterday."

"Not now. Please, just let me sleep."

Frustration rose up in Sarah. She left and walked into the main room just in time to see Simon and Micah heading out.

"You're going back to the synagogue?" she said.

"Jesus is teaching this afternoon," Simon said.

"Jesus? You just saw him yesterday. Can't you stay home for a little while. The past few days it seems like you're never here. You barely stay around long enough to catch a few fish. We've got children to take care of, Simon, and things that need done around here. And sometimes I'd appreciate just a little company."

She could see the attack surprised her husband, but she'd been quiet long enough, thinking he needed to work through some kind of passing fascination with this man, Jesus.

Simon embraced his wife. "I won't be gone long."

"But why go at all?" she said, squirming out of his arms.

"It's the Sabbath."

"You've already gone twice today."

"I know, but I have to go back."

"What do you mean, 'you have to?'"

"It's important. He's… he's…"

"He's what, Simon? What? What can he possibly be that's more important than everything else in your life?"

Simon looked down at the dirt-packed floor and shrugged. "I don't know how to explain it, Sarah. It's what he says. It's what he does. It's everything about him."

He looked at his wife, and a softness swept through his eyes. "You've really got to spend some time with him, get to know him. I'm telling you, he's not like anyone I've ever met."

"What could be so special about him?" she said, following him into the courtyard, "besides the wine thing, I mean. Sure, that got everyone's attention, and I still can't figure out how he did that, but there's something odd about all this. He wanders into Capernaum from out of nowhere, and you all think he's the best thing to ever happen."

"He didn't come from out of nowhere. He's from Nazareth, Sarah."

"Oh, well, that explains it," she said. "Who wouldn't want to spend hour upon hour with some stranger from Nazareth?"

"I can't really put my finger on it," Simon said, ignoring her sarcasm, "but he's different. Everything about him is different. He's got this peacefulness, this clear sense of the law, this kindness, this readiness to reach out that's not like anything else I've ever seen. His perspective on everything is just different." He glanced at the group of men approaching the house. "I've got to go now, but I'll bring him back for dinner tonight."

Before Sarah could protest, he was gone, and she was left alone with a mother sick in bed, two daughters to keep quiet, and the prospect of a guest for dinner.

***

18

Sarah heard them before she saw them, Simon and Andrew, James and John, along with Philip, Nathaniel, and a small group of other men, all excitedly shouting for her.

As they walked in, she noticed Jesus behind them, but before she could welcome anyone, Andrew said, "Sarah, you should have seen it today. With just a couple of words, Jesus sent a demon screaming out of a man."

"It really was amazing," Simon said, as they crowded into the room around her.

Jesus stood by Simon's side, looking at her with a quiet smile that left her unsettled.

"And the teaching this guy did," Simon added, slapping Jesus on the shoulder. "I could listen to you forever."

As they all celebrated what they'd seen and heard, Abigail walked into the room with a cup in her hand, and said, "Mom, Grandma doesn't look so good. I asked if she wanted a drink like you told me, and she didn't answer."

Sarah put her hand on Abi's arm to shush her a moment, and said to Jesus, "You drove out a demon on the Sabbath?"

The others looked at her, surprised at the question, surprised at what they knew was the answer, and surprised they hadn't thought anything of it.

Before Jesus could answer, Andrew said, "But healing is God's work. Is it wrong to do God's work on the Sabbath?"

"It's wrong to do any work on the Sabbath," Sarah said, as Abigail pulled on her arm with force. "What is it, Abi?"

"It's Grandma," she said, "You aren't listening to me. Something's wrong with her."

Simon took his daughter by the hand. "Come on, Abi. Let's go check on her."

They disappeared into the small room, and moments later, Simon came out again. "She's burning up with fever and not responding to anything. Get some wet cloths, quick."

Sarah's heart sank into her stomach, and her thoughts jammed into incoherence, leaving her unable to move even one step forward.

Andrew grabbed Jesus by the arm and went with Simon into the small, dimly lit room. The others followed, and Sarah entered just in time to see Jesus take her mother's limp hand into his own. She stopped at the sight of her mother drenched with sweat, so pale it looked as though her blood had ceased to flow.

Holding Leilah's hand, he brushed her damp hair gently to the side and caressed her cheek in the hushed room.

After a few moments, her eyes opened wide, her cheeks rosy. She smiled into the face of the man looking down at her. "You're that guy from the wedding."

He smiled back and helped her up, as she said, "I hope you brought us some of that wine."

She smoothed her garment, slipped on some sandals, glanced out the window, and said, "Sun's down, and I'm hungry. Sarah, let's get these men some dinner."

Sarah stood in the bedroom doorway and watched Leilah in amazement. Her mother rushed around the kitchen, setting out the food while Abi and Hannah helped get the table ready.

Simon came up beside Sarah and wrapped his arm around her waist. "That's what it's like with him everywhere he goes. I've never seen anything like it." He kissed her on the cheek and joined the rest of the men, who lounged around the table, eating grapes and talking.

Sarah tried to help Leilah, but she couldn't keep her mind on her work. Images of her mother kept flashing through her thoughts, lying there looking sicker than anyone she'd ever seen, and then, moments later, smiling and standing, joking and teasing. She didn't know what was harder to process, her mother's sudden recovery or her almost joyful manner. She looked at the woman who always walked in a dark cloud of judgment and cynicism, and wondered at the lightness of her step, even in her limp, and the almost youthful glee that lit her face.

As Sarah set the last of the food on the table, she saw lights on the road outside their door, torch lights accompanied by a rising wave of voices. As they drew closer, it became clear their intended destination was her home.

Had word gotten out? Did they know about the demon? The Sabbath? Were they going to run him out of town like they did in Nazareth? Or were they just going to burn down her house and be done with it?

She pulled her children to her side and watched as the mob came to the door. People from all over the town extinguished their torches and walked into the house, not even pausing at the threshold for an invitation.

Eli, the innkeeper, led the way as he carried his pallid, almost lifeless wife past Sarah without a word of acknowledgement and went to Jesus. "Please do something. She's growing weaker every day, and I'm afraid I'm going to lose her."

Jesus touched his arm comfortingly, then touched the woman's forehead, and instantly, the woman reached up to take his hand into her own. She grasped it, stood, and embraced him, as her husband wept with joy.

Others filed in behind them, begging Jesus to help their son, their brother, their father, their aunt, to please, please help them see again, hear again, walk again, to free them from whatever it was that possessed them. When they could no longer squeeze into the small house, they reached through the windows and called out from the street.

The crowd pushed Sarah against the wall. She peered over their shoulders and watched the scene unfolding before her, and as he appeared to heal every one of them, she wondered, who was this man?

***

21

The next morning, Sarah arose before dawn. The crowds had left late in the night, each finally returning to his own home, and everyone at her house was still asleep. The mat she had given Jesus lay on the floor, empty. She glanced through the window and saw him in the distance, walking toward the hills, barely visible in the fading starlight. Despite her concerns, her heart stirred at the loneliness in the figure walking through the shadows of a quiet, dreaming world. She watched until the sound of others awakening jarred her back into action.

As the sun began to brighten the rooms, the house came alive with voices and footsteps and the aroma of food. Simon walked into the main room with Andrew and looked around.

"Where's Jesus?" he asked Sarah.

"He left a little while ago and went off toward the hills."

A few minutes later, James and John came into the house.

"Where's Jesus?" John asked.

"Sarah said he left," Simon answered.

"Left? Where'd he go?" John's voice rose with a hint of panic.

"Into the hills. Have something to eat. Then we'll go look for him."

There was a knock at the door, and Micah rushed to open it.

A woman stood at the threshold, a limp child in her arms. "I need to see Jesus."

Sarah looked beyond the woman and saw others making their way to the house.

"You've got to go find him," she said to Simon as she reached around Micah and shut the door in the woman's face. "We can't have all these people in the house again, especially if he's not here. Who knows what they'll do if they can't find him."

As the four men left, they had to squeeze past the gathering crowd, who tried to shove their way into the house.

"He's not here," Simon announced.

Voices out-shouted each other. "Where is he?"

Sarah watched the crowd turn and follow her husband away from her house, out of the village, and into the hills in search of Jesus.

Leilah hobbled over beside her. "I've never seen anything like this in all my years."

"What are you talking about, Mother?" Sarah said. "Charlatans like him come and go every day around here."

"He's different, Sarah."

"He's just better at it than most, that's all. People fall for this stuff all the time, thinking they're healed, seeing miracles because they want to see miracles."

"What about me?" Leilah said.

"Mother, you took a nap. He just woke you up. He didn't heal you. The nap did."

She gazed out at her husband leading the crowd in their search. "But I can't figure out Simon. He has no tolerance for anyone like him. None. You know that." She turned from the window and began picking up the room. "I can only hope he sees the truth about this man soon."

***

The door flew open, and Micah ran in, his face red with excitement. "They're coming back."

Sarah looked past him to see the crowd making their way once again toward her house. She had just cleaned up the last mat and dish, just swept out the dirt dragged in by so many feet the night before. As she searched for something to bar the door, she saw Jesus turn toward the shore. Some in the crowd followed him. Others headed back to their homes while Simon and Andrew broke away and came to the house.

"We're leaving, Sarah," Simon said, as he brushed past her and into their room.

"Leaving? Who's leaving? And where are you going?"

"We're all leaving – me, Andrew, James, John, everyone."

"What?"

"We're going with Jesus."

"Going? Where? What are you talking about? You can't just leave."

"I have to, Sarah," he said, as he tossed some belongings into a satchel. "It'll just be for a few days."

"But what about the children? What about me?"

"You'll be fine. I talked with my father, and he'll be right across the courtyard if you need anything."

"Jonah's always right across the courtyard, but that's not the same as having you here at home with us." Sarah followed her husband around the room as he gathered more items to take. "What's going on with you, Simon? You're the most responsible man I know. You can't just abandon us. This man is turning our whole world upside down."

"I know," he said quietly, avoiding her eyes.

Sarah spun around, trying to keep up with him. "Why would you leave us to follow him? Just because he's worked a few 'miracles?' Every new so-called messiah who pops into town manages to pull off a couple of those. You know that."

"It's a lot more than that," Simon said, as Andrew walked in from the courtyard with a bag under his arm. "Tell her what the Baptist said about him, Andrew."

"Who cares what that nut says?"

"The Baptist isn't as crazy as he seems, Sarah," Andrew said. "John and I have gone down to hear him a lot lately. He talks about Jesus like he's not even worthy to touch the man's sandals. He's so full of awe that he's pretty much stopped preaching himself, saying it's time for him to step back and let the bridegroom take it from here."

"The bridegroom?" Sarah said. "Are you listening to this, Simon? The bridegroom? The Baptist is crazy. The Pharisees have been after him for years, and this is the reason. But still, day after day, the riverbanks are filled with people drinking this stuff in. I can understand John and Andrew. They're young. But you know better, Simon. And you have responsibilities…" Her words trailed off into sadness. She knew he knew he had responsibilities, but he didn't seem to care anymore.

Simon walked around Andrew and led the way to the door.

"I realize it doesn't make any sense, Sarah, and I can't explain it," he said, "but I need to follow him and see where this all goes."

Fresh fear stirred within her at the thought that her husband was falling into some kind of cult, falling so fast and so deep she couldn't even reach him. Simon gave her a quick kiss, then tossed his arm across Andrew's shoulders as they left her and walked out into the dust together to join the crowd gathering at the shore.

Chapter 5

Sarah scraped flour from the nearly empty jar and measured enough for the next day's bread. She could at best stretch it out for two more loaves. After that, she had no idea what she would do. Maybe she could take the boat out and catch a few fish herself and sell them. If she let her long-simmering anger boil, she should have no problem finding the strength to toss a net over the side and pull it back in.

Days had become weeks with no sign of Simon, no word from him at all. Not one single person who had left with Jesus that day had returned. She'd heard talk in the marketplace that they were all wandering from town to town, leaving "miracles" in their wake, attracting more and more people.

She looked out the door and watched his father trying to mend the nets, his aged fingers fumbling to tie knots. He'd returned to the sea after years of letting his sons handle the fishing. Micah hammered a plank on the side of the boat, doing what he could to help his grandfather, but he didn't have much more strength than Jonah. Even the two of them together would never be able to pull in a full net.

What was Simon thinking? Plans consumed her as she weighed every possible means of tracking down her husband to convince him to come home, but she conceded that she likely couldn't compete with miracles.

Whenever the anger abated for a few moments, fear filled her thoughts. Jonah's catches were meager at best. She still had a little to get by on, but she hesitated to spend it. What if Simon never returned? What if the little he'd left her was going to have to last the rest of her life? And how much longer could she tell the children their father would be gone

26

just a short while? How long did he have to be gone before she had to admit to herself that he wasn't coming back?

She never imagined it would end like this.

This kind of thing happened to other families, not hers. She and Simon had a good marriage where everyone knew what they were supposed to do, and they did it. No matter how tired or sick he was, she could always count on Simon to get into that boat and give all his strength to fishing, not coming home until he had enough to take care of his family.

She couldn't remember a single moment when he wasn't either at the synagogue, in the boat, or at home with them. He loved being with his children, arguing the law with Micah, even pulling Abi into their discussions. His deep spirituality and willingness to include her and the girls in their talks always moved Sarah with gratitude that this was the man God had chosen for her.

A chill blew around the edges of the closed shutter behind her, carrying with it distant voices. She opened the shutter and saw people walking down the road toward the house, still too far off for her to make out anyone in the group. Then a familiar laugh floated through the air, momentarily warming her heart. She resisted the urge to rush out to embrace her husband with joy and relief and instead, stood by the flour-dusted table and waited.

Andrew walked in first, talking over his shoulder to some men as Jesus, Simon, John, James, and a crowd of others followed him in.

Simon beamed at his wife and scooped her into his arms, holding her close as he said softly, "It's so good to see you, Sarah."

She wiggled free of his embrace. "You came back."

"We're just picking up supplies. Some food, a few blankets, clean clothes." As he spoke, the men rummaged through her baskets and cabinets, pulling out what little food she had and stuffing it into their satchels.

"What? You can't leave again," she said, nearly shouting even as she tried to keep her composure.

Simon headed into the back room with Sarah following, as he said, "Jesus wants to go to more towns."

"So let him," she said, shutting the door behind them, closing out the group of marauders. It no longer mattered if they stripped her house bare. She needed to free Simon from whatever hold this man had on him. "You have responsibilities here, Simon. Did you even notice your father down by the boat? He's had to go back to fishing, with no one to help him but Micah."

"I noticed, and I'll talk to him. But I'm sure he'll understand."

"Understand? Understand what? Tell me, because I sure don't understand."

"Come with us, Sarah," he said, as he changed into a fresh tunic, "and you'll see."

"Come with you? How can I? Someone has to stay here. We have children, Simon, or have you forgotten?"

"They can join us."

"They'd never last. And Mother can't come. She's better, but she's still in no condition to go walking off to God knows where."

"Then you come. Leave the children with her and join us. Just for a little while," he said, slipping his shawl over his shoulders. "My father's right across the courtyard. He'll help out Leilah, keep an eye on things."

"Do you really think Jonah can handle all this? He was too old for fishing ten years ago."

"He'll be fine. Everyone will be fine." Simon stopped dressing and took her hand in his even as she struggled to break free. "Sometimes you appreciate there are more important things in life."

"More important than what? Your responsibilities? Your children? Me?"

"Come with me, Sarah."

She saw the conviction in her husband's eyes, the zeal tightening its grip on his heart, squeezing her out. And she knew she couldn't fight for him if she wasn't with him, hearing what he heard, seeing what he saw.

"Okay, I'll go, but just for a few days, Simon. Just for a few days."

***

The group that left Capernaum had grown into a mass of hundreds as they made their way through the Galilean countryside, past miles of vineyards, through villages and markets, along the sea and across the deserts. The enormous, suffocating crowd moved Sarah along the road almost without her having to walk. Yet even as they closed in tighter and tighter, a little part of her was grateful for the horde. If it wasn't for the fear of being trampled, she might just fall over and sleep.

Things weren't going as she'd planned. Simon never left Jesus' side, and although she almost ran to keep up with them, more and more people slid in between her and her husband. From time to time, he'd look back and smile at her. Then he'd glance happily at those around her as if he thought she'd become best friends with someone in this dirty, sweaty mob. At night, they all slept on the ground – men, women, children – little separation, no sense of decency, wrapped in their cloaks or blankets, if they'd thought to bring one.

She really didn't get any sleep. Animals might sleep on the ground in the dirt with bugs crawling through the grass. She needed a bed in a house with a door, her bed, in her house, with her door.

She ached to be with her children, fear creeping into her thoughts as she lay in the darkness. Was Micah out sailing alone, thinking he could catch some fish? Was Hannah running around, climbing courtyard walls with the children from town that nobody seemed to watch? And Abi...who was she talking to, sharing her adolescent joys and heartbreaks? Leilah wasn't the most compassionate of souls.

Just about the time she finally did slip into some semblance of sleep, the sun rose, the birds started their cacophony, people began talking and rising and gathering their things, and off she'd go again, along another road, into another town, while Jesus talked on and on and on to those close enough to hear him. She could only hear people asking each other what he was saying.

As they wandered, she knew home was never far away, but each time she thought they were finally headed there, the forward movement would shift, and off they'd go to another town.

She focused on the road ahead, so close to Capernaum that mirages of the familiar village danced on the horizon, but soon Jesus led them yet again in a different direction along the sea.

The chatter of the crowd swelled to a din that overwhelmed the sound of the surf and the call of the birds swooping alongside them in search of crumbs. As he turned up into the hills, some scrambled to catch him. Others plodded with a committed perseverance. Only she seemed hesitant as the surge moved her along the path until the trek abruptly stopped, sending those in back plowing into those in front of them. While Sarah tried to figure out what was going on, everyone else seemed to know, as if they'd received some kind of secret signal.

All around her, men, women, and children scattered across the rocky hillside and found places to sit, with some perched on inclines so steep, she feared a looming human avalanche. Behind them, lilies burst forth from dark crevasses, mingled with the scattered clumps of grass that clung to stone outcroppings too steep even for the most intrepid among them.

As she looked for even a tiny open space, she saw Simon walking toward her. He took her hand, to her embarrassment, and pulled her farther up the hill to the crest where Jesus sat quietly on a rock

"You're holding my hand in public, Simon," she whispered.

"Just to help you up the path."

"But still…" She let the thought drop off into silence before asking, "You don't think it's odd that men and women are sitting together?"

"I guess I didn't think about it," he said. "Everyone's mixed together so much during the journey, it seems to hardly matter anymore."

She stared at her husband. He always obeyed the law. He taught Micah to obey the law. He spent hours every Sabbath after returning from the synagogue discussing with her the vital importance of the law.

They stopped within a few feet of Jesus and sat on the rocky ground. Up close, she noticed the slump in his shoulders, the weariness in his face, and wondered if he was as tired of all this as she. If so, why didn't he just take them home?

He looked out at the hundreds of faces looking up at him. Without turning from the crowd, he spoke so softly that only she, Simon, and the others near him on the hillside could hear, almost as if he were speaking to himself. "Blessed are the poor in spirit." A quiet light lit his eyes and seemed to bring a strength to his weariness. "Theirs is the kingdom of heaven."

As he continued to gaze at the crowd, Sarah too scanned them, noticing the look of expectation on so many.

"Blessed are those who mourn," he said, turning toward her and the others, his posture regaining a determined confidence. "They will be comforted." Then he turned back to the crowd. "And blessed are the meek, for they will inherit the earth."

31

Sarah wondered at what sounded like some kind of affection for this horde.

He stood, and his voice rose, captured by the neighboring hills, reaching across the masses before him. "Blessed are those who hunger and thirst for righteousness, for they will be satisfied."

Hundreds of heads nodded.

"Blessed are the merciful," he said, "for they will be shown mercy. And blessed are the clean of heart, for they will see God."

He grew silent as his words descended over those spread before him.

Sarah waited, then, figuring he was done and her brief rest over, she prepared to stand and begin the walk down the hillside just as he said, "And blessed are the peacemakers, for they will be called children of God."

Shouts shot out from the crowd, and as he continued to speak, she sensed a tide of assent sweeping over the hillside. As the swell washed around her, she felt as if not one single person on that mountain shared her disinterest, her doubt, her certainty that the miracles that drew so many of them were nothing more than tricks of a deft conman.

What had all these people left? Why had they left? Why did they give their attention to every syllable he spoke? Nothing she'd heard moved her the way it seemed to move them. The way it seemed to move Simon.

Jesus' words ceased to be just background noise when he said, "Blessed are those who are persecuted for the sake of righteousness, for theirs is the kingdom of heaven." His voice grew even louder. "And blessed are you, when they insult you and persecute you and utter every kind of insult against you because of me. Rejoice and be glad, for your reward will be great in heaven. Remember, they persecuted the Prophets before you in the same way."

Scattered cheers rose up from the crowd, then grew to a roar of support and unity.

Persecution?

"Wasn't he just talking about peace?" she whispered to Simon, who didn't seem to hear her.

She studied the people stretched out before her and became increasingly uncomfortable as their enthusiasm grew with every word Jesus said.

"You are the salt of the earth, the light of the world. Don't think that I have come to abolish the law. I've come to fulfill it."

"Fulfill the law?" Sarah whispered. "This is why they ran him out of Nazareth, Simon."

Her husband shushed her with a wave of his hand and leaned forward to better hear what Jesus was saying.

Jesus' dusty robe blew around his ankles as he looked from one side of the mount to the other and from face to face. "You've heard it said that anyone who kills shall face judgment, but I say anyone who is angry with his brother is a murderer and shall face judgment."

A murmur ran through the crowd as people pondered the concept.

"You've also heard it said 'You shall not commit adultery,' but I say anyone who even looks with lust at a woman has already committed adultery in his heart."

"His words illuminate truths you haven't even considered, don't they?" Simon said to her. "I mean, when someone is mad at you, it does slice to your heart, killing a part of you. And when someone lusts after a woman even in the most hidden depths of himself, he really has offended the woman, his wife, God."

"That's exactly the problem," Sarah said. "He weaves his dangerous rhetoric into these 'revelations.'"

But her husband didn't agree. He didn't argue. He didn't even glance her way. His focus was again on Jesus.

33

"You've heard it said, 'an eye for an eye, a tooth for a tooth?'" Jesus' voice rang throughout the hillside. "But I say when someone strikes you on your right cheek, turn your other cheek to him."

"Why would anyone do that?" she said to Simon.

"I don't know, Sarah. To show you forgive him? To give the person a chance to act differently the next time?"

She shook her head, unconvinced.

Jesus paused and glanced through the crowd, and Sarah noticed an earnestness in his face that moved her even as she struggled to feel nothing good toward him.

"You've also heard it said 'You shall love your neighbor and hate your enemy,' but I say love your enemies, and pray for those who persecute you."

"What about that? Love your enemies? Pray for those who persecute you?" She looked at her husband, unable to fathom how he could buy all this. "No one loves his enemies, Simon. No one. Avoid them, sure. But love them?"

"I know, but think about it, Sarah." Simon's face glowed with new understanding as he turned toward her. "Shouldn't we? Wouldn't life be more peaceful if we all lived like that? He's only saying what the Prophets say. He's practically reading from the scroll of Isaiah, but the words mean so much more now. They're not something to argue and discuss. They're something to live."

Jesus' voice broke through their whispers. "Don't do good in order to be seen by others," he said, walking from side to side, gazing from person to person. "When you give alms, don't let your left hand know what your right hand is doing."

He looked to those perched high into the neighboring hillside. "Again, when you pray, don't pray like the hypocrites, who love to pray standing in the synagogues and at the street corners in order that they might be seen. They've already received their reward. But when you pray, go to your room and close your door. Pray to your Father in secret. And in praying, don't multiply words as the Gentiles do. They think that by saying a lot of words, they'll be heard. Don't be like them. Your Father knows what you need before you ask him."

A man somewhere in the crowd shouted, "Then how should we pray?"

Jesus looked out as though he could see exactly who had asked the question. "When you pray, say 'Our Father, who is in heaven…'"

Our Father, Sarah thought, what a strange way to start a prayer.

"Whatever happened to 'O God of Abraham, O Lord of Hosts, O Lord God of Israel'?" she said to Simon, who sat so entranced he seemed unaware she was even still beside him.

"…hallowed be your name," Jesus continued even as Sarah tried to ignore him. "Your kingdom come."

At the mention of a coming kingdom, her attention jerked away from the blade of grass she'd been studying. She gazed out at the crowd, hoping not to catch sight of a Roman soldier.

"Your will be done on earth as it is in heaven. Give us this day our daily bread. Forgive us our trespasses as we forgive those who have trespassed against us. And lead us not into temptation, but deliver us from evil." Jesus grew silent as the words resounded through the hillside.

"That's it?" Sarah whispered, looking at Jesus expectantly, certain there had to be more.

"What more do you want?" Simon said.

Jesus began speaking again but had clearly finished the prayer. Sarah once again wondered what Simon saw in this man, what all these people saw in this man. How could they keep following him from town to town to town. How were they supporting their families?

"Don't be anxious about your life, what you will eat, what you will wear."

35

She looked up, expecting to see him looking at her, surprised he knew her thoughts, but then almost disappointed to see him addressing the vast crowd with words that for a moment felt so personal, so intimate.

"Look at the birds of the air." His hand reached toward a sky where seagulls soared and swooped above them. "They don't sow or reap or gather into barns, yet your heavenly Father feeds them. Are you not more valuable than they?"

She had to admit a part of her wanted to think she could trust someone else to take care of things, especially now that it was becoming obvious Simon had abandoned them.

She studied Jesus, who looked at the mob before him as if he cared about them, who spoke with such conviction. For an instant, she saw a glimmer of what captivated people, as if she were peering through the crevice between a wall and a closed door.

His perspective *was* different...on everything. But she couldn't allow herself to fall under his spell. Anyone can weave an enticing web of words.

"Which of you," he said, "by being anxious about it, can add one single bit to his height? And as for clothing, why are you anxious?" He swept his hand across the hillside. "Look at the lilies of the field. They do nothing to clothe themselves, yet I tell you, not even Solomon in all his glory was dressed as beautifully as one of these."

"He sounds as if he knew Solomon," Sarah said, with renewed disdain.

Simon ignored her, most likely never even heard her.

"So don't worry about what you'll eat or what you'll wear or anything else," Jesus said. "Your Father knows you need all these things. But seek first the kingdom of God, and all these things and more shall be given to you."

A tremble ran through Sarah as he again mentioned a kingdom and now a promise of prosperity.

She focused on the ground beneath her, unwilling to look at him any longer, then turned to her husband. "This man is trouble, Simon, no question about it. He's here to stir all these people into a frenzy, convincing them they can have their every dream fulfilled."

"Judge not, and you will not be judged," Jesus said, looking out at the people gathered as far as Sarah could see. "Why do you see the speck in your brother's eye, but you can't see the plank in your own? You are to be perfect, even as your heavenly Father is perfect."

An earnestness filled his voice, as if he wanted nothing more than for the mob before him to understand his words. "Judge not, condemn not, forgive and you will be forgiven, be merciful even as your heavenly Father is merciful. Everything that you want others to do to you, do also to them. For this is the point of the law and of all that the Prophets teach."

He grew quiet for a moment as his words resonated throughout the hillside. Then, gazing intently at the crowd, he said softly, yet somehow loud enough for his words to reach the farthest valley, where every eye was on him, "How narrow the gate that leads to life. And those who recognize it are few."

The sadness in his voice struck Sarah.

He looked out, again seeming to see each person. "Everyone who hears my words and acts on them will be like a man who built his house on a rock. The storms came and the winds blew against the house, but it did not collapse. And everyone who hears my words but does not act on them will be like a man who built his house on sand, and the rain fell and the winds blew against the house, and it collapsed."

Across the hillside, people erupted in cheers.

Sarah glanced through the crowd, wondering at their enthusiastic acceptance of his every word, then said to Simon, "How come no one noticed that regardless of where you build your house, the storm still comes?"

Before her husband could answer, Jesus began walking down the hillside. Simon leapt to his feet and followed, leaving Sarah hurrying to keep up. As Jesus descended through the crowds, everyone they passed praised his words.

"He speaks with such authority," a woman behind them said. "Nothing like the Scribes."

"That's because he lives what he says," a man near her said.

"See," Simon said to Sarah, "that's what I mean. That's what attracts people, and that's what keeps us following him. Think about it, in the time you've known him have you heard him worry about anything, judge anyone, or gossip about anyone? No. And I've never noticed him looking at any woman with inappropriate interest. I'm not just talking about not being crude. There's a level of respect that he shows everyone, a respect that speaks to the dignity of every person he meets."

He pointed back to mountaintop. "You heard him up there. I told you, he teaches the law and the Prophets in a way I've never heard, bringing their words to life, giving them meaning. But more than that," he nodded toward the people behind them, "it's like that man said, he seems to live what he teaches in a way no one else does, not even the religious leaders."

Sarah looked at Jesus, walking a few steps ahead of them. Simon was right. And that was what made him seem so odd to her, the way he lived his life. His peaceful demeanor, his patience, his acceptance, his tolerance.

No one could possibly be that good. Something was wrong. She just couldn't figure out what.

As they continued down the hillside, the crowds parted, giving wide berth to a man who stood patiently waiting for Jesus to draw nearer. Apprehension swept through Sarah as she noticed the man's white skin and disfigured hands and face. She began to turn away, but Simon took her hand and led her alongside Jesus, who didn't stop until he came right up next to the leper.

The man gazed steadily into Jesus' eyes, and said, "Teacher, if you will it, you can make me clean."

If he wills it? Sarah thought. Didn't the man just hear Jesus teaching them the prayer, telling them that only God's will is to be done?

"I will it," she heard Jesus say. "Be made clean."

She turned sharply toward Jesus, but as a cry rose out from the crowd, she looked again at the man, who stood before her with rosy, healthy skin, beautiful, whole, healed.

"Don't tell anyone," Jesus said, locking eyes with the man in a way that seemed to close out the rest of the world, "but go and show the priest that you are clean."

With that, Jesus turned and resumed walking to the bottom of the hill.

As people crowded around Jesus, Andrew leaned toward Simon, and said, "Well, that was confusing."

"What was confusing?"

"He told that man not to tell anyone, but then said go tell the priest."

"He has to tell the priest he's been made clean," Simon said. "You know that. It's the law."

"That's what I don't get," Andrew said. "I know he has to tell the priest. So, why say, 'Don't tell anyone?' Besides, what's there to hide? It's not like a few hundred people didn't see him get cured."

"He means don't tell anyone he's God," Sarah said with disgust.

Andrew and Simon both stopped walking and looked at her.

"You heard them," she said. "That leper said 'if you will it,' and Jesus said, 'I will it.' Weren't you listening to him up there on that hill? He said we should say to God, 'Your will be done.' That leper told him he knew he was God, and Jesus didn't say a thing to stop him. He just told him don't tell anyone else what he knew."

Sarah turned and resumed walking down the hill. "Why even listen to him at all, if you aren't going to pay attention to what he's saying?"

Then she stopped and spun around toward them again. "Maybe that's why you don't see what's going on here. You listen, but you're not hearing a thing he says."

Chapter 6

Grateful to finally be home again, Sarah gazed out her window, past the goats grazing in the courtyard, to the sea. Even as gray clouds mounted across the waters, the peace of her own house soothed her. In just the few days she'd been back, her children and her life had settled into a normal rhythm. Even Jesus seemed content to stay in one place. The crowds remained but didn't pack into her house. Instead, they gathered at the shore where they sat enthralled, hanging onto every word he said.

She glanced their way, wondering what they found so captivating day after day after day. Simon sat on a rock not three steps from him. She didn't know what her husband was hearing, and she didn't want to listen to the nonsense he drank in with such enthusiasm, but at least she knew where he was.

Even in her peaceful moments, waves of fear washed through her. Fear that he would never again be the responsible man she knew. Fear that he was slipping away from her and away from all he once believed. Fear that if she didn't keep him in sight, he would follow Jesus out of her life and never return.

As she watched, Jesus turned from the throng and got into a boat. Simon and some of the other men quickly climbed in behind him. She dropped the bowl she'd been cleaning, called to her mother that she was leaving, and ran out the door to the beach, arriving just as their sail caught a breeze that blew the boat into the sea, beyond her reach.

All around her, up and down the beach, people clambered into boats. She jumped into one of the last to leave shore and tumbled into a man's lap. Others on board stifled laughs as she righted herself, blushing with humiliation, and squeezed into a seat between two women.

Men wrestled with the sail. Others grabbed oars and rowed toward the receding boat. Some leaned over the side, scooping the water away in their eagerness to catch Jesus. As they worked, the sky and sea darkened so gradually no one noticed until the dark became ominous, closing in around them.

Sarah looked out at Simon's boat and back to shore. Neither seemed close, but the shore seemed safer. Why had she even left that shore? She sure hadn't wanted to follow Jesus anywhere. Let him go. Yet in that instant, her heart had told her she needed to follow her husband.

But where? Into a storm? Into this man's insanity?

Lightening ripped across the sky. Thunder rolled out of the darkness. Someone yelled, "Turn around," but the men rowed even harder, determined to get to Jesus.

Winds whipped the sea into a frenzy, tossing them and all the boats about like driftwood. The thick mast groaned under the weight of a twisting sail. Fearing it would snap, people screamed and shoved each other as they tried to get out of the way. Sarah slipped on the wet deck, sliding under another woman's leg. As she lay in a pool of water, she saw three men scramble to support the beam. Other men climbed over those scattered on the deck, trying to get to the wildly flapping sail.

All around her, women struggled to keep their footing and make their way back to their seats. Several men fought to row against the raging waters. Men shouted orders to one another, women wept, and Sarah grew angry…at herself, at Simon, at Jesus.

She should never have gotten into the boat. Everyone knew what gray skies meant on the sea, how quickly a storm could come. For years, she'd watched gathering clouds as she scanned the horizons for signs of Simon's boat, praying he would beat the storm.

And here she was in the middle of one.

She pulled herself off the deck and into a seat and thought of her children, who didn't even know she had left. Of her mother, whose last sight of her was a tossed bowl as she ran out the door to the sea. She was going to die. They were all going to die because of their obsession with this lunatic.

The boat began to take on water from waves crashing against the sides. The men's oars didn't even reach into the sea as it raised the boat above its surface and slammed it back down into its depths again and again. Lightning flashed and thunder roared relentlessly all around them. The woman next to her grasped her hand in a death grip right before the clouds suddenly evaporated.

The sun shone brilliant and warm in a blue sky as the sea settled into a placid cadence. Everyone looked around in disbelief, too stunned even to speak as the men resumed rowing toward Jesus.

Finally, a woman across from her said to no one in particular, "What just happened?"

All around the boat, people shook their heads, exchanging glances that said they had no idea.

When they neared shore, men and women from other boats shouted the same question to one another. The weather on Galilee could be fickle and unpredictable, but no one had ever seen it calm so suddenly.

As soon as the boat floated onto the sand, people jumped out and ran to share what they'd seen. Sarah stepped onto the solid ground, holding the side for a moment to allow her legs to accept that they were on dry land.

From down the shoreline she heard a voice shout, "It was Jesus," to anyone who would listen.

She looked around and saw a man standing on a distant, beached boat.

"I saw the whole thing," he said. "We were just a couple of boats away. I thought for sure we were dead. One minute the storm is ready to capsize us, and the next minute I see Jesus standing at his bow. He reached out and literally commanded the sea to be still. And that was it. The storm vanished."

People ran past her, trying to get to the man, shouting questions.

"I've never seen anything like it," he said. "I'm an old man. I've fished these waters my whole life. I've lived through my share of storms, but I've never seen anything like that before."

Sarah shoved through the crowd, away from the man, and looked along the shore for Simon's boat, peering into shadows cast by the steep mountain cliffs that rose up beyond the sand. She walked through the throng of people and wandered from group to group in search of any sign of her husband. As she neared what she guessed was the front of the mob, she caught sight of him walking next to Jesus. Philip, James, and Andrew inadvertently formed a wall, blocking her way, while others pushed against her from behind as everyone tried to get closer to Jesus.

Reaching past James, she grabbed her husband's arm to stop him from going any farther.

"Sarah," Simon, said, as he fell back to where she stood. "What are you doing here?"

"More importantly, Simon, what are you doing here, sailing off without a word? Did you even think you should maybe tell me you were leaving?"

He dropped his head, and she couldn't help thinking he looked like Micah when he got caught chasing the goats out of the yard. "I'm sorry, Sarah. It all happened so fast. One minute we were sitting on the beach, listening to Jesus, and the next minute he was climbing into the boat and heading off to sea."

"I don't care if he leaves. Why did you go?"

"Because he left."

"That's no excuse, Simon. You don't have to follow him everywhere he goes."

People continued to make their way around them as Simon said, "But I do have to follow him, Sarah. There's nowhere I'd rather be than with him." He smiled a weak half-smile, as if he knew how that sounded, as if he couldn't begin to explain what he'd just said, then turned to follow the crowd.

"Wait a minute." Sarah reached out to grab his arm again, giving no thought to how loud her voice was or whether she should be holding her husband's arm in public. "You can't just say something like that and walk away, Simon. Do you mean you're leaving me, you're leaving us?"

She could hardly string sensible words together. It felt as if the storm had moved into her head.

"No. I'd never leave you or the children. Never. You know that."

He dragged his hand through his hair like he always did when he was frustrated. "I can't explain it. I wish I could. I know I owe it to you, but I can't. I just have to be with him. I can't imagine not being with him. But it doesn't mean I've left you."

Simon glanced at Jesus, who had stopped to talk to some of those nearest to him, and she knew he was eager to be done with this conversation so he could join them.

When he turned his attention again to her, he said, "You saw what happened in the middle of that storm, Sarah. You saw him calm it, right? I mean, how could you have missed it? The sea's so rough, every boat out there was about to capsize, and in one instant, it's calm. The storm is gone. The sky is blue. Not a single rumble of thunder anywhere. You know that was him, don't you?"

"How could it have been him, Simon? No one controls the weather."

"He did." Her husband gazed at her with an intensity she'd never seen. "I thought we were going to die. We all did. And

45

there he was, asleep. Asleep. I shook him awake and told him we were going to die, and do you know what he said?"

She shook her head, more with disbelief that anyone could have slept through that storm than with curiosity as to anything Jesus might have said.

"Why are you afraid? That's what he said. And something about us having no faith. Then he stood up, told the storm to be quiet, and it stopped."

Simon glanced again at Jesus still in conversation with a growing crowd as more and more tried to get close enough to hear him.

Before Sarah could respond, a voice unlike any she had ever heard roared with anger from beyond the road. She and Simon turned to see a man running through a graveyard toward the crowd. Those with Jesus appeared to be held at bay by the man. Chains hung from his wrists, snapped and mangled. His hair was matted, his clothes shredded, his arms and legs covered in bruises and scars. He snorted and glared at anyone who approached, then charged at Jesus and slid to his knees in front of him.

"What have you to do with us, almighty Son of God?" he said, his words twisted, tormented, threatening.

With no hesitation, without even a flinch, Jesus calmly said, "Come out of the man, you unclean spirit."

Sarah stood anchored to the ground, unable to comprehend the scene before her. She should be back in her house making dinner, not watching some macabre act in some Gentile graveyard.

"Have you come to torment us before the time?" the man screamed.

"What's your name?" Jesus said.

"My name is Legion, for we are many." The words rumbled from within the man's very being.

He leapt to his feet, saying, "Don't send us away," and franticly looked around, then pointed to the top of a nearby mountain covered with grazing pigs. "Send us into those swine instead."

Jesus gazed deep into the deranged man's eyes, and said, "Go."

The crowd watched in hushed astonishment as thousands of pigs suddenly raced to the edge of the cliff and plunged into the sea. Everyone stepped back in surprise and fear.

The man dropped to the ground. When he again looked up at Jesus, a calm shone in his face, the fierce, wild madness gone from his eyes. He reached out and grasped Jesus' hand in wordless gratitude and wept with joy.

Low murmurs ran through the crowd. Almost immediately, the murmurs gave way to shouts and cheers as people shoved forward again to get closer to Jesus. Getting bumped and pushed from every direction, Sarah turned in search of escape only to see people rushing in from the nearby village, where they had been watching the scene. Her heart gripped with fear at the anger and terror in their faces.

Their herd was gone. An unclean herd, but still, it was their herd.

As they neared, she looked for someplace to hide, unwilling to go into the cemetery but unsure where else to turn. Before she could make a move in any direction, the villagers swarmed them, trying to get to Jesus. But rather than attack him, they begged him to leave their town.

Sarah stared at him as if she could somehow get her thoughts into his head, praying that he would do what they wanted. After a few moments, he glanced through the mob toward her, then turned and got back into his boat. The crowd around her broke apart and ran to the water's edge, pulling her along with them as she got caught in their swell and lost sight of Simon. In the midst of the commotion, she heard her name and saw her husband waving for her as he climbed into his boat just a short distance away. She shoved through the mob, took his hand, and let him pull her aboard.

As he joined in the excited celebration of the men around her, she slumped into the seat next to him and tried to make sense of what she had just witnessed.

Why would Jesus do that to those poor pigs? They belonged to Gentiles. As far as she knew, they had no law against swine. Then she sat straight, realizing she had slipped into the casual acceptance that Jesus had freed the man from demons and sent them screaming into some pigs. Most likely, he'd made some sound no one else caught, a sound he knew would send the pigs running.

Yet she couldn't stop thinking about the man's words, 'Have you come to torment us before the time?' What time? And if the man really was possessed, why would a demon care about the proper time for anything?

***

Sarah huffed as they walked the steep road. She didn't know whether to be angry or relieved that Jesus hadn't taken them back to Capernaum. Having an entire town of furious pig farmers follow them home wasn't exactly something she wanted her children to see.

As soon as they'd floated onto the rocky shore of a deserted beach, everyone had tumbled out of their boats with excitement and followed him up the into the hills. She trudged along, wondering how people twice her age seemed to climb the twisting, narrow path with ease.

As they made their way around a bend, she looked up to what lay ahead. Gaping tombs carved into the mountainside above them sat in waiting, while heavy stones sealed the entrances to those already taken.

Jesus turned away from the graves and walked along a winding path into a village, where she could only hope they would stop and rest a while. Across the road, a passing procession headed the other way, out of town, toward the tombs. A man too young lay stiff on a funeral bier, his face and hands the color of dusk. Tears streaked the faces of the men bearing him, while several women comforted an inconsolable mother, who shook her head and clutched the young man's hand as if she would never let it go.

Sarah wanted to look away, to give the woman her privacy, but she couldn't. It seemed there was nothing else in all the world to look at but the mother's sorrow.

Jesus, too, couldn't seem to look away.

He walked over to the woman, and said, "Don't cry," and the procession halted in surprise.

Don't cry, Sarah thought. How could she do anything but cry?

The consoling women looked at one another, wondering who this man was intruding on a moment like this.

He touched the bier and gazed at the figure stretched out motionless before him.

Then he brushed the young man's cheek and spoke to him as if in a place where only the two of them existed. "Son, I say to you, arise."

Color flowed through the man. He sat up and glanced around at all those surrounding him. Gasps erupted throughout both crowds.

Seeing his mother, he said, "What are you doing? Why are you crying? What's going on?"

As he leapt off the bier and into her embrace, shouts filled the air. "Praise God... A great prophet has come to us... God has taken care of his people..."

Sarah watched Jesus let them cheer, let them celebrate, never trying to explain that the boy had not really been dead at all.

Chapter 7

The boat slipped onto the sands of home. Sarah stepped onto the ground, grateful to be out of the unpredictable sea. Her husband stood next to Jesus, already encircled by a mob. She felt like the lone sober person among a world drunk on "miracles."

She crossed the beach, pushing through the crowd as more and more people hurried past to greet Jesus. Sensing a presence at her side, she turned to see Simon beside her, talking with excitement to everyone he passed.

She was glad he had deigned to leave Jesus for a moment, but she needed some time to make sense of all they had just experienced. Or at least all they seemed to have experienced. Her husband could talk of nothing else. For him, it had been as real as the sand on which he stood. But for her, it shifted and slipped, leaving nothing solid in her world.

The whole demon-and-the-pigs thing she understood even if she knew her husband would never consider the possibility that Jesus had made some kind of sound no one but the pigs noticed. And the raising of the dead boy? Impressive, but easy to explain. Shallow breathing, something momentarily caught in the boy's throat, some other logical explanation that people eager for miracles ignored. But the storm. How did the storm calm? Simon knew the sea far better than she, and he didn't seem to doubt that Jesus had done it.

But no one controls the seas and skies except God. Jesus must have seen something in the clouds that Simon had missed, something that told him the weather was about to break and break in dramatic fashion.

Seeming to sense her struggle, Simon pulled her close. She allowed herself to relax into his embrace, the familiar roughness of his tunic rubbing against her cheek, before remembering they were not alone. Embarrassed, she pushed away from him. He took her hand, and headed down the road toward home.

"Surely you can't deny what you saw in Nain, Sarah," he said. "Raising someone from the dead?"

"You know as well as I do there are times when people only seem dead, Simon. The boy's breathing probably slowed so much, they assumed he'd died. Then what did they do? They rushed off to bury him as quickly as they could. All that shaking and commotion as they carried him to the tomb is what brought him around. Jesus just got lucky with his timing."

Simon stopped walking.

"What's wrong?" she said.

"Do you have to be so cynical?"

The word stung her as she thought of her own mother's negative perspective of life.

He touched her arm in a gesture meant to convey sympathy, but to her it felt more like pity.

Maybe she was wrong. How could she not see what apparently hundreds and hundreds of others saw?

The excited shouts and cries she'd left behind grew louder. She turned to see what looked like the entire region of Galilee following her, with Jesus at the lead.

"Hurry," she said to Simon as she walked faster.

Micah, Abi, and Hannah rushed out of the courtyard to greet them. She tried to corral her children into the door, hoping to bar it before the horde could get in, but Simon scooped Hannah into his arms, then stopped to examine the rock she held out to him.

"Let's go," Sarah said.

Leilah stood in the doorway. "Did you have to bring the whole town again?"

"Miracles," Sarah said with a roll of her eyes, forgetting her mother believed herself to have been the beneficiary of one of these wonders.

Spying a friend in the approaching crowd, Abi called out with excitement. Sarah looked past her to see Andrew and some of the younger men sprinting toward the house. She grabbed Micah's arm to stop him from running off to meet them, took her older daughter by the hand, and tried to push them into the house. Before she could shut the door, the first of the crowd reached it. Soon, Jesus followed and every room filled with people squeezing into spaces too small for a broom. Still others pushed open the shutters from the outside and reached in, shouting with excitement.

In the corner near a cabinet stood a group of glaring men, Scribes from the local synagogue, none too happy with the crowd, with Jesus, with Simon, with her. Jesus seemed unfazed by the commotion as he warmly greeted Leilah, who melted into hospitality mode and showed him to a stool in the midst of the main room.

He talked with those around him, but Sarah barely heard him as she peered over the heads of people gathered at the door and saw a tidal wave of humanity still making their way down the road to her house. She looked out the window and saw more coming from the other direction. The roar of voices overwhelmed Jesus' until he might as well have said nothing, but still he talked. Outside, men shouted at others to make way for them, but she couldn't imagine where they expected anyone to go. A few moments later, she heard a sound like goats walking on her roof. As she looked up, a small patch of thatch slid to the side above her head, and daylight poured in.

"Simon, they're ripping off the roof," she shouted.

Her husband glanced up toward the ceiling, then smiled across the room at her. She looked around for something to poke at them to get them to stop. Maybe if she climbed on the table she could reach them, but men, women, and children sat on the table and on every bench and stool in the room.

Another bit of thatch slid off, then another. She watched, incredulous, as a man on a stretcher was lowered through the hole and into the room to the floor before Jesus. Sarah recognized him, the motionless young man who had lain on his pallet next to the weaver's booth for years. How many times had she tripped over him in the busy street?

The crowd grew silent as Jesus looked up at the men on the roof, then bent and gently touched the man's forehead. The young man lay still, his useless muscles withered, his limbs contorted, his bones frail.

People squeezed in even closer as Jesus tenderly looked him in the eye. The man gazed up at him with deep gratitude, and Sarah knew it may have been the first time anyone had ever looked at him directly. It was always so much easier to turn the other way.

Jesus lifted the man's limp hand, and said, "Son, your sins are forgiven."

What? Sarah thought. Who cares about his sins? Heal the man, for crying out loud, so these people will get off my roof. Then she saw the Scribes, deep furrows in their foreheads, anger etched into their faces, and she realized the blasphemy of Jesus' words. Who was he to forgive anyone's sins? Only God can forgive sins. But she noticed the man himself didn't say a word. He didn't cry out aghast or beg for a different result. He still lay there paralyzed, and yet he seemed content, as if it were better that he was freed from the paralysis of sin.

Jesus glanced at the Scribes, not with fear or with anger, but with sadness. "Why are you condemning me in your hearts? What's easier, to say to this man, 'Your sins are forgiven' or to say, 'Rise, pick up your pallet, and walk'? But, so that you'll know that the Son of Man has authority to forgive sins on earth," he turned to the young man, "I say to you, son, arise, pick up your pallet, and walk."

53

Sarah watched in amazement as the young man sat up, then rolled to his side and stood on legs no longer frail and withered. He picked up the pallet he had been lying on and made his way through the parting crowd and out the door. As he walked by, people shouted their joy and astonishment to all who could not see what had happened, until the noise became deafening.

Jesus followed him, and the mob poured out of Sarah's house and onto the streets.

Simon headed out behind them, saying to her, "Let's go."

"You're leaving?"

"You saw what just happened."

"What did I see?" Sarah said. "Some poor guy who thinks he's healed, who had some kind of burst of energy for a few minutes. Tomorrow, there he'll be, flat on his back on his pallet in the middle of the road again."

Simon stopped and gently took hold of her hands in the empty house. "You can stay if you want, Sarah. I probably won't be gone long."

"But why go at all?" she said, pushing him away. "People wander into town all the time doing what he does. 'Healing' a couple of people, casting out a couple of demons, and then, after they've made a little money or attracted some rag-tag group of followers, they disappear."

"But what if he's the Messiah?"

"The Messiah?" For a moment Sarah was speechless. "You can't be serious. Look at him. Does he look like the Messiah? If he's the Messiah, then we're in a lot of trouble."

"You have to admit he's different," Simon said

"How? Nothing he's done is different. He just does more of it than others, that's all."

Simon looked wistfully out the door at the departing crowd. His children stood in the courtyard with their grandmother, watching the joyous parade.

"It's what he says that matters," he said, still looking out beyond the confines of their house, "not what he does."

"Well, what he says, Simon, is blasphemy."

"What are you talking about?" He turned his attention back to his wife.

"You heard him. He forgave that man's sins. Who does he think he is? God forgives our sins, Simon, God, and God alone. What does the Psalm, Tehillim, say?"

"I don't know, Sarah."

"Of course you, know," she said. "You just don't want to talk about it. *Against you only have I sinned, O Lord.* We can only sin against God, so only God can forgive our sins. And there he is, telling that man his sins are forgiven. I told you, he's not even claiming to be the Messiah. He's claiming to be God himself."

"You're reading into things," Simon said. "No one would claim to be God."

She watched her husband turn and join the retreating crowd. Never would she have thought he would fall for something like this. He might be impulsive, but he was also faithful. How many times had she heard him pray, "Hear, O Israel, the Lord your God is one God"?

One God.

How could he not see that this man was undermining the single most foundational truth of his existence?

Sarah followed her husband into the village, unwilling to let him out of her sight as he ran to catch up to Jesus in the midst of the crowd.

Merchants struggled to protect their booths as people rushed past. Goats and sheep scattered, their shepherds calling out through the din, trying to gather them back together. As the crowd neared the center of town, she looked down the road and noticed the tax collector sitting at his booth, strategically placed to catch any person who entered the village. He didn't even look up at the mob that swelled past, uninterested in anyone who wasn't bringing something into Capernaum to sell.

Sarah envied his disregard for the excitement of the people running and shouting in front of him. If only Simon had that same disregard.

Then she noticed the man's fine linen and gold, and her heart burned with anger, the same as it did every time she saw him. How could someone so dishonest, someone who took every coin another person had, someone who didn't care about anyone's personal situation, how could someone like that have so much? One of the nicest homes in Galilee, servants, wealth. How could God give him so much?

And yet, she looked at the dark man hunched face down into his account scroll and had to admit, no one seemed to have less joy.

She lost sight of Simon as she slowed to study the man, watching him finally glance toward the crowd and then back again at his ledger. Even if he didn't know about the storm and the demon and the dead boy, surely he'd heard about the young man on the pallet. It's not every day someone rips off a roof just to get into a house. Even now, people were shouting the news back and forth within his hearing. He even likely had watched the man being carried to the house and now saw him running down the street with delight.

Yet he didn't seem to notice anything, including Jesus walking past his table, until Jesus looked directly at him and said, "Follow me."

Sarah watched in amazement as the man immediately stood up, walked away from his money, rushed through the crowd to Jesus, and said something.

A few moments later, Simon came to her, and said, "We're eating at Matthew's."

"Whose?"

"Matthew's…the tax collector."

"You mean Levi?" she said, aghast.

"Jesus welcomed him as Matthew and said we're eating at his house tonight."

"And you don't think that's odd?"

"What?"

"Everything, Simon. Everything. That Levi is now Matthew. That you're eating at a tax collector's house. That Levi is even talking to the likes of us, and that you would have anything to do with the likes of him?"

"Come on, Sarah. Relax. It's just dinner."

***

As Sarah stepped into the house, she almost couldn't take in the opulence. Rich tapestries lined the walls, passageways stretched out before her. Furnishings weren't just wood. They had cloth covers, stuffed cushions. Servants scampered about, rushing to wash the feet of those who entered. Heaps of food lined a table in an adjacent room. She scanned those already at the table and stopped, unwilling to move farther.

"What's wrong?" Simon asked.

"I can't go in there."

"Why?"

"Look at them, Simon. All men you despise. Men who rob everyone who brings anything worth selling into town. I will not stay in the same house as them. Let's go."

"I'm not leaving, Sarah."

She stopped short. "What do you mean you're not leaving? You can't stay here with them. They're unclean. Everything about them is unclean. They thrive because they live on other people's meager incomes."

She watched as Jesus settled in among the guests, taking a place at the table, greeting those already in the room with embraces and smiles.

"You can go if you want," Sarah said, "but I'm not moving beyond this door."

Simon looked at the rest of his friends, who rushed to take their places at the table, then cast an apologetic glance at his wife and turned to go into the house, leaving her on the threshold.

He had taken only a step or two before a man reached past her and grabbed his arm.

"Why does your 'teacher' eat with tax collectors and sinners?" the man said.

Sarah turned to see the angry face of a local Pharisee, a man Simon respected and thought of as a friend. She felt buoyed by the Pharisee's question. Maybe now her husband would come to his senses.

Then she heard Jesus' voice ring out from the other room, addressing those at the table. "People who are well don't need a physician, but those who are sick do. I didn't come to call the righteous, but the sinners."

The Pharisee let go of Simon, freeing him to join the others, while Sarah's hope vanished.

Chapter 8

Sarah sorted through a fruit vendor's heaps of apricots in the midst of the crowded marketplace, the lone person actually shopping. Everyone else gathered around Jesus as he spoke to them, with none closer to him than her husband. She wanted to hear what Simon heard, but she didn't want to hear anything more than what she needed to help him regain some sense of reality.

A small band of dust-covered men passed her and worked their way through the crowd. She hurried to follow as they managed to get close enough to Jesus to speak to him.

"Teacher," a lean young man said, "we've followed John the Baptist for years."

Sarah took in his dirty, torn tunic and unkempt hair and wasn't surprised.

"For days, we've been listening to you and watching you and your followers, and what I don't understand is, why do we and the Pharisees fast, but your followers do not?"

Jesus gave the man his full attention. "Should the wedding guests mourn while the Bridegroom is with them? The days will come when the Bridegroom will be taken away from them. Then they will fast."

The man drank in his words like they made sense. Sarah noticed John and Andrew exchange knowing glances and remembered Andrew once said something about the Baptist, that crazy madman, proclaiming Jesus to be some kind of bridegroom.

Who refers to himself as the bridegroom in the Prophets again and again? God. And here this man was, claiming the title as his own. But no one called him on it. Instead they all embraced it. Even her husband nodded in agreement.

Before she could begin to fathom how he could so readily embrace such blatant heresy, the crowd around her pushed backward in a sudden surge. A man behind her grunted as she knocked into him. All around people scrambled to get out of the way of someone Sarah couldn't see. She stretched to try to catch a glimpse over the heads of those in front of her and saw a man walking through the parting crowd.

A woman near her craned her neck to see what was going on, then mumbled to no one in particular, "No wonder. One of the high and mighty rulers of the synagogue."

Good, Sarah thought, as she glimpsed his silk garb and the authority in his stride. It was long past time for a real confrontation. She'd had enough of the religious leaders watching and criticizing from the sidelines.

She recognized the man, familiar throughout the town but friends with no one. He crossed the road, purpose and intent evident in his gait as he made his way through the crowd. Even Simon backed away as he drew near, but Jesus stood still, quietly focused on the approaching figure. The ruler walked straight up to him, met his gaze, and collapsed to the ground at his feet, his expensive tunic pressed into the dirt.

Reaching out, he cried, "Please, please, I beg you. You've got to come to my house and do something to save my daughter. Please. Please, she's dying. You've got to help…" His words dissolved into sobs.

Some in the crowd gasped. No one even knew his daughter had been sick. Sarah struggled to recall if she'd ever even seen the girl. Seldom did she have reason to go the rich side of town and never did they see a need to come to hers.

Jesus helped the man up and walked with him toward his house with the surrounding crowd moving as one. As they made their way through the marketplace, more people ran from houses and side streets and joined the mob, everyone crushing in closer and closer from all sides. Some ran in front of Jesus, walking backward, tripping and falling over one another as they tried to get his attention. Simon stayed near his side as usual, easily keeping step with him as Sarah struggled to not fall behind.

Suddenly, Jesus stopped so fast the people stumbled over one another. As those around her shouted and blamed everyone else for making them trip, she focused her attention on him.

He looked around from person to person, then said, "Who touched me?"

"Who touched you?" Simon said. "Are you kidding? Look at this crowd. What do you mean, who touched you? Everyone has touched you."

Jesus looked out at the vast multitude. "Someone touched me. I felt power go forth from me."

Murmurs of excitement broke out, and Sarah shook her head. How much more of this nonsense were these people going to take? Still, Simon's words gave her hope. Maybe he was finally seeing a glimmer of light.

A frail woman near Jesus, someone she didn't recognize, fell to the ground trembling, and said, "I touched you."

The murmurs grew louder as people jostled to get a glimpse of her.

"I've been hemorrhaging for twelve years," she said, without looking up as people backed away from her upon hearing she was unclean.

No wonder Sarah had never seen her. What made her think she should come out now?

Tears rolled down the woman's gaunt cheeks and choked her words. "All day, every day for twelve years. I've tried everything, but nothing has helped. Nothing. Then I heard about the works you've done, and someone said you were here, and I thought if I could only get to you. I didn't expect you to touch me, but if I could get close, even if I only touched the hem of your garment, I knew I would be healed."

She slowly looked up into his eyes. "And I was."

A roar rushed through the crowd as people shared the news.

Jesus gently reached out to the woman, took her hand, raised her up, and said, "Daughter, your faith has saved you. Go in peace."

Sarah watched the color return to the woman's face, her frailness faded, a renewed strength evident as she walked with Jesus toward the religious leader's home. The crowd shoved their way around Sarah, calling out to one another while they followed him forward.

She had to admit, she had never seen anyone so good at this healing thing. But it was all drama and deception. No doubt, tomorrow the woman's hemorrhage would start again, and she would just be one in a long line of people so eager to believe he could heal them that, for a minute or two, they convinced themselves he had.

Still, Sarah envied her.

Who believes someone can help you when he doesn't even know you exist? The woman didn't try to get in front of Jesus so he could see her. She didn't grab his arm and turn him toward her. She hadn't even seen him work "miracles." She'd only heard of him from others, and yet she risked everything just to reach out to him.

Within her heart, Sarah told God she wanted that kind of faith.

She looked at Jesus, at the smile that lit not only his face but his eyes, a smile of love that seemed to come from deep within as he'd gazed at the once-hemorrhaging woman. A part of her wanted to let go of her resistance and believe in the miracles she'd witnessed, but she couldn't let herself give in. She couldn't pretend it was all more than an illusion.

Catching her up in its surge, the crowd propelled her onward as they neared the synagogue ruler's house. Even in the midst of well-appointed homes, his stood apart. Sarah looked at the carved columns that lined the entryway, the broad granite steps and portico that served to welcome visitors and stop the unwelcomed.

Before the man got to the steps, several servants came out the door to meet him, somber as they walked down to him.

One of them said softly, "Sir, don't trouble the rabbi anymore. There's nothing he can do for her." He paused and glanced to another servant as if he wanted to look anywhere but into this man's eyes. "Your daughter is dead."

The man nearly dropped beneath the weight of the words, but Jesus caught his arm and said, "Don't be afraid. Just have faith. Your daughter will be well."

The servants glanced at one another, their faces drained of hope. Sarah could see it was too late for Jesus to pull off another 'miracle' this time.

A woman clad in embroidered robes and headdress emerged from the doorway, her face gray and tear-streaked. Without speaking, she stumbled down the steps and into the man's arms and sobbed.

Tears welled up in Sarah's eyes as she mourned for a child she didn't know, for the sorrow of parents she'd never met. Others around her cried openly.

Jesus embraced the couple, then looked past them to where Simon and the others stood. He nodded to the door and led the man, his wife, Simon, James, and John up the steps. They disappeared into the house while throughout the courtyard people wept and wailed. Sarah leaned on a pillar in the hot sun, thinking of her own children. She too wanted to wail, but wailing wasn't her way. Instead, she struggled to maintain her composure as silent tears slid down her cheeks.

Just when she thought she couldn't bear the sadness any longer, the door flew open. Simon, James, and John emerged from the house, bounding down the stairs.

Sarah pushed past those in front of her to get to her husband. "What happened?"

He could barely contain his excitement as people crushed in around them to hear. "We walked into the room and saw this beautiful child lying dead on a cushion, and everyone just started sobbing. Me, too, Sarah," he grabbed her shoulders, "I couldn't help myself. Jesus told us not to cry. He said she's not dead, she's only sleeping. And we literally laughed at him." He turned to all the people gathered around him. "Anyone could see she was dead. Then he took this dead girl by the hand and said, 'Child, arise,' and she immediately sat up. We couldn't believe what we were seeing."

Simon smoothed back his hair, then grabbed her by the shoulders again. "Sarah, I've never in my life seen anything like that before. Never. Even with that boy in Nain, I admit I wondered if maybe he'd only seemed to be dead. I didn't think Jesus would deceive us, but maybe the jostling of the bier or all the commotion jarred him awake."

His sheepish expression told her he was aware that his faith might not be what he thought, that her misgivings might not be so unreasonable.

"But this girl?" he said. "She was dead. There is no doubt in my mind. The girl was dead. And the next thing you know, she's sitting there eating and looking absolutely normal."

James came up beside them and tossed his arm around Simon's shoulders, and the two walked off with Jesus. Sarah watched her husband again disappear into the crowd as she struggled against a little nudge of sympathy for Jesus.

His closest followers laughed at him, having nowhere near the faith of an anonymous woman crawling in the dust just to touch his hem. No wonder he'd noticed her.

Chapter 9

A crowd gathered at Sarah's door and spread throughout her yard and onto the road and beach beyond. Men called to one another. Women chatted excitedly over the heads of their children as they waited for Jesus.

"James said they're heading out again today. Are you going with them?" Salome asked, as she sat on the bench under the vine and watched Sarah take the dried laundry off the courtyard walls. Strangers squeezed between them, bumping Sarah's elbows, kicking her basket in their efforts to get close to the house.

"I don't feel like I have a choice," Sarah said, raising her voice so her friend could hear over the commotion. "If I'm with Simon, maybe I have a chance of getting a little common sense into him. If I don't go, I'm afraid I'll lose him forever."

"I know what you mean," Salome said. "I don't like the idea of leaving home, but I think I'll go this time, too. Zebedee can manage without me. I need to keep an eye on the boys." She reached up and tucked an escaping silver curl into her head covering. " I didn't give it much thought when John spent all that time with the Baptist. Even when he'd come back fired up, ready to take on the world, Zebedee and I would just roll our eyes, figuring he'd grow out of it someday. But this has become a lot more than just spending a few hours down at the Jordan listening to someone rant and preach."

She took a tired linen tunic out of the basket and folded it, smoothing it on her lap without looking up. "James said he believes this Jesus might be the Messiah."

Sarah sighed. "I know. Simon said the same thing." She dropped a garment into the basket and turned to her friend.

"How can they even think that? Look at the man. He's got nothing. No house. No money. No army. No power over anything except this deluded mob. That's their idea of a Messiah? But do your boys listen?"

Salome shook her head.

"No," Sarah said. "And neither does Andrew or Simon. They can't hear anything we say. Their minds are so full of the nonsense he's spouting that nothing else can get through."

The crowd near the door shuffled to the side, parting as Jesus, Simon, and some of the other men left the house. People shoved one another to clear a path without really moving away from him. Someone bumped into Sarah, knocking the clean clothes out of her arms, into the dirt. She watched as the small group of men walked down the road to the shore. When the rest of the crowd realized Jesus was leaving, those on the other side of the house ran past her to catch up.

Salome gave her a long, wary look, then slowly stood and followed them. Sarah saw her mother in the kitchen, watching the people through the window. She struggled against the tide of humanity to get into her house. What little furniture they had was scattered all over the room. Her children stood next to Leilah, looking at Sarah with sad expectation.

"You're going, too, aren't you?" Hannah said.

"I have to go with your father," Sarah said.

Her heart broke as she watched the girls move closer to their grandmother, who wrapped them in a protective hug. Micah stood straight beside them, struggling to appear strong and independent.

"I'm so sorry," she said, "but I feel like I need to be there, at least for now."

"We'll be fine," Leilah said, giving the girls a comforting squeeze. "Jonah's right across the way. And who knows? Maybe they're only going into town. Maybe you'll be back by dinner."

66

Sarah hesitated, reluctant to leave, certain Jesus was taking them farther away than the marketplace, but her mother looked into her eyes, then looked out at the departing crowd, letting her know she was right to leave. Sarah kissed her children and turned away before they could see the tears she fought back. Unable to say anything more, she left.

As she stepped out her door, she saw the mass of people far down the road walking into town. Tossing propriety to the wind, she gathered her tunic around her knees and ran to catch up. She wove between the men, women, and children toward the front of the throng, where she knew she'd find Simon. Over the heads of those who stood in her way, she caught sight of Jesus as he led them up into the hillside. Keeping him in sight, she continued to push and shove her way through, wanting to pause a moment, catch her breath, slow her heart, but afraid to get run over.

Ahead of her, near the top of the hill, Jesus stopped and gazed down at the hundreds who waited below. He stood still a long time as more and more filled the valley, flowing in from roads and paths, trodding through the brush and across streams.

Sarah was surprised to see sadness cloud his face. He should be triumphant, gloating. This mob followed him everywhere he went. They turned when he turned, stopped when he stopped, slept when he slept. What more did he want?

Then he nodded his head for Simon and the other nearby men to join him.

Simon walked obediently to Jesus' side. Determined not to let her husband out of her sight, Sarah shoved through the crowd to the less densely packed wilderness that climbed the hillside. She scrambled through the brush and twigs, tripping on rocks, shoving through overgrown shrubs, and popped out of the brush beside him.

"I wondered if you were coming," Simon said with a smile.

James caught his eye, and he left her to join his friend. Without her husband beside her, Sarah felt exposed and inappropriate among the group of men and slipped back into the scraggly shrubs behind her.

Not a blade of grass was visible in the peaks and valleys below as people covered the hillside.

She heard a branch snap and saw Salome cautiously picking her way through the bushes and weeds to join her. They stood half-hidden in the brush, Salome wheezing beside her.

Jesus continued to look at the people spread out before him to the farthest reaches of the land and said, almost as if to himself, "The harvest is plentiful. But the laborers are few."

The shadows of sadness darkened in his eyes. Then he turned to the small group gathered around him on the hilltop, and his shoulders straightened with a sense of determination as he began to single out men by name.

Simon, Andrew, James, and John moved closer to him when he called them. She watched as Levi took his place with them.

"What's he up to, that he would group Simon with the likes of Levi?" she whispered to Salome.

He continued calling out names, some familiar, but most men she'd only first seen in recent weeks.

She watched Philip step away from the men he'd been standing with to join Jesus. His eagerness to enthusiastically accept every word Jesus said hadn't waned since that day at the market. His black curls always seemed to be bobbing in excitement as he asked those around him how Jesus could have done something he'd just witnessed.

Next Jesus singled out Nathaniel. She no longer saw any trace of the doubt he once had. Instead, he seemed to embrace everything Jesus said and did with quiet acceptance. He stood up from the rock on which he'd been sitting, and walked over to Philip's side. The two men exchanged questioning glances, and Sarah, too, wondered what was going on.

She studied Nathaniel, still puzzled at how quickly he had turned from disbelief to belief.

Jesus' voice broke into her thoughts as she heard him call out Thomas. She saw the stout, ruddy man standing where he usually was, on the perimeter of the group yet always within earshot of Jesus.

After Jesus called his name, she noticed as Thomas gave Simon a wary look. She shared his concern.

Jesus turned to some men standing within a few feet of her. She took a step deeper into the brush, unwilling to have him see her even as she knew he had to have seen her. Salome too crouched in the shadows, certain a couple of branches could make her invisible. His attention focused on a short, quiet young man the others called James the Lesser.

Sarah thought he might trip over her as he shrank back against a rock seconds before Jesus called out his name. She glanced down the hillside toward his mother, a fragile-looking woman who followed Jesus with as much enthusiasm as any man in the crowd. Her face glowed with joy, and she beamed at her son as if she could communicate her fervor to him.

Next to him, Sarah noticed a man named Judas Thaddeus, his clear, confident gaze locked on Jesus in hopeful anticipation. His entire body seemed poised to leap into action. Jesus glanced his way and smiled before saying his name.

Then came a young man named Simon. When Jesus called out his name, he leapt up from the ground and shoved his fist into the sky in elation.

"A little excited, isn't he, " Sarah said, "considering he has no idea what this is all about? Maybe they're just going to run some kind of errand. Hardly worth getting all worked up over."

But deep within, she knew what everyone else on that hillside knew. Something more was going on.

Next to the celebrating Simon stood a man named Judas Iscariot. Sarah barely noticed him most days even though he seemed to keep close to Jesus, pondering what he heard and saw. He would occasionally get into theological discussions with the others but would back off when the conversations grew heated. He seemed surprised when Jesus called out his name.

Jesus gathered the small group of men to his side. As they took their places around him, he looked again at the crowd below, then said, "Don't go to the Gentiles or the Samaritans, but instead go to the lost sheep of Israel."

"Go? Why would they go anywhere at all," Sarah whispered to her friend.

Salome shrugged and signaled for her to be still so she could hear.

"And preach as you go," Jesus said, walking among the men, gazing intently at each one of them as he spoke. "Tell everyone, 'The kingdom of heaven is at hand.' Heal the sick, raise the dead, cleanse lepers, cast out demons."

"Listen to him," Sarah said. "The man is crazy. Surely Simon can see that now."

She tried to catch her husband's eye, but he was focused solely on Jesus. If the hillside were to crumble into the sea, he wouldn't likely notice. He didn't look disgusted or troubled. He looked enthralled, drinking in every word.

"You received without pay, give without pay," Jesus said. He reached out, pulled Levi's money bag from his waist, and held it up. "Take no gold or silver or copper for your journey."

"What journey?" Sarah said, her whispers growing louder.

"I'm sending you like sheep in the midst of wolves." Jesus turned from side to side. "So beware. People will deliver you up to councils and beat you in their synagogues. You'll be dragged before governors and kings for my sake."

Salome gasped.

"How can they listen to this?" Sarah said.

Her friend silently shook her head, her aged hands clutching the branches in front of her.

"When they deliver you up," Jesus said, "don't worry about what you should say, because it's not you who will speak. The Spirit of your Father will speak through you."

The men surrounding him listened without interruption, some as if making mental notes, others with a look of bewilderment. Sarah noticed hesitation on the faces of the younger James, Judas the Iscariot, and Thomas. Then she looked at her husband, captivated by every word, poised to charge off into whatever future Jesus laid out for him, and she wondered why he didn't hear what the others heard.

"Look at them," Sarah said. "I would expect John and Andrew to get all worked up about some new guy who blows into town and draws this much attention. But James? Simon? They're the ones who usually talk some sense into the boys."

Salome's wheeze deepened, sucking away any breath she might have used to reply.

Jesus walked around the tight circle, stopping in front of John and James. "Brother will deliver up brother, and the father his child. Children will rise against parents and have them put to death." He turned to those on the other side, then walked a few steps and stood in front of Simon. "And you will be hated by everyone for my name's sake."

Finally, a cloud of concern crossed her husband's face, but only for a moment.

Jesus walked beyond the small gathering of men and gazed defiantly at the Scribes and Pharisees gathered just below the crest, arms crossed, faces set in uncompromising conviction.

"Don't think I've come to bring peace on earth" he said, loud enough for them to hear. "I've come to bring a sword."

The rising apprehension of the religious leaders seeped into the air.

"Simon isn't stupid," Sarah whispered. "Neither are your sons. Can't they hear this man? It's almost like he's trying to start some kind of revolution or something. And he has the numbers behind him to make him a serious threat."

Salome dropped back deeper into the shadows.

" I don't get it," Sarah said. "This is the kind of man, the kind of talk, Simon would have condemned a few months ago." She turned to her friend. "What's happened to him?"

Jesus spoke again, his words overwhelming hers. "I've come to set a man against his father, and a daughter against her mother." He stepped back into the circle of men, and addressed them even as his words reached everyone on the hills below. "A man's enemies will be those from his own household. Anyone who loves his father or his mother more than he loves me is not worthy of me. Anyone who loves his son or daughter more than me is not worthy of me."

"This is how he controls them, Salome," Sarah said. "It's not the teachings that Simon's always talking about. It's not even the 'miracles.' He's making himself the center of their universe. Somehow, he's managed to strip them of everything that once mattered."

How could she possibly fight this?

"And anyone who doesn't take up his cross and follow me is not worthy of me."

Sarah didn't even try to stifle her gasp. No one in Galilee feared anything more than the Romans' cross. You didn't joke about it. You didn't even speak about it.

"Anyone who finds his life, will lose it," Jesus' words spread over the hushed crowd gathered below, "and anyone who loses his life for my sake, will find it."

Cheers erupted throughout the mountainside, growing louder as he walked down through the crowd, his hair tossed by the soft breeze, the picture of calm. Simon and the others fell into step behind him. People made way for them, then

72

poured down the hill in their wake, deep in conversation over what they'd just heard.

Sarah stumbled through the brush, struggling to still her thoughts as she looked for a way to break the spell this man had on Simon before something unimaginable happened. She tripped on rocks that rolled away from beneath her feet and nearly fell just as a hand took her by the arm.

"Be careful," Simon said. "Come over here to the path, out of the rough."

She grabbed him, no longer worried about proper behavior, and whispered so harshly she nearly shouted, "We have to get out of here. Now."

"Why?"

"He's crazy, Simon. Why can't you see that? You heard him up there, telling you to give your life for him. More than crazy, he's dangerous. Please. Please. Just leave him and come home with me."

Simon stopped and looked at Sarah, his gaze clear and direct. "I can't."

"Of course, you can."

"No, Sarah, I can't. I love you. I love the children. But I can't leave him. He's breathed meaning and purpose into the laws, into the words of the Prophets. Into my life. How can I leave that?" He looked into her eyes a long moment before turning to follow the crowd.

As he made his way down the hill, she ran up beside him.

"Then I will be right behind you every step of the way, Simon," she said. "I love you too much to let you run off alone to wherever this man is leading you."

Chapter 10

Even though Jesus seemed to be taking them back home and not out of town, Sarah found no joy, no relief. Simon and the other men were quiet as they walked, as if trying to make some kind of sense out of whatever had just happened on that hilltop. She walked with her husband, certain there was no sense to be made of it.

The image of the cross seared into her thoughts. Every tree she saw seemed to be nothing more than a crossbar in the making. Who hadn't seen men nailed or tied to beams alongside the road, baking in the sun, their muscles ripping under their skin, a scene so hideous it was unspeakable?

Jesus probably just wanted to make a point, but still there were safer ways to do it.

As they walked into town, swarms of people came from every direction, swelling the crowd. It seemed every one of them reached out to him for something, and although she didn't want to acknowledge it, Sarah couldn't help but notice his unhesitating response as he reached back again and again.

He welcomed children who couldn't walk, old men who couldn't stand straight, people of all ages and shapes who couldn't see, hear, speak, all crying out to him. She could see a look on his face, a light in his eye, a heart broken by the hurt of others.

She understood that he wanted them to be healed, to be whole, to be happy, but still, desire can't work miracles. Yet they all seemed to think it did as they turned back to the crowd, shouting with joy, showing others their strengthened limbs, rejoicing at sights they thought they could now see, sounds they thought they could now hear, souls set free.

Part of her wanted it all to be possible, but how could it possibly be?

As Jesus led the way through the marketplace, people shoved and tripped against the stalls. Sarah felt the distress of vendors who scrambled to keep their wares from tumbling into the dirt.

This man had upended her world, too.

Ahead, she noticed three men head into the throng from a side path. They scanned the crowd, clearly looking for one face. When they spied him, they broke through the mob of people and made their way to Jesus.

Sarah recognized one of them, a young man, fervent and intense.

He fell into step beside Jesus, and said, "John the Baptist sent us to you."

Jesus turned his attention toward the men without slowing his pace.

"Herod had him arrested," the young man said.

"Arrested," Andrew shouted. "For what?"

"For condemning his relationship with his brother's wife"

A few people close enough to hear caught their breath. Others shook their heads. A low murmur ran through the crowd as people passed the word back.

"How would Herod even know what someone like the Baptist says?" a woman behind Sarah asked. "John's out in the desert, nowhere near the palace."

"The Pharisees, no doubt," another woman said. "They've been trying to stop him for years."

"Well, they can lock him up and keep him from speaking of sin, but that doesn't make the sin go away," a man near them said.

"It's more than that," the intense young man said. "It's not just what John says. It's that people listen to him. He speaks truths, and they recognize it. I think Herod saw a rebellion in the making."

Fear gripped Sarah. The king didn't hesitate to tighten his grip around anyone who drew crowds, anyone who might be a threat to his authority and the semblance of peace he had with the Romans.

She watched for Jesus' response, but he kept walking, never breaking his stride even as he listened to the men.

"John sent us to you to ask if you are the one who is to come," the young man said, "or if we should look for someone else."

Jesus stopped and waved his hand toward the vast crowd. "Go and tell John what you see and hear. The blind can see, the lame can walk, lepers are cleansed and the deaf hear, the dead are raised, and the poor are taught the good news."

Those gathered around him cheered at the words while a nearby tanner stopped calling for people to come check his wares. Other merchants grew still as well. Across the crowd, Sarah saw a small group of religious leaders standing on the synagogue steps, their faces clouded with anger.

She pulled Simon off to the side, knocking over a basket in her attempt to get him away from Jesus for even a moment.

"Did you hear that?" she said.

"What?" Simon asked, as he bent to help a frazzled shopkeeper gather the pomegranates that had rolled from the fallen basket.

"What he just said, Simon." She took his arm and drew him up to look at her. "Even I know what he meant. Everyone knows the prophecy of Isaiah. *Say to those who are afraid, be strong, fear not. Behold, your God will come and save you. Then the blind will see, the deaf will hear, then shall the lame man leap like a deer and the tongue of the mute sing for joy.*"

The shopkeeper glanced at her before heading back inside.

"So?" her husband said.

"So? So? Simon, '*God will come and save you?*' He's saying he's God. How can you not get that through your head?"

"I don't think that's what he meant."

"No? Then you're only hearing what you want to hear. I can assure you, the Pharisees and the Scribes got the message loud and clear."

The crowd parted again as John's followers left to return to the Baptist. People tripped over one another, bumping Sarah into another basket. Before a single piece of fruit could escape, Simon caught it and set it upright.

"You're reading into things, Sarah."

"I don't think I am, but even so, look at this mob. How long do you suppose Herod's going to ignore this? The Scribes, the Pharisees hear what he says and see hundreds of people cheering him on. You don't think word of this won't get back to him? Before you know it, Jesus is going to be in prison...," her voice quieted to a whisper, "...you're going to be in prison."

"Me? Why would anyone arrest me?"

"Because you're right there next to him every step, Simon. You don't think others haven't noticed?"

"Don't worry so much. No one cares about me."

He smiled at her and walked back to Jesus' side. As he chatted with others, she wondered how he couldn't be at least a little concerned over what Jesus said, over what the Pharisees heard, over what she felt.

She glared at Jesus even as she noticed he didn't seem caught up in the praise and reaches of the crowd. Instead, as he watched the departing messengers, a shadow darkened his face.

After the men disappeared around a bend, he turned to the people. "When you went to the Baptist, what did you go out in the wilderness to see? A reed shaken by the wind?"

From somewhere deep in the crowd, a man shouted, "No."

Jesus turned toward him. "Then why did you go out there? To see a person dressed in expensive clothes?"

From all around, voices rose in unison. "No."

"No. Those who wear expensive clothes are in kings' houses, not the wilderness." He paused a moment, glancing toward the religious leaders, who stood scowling from the edge of the road, then turned his attention back to the crowd. "So, why did you go out there? To see a prophet?"

The crowd roared its agreement.

"Yes, I tell you, but more than a prophet." Jesus looked out at the throng, to its farthest reaches. "John is the one of whom it is written, *Behold, I send my messenger before you, who shall prepare the way before you.*"

Sarah followed his gaze to the gathering of Scribes and Pharisees, who glared back at him, not caught up in his words as the others were. As Simon was.

"From the day John the Baptist began his ministry until now the kingdom of heaven has suffered violence," Jesus said, clearly speaking to the men who stood on the steps, apart from the crowd. "And men of violence take it by force."

The religious leaders visibly struggled to control their rising anger.

"John is Elijah, who is to come," Jesus said. "If you have ears, hear what I say."

He turned to resume his walk through the town, and Sarah hurried to keep pace with her husband. The crowd behind her grew quiet, pondering his words. Only newcomers called out with excitement as they ran to join the crowd from side streets and courtyards.

John, Andrew, and James didn't talk about his words. They talked about the Baptist's imprisonment, their faces dark with vengeance. She knew Andrew and John were close followers of the Baptist, but the depth of James' anger surprised her. She didn't trust him or his brother. The smallest flicker of a perceived insult could set off an explosion with them. No doubt others in the crowd had followed the Baptist, too, and she feared that any spark might cause a riot.

Simon walked quietly beside her. He had to hear the conversations, feel the mounting tension.

She nodded toward Jesus, and said, "He needs to back down a little, let the people go home. Crowds this big are just going to attract more attention. Bad attention. The Baptist is only the beginning."

"Even Herod's not stupid enough to do anything with this many people around," Simon said.

"But Jesus can't just say whatever he wants," she said. "It's dangerous."

"What do you mean?"

"That nonsense about the Baptist being Elijah. And everyone seemed to accept it as if he'd just said the sky is blue. You know the Scribes and Pharisees aren't as gullible. Did you see their faces?"

"I saw them."

"Why would he say that? Why invite trouble when trouble is already stalking you?"

"Maybe he said it because it's true," Simon said, his voice so quiet she almost didn't hear.

Sarah stopped a moment, then hurried to catch up again. "True? You believe that?"

"I believe him."

"You believe the Baptist is Elijah? You've seen that madman wandering around in the desert. A scrawny mess demanding that everyone in sight repent. That's Elijah?"

"And where is that desert?"

"What?"

"The desert John lives in, the place where he baptizes. Where is it?"

"I don't understand your question, Simon." Sarah was in no mood for riddles.

"I'll tell you where it is. It's right there where Elijah was taken up to heaven."

"Come on, Simon. That doesn't make the man Elijah. Thousands of people have been in that desert since then, more than a few as crazy as the Baptist. You never thought any of them was 'Elijah.' But now, just because Jesus says it's so, you believe it?"

"If it doesn't make sense to me, Sarah, it's only because I don't yet understand."

Chapter 11

Sarah sat on the courtyard bench and drank in the Sabbath quiet. Leaning her head back against the vine-covered wall, she shut her eyes and relaxed into the warmth of the sun until a buzz blew in from the road, and she looked to see a cloud of people on the horizon, heading toward her house. Simon was where she knew he'd be, right at Jesus' side. He practically danced down the road while Sarah searched in vain for a way to signal to him that the mob should go somewhere else – back into town, down to the shore, anywhere.

"You should have seen it, Sarah," Simon said, as he walked past her, pausing for only a moment. "You know the man with the withered hand from the other side of town?"

Sarah nodded. Her heart had ached for the man ever since she was a child, his hand barely a hand at all, his arm stunted and unable to move from his side. How many times had he broken it because he couldn't move it when he fell, couldn't catch himself to stop the fall?

"Jesus healed him, right there in the synagogue," Simon said. "Just like that, his shrunken, useless hand stretched out, healthy and strong. He was waving it around, opening it, closing it. I was amazed. Amazed."

Before she could remind her husband it was the Sabbath, he followed his friends into the house.

Others walked past her, oblivious to her lack of welcome. She had to shove through the crowd to get into her door. Already people crushed into the room so close they could barely lift their arms, squeezing the air out of the small space.

She turned and pushed back through the suffocating mob. Once out on the road, she walked with no destination in mind, leaving Simon safely ensconced in the house to happily relive the events of the day.

Clusters of people stood along the road talking, celebrating the "miracle" they had witnessed, while others streamed by on their way to her house. As she passed a group of men, Sarah noticed they were in deep conversation with some Scribes she didn't recognize.

A few moments later, she overheard one woman say to another, "You know, Scribes have come all the way from Jerusalem to see what's going on here. My husband said they were at the synagogue today and saw the healing."

"How could they miss it?" a man nearby said. "The hand straightened out right before our eyes."

Sarah stopped. That couldn't be good. They'd heard of him even in Jerusalem, and now they've seen him defy the Sabbath law with a visible, obvious work? She made her way through the crowd to get nearer to the group of religious leaders and listened unnoticed in the throng that surrounded them.

"He's gone mad," a man said to them. "We've known him all his life. I know his family. Faithful, devout people. They always obeyed the law. But something's happened to him. He never used to talk like this. And now, he's running around healing people and casting out demons. I don't know what's going on."

"I can tell you what's going on," one of the Scribes said. "He's possessed by Beelzebul, that's what's going on, and it is by the very prince of demons that he casts out demons. Only Satan would 'heal' a person on the Sabbath. And in the synagogue, no less."

"Someone needs to stop him," a thinner, taller, more severe Scribe said.

The men murmured and nodded in agreement as they began to walk toward her house.

Sarah spun around and followed them. She hadn't even thought that Jesus might be possessed. But it made so much sense. How else could he do the things he did? That explained the strange hold he had on people, the cures they thought they saw. He entrances them for a few minutes. No doubt, the man's hand hadn't straightened at all. If he walked by right now, it would still be withered and useless.

The crowd parted to make way for the religious leaders, and she hurried to follow.

As the men entered the door, Jesus greeted them with the words, "How can Satan cast out Satan?"

They all stopped so quickly, Sarah nearly ran into them.

They were right. He was possessed. He couldn't possibly have heard their discussion.

"If a kingdom is divided against itself, that kingdom can't stand. If a house is divided against itself, that house can't stand. And if Satan has risen up against himself and is divided," he looked directly at the Scribes, "he cannot stand but is coming to an end."

Sarah saw the men's scowls deepen and tried to catch Simon's attention, but he sat near her loom with Hannah on his lap, captivated by Jesus, oblivious to her.

While she tried to figure how she could maneuver into his line of vision, a boy slipped past her, squeezed through the crowd, tugged on Jesus' robe, and said, "Your mother and brothers are outside, asking for you."

Jesus turned from the boy and looked at the people sitting on tables and benches, floors, and mats, standing in every corner, gathered at every window, eagerly awaiting every new word he spoke.

"Who are my mother and brothers?" He spread out his arms. "Here are my mother and brothers. Whoever does the will of God is my brother and sister and mother."

His mother. Hope rose just a bit within Sarah. Maybe she's come to get him, to stop him. Sarah looked through the mob outside the house, trying to find the small, dark-haired woman she remembered from the wedding. Finally, she spotted her standing off to the side under a tree, talking with Salome.

She pushed through the people, making her way to where they stood just as the woman disappeared into the crowd.

"What did she say?" she asked Salome.

"Mary? She was just chatting."

"About what?"

"Nothing in particular," Salome said. "The pretty day, the beauty of the fruits beginning to ripen on the jujube trees, the brilliance of the sun sparkling on the sea. She's really pleasant to talk with."

"Did she mention that her son is possessed?"

"What?"

"I heard some men talking, Salome. They think he's possessed. It makes sense. I can't believe it never occurred to me."

"He's not possessed, Sarah," Salome said. "No one possessed by the devil could be so kind, so genuine, make you feel so welcomed."

Sarah looked at her friend. She was one of them. The whole town was entranced by this man.

Chapter 12

Sarah pulled the blanket up around her shoulders and tried to sleep, but the Scribe's words echoed through her thoughts. If evil wasn't the source of Jesus' works, what was? And who, except a man possessed, would claim to be God?

But how could she ever convince Simon that the man who had become the center of his existence was possessed? How could she fight the devil himself?

As she rolled over to face the wall in search of something, anything, normal and solid, a voice drifted in through the courtyard window. A man spoke in hushed tones, as if afraid someone might hear. Even in its whispers, she recognized the deep, resonant voice of Nicodemus, a man Simon knew and liked. A Pharisee. And not just a Pharisee, but a member of the Great Sanhedrin. She'd noticed him in the crowds earlier that day and mentioned it to Simon as they were going to bed, but Simon had dismissed her concern.

Or at least he tried to.

Maybe he didn't share it, but the concern was very real to her.

The local leaders had limited power, but the Court of Jerusalem, the Great Sanhedrin, had the power of life and death. They never shied away from asking Rome to condemn anyone who taught against their interpretation of the law, and all too often, the Roman leaders acquiesced to their judgment.

Nicodemus might be a kind, righteous man in Simon's eyes, but to her he was a symbol of the threat Jesus had become to her husband, her family, her entire way of life.

What could he be doing in her courtyard in the middle of the night? And who was he talking to?

She stared at the wall, trying to decide if she should wake Simon, afraid to listen to the man, afraid to ignore him.

"Rabbi," Nicodemus said, his words clear even if hushed, "we know that you are a teacher come from God, for no one can do these signs that you do unless God is with him."

A teacher come from God? Surely he couldn't be talking to Jesus. Unless it's a trap.

She stood, stepped around her sleeping husband, and walked into the main room. Jesus' mat laid near the fireplace, empty. A shadowy figure sat on the floor across the room, leaning against the wall beside the courtyard door where he could hear and gaze out but still stay hidden in the darkness. When she realized it was John, she drew her cloak tight around her shoulders, quietly walked past all the others scattered and sleeping on the floor, and knelt beside him. Peering out the door through the darkness, she saw Nicodemus and Jesus silhouetted by a small fire in the courtyard. Jesus sat on the bench, wrapped in his shawl in the chill of the night. Nicodemus sat on the ground in front of him, bent forward as if closing off the rest of the world, awaiting a response, but only the crackle of flames and the cry of crickets broke the stillness.

The man couldn't believe what he had said, Sarah thought. It must be a trick, but would Jesus see through him or drink in the admiration? Throughout the day, the religious leaders badgered the people who followed Jesus in search of something with which to trap him. Now, Nicodemus was going directly to the source. A frightening move.

For several moments, Jesus said nothing, then he leaned forward, drawing Nicodemus into an even more intimate discussion.

"Truly," he said, his tone that of someone who wants nothing more in life than to get his message across, "truly, unless one is born again he cannot see the kingdom of God."

"What kind of response is that?" she whispered to John, who shook his head, sharing her confusion.

"How can a man be born again?" Nicodemus asked, aghast. "Can he enter his mother's womb a second time and be reborn?"

"Unless one is born of water and the Spirit, he cannot enter the kingdom of heaven," Jesus said, as if speaking an obvious truth. "Something born of the flesh is flesh, and something born of the Spirit is spirit."

He gazed into the flames as they flickered and crackled, tossed about by the stiff breeze. Was this his way of ending the conversation?

Then he looked again at Nicodemus. "You don't believe me when I say you must be born again?"

Nicodemus shook his head.

Jesus pointed to the fire. "The wind blows where it wills, and you hear the sound, don't you?"

Nicodemus nodded, but even in the dim light his posture was that of a man perplexed. He shifted in the sand and tilted his head as if he actually wanted to make sense of the words.

"Yet, you don't know where the wind comes from," Jesus stretched his arms out to the ends of the earth, "or where it goes, The same is true of everyone who is born of the Spirit. You hear the Spirit even though you don't know where it's from or where it's going."

"How can this be?" Nicodemus asked.

"Are you a teacher of Israel, and yet you don't understand this?"

John looked at Sarah, sharing her concern that Jesus would speak so boldly to a member of the Sanhedrin.

"We talk about what we know," Jesus said, "and bear witness to what we have seen, but you do not receive our testimony. If I tell you about earthly things and you don't believe them, how can you believe if I explain heavenly things to you?"

Nicodemus didn't respond, and his silence troubled Sarah even as she wondered what Jesus meant by "we."

"No one has ascended into heaven," Jesus said, undeterred, as if he thought this made sense, as if he thought he had a right to talk to a man of religious authority like this, "except he who has descended from heaven, the Son of Man. And just as Moses lifted up the serpent in the wilderness, so the Son of Man must be lifted up, so that whoever believes in him may have eternal life."

Sarah couldn't believe Jesus was giving Nicodemus so much to use against him. He had to know the Pharisees were out to get him, and yet, there he was, spouting nonsense about God and Moses and eternal life. Dangerous nonsense.

She didn't care about him so much, but Simon... always right beside him, hanging onto every word, so obviously a follower, and so vulnerable.

Still Jesus kept talking, his tone earnest and passionate. "For God so loved the world that he gave his only Son, so that whoever believes in him should not perish but should have eternal life."

"He's calling himself the son of God, the only son of God?" Sarah whispered.

Israel is God's son. The children of Israel are God's sons and daughters. There is no 'only son of God.' And there's no one akin to God. No one like God. No one equal to God.

Fear rippled through her veins. How could he spout heresy after heresy with such unhesitating confidence?

She looked at John, grateful that someone else was hearing this, but her gratitude quickly dissolved. He didn't look troubled. He looked enthralled, as if he were hearing the greatest truths ever spoken. As if with one sentence, his entire existence made sense.

She left the room, went back to her bed, laid down, and covered her ears, unwilling to hear one more word.

Chapter 13

The fading rays of morning starlight filtered in through the window, and Sarah knew the few minutes of sleep she'd managed to get would have to be enough. Beside her, Simon sat straight up, ready and eager for a new day spent with Jesus.

As he dressed, she said, "Nicodemus was here last night."

"Here?"

"In the middle of the night. I heard him talking to Jesus in the courtyard." She stood and put on a fresh tunic. "He said some really strange things, Simon."

"Nicodemus?"

"No. Jesus. He went on and on about being born again, the wind, Moses, God giving his only son for something."

When she got no response, she said, "He even insulted Nicodemus. Asked him how he could call himself a teacher of the people of Israel if he didn't understand this nonsense." She walked around her husband and stood between him and the door so that he had to face her. "The man is dangerous, Simon. Doesn't it bother you that he's talking like this to a member of the Sanhedrin?"

"Maybe it's something the Sanhedrin needs to hear, Sarah," Simon said, before walking out of the room.

She didn't hurry to join him. Why rush after him? Once, he would have stood with Nicodemus against any hint of heresy. But now...

When she did step out into the morning, she saw, to her surprise, that her husband was on his boat, preparing to do his job, and he'd taken Micah with him.

As they sailed away, she noticed Jesus walking along the shore. He sat on the sand and gazed out beyond the scattered fishing boats to the distant horizon. Waves lapped up, stretching to reach his hand, and she wondered how someone who loomed so large in her life could look so small and lonely.

***

The sun glinted off Simon's boat as it headed in for the day. Sarah walked out and sat on the bench near the door to await him. She noticed Jesus still sitting on the sand in the quiet of midday.

The road began to fill with people headed toward him from all directions, as if they'd received some secret signal calling them together, and Jesus stood to welcome them, reaching out to everyone who drew near.

Men, women, and children soon filled the beach, gathered so close to one another that Simon struggled to find a spot among them large enough to squeeze the boat onto shore. Once he'd maneuvered into a place near a rock, he, Andrew, and Micah jumped onto the sand, pulled out heavy, wet nets, and sorted through the fish, tossing them into baskets. Micah took one basket and emptied it into the ebbing waves. Water splashed as fish too small to sell fell back into the sea. They laid the nets across rocks to dry, then carried the remaining baskets the short distance into town. John and James followed close behind, taking their day's catch to market.

They seemed to be the only people going into town. Everyone else headed out to be with Jesus. Sarah sighed and went back into the house. Simon would not be joining her anytime soon.

She tried to ignore the scene on the shore, but the increasing crowd commanded her attention as people spilled into the road as far as her yard. They pushed to the very edges of the

90

sea, squeezing around Jesus until he finally climbed into Simon's boat in search of space even to turn around and address them. Still people crowded close, knocking the aged vessel against the rocks.

As soon as Simon returned, Jesus called him into the boat and pushed offshore just beyond the beach. Bobbing on gentle waves, anchored in place, he stood and looked out at the people, then began to talk. The crowd grew still while clusters of Scribes, Pharisees, and chief priests hung back along the perimeter near her house, a silent, sullen presence.

"Abi, Hannah, come in now," she called through the window.

"They can stay outside," Leilah said, looking over Sarah's shoulder.

"I want them in. It's not safe."

"Of course, it's safe," her mother said. "You know almost every person out there. Even those from other towns have been hanging around here or wandering Galilee with you for months now." She limped to the table with the bread bowl and punched down the dough. "Admit it, Sarah, you don't want the girls to hear what he has to say."

"It's not what he says that bothers me, Mother. I can counter that when I have to. It's the strange hold he has on these people."

"You talk like he's casting some kind of spell on them."

"Well, how do you explain what's happened around here? How do you explain what's happened to Simon?"

"They like what they hear," Leilah said. "He gives them a different perspective to life, a perspective that makes more sense of life."

"No one cares about what he has to say, Mother. They only want him to do something for them. If they cared about what he says, they'd pay attention and hear what it is he's really saying."

"What do you mean?"

Sarah started to explain, then knew even cynical Leilah wouldn't believe that anyone would have the nerve to proclaim himself to be God.

***

Approaching voices told Sarah the talk by the sea was over. She glanced out the window and saw Simon and Jesus leading the rest of the Twelve to her door. Leilah noticed, too, and began adding to the platters she had prepared.

"Explain what you meant in the parable about the weeds in the field," Nathaniel said, as he walked in with Jesus.

The men sat on mats and cushions around the table. Some pulled fruit off the plate even as Leilah reached between them to set it down. Sarah nodded to Abi to get the jar and pour water into their cups.

"The person who sows the good seed," Jesus said, "is the Son of Man. The field is the world, and the good seed represents the sons of the Kingdom." He paused and looked around the table at the men seated with him. "The weeds are the sons of the evil one, and the enemy who sowed them is the devil."

"So, what about the harvest?" Philip said.

"The harvest is the end of time. The Son of Man will send his angels to gather everyone who does evil and throw them into the fire. Then the righteous will shine like the sun in the Kingdom of their Father."

Sarah was struck by his tone. No gloom and doom or sounds of victory for the righteous. Just a simple statement of fact.

The men pondered his words for a moment before Andrew said, "What's this kingdom like?"

Jesus studied the grapes in his hand as he said, "The kingdom of heaven is like a treasure hidden in a field. A treasure a man finds and covers up. In his joy, he goes out and sells all that he has and buys the field."

He set the grapes on the table and leaned forward. "It's like a merchant in search of fine pearls. When he finds one pearl of great value, he sells everything he has and buys it."

Seeing bewilderment in the faces of those around the table, he gestured toward the sea. "The kingdom of heaven is like a net that was thrown into the sea and gathered fish of every kind. When it was full, men drew it ashore and sorted the good from the bad, throwing away the bad." He leaned back again. "So it will be at the end of time. The angels will separate the evil from the righteous and throw them into the fire. There, men will weep and gnash their teeth."

He looked around at the Twelve before him. "Do you understand this?"

They all answered, "Yes."

Sarah left the house and sat in the quiet of the courtyard. Bits of the ongoing dinner discussion drifted out through the nearby door. She looked up into the night sky and thought of Abraham. Had he felt as alone as she?

It didn't matter so much that they all pretended to understand him. Why did no one else see the danger in his words?

Footsteps drew her attention away from the flickering starlight. Simon walked out of the house, dropped onto the bench beside her, and looked up into the same sky.

"So, what do you think of all that kingdom talk?" Sarah said.

"I thought it was profound."

"It didn't trouble you?'

"Why? Should it?

"Angels separating the evil from the 'righteous'? I'm guessing the righteous, the ones he's promising will be part of the kingdom and finders of treasure, are the people who stick with him. Sounds pretty controlling to me, Simon."

"He's talking about heaven, wisdom, seeing God and his glory, Sarah, not a real kingdom. You know the writings. *If you seek it like silver and search for it as for hidden treasures, then you will understand the fear of the Lord and find the knowledge of God.* That's the treasure he's talking about, the pearl of great value. Wisdom. An awareness of the goodness of God, goodness that is hidden even in the midst of our lives."

She sat silently pondering his words.

"*Wisdom is more precious than jewels, and nothing can compare to her,*" Simon said. "*Her ways are of joy, and all her paths are peace.*"

All her paths are peace, Sarah thought. How she longed for any wisdom that led to peace. Was there anything anyone wanted more?

"We're heading out tomorrow," Simon said.

"Heading out? Where?"

"I'm not sure. Jesus said he wanted to visit some of the nearby towns. We shouldn't be long. Are you coming?"

Her resolve to stick by his side had weakened. She knew he would never hear anything she said as long as Jesus filled his thoughts.

"No, Simon, I'm not. I'm staying here to take care of our family. Mother's looking tired. Besides, we can't abandon the girls and Micah every time Jesus wants to go off somewhere."

"I'm taking Micah with me," Simon said.

"With you?"

"He's old enough, Sarah. He needs to hear what Jesus has to say."

***

Midday. A chance to rest. Sunshine warmed Sarah's soul as she stood in the courtyard and let it wash over her, momentarily easing her guilt that she hadn't gone with Simon, her worry that she'd let him take their son. Leilah napped in the back room, while Hannah and Abi sat near the road, stacking stones, racing to see who could build higher. As she turned to go back inside, she heard Hannah squeal. She looked over her shoulder and saw her daughter run down the dirt road to greet her approaching father.

Even though still irritated that Simon had left and taken Micah with him, Sarah was grateful to see the trip had been a short one. She could live with him wandering off a day or two now and then.

As they neared the house, she noticed the small band seemed uncharacteristically somber. Jesus, especially, looked almost dejected. He separated from the group and walked down to the shore alone. John and James split off and headed to their own home.

Micah greeted her with a hug and a smile.

"How was it?" she asked.

"Okay," he said, as he passed her and went into the house with his sisters following close behind, eager to hear about his adventure.

"Just okay, huh?" she said to Simon. She didn't want to gloat but couldn't hide her relief that her son had been less than captivated by the experience.

"Things didn't go so well in Nazareth," Simon said.

"Nazareth? You took our son to Nazareth? What were you thinking, Simon? You know they ran Jesus out of town. Why would you go back there with him? Worse than that, why would you take Micah?"

"Jesus thought the time was right to return to their synagogue. He hasn't given up on them."

"You went with him to the synagogue? Are you serious? Those people threatened to kill him the last time he was there."

"It seemed like a good idea. It's his hometown. I guess he thought maybe they'd be more open to his teachings now, that maybe they'd heard about how other places have welcomed him."

Sarah clenched her fists and tried to slow her breathing to calm herself. "So. You went to Nazareth. With Micah. What happened?"

"Jesus sat down and started to explain the law and the Prophets like he always does. Next thing I know, the religious leaders are in an uproar, outraged, stirring up everyone else. Men all around us are shouting about how they've known him since he was a boy, he's just the carpenter's son, who does he think he is. And they're shoving each other to get to him, knocking tables over. Knocking people over."

Sarah shut her eyes and dropped her head into her hands, trying to forget that her son had been in the midst of all that chaos.

"Then what?" she said.

"Then he stood and said, 'A prophet is not without honor except in his own country and in his own house.' After that, he really didn't do much in the way of healings or anything. We just left town and headed back here."

Sarah didn't know whether to be angry at Simon or angry at Jesus or angry at both. But even in her fury, the words 'in his own house' hung heavy in her thoughts. Everyone knew that, in the Prophets, a man's house meant his soul. She looked out to the lone figure sitting in the sand on the edge of the sea and was surprised to feel sorry for the doubt. Not hers. His.

Chapter 14

Abi walked into the house with Hannah at her side. "Mom, some men are here, asking for Jesus."

Not again, Sarah thought. Life had calmed considerably since he went to Nazareth. Even the afternoon crowds had dwindled, much to her relief.

She wiped the flour from her hands and stepped into the clouded sunlight. A thin, grave young man stood among the pack. She recognized him as one of the men John the Baptist had sent to Jesus weeks earlier. They stood on the edge of the beaten dirt path that led from the road to her door.

"He's not here," she called out.

"Can we wait?" one of them asked.

"Sure," she said, trying to sound welcoming. "Have a seat on the bench, and we'll bring you some water."

She handed Abi a water jar, then balanced a plate of fruit on her hip, grabbed a ladle and some cups, and carried them out to the men, with her daughter close behind. They accepted the refreshments with gratitude, and she left them waiting in the haze.

A short time later, she saw Simon and Micah walk in from town, carrying their empty fish baskets. Behind them followed Jesus, Andrew, John, and James. Jesus noticed the men and walked ahead to welcome them, greeting each with a warm embrace.

Sarah was struck by the solemnity with which they acknowledged Simon and the others before they all gathered together in a tight circle. As they talked, she strained in vain to try to catch at least some of what they said and didn't hear Leilah walk up behind her.

"Who's that?" she said, glancing over Sarah's shoulder.

"The Baptist's followers. They're here to see Jesus."

Simon looked across the yard to her, his gaze troubled. He left the group and came into the house. After he ushered the girls out of the room, he turned to Sarah, sheltered her with an arm around her shoulders, and said, "The Baptist is dead."

"Dead? What happened?"

He drew in a deep breath and breathed it out, then said, "Herod had him beheaded."

As Sarah's knees buckled, Simon caught her by the arm. He led her to a chair, where she sat, unable to make sense of what she'd just heard. She looked over at Leilah, who looked back at her, concern etched deep into her aged face. Neither said a word.

Simon might have gone back outside. Sarah couldn't be sure. Her world constricted to a tiny crumb of bread on the floor at her feet. To look beyond that was to see the danger, the evil that suddenly seemed to fill the world.

At some point, she realized everyone had come inside. Simon and the others stood near the hearth talking, but Sarah couldn't listen. She wanted to cover her ears and run from the room, but she sat, with nowhere to run.

Only John stayed in the doorway, pacing, his anger growing. "Why would Herod kill him? For what?"

"As a gift to his stepdaughter," one of the men answered.

"A gift?" John said. "What kind of gift is that? What did he do that warranted death?"

The man shook his head.

"John's right," Andrew said. "What did the Baptist do besides teach? You can't kill a man for what he says."

The thin young follower of John glanced at Jesus. "Herod's been talking about you, too. He thinks you're the Baptist, raised from the dead."

***

98

Sarah stumbled through dinner preparations and clean-up, unwilling to listen to anymore of the men's conversation but unable to escape, lost in her thoughts even as she tried not to think.

As she brushed crumbs off a crumbless plate, Simon walked up beside her, and said, "Do you want them to sleep in this room?"

She grabbed his arm and pulled him out into the courtyard. "No, I don't want them to sleep here at all tonight. Let them go to Zebedee's house."

Surprised by the unexpected response, Simon agreed without argument. "Sure. Jesus probably could use the quiet anyway. Better to let the rest go somewhere else."

"Jesus is the one I don't want here."

"Why not? He's slept here every night that we've been in town."

"But I didn't know Herod was out to get him then. He can't stay in this house, Simon. It's not safe. We've got children. Think of them for once."

Almost immediately, she regretted the sting. He was a good father. His children were everything to him. Or at least they used to be.

"We can't send Jesus away, Sarah. This has become his home. He belongs here."

He led her to the bench under the canopy of vines and sat beside her, cradling her hands in his. "I know you're afraid. I understand. But we can't turn our backs on Jesus in his hour of need. We have to be there for him."

Sarah looked through the doorway at the man sitting on a mat at her table, gazing into the candlelight while others around him conversed. She remembered him alone at the beach just a few days earlier, and again, she felt sadness for him. Even in a room full of friends, he seemed so alone.

Chapter 15

As word got out that the Baptist had been executed, people drifted into Capernaum from all over Galilee to gather at Simon's house. More and more came every day. In small groups and large, they slowly filled the yard, the road, the beach for as far as Sarah could see. She didn't have the strength to protest or care. Her head spun with the thought that Herod knew about Jesus. No doubt he also knew Jesus was here, in Capernaum, with Simon.

She felt the world close in around her. Once it seemed so safe in this corner of Galilee, a town nobody gave much thought to. A quiet place to raise a family among friends. Until now, she never appreciated how insulated and isolated she had been from the problems of the real world. Until now, she never thought about the constant fear others lived in as part of their everyday life. Raids on their towns, cities overthrown. She'd hear about their troubles and feel sorry for people, but she didn't really think about what life was like for them. She'd say a prayer or two, then go back to worrying about her own problems.

Now she felt exposed, as if Rome itself had her in its sights. Every fear she had ever felt rose up in her throat, choking her, suffocating her. She felt she'd lost control of her entire existence.

Since she'd heard about the Baptist, she'd barely been able to function. She had no idea if it was sunny or cloudy, no interest in anyone else's business, little thought beyond what she needed to do to take care of her home and her children.

She stood in the doorway and looked out at the sea, surprised to see how green its waves were, how blue the sky.

For days, her world had been devoid of light, a perpetual night.

Jesus walked up and stood by her side. He looked at the crowd of people outside the door, with still more coming down the road. Then he turned to Simon and the others gathered in the room. His face looked drawn and tired. His shoulders sagged as if the weight he carried had suddenly become too much for him to bear.

"We need to get away," he said to Simon.

We echoed through Sarah's head.

"Where to?" Levi asked.

"Somewhere far away," Jesus said. "A desert place, a place alone. A place where we can rest a while."

Lacking even the energy to protest, Sarah watched Jesus, Simon, and the rest of the Twelve walk down to the shore and climb into Simon's boat. As others noticed, the air in Capernaum came alive with people shouting to one another, running to the sea to join them. Some jumped in the few boats beached in the sand. Everyone else ran along the shore, keeping their eyes on Jesus' boat, calling out to him and to one another.

Sarah sighed and stood. She glanced at her mother, who silently nodded. Now was not the time to abandon her husband even if it did seem he had abandoned her…again.

Finding strength in anger, she walked out the door to the road and became one with the crowd. People streamed out of the village from all directions to join them. She looked back at her house, certain her mother and children were the only people left in Capernaum.

Jesus' boat headed out to the middle of the sea. Still, the crowd hurried along the road and the sand. They bumped and tripped over one another as they hurried to wherever he was going. Some splashed through the shallow water along the shore in their attempts to get ahead of the pack. Every door they passed seemed to fly open as people rushed to become a

101

part of the mob. Every village they hurried through seemed to empty as residents dropped what they were doing and followed.

Just as the crowd closed in on the small seaside town they assumed was his destination, they realized the boat had turned, drifting toward a deserted shore far from any town or field worth tilling, a place she never visited because it had nothing to offer.

The mob hurried toward what they decided was now his destination. Still, people flowed in to join them from every road they crossed. Sarah couldn't imagine how word had gotten out so quickly. Farmers, fishermen, merchants, men, women, children of all ages came together. Some carried the lame or led the blind. Some hobbled on weakened limbs while others ran past her. The ever-growing crowd surged forward in one mass. As they neared the isolated beach, the road gradually became more like a trail until it ceased to exist altogether. Scrub bushes, weakly rooted in the sand, fell to the hordes trampling over them in the wilderness.

The boat wove back and forth to the middle of the sea, then again toward land. People arrived at the barren shore before Jesus and filled the stony sand beyond capacity. Sarah climbed onto a rock to peer out over hundreds of heads, all gazing out to sea.

As the boat finally held a steady course and drew near, Jesus stood and looked at all those waiting for him. For a moment, her anger ebbed, and she felt sorry for him.

Despite his weariness, compassion lit his face, a compassion so deep it seemed he drew his strength, his very being from his love for this horde. As soon as the boat reached shore, he welcomed them, embracing all who came to him, reaching out to touch the head, the arm, the shoulder of anyone who got near. Shouts of joy rang out as one after another announced a healing.

For hours, he made his way through the crowd. As he walked past Sarah, he smiled at her, renewed purpose lighting his tired eyes. She wanted to stay angry that he had once again dragged Simon – and her – away from home, but cries of hope and longing, of delight and gratitude from those around her wore down her ire until she, too, felt a spark of longing in her own heart. Not for home. Not for Simon. But for something unknowable.

The sun slipped into the western sky, casting long shadows as it lit the clouds with shocks of pinks and oranges. The chill of evening descended, and some wrapped shawls around children to shield them from its reach. Sarah thought of her own children, grateful they were safe at home. At least, by leaving Capernaum, Jesus would draw Herod's attention elsewhere.

People began to settle in for the night, rummaging through satchels and bags in search of scraps of food but little appeared. They had left so quickly, no one thought to bring any.

Simon approached and motioned for her to come to him. Looking for a path, any path, through the throng, she wove her way over and around people to where he stood.

He took her by the hand and led her to Jesus, just in time to hear Philip say, "What are we going to do with all these people, Jesus? You brought us here to a place with no shops, no groves, no vineyards, nothing, and it's been a long day. Look at them. Everyone's hungry, and there's nothing to eat here, not even a fig tree anywhere in sight. Send them off to the villages to get some food. Tell them you're not going anywhere. You'll be here when they get back in the morning."

Jesus looked at the twelve men who stood near him, each surveying the massive crowd and nodding in agreement. "They don't need to go away," he said. "Feed them yourselves."

The others turned to him, stunned. "Feed them ourselves? With what? There are thousands of people here."

A little boy seated nearby picked up his father's satchel, ran over, and tugged on Andrew's robe. "I have some bread and fish."

Andrew looked into the pouch the boy held, then turned back to Jesus. "Five loaves and a couple of smoked fish? What are we supposed to do with that?"

Jesus embraced the little boy and took the satchel. Then he looked out to all the people, thousands and thousands of people, more people than Sarah had ever seen anywhere, and told them to sit down. In waves, those still standing settled onto the ground and passed the word back.

Taking the few loaves of bread, Jesus gazed up to heaven and said a prayer of thanksgiving for what he had. Then he broke the loaves and handed the pieces to Simon and some of the others, telling them to share them with the crowd. The men looked at each other, hesitant to move out into the crowd with just a few scraps of bread. While they stood still, unsure what to do, Jesus picked up the fish, offered thanksgiving for them, and handed them to the remaining disciples. They stared at him in disbelief, then looked at each other before slowly stepping out into the mob with their meager offerings.

As Simon passed, he glanced at Sarah. She shrugged. What was there to say? These people were either going to laugh them off the beach or riot. Regardless, at least they would all finally know the truth.

But then she watched as bread and fish filled hand after hand after hand, again and again for as far as she could see. Exclamations of surprise and joy shot out from all directions as the offering from the person beside them multiplied each time they accepted and shared it.

Nathaniel tore bread from his scrap and gave it to her. She found a piece in her hand no smaller than what he had started with. She looked at him still holding the same sized scrap, and his eyes mirrored her astonishment. Having no explanation, he reached past Sarah to hand the woman behind her a piece before moving deeper into the crowd.

Sarah tore her bread in half and handed it to the man next to her, who said, "No. I can't take that. It's yours."

"Please," she said, "take it."

He accepted the piece, and ended up with as much as she'd started with. His gaze rose from the bread cradled in his hands. As he looked at the full piece still in her hands, a joyous smile broke out across his face. She pulled some off to eat, and the bread in her hand remained whole.

Her head swam with bewilderment as she tried to make sense of what was happening. Everyone, for as far as she could see, talked and laughed and dined on smoked fish and bread.

But that couldn't be. They must have pulled food out of their satchels, maybe even shared it with those who hadn't brought any. And yet, what were the chances they had all brought the exact same food? And how did that explain what had happened to her?

People all around Sarah relaxed and chatted as they ate until they were filled. Their words floated through the air, mixing together, spinning past her. Chief among them, "How?"

With only the early moonlight to guide them, Simon and the others walked back through the crowd, gathering any food that was left. They returned to Jesus with twelve overflowing baskets of bread and fish.

Sarah looked at the heaps of bread and fish before her. There was no way this much would be left over even if people had shared what they'd brought. Then she looked at Jesus.

Who was this man?

Before they had time to process all that had just happened, he told Simon and the others to get into the boat and sail on ahead of him. Simon motioned for Sarah to join them. Eager to get away from the mob and stay within sight of her husband, she followed him. His gentle grip on her arm as he guided her safely onto the boat soothed any remaining anger over his decision to once again leave home.

She settled into the only available seat, beside Levi, the tax collector. As he slid over to make room for her, she looked him in the eye, the first time she had even allowed herself to be near enough to him to do so, and was caught off-guard by what she saw. Nowhere was the insolent sullenness she had grown accustomed to whenever she'd passed his booth in town. Instead, she saw a joyful, welcoming softness.

The evening breeze brushed against her face as James pushed them off the shore into the sea.

"I don't like that Jesus isn't coming with us," Andrew said.

"He told me he wanted a little time alone to pray," Philip replied. "I think the death of the Baptist hit him hard."

"Well, it should," Sarah said. "If he doesn't stop, he's going to be next."

The men around her looked down at the deck or out into the night.

"It's not just that," Andrew said, his gaze fixed on the distant, night-shrouded horizon. "They were cousins."

"Oh," Sarah said, "I didn't know." The sadness and the weariness in his face took on new meaning. She never thought about him having family. Except his mother.

"So, how's he going to get out here?" Andrew asked as he stood to adjust the sail. "And where are we even going?"

"I don't know," Simon answered. "Maybe someone else will bring him out, or maybe he'll walk back to Capernaum. It's not that far. I assume that's where he meant for us to go."

They sailed away from the shore until Sarah lost sight of the campfires that had lit the night. Overhead, the darkness wrapped around the stars, seeming to bring them down just beyond her reach. She tried to relax, looking up rather than at the sea she never trusted. Again and again thoughts of Jesus and the compassion he had shown those people, when she

106

knew he wanted nothing more than to be left alone, came into her mind and touched her heart.

The men slowly began to talk about what they'd just witnessed.

"How did he do that?" James asked. "People kept reaching up, taking more and more bread out of my hands, but I still always had bread in my hands."

They all shook their heads, no words to express, no way to make sense of what had happened.

Simon leaned toward Sarah, and said, "So?"

"So what?"

"You can't just dismiss what happened back there, Sarah. There were thousands of people there. Thousands. And not one of them went away hungry."

"I'm not dismissing it," she said. "I admit, that was pretty impressive. But I don't have to fall at his feet in adoration because of it. I don't care so much about what he does."

"Then what do you care about, Sarah?"

"Who he is," she answered. But not loud enough for Simon to hear. She wasn't yet ready to say her thoughts out loud. Instead, she breathed them into the night.

Chapter 16

Gazing at the stars, Sarah traced the constellations in her mind, trying not to notice as the wind intensified. When the boat began to rock on rapidly mounting waves, she gripped the edge of her wooden perch. Star by star, the light went out as clouds gathered together, seeming to close in until all she could see was the threatening, suffocating darkness.

She tried to stay calm. The others didn't seem too concerned. Maybe they were used to this, but she seldom ventured out onto the water, and her stomach was not happy with the rising swells. She spotted what she assumed were the flickering lights of Capernaum off in the distance but soon noticed the boat seemed to move away from them rather than toward them. The small vessel dipped farther down into the waves with each surge as the wind whipped wildly around them. Some of the men rushed to readjust the sail. Others began to row, trying to get them back to shore, but the boat persisted in turning away, drifting deeper and deeper into the night.

While those around her struggled against the sea, Sarah kept her eye locked on the receding shoreline of home as if she could mentally pull them toward it.

Behind her, James said, "Look. There's something out there."

She turned, expecting to see a boat. Instead, she saw a figure walking through the spray of the sea. Walking on the sea.

Her thoughts scrambled, unable to make sense of the sight.

Thomas shouted, "It's a ghost."

The men around her leapt to their feet, and she clutched the side of the boat, certain they would capsize it.

It had to be some kind of fish, or maybe a log tossed by the waves. Yet, as it drew nearer, she couldn't deny it was a man even as she knew it couldn't possibly be a man.

Before fear could fully fill her heart, she heard a voice call from the waves, "Don't be afraid. Take courage. I am what you see."

She peered into the misty spray and saw what looked like Jesus walking on the water, his feet making not a splash as he moved closer and closer over the swells.

Simon ran to the stern. "Master, if it's you, tell me to join you."

Jesus reached out his hand. "Come."

Sarah froze, unable to move as her husband climbed over the side into the roiling sea. She wanted to cry out to stop him but not even her voice could respond. Without hesitation, he stepped onto the water and started to walk to Jesus.

On the water, not in the water.

She looked to the sky a moment, certain she must be dreaming. But the wind against her face and the water's spray didn't come from a dream.

As he drew near to Jesus, a gust blew hard against Simon, knocking him off-balance. Panic crossed his face, and he began to sink. Sarah rushed from her seat, not caring if she tipped the whole boat over.

"Teacher, save me," he yelled.

Jesus immediately reached out, grabbed his hand, pulled him to his side, and said, "Oh, you of little faith, why did you doubt me?"

He helped Simon back into the boat, then climbed in beside him. Instantly, the winds and waves calmed, the clouds slid off the stars, and they drifted onto the shores of home.

No one said a word as they exchanged glances. How did they get there? What just happened?

109

Jesus seemed not to notice their hesitation to step onto the sands, afraid the solid ground might be a mirage. He swung over the side and walked toward the road. Simon and the others overcame their fear and hurried to join him while Sarah tentatively touched first one foot onto the beach, then the other. Finally, she let go of the side of the boat and let the ground hold her up.

Simon stopped and waited until she came up beside him.

"Do you believe now?" he said.

"In what?"

"That he's the Messiah, Sarah. I mean, the man walked on water. What more do you need?"

"Come on, Simon. You don't really think he walked on water."

"Then how do you explain what just happened?"

"I don't know," Sarah said. "Maybe there was a sandbar there."

"That's impossible. I got out of that boat, and I wasn't walking on sand. There was nothing beneath my feet but water. Besides, I know that sea better than I know the roads of Capernaum. There is no sandbar there. There has never been a sandbar there."

"Maybe the sand blew, and there's a new one since you last sailed that way."

Simon sighed with exasperation. "That's not how it works. Not in water that deep, and not in the middle of the sea. And even if it had, we would have run aground on it. What are the chances it would have just dropped off right at the point where our boat was? Besides, how would he have known it was there at that exact spot?"

"Well, there's some logical explanation, Simon. There always is. I just don't know what it is yet."

"It's his faith, Sarah."

"What do you mean?" she said, caught short by his quick response.

"That's why he mentioned my lack of faith. He has such enormous faith, and he wants us to have at least a little."

"You're not making any sense, Simon."

" Do you know how much faith it took for him to stand on that water and walk all the way out to us, believing he could do it? I walked what? Maybe five steps before I thought about what I was really doing and sank. But he walked hundreds of steps out from the shore, knowing what he was doing, confident he could do it. Try it sometime," he pointed to the waves lapping at the shore. "Step on that water and believe it will hold you up. And more than that, he believed he could hold me up when my faith failed."

***

Sarah reached to the back of the fireplace and scraped out ash, then dumped it into the bucket at her side. Although dust drifted into her eyes, she barely felt the sting as she wrestled with her new feelings about Jesus and the experiences of the day before. She struggled to deny the works she'd seen him do, to find the logical explanation that surely existed. But more than that, she struggled not to like him.

Leilah walked into the room from the courtyard carrying a basket of fresh-picked figs and sat on a stool near Sarah. "I've been trying to make sense of everything Simon and Andrew said this morning, but I can't." She eyed her daughter. "You really think he walked on water?"

"I don't know what else to think. I questioned Simon every way I could think of as to how he did what he did, and he countered everything. I have to admit, it sure seems like he really did walk on that water."

Her mother pondered the possibility. "I haven't seen everything you've seen, but he's certainly got people's attention. Salome can't talk about anything else. It's almost boring to be around her anymore." She nodded toward the door. "So, where did they go?"

Sarah sat back on her heels and wiped ash from her forehead with a swipe of her arm, then cleaned her hands on the cloth at her waist. "I don't know. Into town, I guess. Jesus headed out early, and there was Simon, running after him."

"You didn't go?"

"I have work to do, Mother. Besides, I assumed they were heading out to fish, to do the work Simon should be doing, but then they took the road away from the sea."

The door opened, and Micah walked in, kicking a rock ahead of him.

"Back so soon?" Sarah asked.

"I was skipping stones with my friends, but the beach got too crowded."

"Crowded?" Sarah stood and looked out the window. People stretched from the shore to the town and beyond.

"I need to see what's going on, where Simon is," she said to her mother, as she hurried out the door, denying to herself that Simon wasn't the only reason she wanted to go.

News had quickly spread that Jesus had fed thousands with almost nothing and then walked on water. Hundreds and hundreds of people from all over Galilee flooded into Capernaum looking for him. Sarah squeezed through the mob and spotted Simon walking with Jesus, heading into the heart of the village. She turned down a side road, running along it to a footpath that took her between buildings and back out onto the main road, deeper into town and closer to her husband.

People filled every nook of the marketplace. Merchants scrambled to move their wares out of the way while boys balanced on covered water jars so they could see over courtyard walls. Windows and doorways overflowed with people, squeezing their heads through any opening just to catch a glimpse of him as he passed.

She pushed through those who stood between her and Simon until she caught up with him just a few steps behind Jesus. As they walked with the crush of people pushing and bumping from every side, she studied the man.

Was it possible? Could he be the Messiah?

Everyone knew the Messiah was coming some time, although she still found it hard to imagine he had come in her time. Yet, she was finding it harder to dismiss the endless healings, people seemingly raised from the dead, thousands of people fed with just a few loaves of bread and a couple of fish. And then, walking on water.

More than all that, though, was his compassion. Unlike anything she'd ever seen. Utterly unselfish. Unmeasured. Unhesitating. Spontaneous, sincere. As if he knew what it was like to be every single person he met. As if he knew every struggle they faced.

When he'd sailed to that far-off shore just a day earlier, grieving the death, the murder, of his cousin, aware he was in Herod's sights, trying to get away, and saw thousands of people waiting for him, she would have understood if he'd ordered Simon to turn around and sail the other way. But he didn't.

Even though he'd still looked tired and beaten up by life, she'd seen a light ignite in his eyes as he reached out with what felt like genuine love to every person there. He understood. He knew the vicious hopelessness and futility of lives spent trying to get enough, be enough, do enough, yet never satisfied. He knew they always hungered for more. And he knew they saw that 'more' in him.

She no longer noticed the people shoving against her but saw only the man leading them forward. Kind, peaceful, gentle even if a bit adamant, loving, humble with a wisdom that took her breath away...when she allowed herself to listen.

Maybe she was wrong to judge him, wrong about his declaring himself to be God. Maybe Simon was right. She was just reading into what he said. Maybe she needed to listen with a more open mind.

Some of those who had dined on bread and fish the night before pushed through the crowd to get to his side, everyone talking at once, clamoring for his attention. "Rabbi, we've been looking for you. When did you get here?... How?... You weren't in any of the boats that left shore... We didn't see you anywhere on the road along the way... Is it true? Did you really walk on the water?"

Jesus answered them as he climbed the steps of the synagogue. "Does it matter how I got here? You've been looking for me but not because of what I've done. You've been looking because you ate the bread and were filled."

At the top of the steps, he looked beyond those nearby to the rest of the crowd and raised his voice so all could hear. "Don't work for bread that perishes but for bread that endures to eternal life, bread the Son of Man will give to you."

"Where do we find bread like that?" someone shouted.

Jesus looked into the crowd as if he knew exactly who had asked the question. "Believe in the one God has sent. He is the one the Father has anointed."

Anointed by God? Sarah snapped out of the daze into which she had allowed herself to be lulled. She saw a group of Scribes and Pharisees in the synagogue doorway behind him, their gaze locked on his every move, and wished she could grab the Messiah insinuation out of the air before it reached their ears.

Still, she no longer felt the anger that such talk once brought. Instead it left her with a curious awe of possibility she saw reflected in the eyes of those around her. An awe she'd seen in her husband's eyes for some time but hadn't understood.

"What sign can you do so that we can believe in you?" someone else called out. "Moses gave our fathers the manna

114

from heaven. You just gave us some bread, bread we can get anywhere."

An earnestness lit Jesus' eyes as he said, "It wasn't Moses who gave the bread from heaven, but my Father, who gives you the true bread from heaven. The bread of God comes down from heaven and gives life to the world."

A woman cried out, "Give us this bread forever."

"Anyone who comes to me will never hunger," he said to her, "and anyone who believes in me will never thirst."

He turned his attention back to the crowd, with hundreds still making their way to him, filling the town from the synagogue to the sea. "I have come down from heaven, not to do my own will, but to do the will of him who sent me. And this is my Father's will, that everyone who sees the Son and believes in him should have eternal life. And I will raise him up on the last day."

A man in front of her said to his wife, "He will raise us up?"

Sarah looked at the religious leaders, leaning in together, talking. Although she couldn't hear them, their ever-present rage pulsed through the air.

Behind her, a man said, "'What does he mean, he's come down from heaven? What's he talking about?"

Another man answered, "I don't know. He's done a lot, but he's still just Jesus. I know him from way back, knew his father, his mother. How can he say he's come down from heaven?"

"Why is there all this murmuring over what I've said?" Jesus said. "Isn't it written in the Prophets, *And they shall all be taught by God*?"

A low rumble ran through the crowd as people began whispering with disdain. Sarah wanted to melt into the crowd, become one with the dust beneath her feet. She had only just begun to let her guard down with him, and for the first time it had felt right to give him her attention. Now, she tried to distract herself, to not hear what he was saying, to no avail.

"Truly, I say to you," he gazed out at the enormous multitude with an intensity so deep it seemed he was addressing each of them personally, "he who believes has eternal life." He looked up at those in the windows above and at the people crammed into doorways, perched on the shoulders of others, sitting on stalls, garden walls, ledges.

"I am the bread of life."

The words echoed off the walls of the town, reverberating to the farthest reaches of the road.

He spoke again, his words unambiguous, his voice strong, his intent becoming increasingly clear. "Your fathers ate the manna in the wilderness, but they still died. This," he pressed his hand against his chest, "is the bread that comes down from heaven, so that a man might eat of this bread and not die but live. Forever."

He paused as people absorbed his words, then said, "The bread that I shall give for the life of the world is my flesh."

The crowd grew silent, but the quiet was not calm. Clouds of anger and confusion darkened the faces of those around her.

A man near Sarah picked up a large stone. Another grabbed his arm and said, "He can't mean what he's saying. Let him get to his point."

Tension shook the streets. If she could have escaped, she would have, but the crowd pushed tighter around her, no longer trying to get near Jesus as much as trying to get at him.

His voice rose above the mounting thunder of derision. "Truly, truly, I say to you, unless you eat the very flesh of the Son of Man and drink his blood, you cannot have life within you. But he who eats my flesh and drinks my blood has eternal life, and I will raise him up on the last day."

Furious voices filled Sarah's ears.

116

"Is he really saying we need to eat his flesh?" a man behind her asked no one in particular.

"If he is, then we'll have to kill him first," another said.

Arms flailed around her, thrust again and again into the air as people tried to get to Jesus. Some grabbed stones and hurled them over her head as the mounting wave of humanity shoved between Sarah and Simon.

She could see her husband next to Jesus, beyond her reach. Now even he seemed to notice what was happening around him. Her chest crushed against the back of the man in front of her, and only the press of people kept her from slipping under their feet as they surged forward.

Still Jesus spoke, his words managing to cut through the roar. "Does this bother you? Then what if you were to see the Son of Man ascending to where he was before?"

As his words fell on them, the tide turned. People began pushing through the crowd to leave rather than get to Jesus.

From all sides, she could hear, "He's crazy... This is impossible... I can't listen to this anymore."

Jesus called out, "It is the Spirit that gives you life. The flesh is of no avail. The words that I have spoken just now are Spirit and life. But," his words trailed off, "there are some of you who do not believe."

By now, nearly no one was left. The crowd had drifted apart, disappearing down the roads out of town and along the shore toward anywhere else. The religious leaders shared smug grins and turned away, going into the synagogue.

Sarah saw her husband, still at Jesus' side, looking bewildered, and she was sorry for him. Her flicker of faith had lasted only hours. His had been the source of his existence for months. While she wasn't surprised at the turn of events, she hadn't expected it all to end so abruptly. She walked over to Simon and took his hand. It no longer mattered who saw. Her husband needed her.

The rest of the Twelve stood around them, among the handful of people still there.

Jesus turned to them and for a moment, the heartache she saw in his eyes startled her.

"Do you also want to leave?" he asked the small group that remained.

"Master," Simon said, "where would we go? Who would we go to? You have the words of everlasting life."

Sarah dropped his hand and stepped back, stunned.

He glanced at the others, then turned to Jesus and said, "We've believed in you all along, and we've come to know you, to know that you are the Messiah, the Holy One of God."

Jesus studied Simon a moment. Then he looked each one in the eye before quietly saying, "Did I not choose you twelve? And yet, one of you is a devil."

Chapter 17

Sarah sat with Leilah on a driftwood log that had long ago washed ashore and watched her children play in the shallow water. The sun warmed her weary face as she gazed out to the calm waves lapping up onto the sand.

Simon had left with Jesus and the others, eager to get out of town. She didn't know where they went, and she didn't care. Weeks had passed, and still she struggled to get over her anger. Anger that Jesus really was a charlatan. Anger that Simon still couldn't see it. And anger that she had almost let herself fall for it.

"I imagine you're glad not to be wandering around all over Galilee," Leilah said.

"I'd be happier if Simon wasn't wandering all over Galilee. But if he didn't give up on Jesus when he said all that nonsense about eating his flesh and drinking his blood, Mother, I don't think he'll ever give up on him."

"So instead, you've given up on Simon?"

Sarah turned from the sea. "What's the point of following him throughout the countryside? Nothing he hears can convince him this man is a fraud. And the religious leaders? Men he once respected? He sees their anger and dismisses it. He knows the danger the same as I do, and he dismisses that, too. Besides, I've got the children to think of. I can't leave them with you any longer."

"Don't worry about us, Sarah. We've been managing just fine. And we're certainly not alone in town anymore. Just about everyone has returned home to their old way of life."

Sarah watched Hannah dig in the sand in search of another shell for her collection. She'd had to toss aside mounds of

119

shells to even get to the sand, but none of those was good enough.

A squeal pierced the air as she jumped up and ran to Sarah, holding a newly-found treasure high in the sky. Sarah pulled her daughter onto her lap and looked at the pearly pink spiral, free of chips, perfect from every angle, and she sighed.

For some reason, shells always left her feeling sad, no matter their beauty or their shape. All she saw was a life that used to be.

***

The basket of grains and fruit threatened to slip off Sarah's hip as she walked down the busy road toward her house. Along the way, she passed stalls selling wares she wished she could buy, but she didn't dare spend any more.

Amid the noise of the market, she noticed someone fall into step behind her. Turning, she saw Simon, smiling. And alone.

Her anger dissolved into joy as she set the basket down and threw open her arms. "You're home."

"Not for long," he said, evaporating the joy before she could even feel it wash through her.

"What do you mean? You're leaving again? So soon?"

"No. We're leaving again, you, me, the children, your mother."

"And where are we going?"

"Jerusalem. It's Tabernacle time."

Sarah measured her words as she picked up the basket. "Maybe you should go without us."

"Why?"

"You know why, Simon. I don't want the children around Jesus, especially after all that crazy bread and blood talk."

"Then there's no problem." Simon took the basket from her. "He's not going."

"How can he not go? He has to go. Every man has to go."

120

He walked a few steps in silence before answering. "It's not safe for him, Sarah. You're not the only one bothered by what he said that day, you know."

"Well, Simon, you have to be honest, he said some crazy things. So crazy, they're impossible to ignore, impossible to even try to comprehend. That anyone would eat his flesh and drink his blood. Really?"

"Like I said, you're not the only one who finds it hard to take."

"I've tried to make some sense of it while you were gone," Sarah said, "tried to give him the benefit of the doubt, but I can't for the life of me imagine what he meant. Mother said she heard the Romans drink the blood of bulls so they can have the power of bulls. Is he saying if people drink his blood they'll have his power?"

Simon shrugged.

"If so," she said, "not only is it heresy, it's disgusting. Did he really think people would jump up and down with joy at the thought?"

She stared straight ahead as they approached their house, unwilling to look at her husband. "I don't understand how you could even want to be around him anymore, but if he's not going, then we'll join you. It's about time something in our life got back to normal."

***

Excitement filled the city of Jerusalem. Not just the commotion of too many people in too small a space, but the joy of people celebrating a holiday. Sukkot structures large and small lined the streets, taking up precious space. Men and boys struggled to carry large palm branches through the crowd while others yelled from above, calling for the leaves they needed to roof their harvest booths. Fruits of the season overflowed sellers' tables for as far as Sarah could see.

She had traveled with Simon and the children along with her mother, Andrew, Simon's father Jonah, and Salome's family. Even though she'd rather be home, she was enjoying the festivities, relieved to be part of a small band, not a wandering mass, feeling invisible in the city, no longer the focus of every Pharisee and Scribe.

Simon had taken Micah into a house along with the other men, leaving the women outside in the cool shadows of the Temple walls. Abi and Hannah clung to their grandmother's hand. They had grown used to large crowds in their own home, but Jerusalem at festival time was another story. Sarah watched people around them barter and buy, and her heart warmed with gratitude. A beautiful fall day. A family to love. Her husband back in her life. What more could she want?

As she gazed into the streets at the people passing by, she noticed Micah leaving the home, talking with a boy she didn't know. Simon walked out behind him, joined by Philip and Nathaniel. Soon all twelve of the men Jesus had singled out came into view. Their families hurried out of the adjacent courtyard and filled the street in front of the house, and her feeling of invisibility melted away.

She smiled at Levi, still not sure what to make of him, and greeted the others warmly. She had become fond of them in the time she'd gotten to know them. Even though she was convinced they'd become some kind of cult, as individuals they were all nice enough. And maybe the cult thing was finally fading.

Laughter and shouts and the sound of thousands of feet making their way down the roads filled the streets. As the group headed toward the Temple steps and the enormous overpass into the Temple itself, the earthy aroma of roasting vegetables gave a sense of welcome.

Sarah drank in the delightful moment, filled with hope for the future, so glad the last few months were behind them. Her joy grew with every cheerful greeting she heard, every happy face she passed.

A solitary figure in the distant shadows of a narrow side road caught her eye. She watched as the person slowly crossed the empty street and disappeared behind the buildings. The sight left her sad that anyone would be alone at a time like this.

The noise of the market soon distracted her again. Everywhere she looked, people gathered and chatted. While he might not be with them, Jesus was still on the minds of many in the crowd, much to her dismay. It seemed he was the subject of conversation in every group they passed. Even though people spoke in hushed tones, afraid the religious leaders might hear, their words drifted out into the streets.

"Is Jesus here?... No, too risky... Why would anyone want to hurt him? He's a good man... Are you kidding? He stirs up trouble everywhere he goes.... He's crazy. Did you hear what he said in Capernaum?... I heard about it. But I can't believe he meant what he said... Then you weren't there..."

Sarah tried to ignore their words. She didn't want anything to ruin this day.

Musicians perched around the Temple walls, their songs ringing through the air. Hundreds of people filled the overpass that crossed above the busy marketplace and led into the Temple courtyard. As the group climbed the steps to the entrance, someone emerged from around the corner of a side road and walked toward them.

"Jesus," Simon shouted.

Jesus, Sarah thought. I should have known.

She had no choice but to stay even though every instinct told her to take her children and leave. All around her, people welcomed him with delight, shaking his hand, slapping him on the back. Others saw him and made their way through the busy streets to where the group stood.

Sarah shrank back, fearing the attention a growing crowd would attract, surprised that so many welcomed him. Hadn't they heard about the bread, the blood, the nonsense?

He stood on the overpass steps near the Temple entrance and spoke to those closest to him, then to those on the ever-expanding edges of the crowd around him. Sarah tried to catch her husband's eye and signal him to her side, far enough away from Jesus that maybe no one would associate him with the group of ardent followers. But she might as well have been trying to get one of the marble pillars to move.

Soon Jesus was no longer just chatting, he was teaching. Sarah pulled the children back against the wall, hoping they would all fade into the stones unnoticed. She tried to distract them, unwilling to have them hear what he said, unwilling to hear it herself, but those around her apparently were listening.

"Where does he get the things he says?" a man near her asked, addressing no one in particular. "He doesn't have any learning, does he?"

"Not that I know of," another answered.

Jesus responded. "My teaching isn't mine. It's the teaching of the One who sent me. If anyone desires to do the will of the One who sent me, then he will recognize whether the teaching is of God or whether I am speaking on my own authority."

She saw him look across the crowd at the gathering group of religious leaders, and she noticed Nicodemus off to the side, apart from them, intently focused on Jesus, taking in every word he said, pondering, weighing, considering, his face curious, not contorted into the familiar scowl of the others. He must not have heard about the eat-my-body talk.

"Someone who speaks on his own authority seeks his own glory," Jesus said, "but someone who wants others to glorify the One who sent him speaks truth. The words he teaches do not serve himself. His words point to the One who sent him."

He gazed directly at the gathering of Scribes and Pharisees. "Did not Moses give you the law? Yet none of you keeps the law. Otherwise, why do you want to kill me?"

All around Sarah, people gasped at the accusation, shocked at his bluntness, not horrified, as she was, by the provocation.

A man deep within the crowd shouted, "You must be crazy. Or possessed. Why would anyone want to kill you?"

"I did one thing that challenges your authority," he said, still looking steadily at the religious leaders, "and you're all focused on that, unable to get past it."

Sarah remembered when he'd healed the man's withered hand on the Sabbath and the fury of the religious leaders she'd seen in the street that day. She pushed harder against the wall, wishing it would swallow up her and her family and take them away from this place.

"You circumcise a man on the Sabbath," Jesus said to the Scribes and Pharisees, "but you want to kill me because I made a man's entire body well on the Sabbath?" He gazed at them a long moment. "If you're going to judge, judge with right judgment."

Anger burned in the faces of the men as his words hit their target. She clutched her daughters' hands more tightly only to have Micah make a move away from her.

"Where do you think you're going?"

"To stand with Dad."

"You stay right here with me."

A man next to her said to his friend, "He thinks they want to kill him, right? Yet, he's standing here speaking openly against them, and they're not doing a thing about it."

The friend shrugged. "Maybe they think he really is the Messiah."

Another man in front of them turned around in anger. "He's no Messiah. We know where he's from. Nazareth. When the Messiah comes, no one will know where he's from. He'll be sent straight from God."

The heated discussion abruptly stopped when Jesus said, "You think you know me? You think you know where I am from? But I have not come of my own accord. I've come from God. The One who sent me is true. And him," he looked again at the gathering of Scribes and Pharisees, "you do not know."

When the unbridled rage of the religious leaders became too obvious to ignore, Jesus stopped talking, and the crowd began to disperse. Sarah wrestled with whether to go to Simon. She wanted to avoid any connection to Jesus, but she needed to talk to her husband. As the crowd thinned, Micah resolved the matter for her, running across the steps to where his father stood in conversation with Jesus and the other men.

She followed him and, letting Abi's hand go for just a moment, took Simon by the arm and pulled him off to the side. In a low whisper, wishing the children were not so close, she said, "Simon, we need to leave."

"I agree," he answered, to her relief.

As she took her daughter's hand and turned to go, he said, "Who are you traveling with?"

"Traveling with? You."

"But I'm staying here."

No. You're going home. You are going to leave this place and this man and take your family home. It's not safe here anymore. How can you not see that? They are out to get him."

"I know," Simon said.

"You know?"

"I heard what he said. I saw their faces, Sarah. And that's why I can't leave him."

Chapter 18

As Salome busily chatted beside her, Sarah looked down from the Temple gallery to where her husband stood among the crowd of men. His face lit with joy as he took in every word Jesus breathed out, and she knew it was more than a friend's loyalty that kept Simon bound to him. Throughout the vast courtyard, men and boys focused on Jesus as he sat on a bench and taught them. Women packed into the balcony space around her, shoving for position, pushing one another precariously close to the low ledge, seeking a place where they could see, or at least hear, Jesus.

She scanned those below for signs of anyone who might be there for a purpose other than listening, grateful Jonah had taken her mother and children back to Capernaum, far from the tension of Jerusalem. She, too, wanted nothing more than to be safe at home with her children as she should be, but her heart and her mother convinced her that her place was with her husband.

Movement in a far entranceway below caught her eye. A group of men walked in and stopped. Officers of the chief priests, biding their time before arresting Jesus. The air constricted with intensifying apprehension and anger as others became aware of them. When she saw that Jesus noticed them, she prayed he would stay still or at least just teach something safe.

Instead, he rose from his seat, and said, "If anyone thirsts, let him come to me and drink."

A shiver raced through Sarah. A low murmur hummed through the crowd, and she heard the echoes of his words 'unless you drink my blood.'

"Not this again," a nearby woman said, as she turned to leave. "I didn't think he'd go back to that nonsense. I can't listen to another word."

A woman beside her said, "But maybe this really is the Prophet, the Messiah."

"It can't be. Look at him," the first woman pointed toward Jesus with disdain. "Besides, the man's from Galilee. Nowhere does it say the Messiah will come from Galilee."

The arguments mounted below Sarah and around her. Voices became angrier as some praised him and others condemned him. Men shoved to get out of the space below, some in fear, others in anger. Sarah saw someone knock Simon off-balance, and she reached out over the balcony ledge as if she could help him.

"Arrest him," people shouted to the officers. "Can't you hear what he's saying?... Somebody has to stop him... Do something."

But the armed officers didn't move from the doorway. Instead, they studied Jesus with a look that seemed more of awe than of anger.

***

As the day drew to a close, the city cleared. People wandered off through the side streets of Jerusalem, chatting and laughing as they headed to their houses, the Temple commotion already forgotten. Sarah stood with Simon in the dusky shadows of the city while he talked to the other men about the day's events. She glanced wistfully down the road that led to the home they would be staying in, grateful to spend the night behind a locked door, wondering how much longer she would have to stand exposed in the evening chill.

Jesus quietly parted from the small group. She watched as he walked alone down the street, through the city gates, toward the mountains. A singular figure in the twilight, he looked not only alone, but lonely. Everyone so caught up in their own lives, no one thought of inviting him into their home.

She continued to watch as he slowly trudged up the distant path, branches reaching out to trip him and snag him, until he disappeared into the darkness. Then she gazed for a long time into the night he'd left behind, wondering at the sadness that broke her heart, the aching desire to reach out and draw him in away from the world.

***

Everyone again gathered at the Temple courtyard early in the morning. Anticipation overwhelmed any lingering tension. As Jesus walked in, Sarah wrestled with the strange new feeling she had about him. She didn't want to care about him. She'd spent the night trying to dispel the image of him alone, a silhouette amid shadows.

He was trouble.

Yet she had to admit, until he arrived, the Temple had felt cold and lifeless despite the gathering crowd. Now that he was there, it had a vibrancy, not because people were happy to see him so much as because he himself gave it life.

He sat again on the bench and spoke words Sarah couldn't hear, and the crowds grew silent. The women in the gallery shoved forward as more and more arrived, pushing Sarah farther toward the front. She looked down at the men and boys who filled every space on the floor below. Columns towered above them on all sides. Heads peered around pillars, and she wondered how no one was crushed.

A commotion at the entrance moved deep into the courtyard. Men scattered below, tripping over one another in the tight space as they made way for someone she couldn't see. She caught her breath as a band of Scribes and Pharisees came into view. They walked with purpose to the seat on which Jesus sat, half-dragging a woman with them. Sarah couldn't see the woman's face for all the hair tossed in front of it, but her posture was angry and resistant.

The men stopped, pulled the woman to a stand, and held her in front of Jesus.

A tall Scribe looked at her with disdain. "Rabbi, this woman has been caught in the act of adultery." He paused to let his words draw their image for all in the room, then said, "You know that in the law, Moses commanded us to stone those caught in the act."

Everyone squeezed closer, and renewed tension filled the air as people waited for Jesus' response. He looked at the men, then bent to the limestone floor, causing them to back up from where they stood. He began to write something in the dust, tracing letters with his finger.

"What are you going to do about this?" another Scribe in the group demanded.

Jesus stood, looked again at the religious leaders, and said, "Let him who is without sin among you be the first to throw a stone at her." Then he bent to the ground and again wrote in the dust.

Sarah watched, captivated, drawn to the motion of his finger as it traced words on the stone.

"What's he doing?" Salome stretched her neck to see around the woman in front of her.

"He's writing something," Sarah said.

"Can you see what it is?"

"No. We're too far away."

She watched Jesus stooping to the ground, writing with his finger in the dust left by their feet. Images of the finger of God carving the words of the law into stone tablets on the heights of the mountaintop rose before her. She shook them off, and as she continued to watch him, a sadness once again tugged at her heart.

He looked so intent, so small and alone in the midst of the vast crowd that surrounded him.

Salome shoved her weight forward, squeezing aside two women who blocked her view. "Maybe it's the law," she whispered excitedly.

Others moved in closer, trying to see for themselves.

"What law?" Sarah said.

"The law the men are talking about, the one about stoning anyone caught in adultery."

Then Sarah realized what he was saying to the Scribes and Pharisees. The law demanded that anyone caught in adultery must die. But you can't catch one person in the act of adultery. Where was the man? By condemning only the woman, they themselves had broken the law.

The religious leaders' glare followed every stroke of Jesus' finger. One by one, they angrily turned and left, defeated but not yet done. When the last one walked out the door, Jesus straightened and looked at the woman who still stood before him, brazen and defiant.

"Where are they, woman? Has no one condemned you?"

"No one," she said.

The room grew so still it seemed everyone had stopped breathing. Jesus studied the woman as she boldly met his gaze.

"I don't condemn you either," he said. "Go, and sin no more."

The defiance that had held her strong before him fell, and she melted into tears of gratitude.

Chapter 19

As Jesus headed out through the streets of Jerusalem, he once again seemed to heal everyone who reached out to him, and the crowd around him grew. Sarah struggled and failed to keep up with Simon as the gap between them filled. She glanced at Salome who, despite her age, seemed to have no trouble keeping pace with her sons.

Although she didn't relish the long walk home, she was grateful to leave the city. After the incident with the woman, word spread that Jesus had outwitted the religious leaders, in the Temple no less. And tension in Jerusalem mounted.

A group of Pharisees and Scribes pushed through the mob and shoved past her. As she struggled to regain her balance, she saw them make their way through the throng, clearly aiming for Jesus, Simon, and the others. The crowd parted to give wide berth to the men, and Sarah hurried to follow before the crowd again closed in.

A Scribe caught up to Jesus first and, keeping step with him, angrily said, "Why do your disciples disobey the tradition of our elders?"

Apprehension gripped Sarah.

"What do you mean?" a man somewhere behind her asked.

The Scribe glanced toward the man, then turned his attention back to Jesus. "We've noticed they don't wash their hands before they eat."

She relaxed a bit. Unclean hands were against the law, but it wasn't the end of the world.

Jesus never slowed his pace as he answered, "And why do you disobey the commandment of God for the sake of your tradition? God commanded, *Honor your father and your mother.* But you tell men they don't need to honor their mother or their father by helping them financially. Instead, you tell them they should give what they have to God – by giving it to you. So," he looked directly at the Scribe, "for the sake of your tradition and for your own gain, you have made void the very word of God."

Without breaking stride, he turned to the other men who accompanied the Scribe. "You hypocrites. Well did Isaiah say of you, *'This people honors me with their lips, but their heart is far from me. In vain do they worship me, teaching as doctrine the precepts of men.'*"

Sarah held her breath, afraid to draw any attention to herself as the religious leaders fell back, letting Jesus move on ahead of them. While people tried to get around them, they stood their ground like immovable obstacles

A few moments later, Jesus stopped and turned to the crowd. "Listen to me, and understand. It's not what goes into the mouth that defiles a man. It's what comes out of the mouth that defiles him."

He looked out over the people and directly into the eyes of the fuming Pharisees and Scribes, then turned and resumed walking.

Nathaniel moved close to him. "You know you offended them, don't you?"

"They're blind guides," Jesus replied. "If a blind man leads a blind man, they'll both fall into the pit."

Simon studied the ground, following Jesus' footsteps, trying to make sense of his words, then said, "What exactly did you mean?"

Jesus gazed at him a moment. "How can it be that you don't understand? Don't you see that whatever you take into your mouth passes through the stomach and leaves. But what comes out of the mouth comes from the heart. Evil thoughts, murder, adultery, theft, lies, slander. These are what defile a man, not whether you eat with unwashed hands."

133

Simon slowed in pensive thought, trailing Jesus out through the city gates. The crowd around them diminished. Some left in consternation, uncomfortable that Jesus would speak to the religious leaders as he had. Others were eager for him to shift into Messiah mode, yet at the same time, wary of the Sanhedrin. They, too, drifted away and headed for the safety of home as the shadows grew long in the city. Rebellion could wait for the light of day.

Sarah walked beside Simon, and said, "He has to stop confronting them like that."

"He's only speaking truth, Sarah. Obvious truths that you can live your whole life and miss. I mean, think about what he just said. Everything comes from your heart, not just good things but words and actions driven by self-love, by your desire for vengeance, for respect and honor, for relationships, for things."

"Maybe so," she said. "But does he have to say everything that pops into his head? Why can't he just let it go sometimes? Is he that oblivious to the danger?'

"He knows the danger," Simon said. "That's why he didn't go with us into Jerusalem for the festival. He needed to keep his distance from the Sanhedrin."

"So then, why did he show up there at all? And not just show up, but confront every religious leader he met?"

"I don't know, Sarah. I guess he decided that being with us was worth the risk."

Up ahead, John left Jesus' side and ran back to Simon. "We're heading to Bethany."

"Bethany?" Sarah stopped and turned to her husband, adamant. "We can't go to Bethany."

"Why not? It's better than staying in the city."

"But a town crawling with destitution and lepers?"

"Other people live there, too, Sarah," Simon said, renewed eagerness energizing his body as he drew her into step behind the rest of the group who were passing them. "Jesus just wants to get us out of Jerusalem. He once mentioned he had a good friend there. I don't expect he's taking us to sleep in the poor house or stay with some leper. "

Certain Jesus wouldn't hesitate to do either one, Sarah reluctantly followed her husband while Salome glanced at her from across the road, her delight evident. They walked amid disparate groups gathered along the way. It seemed everyone they passed whispered his name as they shared word of the day's events with those who hadn't heard.

Scattered structures rose up as they neared Bethany. Chipped plaster marred the facade of a tired building near town. Although a wall encircled it, she glimpsed men, women, and children the ages of her own gazing at those walking freely down the road. Flesh scarred and black with decay covered their faces, the stench so thick she could feel it rubbing on her own skin.

As the small group entered the village, people emerged from their homes, gathering in clusters, curious that the man they'd heard about had come to their town. Some seemed excited, others concerned.

Jesus led them toward a cracked, dirty stone structure that gave those with nothing at least minimal shelter. A sour odor oozed from the doors and windows and seemed to surround the building. Children barely clothed in filthy rags ran through the rocky, dusty courtyard, calling out to one another with a joy poverty couldn't stifle. Weary mothers, bent under the burden of worry, stood along the walls and warily watched Sarah and the group of strangers. Sarah averted her eyes, unwilling to see the hopelessness in theirs, and glanced heavenward with gratitude when Jesus walked past the poorhouse rather than turning into it.

The group entered the center of the village where shops and booths provided welcomed distraction from the desperate realities of people she'd never know, people she wanted to forget. They passed a shop as a woman stepped out into their

135

midst without a glance at anyone. She wove her way through the group, determined to get to wherever she needed to go next. Unaware she was behind them, Salome and the younger James' mother blocked her progress. Rather than ask them to move or bide her time, the woman shoved between them without a word and continued to wherever she was intent on going.

Sarah watched her walk with fierce determination, and wondered that a cloud of such intense self-interest could make someone almost pretty look so bitter and hard.

The woman turned into another shop as Sarah's group continued down the road toward a home perched on a slight incline. The closer they got, the more evident it seemed that this was their destination. To her relief, Sarah could see it looked well-maintained, even a bit prosperous.

A lean man with trimmed dark hair and clean garments hurried out the door to welcome them. Behind him, a slender, plain woman stood just inside the home, as if hesitant to leave what she was doing and come out into the day. The gray of her garment caused her to become one with the shadows within.

Philip embraced the man and introduced him to the others. "This is our host, Lazarus." He turned and peered into the house. "And somewhere in there is his sister, Martha."

The woman Sarah had noticed moved to the doorway and smiled, but her lusterless brown eyes didn't linger on anyone. Instead they glanced to the side, more focused on what she had to do than on anyone standing before her.

"Come in, come in," Lazarus said. "Please, we have dinner enough for everyone." He paused and embraced Jesus, then took him by the shoulders and gazed into his eyes. "You look tired, my friend. A long day, I'm guessing. You were in the city?"

"We were," Philip said.

"So I heard." Lazarus' attention shifted to several local religious leaders standing a short distance down the road, their arms crossed, their attention locked on Jesus.

"Come. Eat, sleep," he said, as he led the small group of travelers into his home and shut the door.

Martha hurried to settle everyone onto a stool or bench or mat. Then she pulled bowls and bread from cabinets and bins. She didn't notice Jesus smile at her as he walked past on his way out into the courtyard.

Sarah watched him through the window, struck again that he could look so small in comparison to the man who had stood strong and militant in the city only a short time earlier. He sat on a bench under the white starry blossoms of a jujube tree, leaned his head against the cold stone wall, and gazed up past the flower-filled boughs above him to the wispy clouds beyond.

Martha reached past her to get into a nearby cabinet.

"Can I help you?" Sarah asked.

The woman seemed surprised by the offer but handed Sarah a platter of cheese. "Thank you. Yes, I'd appreciate it. You can slice this."

As the door opened and someone entered from outside, a chill breeze seemed to blow through the room despite the desert heat. Sarah recognized the woman who had forced her way past them in the marketplace, single-focused on what she wanted and how she would get it.

The woman stopped at the threshold. "What's going on?"

Martha rushed to her side. "Lazarus has invited some friends to stay with us."

The ebony-eyed woman scanned the room icily, glancing from face to face, her disinterest evident as she quickly sized up and dismissed each person. Then she walked past Martha and Sarah and out to the courtyard, heading for the steps to the upper level.

137

Through the window, Sarah saw her cast an indifferent glance toward Jesus. He said something, and she stopped. The friendly chatter in the room behind Sarah overwhelmed his voice, and she couldn't make out his words as he continued talking. He stood, and almost immediately, the woman dropped to the ground, her headdress splayed out around her as she fell face first at his feet.

Sarah set down the platter Martha had given her and moved closer to the window. Jesus bent and gently pulled the woman up. As tears ran down her face, she flung herself into his arms.

Scandalized, Sarah turned back into the room, unwilling to see anymore, and focused on slicing the cheese. A short time later, Jesus walked in with the woman. All conversation in the room stopped as people took in the sight of the woman who had only moments earlier darkened the room with her disdain. She now smiled with joy, warmly looking from person to person. Jesus settled onto a mat next to Lazarus, and Sarah watched in disbelief as the woman sat on the other side of the table, directly across from him.

Conversation resumed, and no one else seemed to notice that the woman was sitting with the men. No one except Martha. She glared at her sister, then turned back to the fish she had been piling onto a dish. Her face looked exhausted and taut. Her gaze flitted around the room as if she were adding up everything that needed her attention.

By comparison, the woman at the table now had a distant look in her once intense eyes. The new calm in her face gave her a rich, glowing depth of beauty.

Martha reached past Jesus to set the fish on the table. "Master, do you not care that my sister has left me to serve alone?"

Sarah was shocked at the bluntness and a little irritated that Martha hadn't mentioned that she'd been helping.

138

Jesus took Martha gently by the hand and gave her his full attention. "Martha, Martha, you worry about so much. There's only one thing you need to be focused on."

He looked across the table at the woman who hadn't taken her eyes off him. "Mary has made the right choice. Nothing can take that away from her."

***

Sarah spent a restless night in Bethany, tossing and turning in what little space she had on the floor of Lazarus' house, squeezed between Salome and a water jug. She might be cramped in a house belonging to someone she didn't really know, but she was grateful to have left Jerusalem and grateful to have the protection of four walls and a door.

Now, as she awoke in the darkness of pre-dawn, she heard someone scuffle around the room, quietly preparing breakfast for the people who slept scattered across the floor. She peered through the dim light of a fading moon and saw what she knew she'd see, Martha busily at work.

Sarah watched her, welcoming the distraction that allowed her to stop thinking about the fury she'd seen in the faces of the religious leaders the day before. She knew the Pharisees and Scribes were not going to ignore what had happened, and she feared what they feared, that Jesus had only just begun.

She heard the footsteps of someone picking his way over sleeping bodies and turned to see her husband kneel beside her.

"Get up," he whispered. "We're leaving."

"Leaving? It's still dark out. We haven't even had breakfast."

"Jesus is already outside. Everyone's getting up to join him."

"When did he go outside?" she said. "I never heard him."

"I don't know. Maybe he slept out there. Andrew just woke me and said it's time to go, that's all I know."

Around them, others began to awaken and rise. As they gathered their belongings and hurried out the door, Sarah glanced toward Martha and saw the dismay on her face and the platters full of food on the table beside her.

She folded the mat she'd slept on and set it next to where Martha stood. "Thank you for everything," she said, as she took some fruit she didn't really want so Martha might not feel her efforts had been a total waste.

Outside, Simon stood with Thomas and Andrew as others gathered in the road alongside them and waited for Jesus.

"I thought you said he was out here," she said.

"That's what I heard," her husband said.

As he spoke, Jesus appeared from around a bend, coming down a road that led out of the hills.

"Did he sleep up in the mountains again?" Simon asked Thomas.

"Yes."

"I wonder what he does."

"What do you mean?" Thomas said.

"When he disappears like that at night and wanders off to the mountains or wherever it is he goes."

"He prays."

"Prays?" Simon said. "How do you know that?"

"I followed him last night." Thomas sounded a bit sheepish. "I thought maybe something was wrong, so after he was gone a while, I went to see what was going on. When I found him, he was deep in prayer. So I left."

"I wish I were so holy I could just pray all night," Andrew said.

Sarah looked at the man walking toward them with purpose, his eye on all those waiting for him. In his stride she saw determination, but in his face she saw a weariness she recognized in her own life when she had too much to do and not enough time.

"Maybe the nights he goes up there to pray," she said, "are the nights he can't sleep."

Chapter 20

Sarah pulled her cloak tight around her shoulders in an attempt to protect herself from the strange world around her. Never did she think she would long for the crowds that had dwindled since leaving the city. Without them, she felt exposed. Now only Jesus, the twelve men, a few women, and she made up the group of travelers.

While she was grateful to be anywhere but Jerusalem, the agora of Tyre was like nothing she had ever seen. No broken baskets of fruit and booths made of sticks here. Merchants sold their wares in storefronts of marble. The smells were vile, the decadence overwhelming. Arenas the size of mountains loomed in the distance, and bathhouses seemed to go on for blocks. Statues of odd figures appeared to hold special place in the market. She tried not to look at them, knowing they were images of "gods," and felt dirty just passing by them.

As they walked the cobbled roads, people cast wary glances at the group. She tried to keep her gaze focused on Simon just ahead of her. If she didn't see the gawkers, maybe they wouldn't see her.

Abruptly, Jesus turned and led them down a short stone pathway and into a house. Sarah hesitated, unsure whether to follow or stay outside alone in these strange streets with these strange people. She decided to follow him, praying he knew someone who lived there.

No sooner had they entered than a woman rushed in through the door behind them, bumping into Sarah as she reached past and grabbed Jesus' sleeve.

"Son of David, have mercy on me."

142

Sarah looked at her and knew she wasn't one of them. Loose dark curls flowed freely down her back, bracelets and rings glistened in the lamplight. No head-covering, no modesty in her dress. How could she call him Son of David? What did a Gentile know of the Messiah?

Jesus ignored the woman and walked into a dining room, where a servant showed him to a plush cushion next to a table covered with ornate painted platters of fruits and meats.

The woman followed him into the room and stepped in front of him, commanding his attention. "Please, do something to save my daughter. She's being destroyed by some kind of demon. I've tried everything, but nothing helps." She pointed out the door. "When you passed by on the road just now, someone told me it was you. I've heard what you've done for others. You have to help her. Please."

Jesus studied the woman but didn't answer.

"Send her away," James said, as he reached for a pear.

Jesus glanced at him, then said to her, "I was sent only to the lost sheep of the house of Israel."

"Please," she said, dropping to her knees before him, "you've got to help me."

"It's not fair to take the children's bread," he said, "and throw it to the dogs."

She reached out and boldly gripped his hand. "Even the dogs hunger for the crumbs that fall from the master's table."

Jesus looked at her, a tender warmth in his eyes. "Oh, woman, what great faith. What you want is done."

The woman collapsed in gratitude, burying her face in her hands as she wept, believing even though she had no visible evidence that he had made any difference in her life.

No one said anything as those around Jesus tried to make sense of what had just happened. After a few moments, the woman stood, grasped Jesus' hand again in wordless thanks, then turned and rushed out the door.

Sarah watched her joyfully make her way down the path. As she watched, she wondered at the thought that Jesus would help someone like that. The Messiah, when he comes, isn't coming for everyone. He's coming for them.

***

Jesus led the small group of followers along the King's Highway as it wound through the countryside. Each time he continued past the scattered pagan cities, Sarah breathed a little easier. But only a little. Rocks, shrubs, and trees lined the long stretches between cities, ideal hiding spots for thieves.

As they walked, the words of Moses came to her mind, words he expressed when he had tried to lead their people through this same land, and Edom had stopped them in a bloody battle. *We will go along the King's Highway. We will not turn aside to the right hand or to the left until we have left your territory,* and she understood the sentiment.

She looked at the wilderness, barely restrained from reclaiming the road on either side, and thought of the countless battles those fields and hillsides had seen since then, centuries of fighting, centuries of blood in a land where peace seemed ever elusive.

Somewhere behind her, she heard the heavy plod of camels. She looked over her shoulder to see a caravan steadily gaining on them. As it drew near, the nutty, musty scent of spices swirled together with the sweet fragrance of frankincense and the pungent odor of men foreign to her.

Dust kicked up into the air as the caravan passed. To her surprise, the men glanced down from their perches, smiled, and nodded to the group of travelers. She watched them until they vanished around a bend farther down the road, feeling a strange sadness that she would never know them.

Through the haze, the walls of yet another city loomed in the distance. Sarah braced herself for the inevitable smells and sounds and chaos that would no doubt fill the marketplace outside those walls. She prayed Jesus would pass by and not turn in at the gates. As the entrance to the city drew near, she glanced toward him, relieved to see he seemed intent on moving forward.

Most people they passed ignored him, immersed in their bargaining as they sought to fill their every need on their own terms. Occasionally, someone recognized him and called out his name while others nearby turned to see the man they'd heard about.

The group passed a fruit seller's stall. As a neighboring vendor shouted Jesus' name, the hefty merchant turned. He stopped haggling with his customer, handed the woman the apples she wanted, and left his booth. Running behind the other sellers' stalls, he came to a young man hoisting wooden crates onto a cart, crates that looked far too heavy for his slender frame to lift. The merchant turned the worker to face him and made wild pointing motions in the air. The thinner man looked toward the road in confusion. He glanced at the hundreds of people crossing in all directions.

A woman at a nearby booth set down a dyed fabric she'd been considering and took the younger man by the arm. Together, she and the merchant pulled him to Jesus.

The merchant turned the thin young man to face him once again, and said, "Jesus."

The man looked at the stranger in a worn, dusty robe, and his face filled with joy. "Eyus," he said, and then shouted with excitement, "es Eyus."

Others drifted over in small groups and large to see what was going on until it soon seemed the entire city surrounded them.

Jesus led the young man away from the growing crowd to a place near the now vacant fruit seller's stall. As the man stood

145

before Jesus and gazed into his eyes with anticipation, Jesus smiled at him. Then he put his fingers in the man's ears. When he pulled them out, the young man glanced off to the side, then up into the air and all around him. Delight illuminated his face, and Sarah knew he was experiencing for the first time the sounds of the city she so disliked. Sounds with a beauty she maybe needed to better appreciate.

Murmurs and exclamations ran through the crowd, but Jesus didn't take the young man back to them. Instead he spat on his finger and touched the man's tongue for a moment. Then he looked up to heaven, sighing so heavily, Sarah could feel it from where she stood, and said something she couldn't hear.

The man, too, said something she couldn't hear. Then he turned to the crowd, and shouted, "It's Jesus. It's Jesus."

Everyone cheered and ran to where they stood. Jesus tried to calm the crowd, but the celebration couldn't be stilled. As he walked back to the road to continue his journey, the group following him was no longer small.

***

Although the crowds were back, Sarah didn't care. There was some comfort, or at least some sense of safety, to be found in their numbers.

Jesus had led them away from the pagan cities, and it felt good to be back in familiar territory, with familiar smells and familiar ways. As they wandered through various villages, she prayed they were headed home, but Jesus seemed in no hurry to get anywhere. He continued to heal, and the crowds continued to grow. For three days, thousands had followed him without stopping except to sleep.

Barren hillsides rose up around them and held in the arid air, giving it no escape, allowing no breeze to lift it. Weary from the heat, weary from the trek, Sarah longed to remove her head-covering for just a moment, to sit before she fainted. She focused her attention on each footstep she took through the dust, trying not to think of the heat, and didn't notice that the crowd had ceased moving until she ran into the woman in front of her. Everyone watched with expectation as Jesus left the crowd and walked slowly up a narrow mountain path to where a large rock had fallen. When he stopped, rather than address them with some grand teaching or proclamation, he dropped heavily onto the rock, his shoulders slumped with exhaustion.

Immediately, people who had not been able to make their way through the moving throng broke out of the crowd to get to him. Some carried sick children in their arms. Others guided blind parents and friends. Still others limped up the rugged, steep path, grasping leafless twigs that protruded between rocks to pull themselves up, determined to let nothing stop them.

Jesus greeted each soul with a quiet smile. He had to be as hot, as hungry, as tired as she, but still he found the energy to be welcoming and patient. Cries of joy rang out as newly healthy children ran down the hillside and once blind men walked the path with ease, tripping only because they were so engrossed in looking out rather than down.

John stood near her and watched Jesus' compassionate interaction with each person. "How does he do it?"

"I know," Sarah said, with grudging admiration. "I could never be so patient. Not when I'm this hot and worn out."

"Not that," John said. "How does he heal these people again and again and again? Every last one of them? All this time with him, and I still don't understand. He's not calling down any power from heaven or praying over them. It's like, just because he wants them to be well, they're well." He turned to Sarah. "I want them to be well, too, but that doesn't make it happen."

As the sun climbed to its highest point, with nothing to block its relentless heat, Jesus stood and looked out to the thousands of faces gazing up at him. Then he called Simon and the others to his side. Sarah followed, not waiting for an invitation.

"I have to do something for these people," he said. "They've been with me for days with almost nothing to eat."

"Just tell them to leave," Nathaniel said. "We're not that far from the sea. There are villages all along the shore just a few miles from here. Besides, it's got to be cooler there."

" I can't send them away hungry," Jesus said. "They might collapse with hunger before they get where they're going."

Sarah looked at the weary slouch of his shoulders and felt he might collapse before they did.

"You need to feed them," he said to the men standing around him.

Twelve stunned faces stared back at him.

"Where are we supposed to get enough food for all of them?" Thomas said, while the others nodded with bewildered agreement. "Look around you. We're in a desert."

"Even if we head to the villages," Andrew said, "we don't have anywhere near the money we'd need to feed this many people."

Sarah wondered if they had forgotten about the seaside meal for thousands. Or maybe they, like she, suspected they had somehow been tricked back then even if they wouldn't admit it.

"How much bread do you have?" Jesus asked them.

Those nearby pulled satchels off their shoulders and held them open.

Nathaniel glanced into the gaping bags, most of them empty. "Seven loaves. And a few small fish," he said, exasperation edging his words.

Jesus looked out at the people, and said, "Everybody find a place to sit." His voice echoed off the neighboring hills.

Then he took the seven loaves and the fish and thanked God for what they had. He broke the bread and gave the broken pieces and the fish to the twelve men, telling them to give the food to the people.

Simon and the others hesitated before making their way through the hot, hungry crowd. As they walked down the hillside and along the road, hand after hand reached out to take the bread, passing it along to those beside them while still eating their fill themselves.

After everyone had eaten, Simon and the others struggled to bring seven overflowing baskets back to Jesus. Throughout the desert, men, women, and children sat and ate and exclaimed their certainty that this was, indeed, the Messiah.

Sitting on the ground near him, Sarah studied the man and couldn't believe he had done it again.

***

After eating their fill, people drifted off to the seaside villages, unwilling to spend another night in the desert heat. Sarah and the few others that remained followed Jesus along the dusty road to a more distant shore. Scattered houses lined the water's edge. Boats and nets rested in the late afternoon shadows, awaiting the work of a new day. Nearby, a handful of men chatted just beyond the reach of the waves.

Sarah fell to the back of the small group of travelers, so tired she struggled to keep pace with them. When Jesus stopped to talk with the fishermen, she wanted nothing more than to drop onto the rocky ground and fall asleep.

Just when she thought she might lose her fight to stay upright, Simon left Jesus' side and walked back to where she stood.

He nodded toward a fisherman, and said, "He's lending us his boat."

Too tired to ask why or where, grateful just to be able to sit, she climbed into the boat. While she noticed the patches and marring in a vessel that had no business putting out to sea, she couldn't even muster the energy to worry.

Calm waters and gentle winds moved them toward Capernaum. As they sailed west, Sarah shut her eyes and lifted her face to the descending sun, the breeze brushing against her cheek.

Her head dropped with momentary sleep, and when she opened her eyes, she saw the shores of home were no longer straight ahead. Instead, shades of sunset shone on limestone columns that rose up from the sands, lining the road of some other town. She stifled a shout of protest as the group floated ashore amid fishermen finishing their tasks in the dimming light of day. Beyond the sand, a separate group of men gathered and waited on the road. She looked at the angry faces of the Pharisees and knew word had already reached them about the bread and the fishes.

As Jesus walked across the beach to the road, one of them said, "We demand you give *us* a sign from heaven. Prove to us you are the Messiah."

He looked at them and sighed with a frustration so deep it seemed to come from his very spirit. She understood and wanted to sigh herself. What more do they want? He's healing everyone in sight. He just fed thousands of people with a few loaves of bread and a couple of fish. Again. He's walked on water, he's raised the dead. What more can the man do?

Then she stopped, surprised at herself.

"Why does this generation demand a sign?" Jesus said. He pointed to the horizon. "If you see a red sky in the evening, you think it's a sign it will be fair tomorrow. And if you see a red sky in the morning, you think it's a sign the day will be stormy. How is it you can interpret the sky, but you can't interpret the signs of the times."

They stood firm before him without response.

"An evil and adulterous generation asks for a sign," he said, "but no sign will be given to it except the sign of Jonah."

He turned and walked back to the boat. Simon and the others quickly followed as Sarah rushed to join them, her hope rising anew that they might finally head home. But within moments the hope deflated as the sails filled and the wind blew them in the opposite direction.

Unwilling to fruitlessly nurse the now-familiar disappointment, she settled into the boat, looked at the others, and wondered if any of them had any idea what he'd meant by the sign of Jonah.

As the boat sailed across the calm sea, John turned over a nearby basket and scooted forward to peer under the seat across from him.

He dragged a sack out from beneath it, reached deep into it, pulled out a small loaf of bread, and said, "We've only got one loaf."

"What do you mean?" Philip said.

"One loaf, look." He held the bread in the air.

Jesus gazed out at the shore they had left behind, and said, "Beware of the leaven of the Pharisees and Sadducees."

"I'll take anyone's leaven if it means we eat," James said. "What are we supposed to do with one loaf of bread?"

Jesus looked at Sarah. She shook her head and offered a silent, sympathetic shrug.

Then he turned toward the men. "Why are you worried about bread? Don't you remember the five loaves and the thousands of people? How many baskets did you gather after that? Or the seven loaves and the thousands of people. How many baskets did you gather then? How can you not understand that I'm not worried about bread. I'm talking about the corrupt leaven in the teachings of the Pharisees and the Sadducees. How can you not understand?"

Chapter 21

As Jesus led his followers along a road, the sun of yet
another day slid toward darkness. Sarah walked behind him in
the dusky shadows of Caesarea Philippi, a city mounted on
towering rock walls that rose straight up from the earth,
eclipsing fertile fields as if in defiance.

The past few days, she'd relaxed into their routine, less
anxious about Simon, less eager to return home. She didn't
know if she had just given up or if it was the small group of
familiar traveling companions. No shoving, no pushing, no
wrestling for position near Jesus, no religious leaders dogging
their every step. Even Jesus seemed less intense, more
instructive than rebellious.

But now, the old worries and concerns stirred within her as
she glanced up at Roman temples carved into the cliffs. Their
pagan images burned into her brain even as she tried to look
away.

Jesus unexpectedly turned from the road toward the rocky
fortress, and Sarah hesitated. Even if Simon followed him, she
could not go into that city. She'd heard of the decadence in
their lifestyles, their values, their worship. The very air hung
heavy with perversion and evil.

As she slowed her steps, unwilling to follow him any
farther, Jesus turned again, led them up a rugged hillside
under dead, low-hanging branches, and stopped just short of a
place devoid of brush and trees. Beyond, a frantic spring
surged out of a cave. Sarah watched as its waters rushed down
the stones, the thundering cascade fighting to escape into the
distance beyond her sight.

"Why did he stop here?" James whispered to Simon. "Doesn't he know what this place is?"

She didn't know, but she didn't want to know. It felt dirty even in its beauty.

Salome climbed the rock-strewn trail to where she stood. "I just heard Philip say the Romans think this cave is the entryway into the underworld."

Together they stared into the dark depths from which the water erupted almost as if spit out. The sound it made as it crashed down the rocks was more disturbing than soothing. Even though Sarah knew the thought that this was the entrance to anything was ludicrous, she couldn't shake the ominous aura that surrounded the place and the sense that she shouldn't be there. She tried to divert her gaze from the gaping mouth of darkness only to see what appeared to be bones scattered on the ground before them. Human bones. Bones of sacrifice.

Nausea rose up within her as she walked to the edge of the clearing, away from the bones, and pondered how safe she would be if she returned to the road below. The impropriety of a woman alone no longer mattered to her, but the thieves that controlled the night did.

When it became obvious that Jesus wasn't leaving, everyone settled in for the night. Sarah watched as the others moved away from the bones, setting their mats in the dirt along the path that led down the hillside. Salome sat far from the bone-covered clearing and chatted with several other women. Newly lit fires glowed, and voices hummed along with the crickets. Did no one else sense the reverberating terror, the suffering, the heartbreak held in the shadows?

Sarah stepped around those scattered between her and her husband and stood in his line of sight, signaling with a nod that they needed to leave. He glanced at her and smiled, then turned back to his conversation with the rest of the Twelve.

Just as she opened her mouth to demand that they leave, Jesus walked over and stood by her side, looking past her to the waters that thundered along the rocks, deep in thought.

After a few moments, he spoke without turning from the torrent. "Who do people say that I am?"

The men shot out answers. "Some say John the Baptist.... Others say Elijah.... Jeremiah.... One of the Prophets."

He turned to them. "But who do you say that I am?"

Everyone looked at him.

Sarah considered the question – fraud? charlatan? a nice enough guy but maybe a little crazy? – when she heard Simon say, "You are the Christ, the son of the Living God."

"Blessed are you, Simon, son of Jonah." Relief and conviction lit in Jesus' eyes. "This was not revealed to you by flesh and blood, but by my Father in heaven. And I tell you, you are Peter, you are Rock, and upon this rock I will build my church." He looked again to the chaotic waters. "And the gates of hell shall not prevail against it."

You are Peter? You are Rock? Sarah looked at Simon, wondering what Jesus meant and wondering why Simon didn't ask.

"I give you the keys to the kingdom of heaven," he said to Simon. "Whatever you bind on earth will be bound in heaven, and whatever you loose on earth will be loosed in heaven."

As he told them not to tell anyone what Simon had said, his words 'keys to the kingdom' echoed in Sarah's ears. She'd hoped he was done with all that kingdom talk. But not only was he not done, he'd dragged Simon into it.

Jesus continued talking, but Sarah didn't hear. The bones seemed to rise up in witness to the horrors such words could bring.

Glancing through the trees, she thanked God no Scribes or Pharisees were anywhere around. No Romans seemed to be watching them from the walled city. But she wondered about the others.

154

John and James scowled with fury, clearly not happy that Jesus seemed to single out Simon. She looked behind them and saw their mother glaring at Simon while the others seemed more confused than angry.

Jesus' voice again made its way into her consciousness. She tried not to listen to him talk about someday being rejected by the chief priests and killed, but when he said he would then rise again on the third day, she turned away, unwilling to stay there any longer.

Before she could leave, Simon jumped up, nearly knocking her over.

He took Jesus by the arm and pulled him off to the side. "God forbid. This will never happen to you."

"Get behind me, Satan," Jesus said. "You're not on the side of God, but of men."

Simon stood dumbstruck. Sarah felt sorry for him while at the same time relieved that he was evidently not the threat others might have thought he'd be.

Jesus turned and addressed the rest of the group. "If any man wishes to follow me, let him deny himself and take up his cross and follow me. For whoever loses his life for my sake will save it."

With his words, Sarah's relief turned to cold fear.

He looked up at the craggy cliffs of the city. "Whoever is ashamed of me and of my words in this adulterous and sinful generation, of him the Son of Man will be ashamed when he comes in the glory of his Father with the holy angels. Then he will repay every man for what he has done."

His gaze moved through the small group assembled before him. "Truly, I say to you, there are some here today who will not taste death before they see the kingdom of God come with power."

He walked off alone, sat on a ledge, and peered into the tumultuous waters.

People around her seemed to shrug off his outburst and tried to get comfortable bedding down on the rocky ground. Sarah walked away from them and sat on a stump next to her husband. Unwilling to look at ground darkened by so much sadness and horror, she focused instead on the stars that seemed to hang right above her.

"So, what do you think now?" she said, without looking away from the sky.

"About what?" Simon said.

"The whole name change thing."

"I guess I don't know what to think."

She turned toward him and saw he was studying the same stars.

"Well, I'll tell you what to think. No one changes someone else's name. No one. Except God. Have you forgotten Abraham? Jacob? God changes names, Simon. I told you, the man thinks he's God."

"He doesn't think he's a god, Sarah."

"You're right, he doesn't think he's a god. He thinks he's God himself. The one God. The God you have committed your entire life to. The God you pray to night and day."

"I don't pray to Jesus," Simon said, as he laid out his cloak to go to sleep.

"You also don't pay attention to what is happening right in front of you."

Chapter 22

Sarah sat next to Salome, their perch jutting from the base of a mountain that rose high above them. Some of the others sat or stood in small clusters among the surrounding scattered shrubs. The sun beat down relentlessly, but no one complained. No one longed to return to Philippi with its dark cave, frantic waters, and bones.

Shielding her eyes with her hand, Sarah scoured the area in search of one small shady spot no one else had found. Earlier a cloud had passed overhead, and for a moment she thought they might get some relief from the heat, but it no sooner appeared than it was gone.

She adjusted the head covering that persisted in slipping down her sweaty hair. Coils of frizz sprung out from its edges. Her linen tunic felt heavy with perspiration and dirt. Never would she have imagined going so long without washing it.

Around her, everyone talked, swatted at bugs, and glanced up toward the peak. Everyone except Simon, John, and James. They alone had been invited by Jesus to join him as he walked the winding pathway to the top. Sarah had watched the foursome until they disappeared around a bend.

"What do you think is going on up there?" she asked Salome. "They've been gone a long time."

"I can't imagine."

"I'm never comfortable when he singles out Simon like this."

"He seems to single out John and James a lot, too," Salome said, with an air of pride. "I'm glad he includes both of them. They're so competitive. Even when they were little, they always tried to out-achieve each other." She wiped the sweat

157

from her cheek and looked up the mountain for some sign of them. "What about Andrew? How does he feel about being left out?"

"He doesn't seem to mind," Sarah said. "He's pretty easy going. And with the age difference, I don't think he worries too much about what Simon does."

"I'm a little surprised the others haven't complained."

"Me, too," Sarah said. "Especially Levi. I can't believe he takes it so well. He always thought he was so far above the rest of us."

"It's not Levi I was thinking of," Salome said.

Before Sarah could ask what she meant, a commotion roared from down the road. She climbed up on the rock to see what looked like the entire nearby town headed their way. Ahead of them, a man struggled to carry a thrashing boy.

Philip, Andrew, and the others jumped down from the rocks and ledges on which they'd been sitting to meet him. The man held the child out to them, and they stepped back beyond the reach of the boy's violently flailing arms and legs.

"Where is he?" the man said.

"He isn't here," Philip said.

"Where is he?" The man spun around, searching the mountainside.

"Up there." Andrew pointed to the distant peak.

"I can't carry him all the way up there." Tears filled the man's eyes.

The townspeople moved in, calling for Jesus, demanding he come down.

The man again held out his son. "If he's not here, then please, you do something for my boy."

"What do you want us to do?" Levi said.

"You're one of them, aren't you? One of the men always with Jesus? Do something."

The disciples looked from one to the other. A couple of them reached out tentatively to touch the child while others

158

uttered strings of words Sarah couldn't hear. Still the boy thrashed and threw himself on the ground, going rigid before jerking wildly again. The man became frantic while the disciples ran around the boy. They outshouted one another and flailed in frenzied gestures in the mounting chaos. People closed in around the scene, trying to see over those in front of them, angrily calling back to others that nothing was happening. The boy still thrashed.

"There he is," a woman in the crowd shouted, pointing up the mountain.

Sarah turned and saw Simon, Jesus, and the others coming down the path to rejoin them.

The man picked up his son and held him above the crush of people. He looked out from the midst of the throng to Jesus. "Master, do something. Have mercy on my son."

Simon, John, and James stared down at the scene, confused. They'd left no more than a few dozen people behind. Now hundreds stretched out before them.

The man called out again, "Please, Master, my son. The demon won't let him go." He laid the writhing boy on the ground and pointed to him with both hands, as if there was nothing else anywhere in the world to see. "It never ends, and nothing I do helps. It throws him into the water, into the fire."

He wiped tears from his eyes, unashamed of his desperation. "I brought him to your followers," he nodded his head toward the hapless Nine, "but they couldn't do anything. Please. You've got to help him."

Jesus looked down the hillside past the man to the disciples, who stood huddled together, pointing blame back and forth from one to the other.

"I tried," Levi said.

"You didn't try," Philip said. "You threw your hands in the air and started shouting at the boy."

"What did you do?" Levi said. "Nothing. Nothing at all."

159

"Oh, faithless and perverse generation," Jesus said. "How long do I have to be with you? How long do I have to put up with this?"

The men stopped short and stepped away from one another. Sarah didn't know if she'd ever seen grown men look so embarrassed.

Jesus turned to the father. "Bring your son here."

The man struggled to carry his writhing child through the crowd to the bottom of the steep rocky incline. People stumbled backward against one another, trying to make way while still trying to see the man and his boy. They closed back around him as he drew near to Jesus. Salome stood next to Sarah on the rock, where they peered over the heads of men, women, and children. Everywhere people scrambled for position, craning their necks to see.

The man stopped in front of Jesus and laid his thrashing son before him. "Have pity on us. Heal him, if you can."

"If I can?" Jesus said. "All things are possible, if you believe." He glanced toward the dismayed disciples and then turned his attention back to the father.

"I do believe," the man said, "but help my unbelief."

Jesus let the man's words hang in the air a moment, then said to the boy, "You mute and deaf spirit, I command you, come out of him and never return again."

Immediately, the boy convulsed and collapsed.

The crowd moved in even closer around the child, who lay lifeless on the ground, then somberly passed the word back. "He's dead."

Salome grabbed onto Sarah's arm. Sarah clutched her friend's hand as her own heart broke with sadness. But the man didn't despair. He stood steadfast and confident as Jesus reached down, took the motionless boy by the hand, and lifted him up. The boy arose, standing strong on his own. He looked with bewilderment at the hundreds of faces staring at him before his father scooped him up in a joyful embrace.

160

As the crowd shouted the news out to all who couldn't see, Simon ran to Sarah.

"Did you see that?"

"I was standing right here, Simon. It was kind of hard to miss."

"Can you believe it?" His eyes glistened with excitement.

""I want to, Simon. I really do. But I know that as soon as they get back home that boy will be flat out on the ground, thrashing around again."

A shadow crossed her husband's face, but the light in his eyes didn't dim. "Why can't you believe, Sarah?"

"Because I don't understand what it is I'm supposed to believe."

They walked together along the base of the mountain in silence, weaving in and out around the celebrating groups.

"So, where did he take you?" she said.

"Up the mountain."

"I know that, but why? What did he do there that he couldn't do here?"

"I'm not supposed to say anything," Simon said.

Sarah stopped walking. "What do you mean you're not supposed to say anything? Who said?"

"Jesus."

"Well, that's not going to happen. I need to know what you did up there."

"I didn't do anything."

"Then I need to know what everyone else did."

Simon studied the ground. "I don't know how to explain it, Sarah. We climbed to the very top of the mountain, and then all of a sudden, Jesus stopped and turned to us, his whole face, his whole being lit up."

"Lit up?"

"There's no other way to describe it. He just glowed with this really bright white light, brighter than the sun. But we could look at it. It seemed almost like his clothes, even his

161

flesh couldn't contain this light, this brilliant light that I felt I could have gazed into forever. A light I felt I could fall into. A light that seemed to contain every color and every thing even though it was the purest white you could imagine."

"So, all that time you were up there looking at some light?"

"No," he said, measuring his words, "then we saw Moses and Elijah."

"What do you mean, you saw Moses and Elijah?"

"I don't know what else to say, Sarah. We saw them. All three of us. They were standing there next to Jesus, talking to him."

"About what?"

"I didn't hear."

"You saw Moses and Elijah," Sarah said.

"We did. It might sound crazy, but I know what I saw."

They walked up into the hillside, away from the crowd, before Sarah finally said, "So, what did you do when you saw Moses and Elijah?"

"I suggested we make three booths," Simon said, a bit chagrined.

"Three booths?"

" You know, one for each of them and one for Jesus."

"And did you?"

"Well, no. I hadn't even finished suggesting it when this cloud came from out of nowhere and surrounded us, and this voice came out of the cloud."

"A voice," Sarah said. "You heard a voice. Whose voice, Simon?"

"God's," he said, looking her steadily in the eye.

Sarah dropped down on a rock. "You heard God?"

Simon nodded.

"And what did God say?"

"This is my beloved son, with whom I am well pleased. Listen to him."

She let the words sink in, then stood again, her hands on her hips. "Okay, so what did you do then? Start chatting with God?"

"No. I fell to the ground. We all did, James John, me. We buried our faces, afraid to look up. What would you do?"

"I don't know," she admitted.

"Anyway," Simon said, "I have no idea how much time passed, but eventually I heard someone say, 'Arise. Don't be afraid.' We looked up, and there was Jesus by himself, looking down at us."

"And?"

"And that's it."

"That's it?" she said. "You looked up and saw Jesus, and everything just went back to normal again?"

"Yes."

Sarah was silent a few minutes, studying the bramble bush before her. Then she said, "This light…"

"Yes?"

"You said it didn't shine on Jesus?"

"No."

"And it didn't shine around Jesus?"

"No," Simon said. "It was like the light *was* Jesus."

Sarah absorbed this a moment, before saying, "And you fell face down into the dirt at the presence of God, but when you looked up and saw no one was left but Jesus, you got up, dusted yourself off, and headed back down the mountain again because you figured God was gone."

"Yes. Why?"

"No reason," she said, as she turned and headed back to the crowd.

Chapter 23

As the small group trudged along the shore, the knowledge that home lay just beyond the horizon gave Sarah the strength to walk the remaining distance. After the mountain stop, the crowd had again grown, but when Jesus turned toward Capernaum, people seemed to understand it was time to go home. Group by group, they had peeled off along the way. Now only a few remained. Jesus had moved farther on ahead of them while Simon and the rest of the Twelve fell back to join her and Salome.

Familiar smells of sea, sand, and citrus blossoms comforted her. The sun sparkled on the waters, and the constant buzz of hundreds of voices had quieted into the soothing cadence of conversation. But as they neared home, words drifted out of those conversations with an edge that sliced into Sarah's consciousness.

"Look at that sea," Simon said. "I could fill the boat on a day like this."

"You couldn't fill a boat on the best of days, Peter," James said.

Sarah bristled at the name even though James said it with sarcasm. Her husband's shoulders hunched with anger, and she noticed as Andrew held him back with a single grab of the arm. Still, he couldn't stifle the fire shooting from Simon's eyes.

"He could out fish anyone here," Andrew said.

"Well, he could out fish you, anyway."

"He's just a kid," Philip said. "Let it go."

"Who's a kid? I'm as good as any of you, better than most."

The other men scoffed, then came together only in their efforts to belittle one another, going far beyond good-natured teasing, and the air grew heavy with resentment. As their barbs continued, Simon exchanged bitter words with men he held as close to his heart as brothers, and she feared life-long relationships might suffer irreparable wounds.

Sarah exchanged glances with Salome before wandering closer to the sea in hopes that the gentle lapping of the waves would drown out the rising tension and voices.

She'd known this moment would come ever since Jesus said all that nonsense about giving Simon the keys to the kingdom. She looked down the beach at Jesus as he walked alone, the wind blowing his frayed garment about his legs, sea birds calling each other over his head. Again, she was struck by his loneliness. And again, she felt a strange tug in her heart.

She tried to resist the feeling... pity... sympathy... something deeper? And she tried to shake the understanding she had come to on that mountain with Simon.

He couldn't have seen that light or heard that voice. It must have been a dream or maybe some kind of induced trance. But when he said that it seemed like the light *was* Jesus, a truth resounded in her soul unlike any truth she'd ever known. It seemed every other truth in her life immediately rebuilt itself around this singular reality.

She struggled to deny it. God had no son. It was heresy to even consider such a thing. If he did, they'd be no different than the Romans with their statues of gods and goddesses, sons of gods, daughters of gods. Hollow statues made of clay. Worthless, violent superstitions. She'd heard what it took to pacify their lifeless gods. A god who could be broken, stolen. A god who needed a man to even give him shape.

She didn't want a god like that. There is only one God, an unfathomable God, an invisible God, a God without body of stone or brass or clay or flesh, a God who cares for the

165

children of Abraham, a God who has chosen her people as his own. The Almighty God, majestic, protecting, steadfast, Creator of all that is. The Living God. The Eternal God. A God that needs no other gods.

Sarah continued to watch the lone figure as he walked silhouetted by the sun. This was not a god. There was no sense of wrath or vengeance or power about him. He was almost meek sometimes, gentle, kind, even humble. Eventually she knew he'd start to proclaim himself some kind of king or messiah, but so far, Sarah had to admit there was no sense of pride, superiority, or arrogance in him. He laughed, he chatted, he enjoyed being with people, he got tired and hungry and frustrated. What kind of god gets frustrated?

She'd followed him for months, listening to him, watching him, but she felt she didn't know him at all. Something about him seemed ultimately unknowable. And yet, in spite of herself, she wanted to know him.

As she neared the path to her door, the few families still with them broke off from the group and headed to their own homes. Salome shouted a good-bye to Sarah, but James and John, still engrossed in the roiling argument with the others, ignored their mother and walked with the others toward Sarah's house. She wondered if they even cared that Jesus would most likely go there or if they just wanted to ensure that no one else had a chance to be alone with him.

As she turned onto the path, she saw Micah cross the courtyard with a bucket of goat milk in each hand. He nodded a greeting toward her and tried to squeeze past his sisters as they rushed out the door.

In her excitement to run to her parents, Abi knocked the milk out of one his buckets. Hannah, followed, screeching for joy. Simon scooped his youngest into his arms while Sarah hugged Abi and let her take her hand to lead her up the path. In the short distance to the door, Abi filled her mother in on everything that had happened in the house, in the town, and in her adolescent life.

The men broke off their conversation as they followed them through the door. Some tousled Micah's hair with no joy or enthusiasm while others dropped down onto the cushions around the table.

Jesus walked in a short time later. He stood at the window, looking back along the way they had just traveled. Hannah ran to him and stayed by his side, saying nothing. Joy lit her eyes as if she were glad just to be near him even if he didn't seem to notice her.

Sarah helped Leilah gather some food and ladle wine for the men. Although she eyed the cushion by the fireplace with exhausted desire, she felt she had to help her mother. One look at the weariness etched into her face told Sarah God never intended for a woman Leilah's age to mother three children.

The sound of no one speaking permeated the air. Even the children grew still, aware that all was not well.

Jesus, still gazing out the window, asked the others, "What were you talking about on the way here?"

No one answered.

He turned, walked to the table, and sat on a mat beside Philip.

Pulling some grapes off the bunch Leilah had just set in the middle of the table, he said, "If anyone would be the greatest, he must be the least of all."

The men gazed down at their cups and up at the ceiling, convinced that if they didn't look at Jesus, he wouldn't see the guilt in them. Silence grew so loud it seemed to fill the room, closing in on them.

Finally, Levi said, "If the least is the greatest, then how can anyone be the greatest in the kingdom of heaven?"

Jesus called Hannah to him and took her into his arms. "Unless you become like little children, you will never even

167

enter the kingdom of heaven. Whoever humbles himself like this child, he is the greatest in heaven."

The others shifted in their places, secretly blaming each other for starting the whole argument.

As Sarah slid a basket of bread onto the table, he continued. "See to it that you don't despise even one of these little ones, for I tell you their angels in heaven always behold the face of my Father in heaven."

Sarah focused on slicing cheese, her back to Simon and the others, and still she could feel the tension and anger of those sitting with Jesus. No one wanted to lean toward another as she struggled to reach between the men to set the dish on the table. Her heart ached with sadness that friendships generations old were now broken, maybe forever severed.

James was as unforgiving as they came, and Simon could hold a grudge with the best of them. She knew he felt especially betrayed by someone as close to him as James, someone he always counted on to have his back, someone closer to him than his own brother.

Jesus took the plate from her, handed it to Philip, and said to no one in particular, "If your brother sins against you, tell him his fault between him and you alone. Truly, I say to you, whatever you bind on earth will be bound in heaven, and whatever you loose on earth, will be loosed in heaven."

Simon struggled to contain his anger as he said, "So then, how often do I have to forgive someone? As much as seven times? When is enough enough?"

"You don't have to forgive someone seven times," Jesus said.

Simon nodded with smug satisfaction before Jesus continued. "You have to forgive him seventy times seven."

He leaned on the table toward the men as if what he was saying were the most important words they'd ever hear. "The kingdom of heaven is like a king who wants his servants to settle their accounts and pay what they owe him. A servant,

168

who can't possibly pay all he owes, begs for mercy, and the king forgives his debt, but then the man refuses to forgive another. The king then turns the servant over to be tortured until he has paid back all he owes. This is how my heavenly Father will treat each of you unless you forgive your brothers of everything. Not just with words, but from your heart."

Sarah watched the men who had been arguing only a short time earlier. Their efforts to maintain their ire wrestled with their realization that Jesus was calling them to let it go, free their hearts for love, not revenge. The tension eased from their faces. Several began to chat, and soon the room filled with laughter and camaraderie. Even James relaxed and joked with the others.

She saw their relief and wondered at the liberation that came with forgiveness. Was there anything more difficult or more healing? Then she looked at Jesus and for the first time felt he had worked a miracle.

***

That night, Sarah lay beside Simon, unable to still her thoughts enough to allow herself to slip into sleep. She gazed at the moonlit ceiling and thought about the men who had once ripped off her roof just to get to Jesus. Memories raced through her mind. Pleading faces, grateful faces, angry faces, hopeful faces, trusting faces.

The one thought she'd tried to forget, thoughts of Jesus and the light, overshadowed the rest. A light Simon was certain he had seen. And the voice. Of God. Was that possible? Had Simon and the others seen what he insisted they'd seen, heard what he says they heard?

A light unable to be contained by Jesus' clothes or even by his flesh. A light that seemed to contain everything. A light you felt you could fall into forever. A light she knew could only be divine. The light of God himself.

Could it be, Sarah wondered. Could it possibly be? But how could it be?

Images of Jesus hung before her in the shadows. He healed everyone. Reached out to everyone. Never seemed to hesitate or consider whether he should reach out. Never seemed to measure or hold back his compassion. Spontaneous in his love unlike any person she'd ever known. Ever.

Maybe he's an angel. But that couldn't be. Angels in the writings of Moses come and go. They don't stay months. Years. They don't have parents and cousins and friends.

But he couldn't be a god. There's only one God. Sarah was as certain of that as she was that she existed. And he couldn't be God himself. God doesn't have parents. God has no beginning. She'd met Jesus' mother and heard from Salome that Jesus was born in Bethlehem. God isn't from anywhere.

And God doesn't have flesh.

Simon rolled over toward her. "Are you still awake?" he asked, falling back to sleep before his words made it to her ears.

Still gazing at the streaks of moonlight, she said, "Moses saw the back of God, right?"

"Huh?"

"In his writings, Moses says he saw the back of God."

"So?" he said, still not awake.

"And Abraham entertained God. Saw him. Fed him. Talked with him. Walked with him." She rose up on one elbow and faced her husband. "And Jacob. He wrestled with God. I mean, he got down in the dirt and wrestled with God, right?"

"I guess," Simon said, his voice cloudy with sleep.

"But those were like visions, don't you think? They didn't really see God himself. The law says if you see the face of God, you die." She was still a moment before giving word to her thoughts. "But Jacob named the place where they wrestled Penuel, The Face of God, because he did see the face of God. And he didn't die."

170

"That's not what it means to see the face of God, Sarah. To see the face of God is to see God in all his glory. When we say we can't see his face, it means we can never see the fullness of God's glory. It's impossible. It's too big, too much. We couldn't begin to comprehend it."

Sarah lay back again and considered her husband's words, before saying, "What is his glory?"

"It's his glory. What more can you say about it?"

"But when we die, Simon, and someday see God in all his glory, what will we see? And what do the angels see? Even Jesus said they always see the face of God, so they always see his glory. But what is it they see?"

"I don't know, Sarah," Simon said, rolling away from her and pulling the blanket up to his shoulders. "Let's talk about this tomorrow, okay?"

"It's his goodness," she said, with certainty. "That's what the angels see. That's what we cannot even begin to fully comprehend."

As her husband slipped into the quiet rhythmic breathing of sleep, she thought again of Jesus. Goodness. She couldn't think of any word that better described him.

Chapter 24

"We're heading out in the morning," Simon said.

Sarah stopped beating the dirt out of a wet tunic. "So soon?"

"I guess so. Jesus seems eager to get going."

"But we just got home. We can't leave Mother again. More than that, we can't leave the children again."

"We could take them with us, Sarah. Everyone else does." He took the club from her hand and set it against a rock, then wrung the water from the garment.

"I still need to rinse that," she said, taking it from his hands. "I know other people bring their children, but how can it be good for them to roam the countryside like a flock of sheep, sleeping on the ground, bugs everywhere? No. Their place is here at home, and our place is here, too."

She dipped the tunic in a barrel filled with water. "Besides, I haven't finished washing our clothes, and they still have to dry. And you've got fish to catch, nets to mend. You can't keep letting your father support your family, Simon. They're your children. Let Jesus go without you for a while. You don't need to follow him every step of the way."

Simon sat on the rock and studied the ground at his feet. "We were talking today, and he said something about his future, about being delivered into the hands of men who will kill him."

"Well, that's even more reason not to go. Besides, I think he says stuff like that just to keep all of you from leaving him."

"But I'd never leave him, Sarah. Would you?"

***

Sarah shifted her satchel from one shoulder to the other as she walked with Simon and the others. Once again a crowd of people had joined them, trudging down yet another dirt road to yet another hot, dusty town, but she was surprised not to care. Even though she still longed to be home, more and more she felt she needed to be on this road.

Ahead, she saw Jesus talking to a woman and smiling. The sea beyond him sparkled with sunshine, and she wondered at the feeling that swelled within her heart. Even as she tried to stay on her guard, she found every move he made seemed to touch a chord deep within her, filling her with a gentle, pervasive...something.

"Another day, another journey," Salome said, walking up beside her.

"I know."

"Where are we headed this time?"

"I'm not sure. Simon thought maybe Jerusalem."

"Jerusalem?"

"That's what he thought."

"Maybe it's time to get this kingdom thing started," Salome said, a lilt in her voice.

Sarah looked at her, surprised at the excited anticipation in her words. Didn't anyone else fear the thought of a Messiah or a kingdom challenging Rome, the thought of anyone challenging Rome?

As they drew near to a city, the houses alongside the road grew in size and ostentation, with detailed tile frescos and stone carvings so ornate they verged on decadent. Townspeople stood outside the walls of the houses and courtyards, wondering at the large, diverse parade that passed. Some fell into step with the crowd as they questioned who they were, where they were going, how long they had traveled. Others shouted Jesus' name.

173

She watched children playing alongside the road, and her heart ached with the desire to be with her own. But she could no longer blame Simon for taking her from them. This had become a journey she chose to make. A journey she knew she had no choice but to make.

As they passed a villa, a young man ran across the column-lined portico and down the broad granite steps into the street. He squeezed through the crowd, rushed up to Jesus, and dropped to the ground before him, stopping him from going any farther.

"Rabbi, please," he grabbed Jesus' cloak, "please, tell me. What do I have to do to gain eternal life? I'll do anything. Anything."

The crowd gathered around them. Sarah studied the young man, his hair slick in the well-oiled style of the rich, his tunic silk, his rings glimmering gold.

"Why do you call me good?" Jesus said. "No one is good but God alone."

Sarah shot her attention back to Jesus. He glanced toward her for a moment before looking again to the man in the dirt.

"You know the commandments?" he said.

The man nodded.

"Do not kill," Jesus said. "Do not commit adultery. Do not steal. Do not bear false witness. Do not lie. Honor your mother and your father."

"I do all these things, Rabbi."

Jesus gazed at him, and Sarah drew in her breath at the depths of love she saw in his eyes for someone he didn't even know.

"But there's one thing you haven't done," he said. "Go, and sell what you have and give to the poor, and you will have treasure in heaven. Then come and follow me."

The young man's shoulders drooped, and his head dropped as he slowly stood up from the dirt. He looked at Jesus a moment, then wordlessly walked away, back to his house, oblivious to the people parting to make way for him to pass.

Jesus watched him leave, and said, "How hard it will be for those who have riches to enter the kingdom of God. It's easier for a camel to pass through the eye of a needle than for a rich man to enter into heaven."

Someone from within the crowd said, "Then who can be saved?"

"For men it is impossible," Jesus turned back to them, "but with God all things are possible."

Simon grabbed his arm. "But we've given up everything to follow you."

Again, Sarah was struck by the look of compassion in Jesus' eyes. "Everyone who has left his house or brothers or sisters or mother or father or children or lands for me will receive a hundredfold even now. Although with persecutions. And a hundred-fold in the age to come, in eternal life. But," he gazed out over the crowd, "many who are first, will be last, and many who are last, will be first."

Then he nodded toward Simon and the other men standing nearby and led them off to the nearby shore apart from everyone else. Sarah watched as people all around her dropped their bags, sat, and stretched out, settling onto the sandy road. No one tried to follow them or even seemed to care that he had left them behind, that he had clearly singled out a handful of men.

But she cared.

She wove her way behind boats and net-draped rocks to a spot behind a pile of baskets where she could hear what he had to say without being seen.

He looked earnestly at each of the Twelve, then in a quiet voice said, "We are going up to Jerusalem, and everything the Prophets have written about the Son of Man will be accomplished. He will be delivered to the Gentiles, and they will mock him. They will spit on him and scourge him. And they will kill him."

Even though Simon had told her something similar only the day before, the image Jesus drew was far more graphic. Far more real.

"And after three days," Jesus said, "he will rise."

He paused for a reaction, and Sarah waited for someone to ask him what in the world he meant. But it looked as if they hadn't heard a word he'd said.

John glanced over at James and then at their mother, who stood at the edge of the crowd, watching them. Salome nodded so slightly Sarah was certain no one else even noticed. Then the two brothers moved closer to Jesus.

"Master," James said, "we want you to do something for us."

"What?" Jesus said.

John stepped in front of his brother. "When you come into your kingdom, grant that we're seated at your side, one at your right hand and one at your left."

The others started to shout in protest, but Jesus said, "You don't know what you're asking for. Are you able to drink from the cup that I drink from? Or be baptized with the baptism I'm baptized with?"

As Sarah tried to figure out what he was talking about, they both shouted, "Yes."

Jesus looked from one brother to the other before saying, "You will drink from the cup from which I drink, and you will be baptized with the baptism I'm baptized with, but it's not for me to decide who will sit at my right hand or my left. That is for those for whom it has been prepared."

The others could hold back no longer. Their angry words tangled in the sea air.

Sarah retreated deeper behind the baskets, certain a fight was about to break out. She saw the veins pop up on Simon's forehead and understood the indignation he felt but still, it wasn't worth a fight over some imaginary seats in some imaginary kingdom.

She felt the warmth of a gaze and peered through the baskets to see Jesus looking at her. As she fell back into the shadows in embarrassment, she noticed he didn't seem angry or surprised to see her. He seemed more like someone who needed a friend, and he was looking her way.

Then he turned his attention back to the battle before him. "You know those who rule the pagans think they're more important than everyone else and can order them to do whatever they want. But it won't be like that with you. Whoever would be great among you must be your servant. Whoever would be first among you must be your slave."

The men struggled to control their anger. Tense muscles barely relaxed, breathing slowed only a little. Philip ran his fingers through his dark curls as if that might control his emotions. Levi's face still burned red with fury as he turned from Salome's sons, walked to a nearby rock, sat, and stared out to sea. The two Judases stood on the perimeter of the fray. One visibly calmed to a simmer while the other, the Iscariot, seemed to be trying to make sense of what he'd just witnessed and heard.

"Even the Son of Man didn't come to be served, but to serve," Jesus said, his voice quiet in the midst of the storm swirling around him. "And he will give his very life as the price of redemption for many."

He left them to rejoin the people, and the Twelve rushed to take their places at his side.

The midday heat of the desert competed with the heat of anger still burning in the curt words and attitudes of the men who walked nearest to him along the road to Jerusalem. Sarah followed in silence, unwilling to chat with Salome, certain her friend would detail for her exactly why her sons should be in a superior position in the 'coming kingdom.'

177

Jesus gradually slipped to the back of the group, letting the others keep a faster pace. His shoulders slumped, and she wondered if he was thinking of giving up on the whole bunch.

Simon walked back through the crowd to her side. "We're taking the shortcut."

"What shortcut?"

"Through Samaria," he said, his tone upbeat as if to counter the response he knew was coming.

"Samaria? Is he mad? Or maybe he plans to abandon us there like they abandoned God. It would serve you all right, leaving you there to be stoned by infidels."

Simon smiled as if she were kidding, but she knew he, too, couldn't be comfortable with this.

Chapter 25

Off the road that led from Galilee to Samaria, the remnants of a decaying building stood alone in the rocky, barren emptiness. A group of men gathered outside it, huddled together, their backs turned to those walking past while others sat in the windows, gazing out at a world of which they could no longer be a part. A sole figure stood at the desolate courtyard entrance. Sarah saw one of the men in the windows push back his head covering, revealing an empty eye socket and rotted cheek, testament to his sin and disease.

"It's Jesus," he shouted, pointing a hand wrapped in filthy bandages.

The others turned and looked at the group of travelers.

Salome gripped Sarah's arm as the lepers ran from the house toward them. Although the men stopped in the field a fair distance away, Sarah didn't know how close was too close. She noticed one wore what looked like the frayed scraps of a Pharisee's cloak, while another younger man, the one who had been standing alone, kept back, apart from the others. It seemed he was not even welcome among lepers. The blue fringe of his shawl revealed the depths of his sin. A Samaritan.

She looked away, unable to bear the sight of what was left of their faces.

"Jesus, help us... Master, have pity on us... Do something...," they cried.

Jesus stopped and gave each man his full attention, turning even to the leper among lepers, and Sarah wondered how he could bear to look at them. She wondered too at his audacity, gazing at the Samaritan with the same compassion as he showed his own brothers.

As he crossed the road and drew nearer to them, he said, "Go. And show yourself to the priests."

They looked at each other, their flesh still black, what flesh they had. One of the men, the one who had been standing apart, looked back at Jesus, then ran through the field toward a nearby village. The others raced to follow him.

They stopped midway, held up their hands, grabbed one another's faces and arms, and shouted with joy. Most of them continued running to the town, but one, the one who first trusted Jesus, turned back and ran to him.

"Praise God," he cried, "Praise God." He fell to his knees at Jesus' feet, weeping into healed, whole, beautiful hands. When he looked up, his ruddy, healthy face beamed with joy and gratitude.

Jesus said, "Weren't all ten of you made clean?"

The man nodded, unable to speak through his tears.

"Then where are the others?" Jesus looked out over the field to the departing men. "Has no one else returned to give glory to God except this foreigner, this Samaritan?"

He took the man by the hand, said, "Arise," and helped him stand. Still holding the man by the hand, he looked intently into his eyes. "Go your way. Your faith has made you whole."

Sarah watched the man head off to the town, his flesh as healthy as those who hadn't returned, but his soul made whole with gratitude.

***

Although Jesus' pace had slowed considerably, he seemed unwilling to stop, clearly heading for a town not far off. He sent Andrew and Philip to go ahead of them and find a place in the village where they could rest. The two men exchanged uncertain glances, then walked up a hill along a deer path more direct than the twisting road.

Sarah leaned toward her husband. "Is that still Galilee?"

When he didn't answer, she knew. Jesus had sent them into Samaria.

They melted into the distant marketplace but soon reappeared, hurrying back to the small group of travelers.

Andrew got to Jesus before his older companion, and said, "They ran us out of town."

Philip came up behind him and stopped, leaning forward, his hands on his knees, trying to catch his breath, as Andrew continued. "They asked where we were heading, and I said Jerusalem. I thought they were going to kill us right then and there. They started throwing rocks at us. Some drew their knives."

John and James shot forward, pulling their own fishing knives from their belts.

"Let us at them," James said. "We'll call down fire from heaven to consume their filthy town."

Jesus shook his head and silently led them farther down the road, away from the village.

"He should have known better," Sarah whispered to Simon. "What was he thinking? Why would he even bring us this close to Samaria?" She spit the word as if it made her mouth unclean.

As they walked, the road curved closer toward other foreign towns. Sarah strained to see where it must surely turn away again. Shepherds scattered on the hillsides warily kept their eye on the small group of strangers. One quickly led his flock from a well when it appeared they were heading toward it.

"Jacob's well," Simon said.

Sarah stopped a moment, then hurried to catch up. "That's in Sychor. I'm not crossing the border into that heathen territory."

"Too late. You already have."

She drew her cloak tighter around her shoulders as if she could cocoon herself safely inside.

Jesus paused at the well, leaning against its thick stone walls. He sat on the edge and gazed into its depths, almost as if he could see the generations of faithful and fallen who had drank from its waters through the centuries.

After a few moments, he looked up again, his eyes revealing a weariness so heavy Sarah could feel it.

"Go on ahead," he said. "I'll join you later. I'm just going to sit here and rest a little while."

"When did you last eat?" Nathaniel said. He looked into his bag and turned to the others. "Does anyone have any food left?"

Simon and the others rummaged in their satchels, then shook their heads.

"There's got to be some place around here where we can get him food," Nathaniel said.

Without waiting for a response, he headed toward the village. Simon and the rest hurried to join him. Sarah hesitated, unsure whether to venture one step deeper into Samaria, before deciding she had no choice but to go wherever her husband went. She couldn't stay there alone with Jesus. It wasn't proper.

She glanced back at him, and the exhaustion in his posture touched her heart. Even though she didn't hang on to his every word as the others did or feel the need to stay close by his side, she wasn't sure she wanted to walk on without him. The farther they got, the more she felt his absence.

As they neared the town, they passed a woman heading in the opposite direction, a water jar perched on her hip, held in place by an arm draped in jangling bracelets. Her veil blew back in the breeze, carelessly revealing long russet curls.

Sarah was grateful to see Simon avert his gaze.

As they entered the marketplace, venders and shopkeepers watched the group as if they were thieves. Sarah wanted to

182

tell them she had no interest in their wares. Simon, however, did.

Casting aside all propriety, he approached a baker. "I'd like to buy some bread."

"I'm closed," the man answered.

Simon fell back a step and pointed to the mound of loaves. "You're clearly not."

"I sell to my own," the man said, turning to take care of the needs of a woman on the other side of his booth.

"Forget it," Sarah whispered. "Let's just go back. We shouldn't be here anyway. I've got a couple of figs in my bag. They're almost rotten, but they're better than anything we'll find here."

"We're not leaving without food for him."

She followed her husband from stall to stall and shop to shop, while the others ventured out on their own, all in search of something to take back with them. Simon led her to a vender tucked in a corner of one of the few side roads in the small village. A stooped woman older than Leilah sat behind stacks of bread.

"I'll sell you what I have," she said before Simon could say anything. "It don't matter to me who you are."

Simon gratefully filled his satchel and paid the woman. He called out to John and Andrew, "I've got enough," and the others joined them for the trip back to the well. Sarah didn't have to struggle to keep up. She was eager to get out of the town and hoped she would soon be out of Samaria entirely.

The well rose up in the distance, the lone structure on the dusty horizon, and she noticed what looked like two people talking. As they got closer, she could see one was Jesus, still sitting where they'd left him. The other was the woman with the water jar.

There they were, in the middle of nowhere, alone together, chatting like it didn't matter that he was a Jew and she was a Samaritan, that he was a man and she was a woman, that he was a man and she was the kind of woman no decent person should talk to.

The woman suddenly turned and left Jesus. She ran past the small group but didn't seem to be running from them. She didn't even seem to notice them. Her face was ablaze with some kind of inner fire. Nothing about her appeared sensual as it had only a short time earlier even as her garments swept around her legs in her eagerness to get to wherever she was going.

Salome openly turned to watch her race toward town while others tried unsuccessfully to pretend they hadn't seen her. No one said anything.

Simon reached into his bag, pulled out some of the bread he had just bought, and offered it to Jesus. But Jesus seemed not to see anything but the woman who had just left his side.

"I thought you were hungry," Simon said.

"I have food to eat that you cannot appreciate," Jesus said, still watching the woman.

James, Andrew, and the others looked around at one another, confused. Sarah searched for any sign of crumbs in the straggly grass along the walls of the well.

"Did someone else already give you something to eat?" James said.

Jesus turned to them. "My food is to do the will of the One who sent me. To accomplish his work."

He gazed out to the fields that lay between him and the town. "Don't you say there are a few months yet before the harvest? Well, look up and see that the fields are already ripe and ready."

From the distance, a cry filled the air, roaring out of the village. People poured out of the town and onto the road leading to Jesus. Simon and the others looked at him, waiting for a signal to leave, but none came.

Soon dozens of men and women surrounded the well, yelling out Jesus' name with what seemed to be joy.

"She said you told her everything she's ever done," a man shouted.

Sarah recognized him as the one who sold only to his own. Now, he smiled at Simon and shook hands with James, slapping Levi on the shoulder in friendship and solidarity, and leaving the men too stunned to resist the touch of a Samaritan.

He looked at Jesus still perched on the well. "She said you have the water of everlasting life."

Jesus smiled.

"Well, we want that water," the man said, as others around him cheered.

Chapter 26

The walls of a fortress loomed in the distance, perched on a mountain rising out of the sands of the desert. Sarah gazed at the guard towers, uncomfortable with the knowledge that they were being watched as they made their way along the road leading through Jericho. On the horizon, the gleaming marble of Herod's winter palace shimmered in an emerald oasis, as if a mirage. She couldn't imagine the decadence of life behind those walls, and she didn't want to give it any thought.

The crowd had grown since they were no longer in enemy territory. Or at least, they were no longer in Samaria. People walked apart from one another in the heat. Laughter and conversation floated off over the desert. Some had moved ahead of Jesus as he fell back into the middle of the pack and chatted with those around him.

The crowd merged with other travelers anxious to get to their own destinations. Merchants' booths increasingly lined their path. The sounds of the city echoed off the mountain cliffs that hung above them. Sellers promoted their wares, and buyers offered their price. Over-dyed fabrics swirled from booths and from people in the arid, perfumed air. Even with the open desert nearby, Sarah felt closed in by the chaos.

She slowed her pace at the sight of Roman soldiers riding out of the city. They stopped and glared down the road at the approaching mass of people.

Averting her gaze in hopes of not drawing their attention, she saw a beggar sitting by the side of the road a short distance ahead. He looked blankly at the passing feet that kicked dust in his face as oblivious people shuffled through the dirt.

A woman near the edge of the crowd noticed him and stopped, forcing those behind her to make their way around her.

She bent down to the man, and said, "Jesus of Nazareth is passing by."

His eyes stared into the crowd, seeing nothing as he called out, "Jesus, Son of David. Have mercy on me."

Others nearby scolded the man as if he were a child, "Be quiet. Leave Jesus alone... Don't bother him... He can't even hear you in this mob."

But the man cried louder, "Son of David. Have mercy on me."

As the plea reached him, Jesus stopped and searched for the man who sat hidden by everyone who stood in his way.

While voices rose to quiet the man, Jesus said to no one in particular, "Bring him here."

Two men moved through the people to where the beggar sat. They reached down, took him by the arms, and helped him stand amid the crush of the crowd, then led him through the throng to Jesus. Those farther ahead, who had tried to silence the man, stopped and gathered in small groups, unable to see why the forward movement had stopped as they waited for Jesus to catch up to them.

Jesus acknowledged the two who had made it their job to get the man to him, then turned his attention to the beggar. "What do you want me to do for you?"

The man's grimy hand searched the air around him before finding Jesus' arm. Grabbing on to it, he said, "Master, I want to see."

A soft smile crossed Jesus' face. "Receive your sight. Your faith has saved you."

Immediately, the man focused from staring into the nothingness that had been his life and looked into the eyes of Jesus.

"Praise God. I can see."

Throughout the marketplace, people called out the news, sending it through the crowd, their joy as fresh as it had been the first time they saw Jesus cure someone.

Jesus turned to continue his journey, and the beggar followed close behind. Sarah studied the man who walked with his newly lit eyes locked on Jesus, as if determined never to let him out of his sight, as if this was why he had sight.

She glanced around at the people and the buildings and the sky and the colors that surrounded them. Then she looked again at the beggar and wondered that a person who couldn't see any of the world before today seemed to have no desire to see anything more than a man in a tattered tunic leading him down a dusty, winding road.

***

Towering date trees lined the street into Jericho, fronds blowing in the arid breeze. Caravans wove through the crowd. As those perched on camels rode by, the harsh aromas of pepper made Sarah's eyes water. Near the gates, Roman soldiers sat atop snorting horses and watched the passersby. With each step, she prayed that Jesus would speed up and get them through the city quickly.

Along the way, people ran out of houses and shops to join the crowd, putting distance between her and Simon. A man no taller than she pushed against her. His purple cloak and heavily fringed sash screamed status as did the high headpiece atop his flowing hair. The smoky scent of expensive balsam oil reeked into the air around him. Some from Jericho seemed to recognize him and shuffled aside, giving him wide berth more than respect.

As still others shoved in front of him, he stretched his neck, and said to Sarah, "Where is he?"

Assuming he meant Jesus, she said, "I think he's behind us."

188

The man stopped and twirled around. Dozens of people tripped over one another to get around him. He ran to a sycamore tree, it's massive trunk gnarled into an endless web of branches reaching out in every direction. Some hung so low she could touch them while others stretched toward the heavens. Still others snaked around the tree, thick and coiling, hidden under the large leaves.

He climbed up the trunk and scooted out on a limb bent over the road, twigs tugging at the threads of his robe. Branches knocked his headpiece to the ground, but still he pushed forward to his goal.

Sarah moved under the tree, no longer surprised at the lengths to which people would go to see Jesus, and waited for Simon to catch up. When he and the others came into sight, she stepped into the street again just as Jesus looked up into the sycamore tree.

"Zacchaeus," he said, "come down here. I'm eating at your house today."

Sarah's heart sank with disappointment as hopes of passing quickly through town faded.

Around her, the cheering crowd quieted while some murmured, "Does he know who that man is?... He must. He called him by name... He's eating with the chief publican? With that sinner?"

The man jumped down from the branch and ran to Jesus, standing before him short, strong, and confident as he said, "Master, I will give half of all that I own to the poor, and if I have ever defrauded anyone, I will pay him back fourfold."

Jesus turned to Simon and the others. "Today, salvation has come to this house. For the Son of Man has come to seek and to save what was lost."

Together Jesus and Zacchaeus walked deeper into the city, leaving behind the sycamore, threads of who the publican used to be clinging to the wood of the tree.

Chapter 27

Sarah waited with Salome and the horde outside the walls of Jericho while her husband joined Jesus and the others at Zacchaeus' house. Passersby cast a wary eye toward them, and she could feel the cold glare of Roman soldiers posted in the towers above. While grateful to avoid spending even one more moment in the city, she felt vulnerable without Simon and, unexpectedly, even more vulnerable without Jesus.

The crowd around her came to life, and she knew he had reappeared. Peering over the heads of those between her and the city gates, she caught sight of Simon walking down the road toward her, close by Jesus' side. James, Andrew, and the others followed, accompanied by a woman she hadn't seen before.

"Who's that?" she asked Simon before he could greet her.

He followed her gaze to the woman draped with expensive embroidered fabrics and jewels, a woman unlike most who followed Jesus, a woman who would seem to have no need of the diversion and hope he offered.

"Joanna," he said. "She and her husband were at Zacchaeus' house."

"So, where's he?"

"The husband?" Simon glanced around. "Not here, apparently. He probably couldn't leave his job."

"Well, none of these people should have left their jobs," she said, "but that doesn't seem to have stopped them. What's he do that's too important to leave?"

Simon hesitated before answering. "He's Herod's household steward."

"Herod's steward?" People nearby turned, surprised at her outburst. She lowered her voice. "Are you serious? And you don't think it's crazy to be associated with anyone who's associated with Herod?"

"We can't tell her to leave, Sarah."

"What's her excuse for even coming out here with us?"

"I don't know. Does she need an excuse?"

Having no response, Sarah started to walk away, then spun around to confront her husband again. "What in the world happened in that house that would justify someone associated with Herod being with us?"

"I have no idea," Simon said, looking at the woman. "She was in the courtyard with other women, and Jesus went out to talk with them. She actually caught my eye because, as I watched him through the door, I noticed she turned away from him. I wondered if it was an intentional snub or if he was just that irrelevant to her. Then he said something, and she separated from the women she'd been with and walked over to him. He said something else, and the next thing I know, she's sobbing into her hands. After a few moments, she grabbed his hand, kissed it, and dropped into the dirt at his feet."

He turned back to Sarah. "I admit, I didn't know whether to be scandalized or amazed."

Sarah thought of a similar scene with Lazarus' sister, and she knew how he felt.

***

The oasis city receded behind them as Jesus led the small band of people toward Jerusalem. Lavish villas gave way to more modest structures, then eventually to no structures at all. Sarah was glad to leave Jericho but uneasy traveling a road infamous for violent gangs of thieves.

191

As the road climbed up from the desert floor, she looked out at the steep, treacherous cliffs of a gorge. The jagged peaks cast shadows that kept the valley in perpetual night. Far below, deep in the dimness, the shadowy path of a river traced onward in its never-ending trek. How strange that something so life-giving could be hidden in the depths of such darkness.

She glanced up and noticed that Jesus had been watching her. For a moment, her fear of thieves left. For a moment, her fear of everything left.

But only for a moment.

***

The walls of Jerusalem rose up over the road ahead, filling Sarah with dread even as those around her shouted with joyful anticipation.

"Why does he have to go to the city again?" she asked Simon.

"It's almost Passover."

"Still, we should get as far away from there as we can, not go rushing back into it." She tripped on the rutted road. "No good can come from this, Simon."

When he didn't respond, she knew he too was uneasy.

Just as everyone prepared to turn into the gates, Jesus turned toward the mountains opposite Jerusalem. The enthusiasm that had pulsed through the crowd quickly turned to cries of disappointment .

"What's he doing?" Salome said "We're so close."

Sarah didn't answer. While the wilderness seemed safer than the city, she didn't look forward to another night on the ground.

A vendor passed with his cart of unsold goods, chickens scrawking from their cages, chickens that would get to sleep in a coop. She watched them roll by and didn't even care that she was envying chickens.

Jesus led them up the hillside and stopped near the top. Taking the cue that this was their lodging place for the night, people opened satchels and pulled out cloaks to lay on the rocky ground and food that would have to suffice. Sarah glanced past a straggly shrub to where a group of women settled into the gravel and wondered how long Herod's steward's wife would be one of the party now.

The woman removed a velvet wrap and tossed it onto the dirt as if it had been a weight from which she was grateful to be free. She dropped down onto it, her silk garment splayed out around her, gems glittering even in the dusky gray of twilight, and laughed with the others like someone who couldn't imagine being anywhere other than where she was.

Sarah sat on her own worn and dirty cloak and gnawed on old bread, offering a chunk to her husband. He gazed up into the darkening sky, and for a moment she wanted to brush back the unkempt curls around his face just to feel the touch of his skin.

What had happened to them? Clean had become an almost foreign concept. Even the bread tasted like dust.

James walked over to their cloak-sized piece of the world, crossed his arms, and looked out at the city. "Might just be time to get this kingdom thing going, don't you think, Peter?"

"Might be," Simon said, and she wondered how he could so readily embrace a name that wasn't his. She wondered even more at the casual way James used it, no longer bitter and angry.

The two men wandered over to the rest of the Twelve to talk about the kingdom. Salome chatted with those nearby about their own hopes and plans for whatever Jesus was about to finally do.

A small group of men gathered under a dead olive tree, religious leaders who had followed them from Jericho. The thick branches hung low, casting them into distorted shadow. They shared none of the people's animation and anticipation.

Jesus sat perched on a rock, away from the crowd but not so far that he couldn't hear their discussions. In the dim moonlight, Sarah saw concern in his eyes. Maybe he was having second thoughts.

He stood and walked slowly to where the people were, then said, "A nobleman went into a distant country to receive his kingly power and then return to rule his kingdom."

At the word *kingdom* everyone quieted.

"He called ten of his servants, gave them each a mina, three months' wages, and said, 'Trade with these until I return.' But his people hated him. And they sent a delegation after him, saying, 'We don't want this man to reign over us.' But still, the man returned from the distant land to rule them as king, and he commanded that those servants to whom he had given money be called to him to give an account of what they had done with what he had given them."

He walked slowly through the gathering. "The first said, 'Master, your mina has made ten more.' And the king said to him, 'Well done, good and faithful servant. Because you have been faithful with a little, you shall have authority over ten cities.' The second said, 'Master, your mina had made five more.' And the king said to him, 'Well done, good and faithful servant. Because you have been faithful with a little, you shall have authority over five cities.' Then another came to him and said, 'Master, here is your mina back. I kept it safely to myself because I feared you, thinking you cruel and uncompassionate.'"

Jesus paused and looked with deep sadness at the people stretched out before him.

He moved into the crowd until he stood only a short distance from the religious leaders under the dead tree and looked directly at them. "The king said, 'I will condemn you through the words of your own mouth, you wicked servant. Why did you not invest my money, and at my coming I would have collected it with interest?'"

194

Turning to Simon, James, and the others, he said, "And the king said to those who stood by, 'Take the mina from him and give it to the one who has ten.' For I tell you that to the one who has, more will be given. But from the one who has not, even what he has will be taken away." He gazed again at the religious leaders standing in the shadows. "But as for these enemies of mine, who did not want me to reign over them, bring them here, and slay them before me."

Chapter 28

The morning couldn't come soon enough for Sarah. She'd lain in the dark amid the brush and grasses of the mountainside unable to sleep, thinking of the threat she'd heard in Jesus' words. She couldn't imagine how much more the religious leaders would take. Every time she almost drifted off, a twig would snap in the distance, and she'd jolt back to consciousness.

As she stood in the dawning light of a spring day, she began to feel a little better. Maybe Jesus wasn't worth their effort. Maybe they were willing to let this all play out, let the crowds eventually dissipate.

But would people stop coming to him?

Could she?

A flock of sheep grazed farther down the hillside. Their shepherd leaned on his gnarled staff, looking lonely and tired. She knew he spent every night sleeping on this rocky ground with its piercing blades of grass and bramble. But he was all the sheep had. If he didn't risk his life, lying in the dirt, blocking the entrance of the enclosure where he led the sheep for the night, every wolf and hyena in Judah would dine on mutton.

No doubt the life of a shepherd was a hard one, but the sight of a man gently guiding his flock always gave her peace, always brought to mind the words of God, *I, I myself, will search for my sheep, and I will rescue them from all the places they have been scattered. I will seek the lost and bring back the straying, bind the crippled, and strengthen the weak. And I will feed them on the mountains of Israel. I myself will be the shepherd of my sheep.*

Jesus walked past, looked at her, and smiled, and she knew it was time to go.

The small group followed him down the Mount of Olives and into Jerusalem. Already the city was awake with people making their way to the Temple for the Sabbath. Some called out to Jesus with delight as he led those following him through the streets.

As they neared the overpass, Sarah prayed he would take them anywhere but the Temple. Why couldn't he find a stool in some quiet corner of the city? Somewhere far from the eyes and ears of the Sanhedrin.

He bounded up the stairs, across the walkway, past the walls and columns gleaming with morning sunlight, and into the broad, open courtyard. As he sat on a stone bench against the far wall, people flowed in and filled the plaza before him.

The odor of too many bodies in too small a space choked her, and the sea of brightly dyed garments and never dyed garments was more than the courtyard could contain. People climbed onto ledges enclosing the area and pushed and pulled each other up onto the roofs of surrounding structures.

Jesus rose to speak, and a hush fell over the area. He looked at all the people, those who had followed him from the beginning and those who were about to hear him for the first time.

"You are truly my disciples if you keep to my teachings. Then you will know the truth, and the truth will set you free."

A man standing against a column shouted, "Set us free? We're children of Abraham. We've always been free."

Another man beside him said, "I'm not anybody's slave."

Others in the crowd murmured their agreement and confusion, and the hint of renewed tension rose into the air. Sarah moved close to Simon but kept her eye on Jesus.

"If you've committed a sin," he said, "you are a slave to sin. But the Son can free the slave. And if the Son sets you free, you are free, indeed."

197

He looked at the religious leaders standing in the entryway. "I know that you are descendants of Abraham, and yet you are out to kill me."

Surprise, consternation, and bewilderment spread through the courtyard.

"I speak of what I have seen with my Father," he said, "and you seek to do what you have been told by your father."

One of the Scribes, unable to remain still, said, "Abraham is our father."

"The devil is your father."

No one dared speak or draw attention to himself. Mothers pulled children close and shielded them with their cloaks while Sarah wanted only for him to stop. Please stop. But she knew he wouldn't.

"Satan was a murderer from the beginning," Jesus said, as if he were talking about someone he knew, as if he were speaking a reality no one else could fully understand. "He hates the truth. And so, because you are a son of Satan, you cannot recognize the truth when I speak it."

He turned away from the furious leaders and looked out over the people spread before him. "I tell you, if anyone keeps my word, that person will not die."

A tall, thin Pharisee strode through the crowd as if hundreds weren't sitting in his way, forcing people to lean and jump aside.

He came close to Jesus and pointed at him. "Now we know you are possessed. Abraham and all the Prophets died. Are you saying you're greater than our father Abraham? Who do you think you are?"

Jesus gazed steadily into the man's eyes. "Before Abraham was, I Am."

Gasps arose from the crowd, and angry words rumbled through the air as people argued over what he could possibly have meant equating himself with God.

Even in the midst of the shouting, Sarah felt the crowd, the commotion, and the chaos recede around her until she seemed to stand alone with him, his words sinking deep into her soul, resonating a truth she couldn't yet comprehend.

The Scribes and priests in the archway roared with rage and picked up stones to throw at him. Sarah shielded her head, certain she was in their line of fire, but Jesus slipped through a nearby exit and left the courtyard before a single stone could be hurled.

People everywhere called out and tripped over one another, some trying to escape the mayhem, others trying to get at Jesus.

Simon took Sarah by the hand and hurried out, struggling to keep Jesus in sight. John, Andrew, and the others ran with them, weaving in and out of the crowd. With guilty relief, she saw James help his mother keep up, unwilling to slow down herself to help the woman.

They ran down the steps and into streets filled with more people than they had left in the Temple.

"I see him," John said.

The others followed past closed booths and shops, dodging children and sheep.

Simon lost sight of John and stopped. "Where did he go?"

"He's with Jesus. Right there," Sarah said, "standing by that man."

"What man?"

"The one sitting on the mat by the spice booth." She took Simon by the shoulders and turned him. "There. Just a couple of shops away. See the man sitting against a stall, staring into space?"

At least, Sarah thought, he was kind of staring. Having only the whites of his eyes, she didn't know if staring was the right word.

Simon led her through the crowd to where Jesus stood watching them come to him, patiently waiting for them to catch up.

As the small group gathered around him, James said, "I thought I was going to have to take down a Pharisee for a minute there."

Jesus didn't respond, and the others shuffled uncomfortably, unsure what to say.

To change the subject, Philip pointed to the nearby blind man. "Master, who sinned? This man or his parents?"

"What do you mean?" Andrew said.

"Well, the man was obviously born blind. So it doesn't seem this should be a punishment for his sin, does it?"

"No one's sin caused this man to be born blind," Jesus said, gently pulling the man to his feet. "He was born blind so that the goodness of God could be made known to everyone through him."

Who could look at this filthy, hopeless man and see the goodness of God, Sarah wondered.

Jesus scooped up a palmful of dirt and spit into it, rolled it in his hands, and then spread the mud on the man's eyes.

"That's disgusting," a woman standing nearby shouted. "What's he doing?" She looked around for help. "Somebody stop this man."

Jesus ignored her and kept his focus on the blind man. "Go, wash in the pool of Siloam."

He nodded to Philip, who took the man by the arm and led him to the narrow, man-made pond beyond the remnants of the old southern wall and out of their sight. Sarah and the others stood in the tiny corner of the marketplace, waiting for Jesus to make a move or lead them somewhere.

"Why would he spit in the dirt like that and then rub it all over that poor man's eyes?" Sarah whispered to Simon. "It's not only disgusting, it's humiliating."

Simon shrugged.

" I mean," she said, "he obviously can't 'heal' the man. This is more than some guy who thinks he can't see. The man has no eyes."

A few moments later, an uproar arose from down the street, overwhelming the cacophony of musicians and conversations that already filled the city. The din grew louder as more and more people joined in the commotion.

"Sounds like a riot," Salome said.

Sarah peered down the road, trying to see what was going on. She noticed Philip and the blind man struggling to make their way back to where Jesus stood, their path blocked by people engulfing them from all directions.

A nearby fruit vendor, guarding his closed booth, trying to protect it from the mob in the streets, called out to another man across the road. "What's going on?"

"It's the blind guy," the man said.

"What blind guy?"

The one who's always sitting there." He pointed to the empty mat at Jesus' feet. "People are shouting that he can see."

"How can he see?" the vendor siad, as he looked for the man in the crowd. "He's got no eyes."

A beaming Philip led the man to Jesus' side. "You should have seen it. He did like you said, Jesus, and washed the mud from his eyes. Then he stared off into space a minute, turned to me, and said, 'I can see.' I looked at him, and he had eyes."

Philip turned from one person to another. "Can you believe it? He's got eyes." He grabbed the man by the arms. "Go ahead, show them."

He didn't have to show them. No one in the city could miss the fact that a man who had no eyes now had eyes. All around them, Jerusalem erupted.

The fruit vendor abandoned his booth and ran over to the man. "You're the guy who's sat here begging for years, aren't you."

"Yes," the man said, his joy uncontainable.

"But what happened?" the vendor said, as people crowded in on them from every corner of the market.

"That man put clay on my eyes. I could feel the warm mud on my face. Then he told me to go wash in the pool of Siloam. So I did. I went to the pool, washed my eyes, and now I can see."

"Where is he?" the vendor asked, looking around.

"I don't know," the once-blind man answered.

Sarah and the others looked, too, and saw that Jesus had disappeared into the crowd.

Word shot like lightening through the streets. Jesus had put eyes where there were no eyes. Before the Twelve could go in search of him, a group of local Pharisees descended on the man with new-found sight.

One of them grabbed him and spun him around. "Look at me."

The man gazed at him with lucid, hazel eyes.

The Pharisee fell back a step, then said, "What's going on here?"

"It was that man, Jesus," he said. "He put mud on my eyes, told me to wash, and now I can see."

"He did this today?" the scowling Pharisee said. "On the Sabbath?"

The man nodded.

The religious leader turned to the others in his group. "This Jesus is not from God, or he would keep the Sabbath."

Another Pharisee, standing toward the back of the group as if he wanted to separate himself from them and take in what he saw, said, "But how can a man who is not from God do something like this?"

"Well," said the first Pharisee," obviously he can't."

He looked at the man. "Where did you wash?"

"In the pool of Siloam?"

"And how did you get there? You couldn't see, right? And you had mud on your eyes, right? So, how did you make it out of the city through this crowd?"

"This man took me." He pointed to Philip.

The Pharisee glared at the man and then at Philip. Then he turned to the crowd. "Clearly this isn't the same person. It's his brother or someone else who looks like him." He walked over to Philip. "Admit it. When you took the blind man out of the city, you switched him with this man, didn't you?"

"No," Philip said. "This is the man I left with, the one who had no eyes."

The Pharisee snorted, grabbed the man by the arm, and pulled him down the street. Sarah stood rooted to the ground, wondering how these men could not see the good, could not rejoice in the good, could only call good evil even as it stood in front of them, so evident, so beautiful.

Simon took her hand as the crowd swelled forward, following the band of angry, determined religious leaders. As they passed a shuttered fish mongers' shop, they met a man and woman hurrying into the marketplace from the other direction. The woman stopped in her tracks and looked at the once blind man.

Then she caught him up in her arms and wept. "It's true. I couldn't believe it when they told me, but it's true."

The man with her hugged them both and sobbed with joy.

"Is this your son?" the Pharisee asked.

"It is," the man answered, as he wiped tears from his face.

"Are you sure?"

The man looked surprised at the question. "I know my son."

"And do you claim he was born blind?"

"He was."

"Then how do you explain this?"

"I can't." The father's words choked with delight. "I assure you this is my son, and I assure you he was born blind. But I have no idea what's happened. Ask him. He's an adult."

"It was Jesus," the man with new sight said.

The Pharisee shoved the elderly father to the side and pulled the man out of his mother's embrace. "You are to give glory to God. This Jesus is not God. He's a man, a sinner, a servant of Satan."

"Maybe he is a sinner," the man said, "I don't know. All I know is I couldn't see, and now I can."

An older, shorter, even angrier Pharisee said, "What did he do to you?"

"I already told you," the man said, "but you don't want to hear it, so why ask again? Never, since the world began, has a man given eyes to someone born without eyes. How can he be a servant of Satan? If this Jesus were not from God, how could he do this?"

Rage clouded the Pharisees' faces, as the older one said, "You were born in sin, and yet you presume to teach us? You are never to return to the synagogue again, do you understand? You are banned. Forever."

With that, the religious leaders turned and left, but Sarah noticed the one who had stood on the edge looked back over his shoulder. In his face she saw a yearning to be free enough to rejoice at what he'd seen.

The Pharisees strode down the busy street and stopped at a distant corner. There, they glared at the crowd still shouting and celebrating the good news.

"Look at them," Simon said. "They thought everyone would run away from the man once they banned him from the synagogue. But no one's going anywhere. They've lost the only power they had."

Sarah saw the darkness in the faces of the men huddled on the corner and feared they had not yet come to the end of their power.

Chapter 29

"Where's Jesus?" John asked. "Does he know the Pharisees have banned the man from the synagogue?"

The others glanced through the mob in the packed street, trying to catch a glimpse of him. "There he is," Salome said.

Sarah turned to where she pointed and saw Jesus standing on the walkway to the Temple, above the jubilation of the marketplace. Dwarfed by the enormous steps and the massive stones of the Temple walls, he watched the crowd below, where people still shouted news of the blind man's eyes to anyone who hadn't heard.

"Let's go," Simon said, as he took her hand and led her through the crowd to the steps. The others followed, making their way between the groups of people and up the steps until they got to Jesus' side.

He didn't turn to acknowledge them but continued to look out into the streets. Sarah stood beside him, leaned against the low wall, and gazed down at men and women pointing up at him as they told yet another person of the amazing event. Others, who had been on their way into the Temple, stopped and crowded in to be close to him.

She glanced toward the entrance at the end of the walkway and noticed Scribes, Pharisees, and priests spanning the passage, arms folded, eyes locked on Jesus. She looked down again to the road and saw more Pharisees standing their ground on the corner, their numbers increasing as others joined them. A group of Scribes pushed through the throng to talk with them, consternation and anger etched deep into their faces. She glanced over at Jesus and realized this growing band of religious leaders was what he'd been watching as well.

He turned toward the men who blocked the Temple entrance, then spoke, his words quiet but clear. At the sound of his voice, conversation ceased. Up and down the steps and throughout the streets below, Sarah could hear people telling one another to be still. *He's talking.*

"Truly, truly, I tell you, I am the door of the sheep." He swept his hand out toward the religious leaders below and to the men at the entrance. "All who came before me are thieves and robbers, but the sheep did not listen to them.

"I am the door," his voice rose, reaching out to all those gathered before him. "Anyone who enters through me will be saved and will go in and come out and find pasture. The thief comes only to steal and destroy."

Several of the nearby religious leaders lunged forward while others held them back.

"But I come so they may have life, and have it more abundantly. I am the good shepherd. And the good shepherd lays down his life for his sheep."

He glanced at Sarah for a moment, then turned to address those on the other side of the stairway. "A hireling is not a shepherd. He cares nothing for the sheep. But I am not a hireling. The sheep are mine. I know my sheep, and my sheep know me."

He again looked at the religious leaders in the entranceway and at those on the corner of the city street. "No one takes my life from me. I lay it down. I have the power to lay it down, and I have the power to take it up again."

All around her people began to argue. "The power to take his life back up again?... Raise himself from the dead?... The man's crazy... He's possessed... Why listen to him?... But can a madman open the eyes of a blind man?... Can a demon give eyes to someone born without them?"

Contentious words rang through the streets below as well. Again, Sarah feared a riot was about to break out. From all sides, Scribes, Pharisees, priests, and elders moved in toward him, shoving people aside if they weren't fast enough to move, no longer caring if they became unclean.

A well-fed Pharisee led the group, his ebony side curls flying back from his headwear, the fringes of his prayer shawl flailing around him.

He strode up to Jesus, and said, "How long do you plan to keep us in suspense? If you're the Christ, the Messiah, say so."

"I did tell you," Jesus said, "but you don't believe what I said. The works I do in my Father's name speak of the truth, but you don't believe them. You don't believe because you do not belong to my sheep."

He looked beyond the Pharisee to the thousands gathered on the walkway and streets, and the harsh edge to his voice softened. "My sheep hear my voice. They hear my words, and they follow me. I give them eternal life, and they will never perish." He turned his attention back to the Pharisee. "And no one will snatch them from out of my hand."

Rage rippled through the group of religious leaders.

"My Father, who has given them to me," Jesus said, "is mightier than all, and no one is able to snatch them out of the hand of my Father."

He leveled a steady gaze at the Pharisee standing before him. "I and the Father are one."

The Scribes, Pharisees, and priests picked up stones to hurl at him, while people screamed and scrambled to get out of the way.

"Which of my works do you stone me for?"

"We're not stoning you for any of your works. We're stoning you for your blasphemy. You, a man," the Pharisee spit the word to the ground, "declaring yourself to be God."

"If you don't believe me, then believe my works. Maybe then you'll understand that the Father is in me, and I am in the Father."

He led the crowd down the steps, to the road, and past the enraged religious leaders. Sarah noticed some still cradled their rocks, weighing the risks of following through on their desire to destroy him.

Chapter 30

They had walked hours to the Jordan, passing through towns and villages stretched along the road. The journey was tiring, but Sarah thanked God for every footstep he put between them and Jerusalem.

With the moon as their only light, they crossed the river at a narrow ford and came to a stop. Quiet conversation hummed in the night breeze as people found places to settle in until morning.

For the entire day, Simon had never allowed Jesus to get more than two paces away from him, but now her husband sat alone on the bank, watching the water flow over and around smooth, worn rocks.

She walked to his side and drank in the peace of the gently rushing stream.

"So," she said, "what do you think now?"

"I think he might be heading back home."

"Well, I'm glad, but that's not what I meant. What do you think about what he said today, about the Father and him?'"

"We always knew the Messiah would be sent from God, anointed by God," Simon said. "So he'd have to have a close relationship with God."

"As close as God himself?" she said.

"Nowhere in the law or the Prophets does it say the Messiah is God, Sarah, and Jesus would never say something like that. He meant he and God are one in mission. The Scribes and Pharisees just read into what he says, looking for something to turn people away from him."

"Then what about him being the good shepherd gathering his flock? When Ezekiel said, *I, I myself, will search for my sheep*, he was talking about God, Simon. God himself."

"Isaiah meant God working through the Messiah, through Jesus. Jesus is not God himself. That's sacrilege. He wouldn't twist those words to mean he's God." Simon stood and dusted dirt from his hands. "I know you think he's a charlatan, but I can't understand why you think he's saying he's God. You skipped over Messiah completely."

Leaving her alone, he walked around several small groups of people to join Levi and Nathaniel. She sat on the gravelly sand alongside the Jordan and gazed into the night sky where stars glimmered. It seemed the more she looked, the deeper she saw.

She wasn't accusing Jesus of saying he's God. She was asking, what if?

Chapter 31

Sarah looked at the land around her, an area that once bustled with those eager for the Baptist to plunge them into the murky waters. Now, in the evening darkness, people quietly talked around fires. Simon sat on a fallen tree, engaged in earnest discussion with Nathaniel and Levi. Salome chatted with several other women.

Sarah could join them, but she preferred to stay where she was. In the quiet with the incomprehensible.

A star shot across the sky in a moment of distant fiery illumination before it evaporated into the night. Every time she saw a shooting star, she thought of Elijah and his flaming chariot sweeping up into the heavens. She found comfort knowing that someone who lived with such devotion to God spent eternity with him.

A chill wind brushed over her. As she pulled her cloak up to her neck, she noticed Jesus talking with those near him. The men and women gathered in his small circle listened attentively, taking in his perspective, a perspective unlike anyone else's she had ever known. And she wondered what it must feel like to be him. Alone in his understanding. Alone in his courage.

Alone in his love.

The darkness deepened. She walked around some rocks and between clusters of people to where her husband sat gazing into a fire, his friends now engaged in discussions with others around them.

She dropped onto the stump beside him, and said, "I hope you're right and we're heading home. The city isn't safe. For him For you."

Simon didn't answer. The crackle of flames snapped, loud amid the quiet conversations around them.

Shadows moved along the road toward their camp. Her first thought was thieves. Or worse yet, Pharisees. As they drew closer, Sarah could see two young men searching for a face amid the crowd. No doubt yet more miracle-seekers. She saw the flicker of recognition as they spotted Jesus and approached him. Others stopped talking to see what wonder he would do for them.

"Lazarus is sick," one of the men said, as he knelt in the dirt beside Jesus. "Really sick. His sisters sent us to find you and bring you back to the house."

Reflections of firelight darted across Jesus' face as everyone awaited his response, poised to leap to their feet and follow him into the night. But he said nothing. Instead, he stood and walked a short way up the river, tossed his cloak on the ground, and laid down.

"What's he doing?" she asked Simon.

"He's going to sleep."

"I can see that. But why?"

"I don't know, Sarah. My guess is he's planning to leave at first light, which means we need to get some sleep, too."

"Do you really think he's going to go running back to Bethany? So close to Jerusalem? Hardly sounds like a good idea," Sarah grumbled as she settled onto her cloak, dreading yet another restless night spent on the ground. "Besides, Lazarus is a young man. He can't be that sick."

***

First light came and went and came again, and still Jesus made no move to leave. While many from surrounding villages wandered by to see and hear him or seek healing or freedom from some demon, those camped by the river had spent the entire time packed and ready to head out. But he acted as though he had nowhere to go.

As the sun rose high in the sky for a second day, Sarah looked down the road that led to Capernaum and ached to be home. Maybe he was just letting everyone rest before sending them all off to their homes. He obviously wasn't going to Bethany. He hadn't even mentioned Lazarus.

***

Yet another night passed. Sarah awoke to the sound of others gathering their belongings and saw Simon nearby, digging into his satchel.

"What's going on?" she asked him.

He handed her some dried figs. "I don't know."

Jesus walked past, talking with Philip, John, and Levi. Simon stopped him. "Are we leaving?"

"We're going to Judea," Jesus answered.

"You're going back to Jerusalem?" Simon's surprise mirrored that of everyone close enough to hear as Sarah's heart sank.

"You can't be serious," John said. "Just a couple of days ago the priests tried to stone you, and now, you want to go back?"

Jesus looked to the rising sun, its blush dusting the treetops with a soft peach glow. "We're going to Bethany. Our friend, Lazarus, needs me. He's fallen asleep, but I'm going to him, to wake him."

"If he's sleeping, that's good," John said. "Why would you wake him?"

Jesus studied him in silence, then looked at those gathered around him, and said, "Lazarus is dead."

Stifled gasps ran through the crowd.

213

Dead? Sarah couldn't imagine how someone so young, someone who had seemed so alive just weeks ago, could be dead.

Salome leaned toward her. "I bet he feels pretty bad about not going to him when the girls sent for him. I can't imagine what he was thinking. We didn't accomplish anything hanging around here."

"I think he was afraid to go to Bethany," a woman behind Salome said. "It's so close to the city. Besides, it wouldn't have done any good. Dead is dead. But it doesn't make sense to go there now. Why take a chance? Why get anywhere near Jerusalem? Let things cool down a little."

Jesus started toward the river, then stopped and turned back to them. "I'm glad I wasn't there, for your sakes, because now I can go to Lazarus, so that you might believe."

Sarah stood by a tree, hesitant to take a single step closer to the city as he led the crowd west.

Thomas ran past her, shouting to the others, "Let's go. If Jesus is willing to risk this, then we can, too. If he dies, we die."

John, James, and Andrew cried out their agreement as they rushed to join Jesus.

Salome walked behind them and nodded at her sons and their enthusiasm as she passed Sarah. "They're always ready for a fight."

Simon took his place at Jesus' side, every bit as enthusiastic as Salome's sons. And Sarah knew she couldn't leave her husband as he walked into whatever lay ahead. At the same time, even though every instinct screamed at her to do so, she couldn't bring herself to demand that he let Jesus face this alone.

***

214

The road bent toward Bethany, and the chipped walls of the structures housing the poor and the lepers came into sight. Even from this distance, Sarah could smell the putrid odor of poverty and rotted flesh. As those following Jesus neared the village, they merged with other groups headed for the same destination, some weeping, others stone-faced and somber.

Pharisees and Scribes gathered at the side of the road, watching Jesus and those with him. Fear nagged Sarah to turn around, but she told herself they wouldn't be foolish enough to do anything now while the streets were full of people mourning a dead man.

"I didn't expect so many," she said to Salome.

"Well, Jerusalem isn't that far. And with people from all the nearby towns," Salome said with a sniffle, wiping tears from her eyes.

Sarah looked at her friend, surprised to hear the catch in her voice. They hardly knew the man. Then she glanced at Jesus, quietly leading the group forward, and realized he did know him. He'd lost a friend. A good friend. A close friend.

Why hadn't she thought of that? It never occurred to her he might be grieving, that maybe he hadn't rushed to Bethany because he had a feeling his friend might die, and he couldn't bear to be there when it happened.

Sometimes she forgot he was a man like everyone else.

While she was lost in thought, Salome poked her side and pointed. "Martha's coming."

Lazarus' sister walked toward Jesus with quiet intent. She looked small in the crowd that parted to make way for her, her eyes red, her skin sallow, shoulders slumped under her cloak.

She stopped in front of him and looked him in the eye. "If you had been here, Master, my brother wouldn't have died." Her words caught in her throat a moment as her head dropped in sorrow. "Instead, he's dead…dead and buried. Four days in the tomb."

Deep sadness darkened Jesus' face. Sarah studied the woman who worked so hard to keep everything under control. How unbearable to now have it all spin so wildly beyond anyone's control.

Martha lifted her head and again gazed steadily into Jesus' eyes, the sober calm in her face surprising. "But still, I know that whatever you ask, God will do it for you."

With her words, Sarah saw a light dawn in his darkness, a light that seemed to glow from within, as he said, "Your brother shall rise."

"I know he will rise at the resurrection, on the last day."

"I am the resurrection and the life." He gently took her hand in his. "Anyone who believes in me, even if he dies, will live, and whoever lives and believes in me will never die."

Although his words made no sense, Sarah was struck by his earnestness as he asked Martha, "Do you believe this?"

"Yes," she answered softly. "I believe you are the Christ, Messiah, the Son of God, who has come into the world." Then she turned and went back to the house.

Sarah made her way through the crowd to Simon, aware of the men standing along the road into town, arms crossed, eyes focused solely on Jesus.

The flash of a cloak caught her eye, and she turned to see Martha's sister, Mary, running to Jesus, accompanied by what seemed to be half the town of Bethany. The air filled with their wailing and weeping as she dropped to the ground before him, face-down in the dust.

She looked up, and tears choked her words as she said, "If you had been here, my brother would still be alive."

Nearly everyone on the road sobbed at her grief. Sarah shifted uncomfortably, thinking she should probably feel at least a little sorrow herself. She noticed the dark shadow cross Jesus' face again, and his eyes looked sadder than any she had ever seen.

He glanced at the mourners who accompanied Mary, and said, "Where have you buried him?"

Their grief gave way a bit too quickly to enthusiasm as they shouted, "Come and see."

The words seemed to pierce through his heart. The cloud that had darkened his eyes burst. And Jesus wept.

Some of those close by said, "Look. See how much he loved him," while others scoffed, "Then why didn't he do something? He gave eyes to a blind man. Couldn't he have kept Lazarus from dying?"

Jesus seemed not to hear as he helped Mary to her feet. She cried softly into the cloth of her veil as he walked with her to the village, following the lead of people eager to show him the dead man's tomb.

Sarah trailed close behind Simon, holding her breath against the stench as they passed the decaying home for lepers and the poorhouse. They walked by shuttered shops and vacant booths, and she wondered if the entire town had shut down in mourning.

As they turned down a side road, Sarah noticed people gathered in front of Lazarus' house. When they saw the crowd surrounding Jesus, lamenting the late Lazarus, and realized they were headed for the tomb, they left the house and ran to join in.

Beyond the edge of the village, they came to a hillside carved with caves. Some had rocks rolled into the openings, others lay exposed, gaping, waiting. Jesus stopped before one where the dust was still parted from the recent rolling of the stone.

"Take away the stone," he said, to no one in particular.

Shocked exclamations arose from the crowd.

Martha moved close to him, and Sarah could barely hear, as she whispered, "Master, he's been in there...dead...for four days. The odor will be...unbearable."

"Did I not tell you," he said, turning to her, "that if you believe, you would never die but would see the glory of God?"

Others around Sarah murmured that they had seen Lazarus before his burial. He'd been stiff and drained of color even then. No doubt his body had begun to turn to dust by now.

Jesus looked to the crowd for someone to roll the stone away from the tomb, and a band of men, young and old, came forward. As they wrested the rock from the opening, people stepped back from what they didn't want to smell, some covering their faces with their veils and cloaks. They braced themselves against whatever might take up residence in a closed cave, certain that bugs, bats, and rodents would race out at the intrusion of light.

When the men finally pushed the stone aside, nothing greeted them but darkness. No odor. No sound stirred within. Sarah peered over Simon's shoulder but could see nothing.

Jesus looked up to heaven, and said quietly, "Father, I thank you that you have heard me. I know you always hear me, but I say this that they may believe that you have sent me."

Then his voice rose until it seemed the entire universe could hear. "Lazarus, come out."

People shoved forward, crushing Sarah against her husband, as they tried to see what, if anything, would happen. She continued to look past Simon, into the darkness.

The sound of footsteps came from the depths of the cave, followed by the sight of a man wrapped head to toe in burial cloths.

Women screamed. Some fainted. Men struggled to remain calm. Sarah grabbed onto Simon's arm to steady herself.

Jesus turned to the men next to him. "Unbind him, and set him free."

The men hesitated, looking from one to the other until finally one walked over to what Sarah could only guess was Lazarus and removed the cloths that encircled his head.

Lazarus gazed into Jesus' face.

When they saw it was their brother, alive, vibrant, healthy, Martha and Mary ran to him and began to free him from the other wrappings of death. They hugged him, tears of joy running down their cheeks.

The men who had rolled the stone aside peered a moment into the darkness of the tomb, then shrugged and left to join the jubilation.

Sarah's heart raced, the blood pounded in her head as she struggled to make sense of what she had seen. "He couldn't have been dead," she said, unaware she had spoken the words out loud.

James heard her, and said, "Of course, he was."

"It's impossible" she said. "They must have just thought he'd died."

"Sarah," Simon said, "you saw him. His face was completely wrapped in burial cloths. Even if he'd been alive when they buried him, after four days in a sealed tomb with those cloths tight around his face, he would have suffocated."

"He must have wrapped the cloths around his face himself then," she said, still trying to comprehend what she'd seen, "before he came out."

"His hands and arms were wrapped, too, Sarah. You saw him. And you saw those men look in. There is no one else in that tomb."

"That's why he waited," James said.

"What do you mean?" Simon said.

"That's why Jesus stayed by the river instead of heading for Bethany right away. He wanted us to see that Lazarus had to be dead, long dead."

Sarah walked away from the scene in front of the tomb, trembling, trying to accept that he had actually raised a man from the dead. Not just someone who seemed dead, but someone who was dead. Dead and buried.

Simon came to her and put his arm around her waist. "Are you okay?"

She gazed back at Jesus, surrounded by the celebrating crowd.

"Do you understand what he did?" she said. "He didn't just raise a man from the dead. He raised a man from the dead by his own power. He didn't call on God like the other 'messiahs' do when they 'raise' someone from the dead. He took a man who was dead and brought him back to life by his own command." She turned to her husband. "No one does that, Simon. No one."

People ran to share the news beyond the small village. They joyfully raced past the Scribes and Pharisees, who had watched the scene from beyond the crowd. Even some of them looked stunned, but Sarah knew it wouldn't take long for the bewilderment to turn to fury. As angry as they'd been about the blind man, she knew they would be livid when word got out in Jerusalem that Jesus had raised a man, dead and buried, from the grave simply by calling his name.

Chapter 32

Excitement ran through the crowd as the walls of Jerusalem came into sight, but dread mounted within Sarah. Simon had tried to convince her that they had to go to the city to celebrate the upcoming Passover, but she saw nothing to celebrate there.

Word of the blind man and Lazarus had spread far beyond the region. As they walked the road from Bethany, people flocked to join them. Things were escalating too fast. She knew those around her expected Jesus to finally fulfill the role of the Messiah, overthrow Rome, and re-establish the kingdom. She prayed he wouldn't.

Salome walked beside her, chatting endlessly with everyone about anything.

She turned to Sarah, and said, "Can you believe it? We're almost there. It's about time. I really thought he would've gotten this kingdom thing going by now, didn't you?"

Sarah knew she should relax and enjoy the moment. Maybe she really was living in the midst of a great historical epoch. Maybe it was possible that, of all the moments in time when the Messiah could come, he'd come in hers.

But that was ridiculous. For centuries, every time some charlatan worked a couple of 'miracles,' people thought the Messiah had come. Hundreds of generations had waited and watched for any sign he was with them.

She looked at Jesus walking with Simon and the others. Everyone knows that when the Messiah finally does come, he isn't going to look like that. No army. No authority. Not even a house or a goat of his own.

At the foot of the Mount of Olives, he suddenly stopped. People around her mumbled with disappointment. The city gates were so close they could see them. But she just felt relieved and hopeful that maybe he was having second thoughts.

A nearby rock invited her to sit, and she headed toward it.

As she passed her husband, she saw Jesus point into the distance and heard him say to the two men closest to him, "Go into the village opposite of here. When you get there, you'll see a colt tied to a post, a colt no one has sat on. Untie it, and bring it here."

"You want us to steal a colt?" one of them said.

"If anyone tries to stop you, just tell him the Master needs it."

They looked at one another, then hesitantly set out across the road toward the nearby town.

"What's he doing?" she whispered to Simon.

"He needs a colt."

"So he steals one?"

"He wouldn't steal anything, Sarah. I don't know, maybe someone in the crowd gave him the colt. He must have some reason to think it's his."

She walked to the rock and sat down, separating herself as much as she could from the group while still not losing sight of her husband. The men headed off to do something they would never have done on their own, and her head pounded with fear at the level of devotion they had. She knew they weren't alone. She knew Simon shared their commitment.

Soon, the two made their way toward Jesus, pulling a colt along with them. She braced herself, certain that men would run from the village after them, that stones would fly through the air to stop them. But no one came. Calm prevailed.

Without a word, the two men removed their shawls and threw them over the colt, then stepped aside as Jesus mounted the tiny animal. All around her, people erupted in cheers and ran to get in front of the donkey. They tripped over one another, laying their garments on the road before him as he slowly rode toward Jerusalem.

Simon shook hands with Levi and John and slapped men she didn't know on the shoulders as they called out to one another in triumph. He signaled for Sarah to join them. When she did, he didn't seem to notice her reluctance but instead embraced her, breathless with excitement.

They followed Jesus, and John turned to her, his face aglow with joy. "It's happening. He's fulfilling the prophecy of Zechariah. *Rejoice, rejoice, people of Zion. Shout for joy, you people of Jerusalem. Look, your king is coming to you. He comes triumphant and victorious, but humble and riding on a donkey, on a colt, the foal of a donkey.*"

"Anyone can fulfill a prophecy," Sarah said. "You just have to steal someone's colt."

He gave her a curious look, then turned to celebrate with the others.

The cheers caught the attention of nearly everyone in front of the city walls, and she tried to disappear into the mob as she walked near Simon. She glanced up and saw Roman soldiers perched on the walls, looking down at them. Hundreds of people ran out of Jerusalem, the commotion stirring their excitement to greet Jesus.

Some ripped palms off trees and threw them on the ground before the approaching colt. Others waved fronds and bundles of branches high in the air. Everyone seemed to be shouting, "Hosanna... Save us, O Lord... Hosanna, Son of David... Blessed is he who comes in the name of the Lord... Hosanna in the highest."

Sarah bristled at every word. Couldn't they hear themselves? Shouting as if he were the very fulfillment of the Prophets themselves. Calling out to him in words of praise, words of salvation, of freedom. From Rome. And why did he just drink it all in? Surely he knew how dangerous this was.

She moved closer to Simon as a dark, glowering cloud of Pharisees emerged from the city gates and waited to confront Jesus.

As he drew near, they said, "Rabbi, stop these people."

From his mount on the colt, Jesus gazed steadily at the religious leaders. "I tell you, if they were stilled, even these rocks would cry out with joy."

The din grew deafening, and Sarah watched Jesus continue to move steadily forward. All her ponderings and wonderings about him sank into the darkness of anger. How dare he? How arrogant to allow all these people treat him like some kind of king. And in front of the Romans. Didn't he care about any of them?

She glared at him in fury, her fists clenched. If only she could stop and let all these people leave her behind, safe outside the walls, but rage and deepening concern about Simon's safety propelled her forward behind the tiny, plodding animal.

People young and old, some with a leap, some with a limp, pushed against her. As she stumbled along, her anger boiled until she decided it was time she finally confronted Jesus herself. She shoved through to the colt's side and tripped, falling against Jesus' leg. She steadied herself and looked up, prepared to freely release all the cynicism and anger she'd been holding back since the day he first walked into their lives. But the words stopped unspoken when she noticed tears in his eyes.

While everyone else shouted and jumped for joy, she saw Jesus look at the approaching city and silently weep with sadness. Within her, the rage melted.

"Oh, Jerusalem," he said, so softly she didn't know if anyone else heard, "if only you knew the things that could bring you peace. But now they're hidden from your eyes. The days will come upon you and surround you and hem you in on every side and hurl you to the ground, you and your children.

And they will not leave one stone upon another in you, because you did not recognize the time of your visitation."

Sarah stopped walking as the crowd surged past her. His sadness touched her, but his words froze her in place. People rushed by, filling the growing distance between her and Jesus. She looked down the road and watched as they also filled the distance between her and Simon. Her heart wrestled with common sense. She needed to go home. Jerusalem wasn't safe. If trouble was coming, and she knew it was, she needed to be with her children.

But Simon...Simon. He wasn't just an anonymous follower, a face in the crowd. Jesus had singled him out again and again. She had no doubt the Sanhedrin, Herod, maybe even Rome, had their eye on him, too.

The mob moved through the gates and into the city. She slid between the people and the walls of the buildings, trying to make up the ground she had lost, fighting her way to the front of the crowd. An elbow caught her on the cheek, and a foot tripped her, but she had nowhere to fall. Bracing herself for a moment against the doorway of a shop, she regained her balance and resumed her struggle.

Around her, the throng still cheered. Those just coming upon the scene from side streets grabbed the arms of strangers, and asked, "What's going on?"

"It's Jesus of Nazareth," the crowd shouted back. "The prophet from Galilee... The one who healed the blind man... The one who raised the man in Bethany."

The Temple lay ahead of them, and the crowd crushed her against a post as they funneled tighter to squeeze into the Temple doors, backing up deep into the city, everyone so caught up in trying to see what Jesus was doing, where he was going, they barely noticed Sarah as she shoved them aside. Herds of lambs destined for sacrifice blocked her way. She wove through them and finally made it to the entry of the

Temple courtyard just in time to see Jesus climb down from the colt.

Before she could reach her husband, Simon followed Jesus inside. As she tried to get to him, she heard a loud crash and screams, then more crashes and angry voices yelling out. She looked over the shoulder of a man in front of her and saw Jesus overturn tables and shove pots, baskets, and piles of coins to the stone floor. Vessels of all shapes shattered, and shards flew through the air. Animals broke away from their handlers and scattered, running into the crowd and out onto the streets as doves flew free from broken cages and filled the sky.

"Is it not written," he said, "*my house will be called a house of prayer*? But you've made it a den of thieves."

Outraged money-changers shouted and hurled stools and broken pottery at him. Sarah watched the scene before her in disbelief. She knew trouble was coming, but she hadn't expected it to go so wrong so fast.

Pharisees and Scribes furiously rushed to get to him as he blocked anyone from coming into the courtyard to sell or trade anything.

"Destroy this temple," he said, looking directly at the religious leaders, "and in three days I will raise it up."

In the midst of the commotion, a deluge of people flowed around them, crying out for Jesus to help them, heal them, save them, and the religious leaders backed off.

Now was not the time.

Sarah pushed her way past anyone who was between her and Simon. When she got close enough for him to hear, she said, "We've got to get out of here."

For once, he didn't look puzzled at her concern. Instead, he led her out of the Temple. They stumbled down the steps into the street while hundreds of others fought to get into the Temple and to the source of the pandemonium that spilled out onto the surrounding roads.

They struggled against the tide as vendors tried to protect their wares from the people streaming around them. Shepherds scrambled to round up stray flocks. Mothers searched for children, and men searched for news of what had happened. Roman soldiers moved into the streets, trying to find the cause of the commotion.

Simon didn't stop until they came to the city gates. Nearby merchants ventured from their stalls and gazed down the road at the scene, a scene unlike any they had ever witnessed in Jerusalem.

As Sarah caught her breath, Simon turned and looked back at the Temple and the mayhem that still surrounded it.

"What was that about?" he said

"You heard him. You know the Prophets better than I do. The words of Jeremiah. *Has this house, which has been called by my name, become a den of thieves? Behold, I myself have seen it, says the Lord?* Does any of that sound familiar to you?" Sarah struggled to control the anger rising up anew within her. "'*I myself have seen it, says the Lord?*' Are you paying any attention to what is going on here, Simon?"

Her husband watched the frenzy still playing out before him and shook his head but had no response.

"I like him," Sarah said. "Believe it or not, I really do. But he has got to stop proclaiming himself God."

Simon didn't seem to notice that her protest was against Jesus' proclamation, not his claim.

The movement of the crowd shifted as people began to turn away from the Temple and into the streets of Jerusalem. She watched them head down side roads and hoped this meant things had calmed down enough that everyone was going home.

As people drifted out of the courtyard in large and small groups, Simon took her hand and led her away from the gates, back into the city.

"What are you doing?" She planted her feet in the dust, refusing to take one more step forward.

"They're still at the Temple."

She saw a group near the entrance, gathered around someone, someone she could only imagine had to be Jesus.

"We are not going back there," she said.

"The trouble's over, Sarah."

Feeling she had no choice, she followed her husband, certain the trouble had only just begun.

Simon led her up the stairs to James and some of the others gathered near Jesus. They all chatted as if it were just another spring day. She noticed Jesus said nothing but stood in the shadows of the Temple walls and watched as people walked past him into the house of God. Most pointed him out to those with them and whispered of the day's events. Everyone seemed willing to give him wide berth for once.

Andrew gazed up at the enormous stone blocks that rose into the sky above him.

He caught Jesus by the arm, and said, "Would you look at these walls? Can you imagine the work that went into building this place. "

John joined in with equal enthusiasm. "I know. They're huge. Every time I see them, I wonder how men could've lifted them into place."

"And the fit," Andrew rubbed his hand along the rock. "So tight you couldn't fit a feather between them."

"Do you see these buildings?" Jesus said. "Believe me, there will not be a single stone left on top of another, not a single stone that won't be thrown to the ground."

He turned and walked away, leaving John and Andrew stunned. The others glanced at one another, but their questions stayed unspoken

"Come on," Simon said, as he turned to follow Jesus.

Sarah kept close to her husband, aware that others had heard Jesus' outburst, including priests and Scribes in the area. Even the Roman soldiers in the street below must have heard him.

He led the small group through the crowded streets, out the city gates, and up into groves of the Mount of Olives. Then he walked alone to a large rock and sat opposite the Temple.

Chapter 33

Sarah stood alone on the mountainside as night approached. The sun slanted deep into the afternoon sky, and the sweet scent of apricot blossoms swirled through the air. She looked out at the dusky golden fields of softly blowing wheat and wished she could enjoy the sight.

Simon walked up behind her and inhaled the aroma, then breathed out a satisfied sigh.

"I don't know how you can be so relaxed," she said, "especially this close to Jerusalem."

A young man she didn't recognize climbed the hillside path toward them, clearly aiming for the rock on which Jesus sat. He said something to him, and Jesus smiled with delight. Philip walked past Simon and said a few words she couldn't hear.

Her husband turned to her. "We're heading back tomorrow."

"We are?" Her heart swelled with hope, grateful that Jesus realized there was only one place he could go now. Home.

***

Sitting on a stump by the path, her satchel at her feet, Sarah grew more impatient with every downward slide of the sun. She'd awakened early, unable to sleep as the anticipation of going back to her children wrestled with the worry that she shouldn't bring the danger to them.

Jesus had said he was leaving, but he made no move to do so. Instead he'd spent the day strolling through the groves of olive trees, chatting with the few people gathered around barely burning fires. While they all had packed up their belongings, no one seemed in a hurry to go. But she couldn't leave soon enough. She kept one eye on Jesus and the other on Jerusalem, aware that at any moment an army of angry religious leaders could come roaring through the gates and up into the hillside to seek their revenge.

Finally, just as she began to think she wasn't going anywhere after all, he headed down the hill. She, along with everyone else, jumped up and hurried to follow.

As they walked to the road, she noticed he led them south away from Capernaum, away from home.

She rushed to catch up with Simon, and said, "What's he doing?"

"Going to Bethany."

"Bethany? I thought you said we were going home."

"I said we were heading back, Sarah. Back to Bethany."

Disappointment and fear filled her very soul. "Why? Why would he even think that's a good idea? Can you imagine what the priests and Pharisees there will do when they see him return after what he did at the Temple yesterday? They're already livid about the Lazarus thing."

"The Lazarus thing? Come on, Sarah, you can't minimize what he did there. He raised a man from the dead."

"I don't want to go back." Not only did she not want to risk whatever danger awaited them, she really didn't want to see either of Lazarus's sisters so soon.

Martha was nice enough, but she couldn't imagine how the woman put up with the insolence of the other one. Sarah wasn't in the mood to do whatever Mary should be doing while at the same time struggling not to snap at her.

As the small group walked the short distance to the town, they passed the courtyard filled with dirty children in rags. A stench filled the air, a stench that had become too familiar. Some turned away as if the air was purer over their left shoulder. Jesus seemed not to notice as he turned abruptly down a side road, throwing off those who had walked ahead of him. The handful of people scrambled to change direction and catch up as he led them to a house that was not Lazarus'.

Nathaniel leaned in toward Simon, and Sarah moved closer to hear what he had to say.

"That's Simon's place."

When her husband gave him a blank look, she knew it meant no more to him than to her.

"You know, the Pharisee who had leprosy."

Leprosy? Sarah stopped in mid-step. She was not going into a leper's house. Neither was her husband.

She rushed to his side again in time to hear Nathaniel say, "You remember. He was one of the men Jesus healed on the way to Jericho."

Sarah tried to think back to what he meant. The days, the months, the villages and towns, the healings, the fleeing demons, everything had run together these last three years.

It didn't matter who he was anyway. He had leprosy. That's all she needed to know.

Her husband didn't falter in his stride but kept pace with Jesus. She thought of turning back but had nowhere to go. She couldn't sit on the side of the road by herself and wait for them. Instead, she tried to focus on the "had" and trust that the leprosy was indeed gone. But if she saw so much as a pimple or a scab on the man, she was leaving.

A lean, short man in familiar Pharisee garb stood at the door, smiling a greeting to them. Sarah's step slowed again. The thought of leprosy so consumed her, she'd forgotten the Pharisee part.

"Why would he take us to a Pharisee's house," she whispered to her husband.

"He invited us for dinner."

"Dinner?"

"Dinner," Simon repeated.

"We're having dinner with a Pharisee? After what happened yesterday?"

When her husband didn't answer, she said, "It's a trap, Simon. It has to be. They're setting him up. We don't have to go with him. We can wait outside of town until he leaves and then join him again."

"We're just going to dinner, Sarah," Simon said, taking her hand.

She knew he meant for the gesture to comfort her, but it did nothing to allay her concerns.

The man stood by the door, waiting for everyone to enter. She tried not to be obvious as she scanned him for any obvious flaws. The hand that pointed the way into the house looked whole. The smiling face seemed complete. Still…

She sucked in her stomach, thinking that might keep her from brushing against him as she walked into the house. Then she realized he had positioned himself so that he couldn't be touched. Not because he was unclean, but because they were.

Sarah followed Salome and the others into a large room. Furnishings finer than hers filled the space and lined the walls, but they looked tired and worn.

The men settled onto the cushions and mats around the table while Sarah shuffled into a corner next to Salome, Joanna, and the other women. She wondered if the Pharisee would throw out the furnishings that couldn't be washed after they left.

She tried to distract herself from the discomfort of being welcomed into a home in which she really wasn't welcome at all. She looked around for some chore to help with, but servants seemed to have everything under control. A rotund woman scurried among them, giving orders, pointing and gesturing with urgency. Sarah assumed the woman was the Pharisee's wife. She had the air of self-importance that seemed to go with the position.

233

A knock at the door interrupted her musings. A servant opened it to reveal Lazarus and his sister, Mary. Sarah bristled at the sight of her crisp, fresh headdress and imperious posture. Just what she needed. As if she didn't already feel unworthy enough, now she had this woman to drive home her insignificance.

Mary clutched an alabaster jar against her breast, and Sarah wondered if the Pharisee's wine might not be good enough for her. But as Mary rushed past her brother and moved into the room toward Jesus, the haughtiness seemed gone.

She walked up to him, her head bent in some semblance of humility, her face shadowed by the embroidered covering that draped over her hair. Sarah glanced at Salome, scandalized that the woman would approach a man so boldly. Then, Mary dropped to the floor.

Salome moved closer to Sarah to see around the servant in front of her as Lazarus' sister pulled the stopper from the pearl-white jar. The light of the flickering lantern on the wall lit the alabaster as if from within. She tipped the jar, and thick ointment poured out over Jesus' feet. The dusky lavender aroma of myrrh filled the room, and gasps erupted as she bent and rubbed the salve onto his feet with her veil. Sarah knew she should look away, should leave the house altogether, but she couldn't. The scene was so unexpected, it anchored her to the floor.

Jesus looked down at Mary, but he didn't pull away or tell her to stop.

Suddenly, she ripped the covering from her head. Long, ebony curls spilled across her shoulders as she wiped his feet with her hair.

The Pharisee's wife fell back in a swoon, and men stood in surprise, turning as if they should avert their gaze. But like Sarah, they couldn't stop watching. Tears streamed down Mary's face and fell onto Jesus' feet. Just when Sarah thought the scene couldn't get more indecent, the woman bent her head to the floor and began to kiss his feet.

Salome grabbed onto Sarah's arm to steady herself. Their host leapt up from his seat, horrified at the woman's sin. And in his house.

Gazing down at Mary, Jesus addressed the leprous Pharisee. "Simon, I have something to say to you."

"What, Master?" the Pharisee asked, struggling to maintain his composure, sarcasm wrapping around the term of honor.

"If someone lent one person five-hundred denarii and another person fifty, and then forgave both of them their debt, which of them would love him more?"

The Pharisee rolled his eyes under heavy lids, as he said, "The one who felt he'd been forgiven more, I suppose."

"You're right."

Jesus touched Mary's head as she still massaged her tears and salve into his feet.

"Do you see this woman?" He turned to the Pharisee, who stood staring down at her. "When I came into your house, you didn't so much as give me water to wash my feet. But she? She has bathed my feet with tears, and wiped them with her hair. You didn't so much as brush my cheek with a kiss, but she has not ceased kissing my feet. You didn't anoint my head with even a little olive oil in greeting, but she anointed my feet with ointment."

The leper scowled, unmoved, unwavering. Sarah could see him wrestle with how to order them out of his house.

"I tell you," Jesus said to the leper, "her sins, as many as they are, will be forgiven because of her great love. But someone who doesn't recognize how much he's been forgiven, loves little."

He took Mary's hand and raised her up, wiping tears from her face. "Your faith has saved you. Go in peace."

As she turned to leave, Judas, the Iscariot, stepped in front of her, pointed to the jar lying on the floor in a pool of ointment, and said to Mary, "Why would you waste all this?"

The others looked at him in surprise. Sarah couldn't think of a single time when he had made himself stand out. He always seemed to take in all that he saw and heard, talking with Jesus or the others quietly but never stepping forward from the crowd.

"This could have been sold for three-hundred denarii," he said, then looked at the others. "We could have given the money to the poor."

Sarah thought of the children she had avoided looking at, of mothers with haunted, hollow eyes, and understood his desire to help. Then she noticed John glare at him and glance down at the moneybag Judas kept strapped to his side.

"Let her be," Jesus said, looking steadily at Judas. "She is preparing me for my burial. You will always have the poor. You will not always have me."

Unspoken anger darkened Judas' face as his shoulders straightened. Everyone else appeared to be still trying to take in the sight of the broken alabaster jar and the woman with the tear-streaked face and dangling hair, leaving no one but Sarah to wonder what Jesus meant.

Chapter 34

Jerusalem's walls drew near once again, a fortress in the hills, a sanctuary from the wilderness, but the sight offered Sarah no comfort. She saw a city too small to contain the tension it held, a riot waiting to happen. No doubt the leper had been quick to send word to Jerusalem of the previous night's dinner at Bethany. Not that the Sanhedrin needed more fuel for their fury.

Jesus stopped in the middle of the road and gazed a long time at the city rising up before him. Sarah recognized the sadness she had seen when he rode in on the colt. Then he walked off the road and up the incline of a nearby mountainside into a small grove of fig trees.

"What's he doing?" she asked her husband.

"How should I know? I'm guessing he's hungry."

"But the fig hasn't even blossomed yet."

Reaching into the newly-sprouted leaves and buds, Jesus rustled among the branches, then pulled out an empty hand.

He looked at the barren tree, and said, "May you never bear fruit again."

The startled followers watched as the tree withered, roots rising up from the ground, leaves falling, and boughs bending toward the earth, a once thriving tree now turning in on itself, no longer reaching out to the light, no longer searching deep for life-giving water.

Jesus turned from the plant. "Truly I tell you, if you have faith and never doubt, you will not only do this to a fruitless fig tree, you will say to this mountain, 'Arise, and crumble into the sea,' and it will arise and crumble into the sea." He glanced again at the tree, then looked back to those gathered around him, an earnest intensity burning in his eyes. "Whatever you ask in prayer, you will receive. You just have to have faith."

No one spoke as they resumed their walk toward the city gates. Sarah glanced around her and wondered if they weren't speaking because they didn't know what to say. She couldn't begin to make sense of what had just happened. Why would he curse a tree? It wasn't even the season for figs. What did he want from the poor tree? He was asking…no, demanding…the impossible from it, as if it should always be the season for fruit.

After a few moments, he turned to address the group while still leading them forward. "Whenever you stand before God and pray, forgive. If you have anything against another person, forgive him. Then your heavenly Father can forgive you."

As he turned back toward the road ahead, Sarah wondered what forgiveness had to do with what he had just done to that tree. Could it be that he was sorry for cursing it? Maybe even sorry for what he'd done in the Temple?

She thought about the scene in the Temple a few days earlier. Even though she knew his actions were certain to cause trouble for all of them, she grudgingly admired him. She hadn't had time to fully take in all that had happened while in the midst of it, but in the chaos of his rampage, she had been struck by his words, the quotation from Jeremiah, *You've made my house a den of thieves*.

A shiver ran through Sarah as she again recalled the rest of the passage, *Behold, I myself have seen it, says the Lord.*

She studied the man walking ahead of her, small in the shadow of the mountain, alone even among this group of friends. Then she thought of what Jeremiah had said just a few lines later, *Behold, says the Lord God, my anger and wrath will be poured out on this place, upon man and beast, upon the trees of the field and the fruit of the ground.*

238

And again she wondered, who was this man?

***

As the small group drew near to Jerusalem's gates, people noticed and joined their ranks. Men and women called out to those in the shops along the way, and Sarah watched as people left their bargaining and followed Jesus. Beggars and blind men stumbled to their feet while those lying on mats, unable to move, pleaded for someone to take them to him.

With each new person who joined them, she moved closer to Simon. Any hope that the religious leaders might not notice them faded as the band of followers grew once again into a mob no one could ignore.

Jesus led them into the city, past the musicians and singing priests at the Temple entrance, along the walkway, through the towering arches, and across the wide outer temple courtyard. Sheep and oxen merged with thousands of people from throughout Judea, but despite the approaching Passover, Sarah didn't sense a holiday spirit. Tension pulsed through the crowd and reverberated against the polished limestone walls.

Caged doves and money-changers' tables had reclaimed their spots. The angry, apprehensive faces of those seated behind them glared at Jesus. He passed without a word, as if he had nothing more to say to them, and walked into the courtyard, past the colonnades, to a bench in a corner. As he sat, the crowd grew silent and settled onto the cold stone floor or perched and stood on other benches. Some climbed ladders to the rooftops and walkways surrounding the courtyard. Sarah leaned against a pillar and looked behind her to see still more people packed into the entryways and beyond.

Before he could address the crowd, murmurs caught Sarah's attention. Those near the entry stood and shuffled aside, making room for people she couldn't see. As they came into sight, she realized it was a large group of chief priests,

239

Scribes, and elders struggling to pick their way through the mass of humanity, careful not to touch anyone lest they might become unclean.

Simon whispered to Levi, "Looks like the entire Sanhedrin is here," and she noticed James and John move closer to Jesus.

As the religious leaders drew near to him, the crowded courtyard grew icy cold with the chill of their barely restrained fury. They stopped before him, forming a wall between him and those gathered in the courtyard.

"By what authority do you do the things you do?" asked a stout priest in black garments, tassels trembling from beneath his hem, rage quaking under his efforts to appear calm and in control. "And who gave you this authority?"

Jesus leaned back against the wall, resting one elbow on the bench. "I have a question for you. If you answer my question, I'll answer yours."

Sarah squirmed and looked for an escape route as people squeezed in on her to try to see around the men. Simon had moved nearer to Jesus, on the other side of the human barrier, only a few feet away and yet beyond her reach. She tried to catch his eye, to signal to him to come to her, but he was focused on Jesus and oblivious to her.

Jesus gazed steadily at the men in front of him. "The baptism of John, where was that from? From heaven, or from men?"

The leaders shrank back a step. Sarah strained to catch fragments of their sentences as they whispered to one another.

An older priest, whom the others seemed to hold in high esteem, stroked his neatly trimmed beard, and whispered, "We should say from heaven."

"But then," said a thin Scribe with a rigid posture, "he will ask why we didn't believe him."

Another priest pulled his shawl around his shoulders and leaned in. "Well, we can't say, from man." He glanced back at the mob behind him. "They all think the Baptist was a prophet."

The older priest stepped forward and addressed Jesus. "We cannot tell you by what authority John baptized."

Jesus studied the man before saying, "Then I will not tell you by what authority I do the things I do."

He sat up straight under their glare. "What do you think of this? A man had two sons, and he went to the first and said, 'Son, go and work in the vineyard.' And the son said, 'I will not,' but soon repented and went. Then the man went to the second son and said the same thing, and the second son said, 'I will go, sir.' But he did not. Which of these two did the father's will?"

Several of the religious leaders answered, "The first, of course," and glanced at the others as if in wonderment that this man could captivate people with words like these.

"Truly, I say to you" Jesus said, looking intently at each man standing before him, "tax collectors and harlots will get into the kingdom of God before you."

Cries of shock rose from those close enough to hear, and people shoved to get a clearer view of the fuming men.

"John came to show you the way of righteousness," Jesus said, "and you did not believe him. But the tax collectors and the harlots? They believed him. They repented. And even seeing this, you still did not repent and believe."

Murmurs ran through the crowd as people relayed Jesus' words to those behind them. Sarah watched the reactions of those around her as word spread that Jesus was besting, not bowing to, religious authority, and the tension became oppressive.

A tall, slender Scribe entered from a side archway and stood near Sarah, drawn in by a man who must have sought him out. He stood among the crowd and crossed his arms, taking in the scene before him.

Jesus rose up from the bench and spoke to those who filled the space beyond the religious leaders. "There was a homeowner who planted a vineyard and surrounded it with a hedge. He dug a winepress in it, built a tower, and leased it out to tenants to care for it. The man went into another country, and when the season for fruit drew near, he sent his servants to the tenants to get the fruit. " He eyed the men still standing before him. "But the tenants took his servants and beat one, and killed another, and stoned another."

The religious leaders moved closer together, firming their barrier, finding strength in one another.

"Then," Jesus said, "the man sent other servants, and the tenants treated them the same way. Finally, he sent his son saying, 'Surely they will respect my son.'"

He stopped, and Sarah wondered at the look in his face, not the anger she expected, but a sadness deeper than any she'd seen before.

"When the tenants saw the son," he said, "they said to themselves, 'This is the heir. Let's kill him and take his inheritance.' And they took him out of the vineyard and killed him."

He paused a moment before asking the crowd, "When the owner, then, returns to his vineyard, what will he do to those tenants?"

Someone called out, "He'll kill them."

"He'll take the vineyard away from them," someone else shouted, "and give it to people he can trust to give him his fruit when it's time,"

Jesus sat down again and spoke directly to the leaders before him. "Have you never read in Tehillim, *The very stone which the builders rejected has become the cornerstone*?"

The men stiffened, their shoulders arching back with resolve.

"The kingdom of heaven will be taken away from you," he said, as if speaking to each man individually, "and given to those who will produce the fruit of the kingdom."

Several of the leaders lunged forward, reaching out to take hold of Jesus, but the others grabbed their arms and pulled them back, nervously glancing at the mob behind them.

A low roar rumbled through the crowd, and Sarah saw anger and rebellion in the eyes of those around her. She stood against the pillar, unsure whether to flee or run to Simon. Jesus was still speaking, but she didn't care. She looked out at the sea of people that blocked her escape and wondered if she might be better off trying to get to a ladder and heading up instead of out.

As Jesus continued whatever he'd been saying, the people grew quiet, trying to hear him.

"The wedding feast is ready," he said, "but those invited were not worthy."

The older priest turned and walked out of the courtyard. The others followed him, struggling against the crowd who stood and sat in their way. Commotion filled the space as some scrambled to clear a path, tripping over others who refused.

Watching their retreat, Jesus said, again more with sadness than anger, "Many are called, but few are chosen."

No one spoke for a moment as his words hung over the crowd, but soon the air filled with hushed discussion and loud catcalls at the heels of the departing men.

Several Sadducees, who stood off to the side taking in the scene, stepped forward. Jesus watched as they too struggled to walk around the people. Their embroidered garments stood apart in the crowd, gold threads blinding in the sun.

One, whose headpiece gave a false impression of height and prominence, bent toward Jesus, and said, "Teacher, Moses tells us that if a man's brother dies and leaves a wife but no children, the man must marry his widow and raise up children for his brother."

He paused to let his words sink in, as though he had spoken a most profound truth. Jesus gazed steadily at him with no response.

The man continued. "Let's say there are seven brothers. The first took a wife and died without leaving children. The second married her and likewise died without leaving children. The third did likewise, as did all the rest. Seven brothers marrying the same woman and dying, all without leaving children. Finally, the woman dies. In the resurrection, whose wife will she be?"

Jesus studied the man, then said, "You know neither the law nor the power of God."

The room grew still. No one even shifted on the floor as all wondered how the Sadducee would respond.

The man straightened and stepped back in line with the others.

"When the dead arise," Jesus said, "they neither marry nor are given in marriage but are like the angels in heaven. As for any doubt about the resurrection of the dead to new life, have you not read the book of Moses?"

Sarah shrunk deeper into the crevices of the wall, surprised he would go so far as to challenge the Sadducees on their refusal to believe in the resurrection and then infer a priest of this magnitude had not read Moses.

"Does God not say to him, *I am the God of Abraham, the God of Isaac, and the God of Jacob?* He is not God of the dead, but of the living. Yet he is the God of these men, so they who died must live anew. That would mean you are completely wrong in refusing to believe."

Even though the men had no response, Sarah could see the rage in their posture as they stood before him a moment before turning to leave. She looked away, unwilling to make eye contact with them as they walked along the wall toward an exit. She noticed Nicodemus, the Pharisee from the Sanhedrin, standing off to the side of the passageway, taking in the scene, and thought of his night visit to Jesus. What must he think of him now?

The Scribe, who had stood near her unmoved throughout all that had taken place, watched the men leave, then walked past Nicodemus and through the crowd to Jesus. Jesus watched him approach and waited.

"Teacher," the man said, "you have answered them all well. Can you answer a question for me?"

Jesus leaned toward him, inviting the question.

"Which is the greatest commandment?"

"*Hear, O Israel*," Jesus said with no emotion, as if the question needed no answer, "*the Lord your God is one God, and you shall love the Lord your God with all your heart, and with all your soul, and with all your mind, and with all your strength.*"

The Scribe nodded and began to turn away.

"The second follows," Jesus said, stopping the man in mid-turn. "You shall love your neighbor as yourself." His voice softened as he looked steadily at the man. "Love them as you, yourself, are loved by God."

The man drank in his words with no response, letting them settle into his soul.

"There is no commandment greater than these," Jesus said.

"You are right, Teacher," the Scribe said in a quiet voice that carried throughout the hushed courtyard. "You have spoken truly. God is one, and we are to love him with our whole heart, our whole soul, our whole mind, and with all of our strength, and love others as God loves us." He looked at Jesus with an understanding that went beyond his words. "This is worth more than all our burnt offerings and sacrifices."

Jesus smiled. "You are not far from the kingdom of God."

Several Scribes rushed to their brother and spoke to him in words too low for Sarah to hear. The man glanced at Jesus, then turned away and left with them, their cloaks brushing over the heads of those seated on the stone floor.

As they picked their way over the people, Jesus said, "Beware of the Scribes who like to go about in long robes and to have salutations in the marketplace and the best seats in the synagogue and places of honor at feasts, who make a pretense of long prayers to God."

The room quieted as all around her people sat motionless, afraid even to exhale, afraid to draw any attention to themselves, aware that the religious leaders were not yet out of earshot.

"These Scribes," he said, his words filling the stilled courtyard, "will receive a greater condemnation."

Sarah felt the room shake with the anger of the men who had come to escort one of their own from his presence.

Would he never stay quiet? Did he always have to have the last word?

She threaded her way through those sitting along the wall until she came up to Simon.

"Did you hear that?" she asked him.

"I heard him, Sarah. I'm standing right here."

"That was a direct hit, Simon. No one can pretend he didn't aim those words directly at those Scribes."

"He's just frustrated with them. The rabbis in the synagogues work week after week to teach us about God and about how his laws can make us a holy nation, a holy people. But these guys, the Scribes, the Sadducees, even the Pharisees? Most only worry about how they can twist the laws to control the rest of us. They seldom mention God at all."

"That might be true, but does he have to enrage them?"

"They choose to be enraged," Simon said.

"But he chooses words that ignite their anger."

246

She looked at the people spread throughout the courtyard and beyond and wondered that no one left. Didn't anyone else understand the threat? Instead, more tried to make their way into the space, curious about what was going on, drawn in by what they heard from others or by the sight of so many people.

As a group of elders made their way past her, she heard one say to his companions, "I hate what this man is doing to these people. I hate how they cling to his words. And I hate how they follow his every twist and turn."

His words dissipated into the air as he moved out of the courtyard, but "I hate" echoed within her. How sad that all she would ever know of this man is that he hates.

***

Not everyone in the area was there to hear Jesus. Some had stopped by to make their temple donation. Sarah noticed the surprised expressions of men and women as they turned into the courtyard and saw the sea of humanity spread out between them and the treasury.

Jesus gazed at the people making their way along a wall opposite him and dropping money into a temple donation box. One by one, they fulfilled their obligation to God, oblivious to him sitting in the corner.

Men and women modestly dressed and those in garments more elegant than any she had seen outside Tyre put money into the carved wooden container. As the coins traveled down the curved bronze receptacle and into the box, the chime of donations filled the room. Occasionally some in the crowd would comment at the sound of an especially significant contribution.

A lone woman walked in, barely tall enough to be seen above the seated throng, her cloak so ragged Sarah wondered what kept it on her body. Her gray hair coiled out from under a covering too frayed to contain it.

Jesus watched the woman intently as she reached into a threadbare bag, pulled out her coins, and dropped them into the treasury. The sound they made was almost inaudible. No one else in the room even seemed to notice her. They appeared more captivated by the wealth of those impatiently waiting for her to finish.

He turned from looking at those near the treasury and leaned toward Simon and some of the others. "Do you see that poor widow?" He nodded toward the woman. "What did she give? Maybe two mites? Yet truly, I tell you, she gave more than everyone else."

The men looked at the destitute woman and then at each other in confusion.

"They've all given out of their abundance. She, though," he looked at the woman, and Sarah saw again a love that touched her down to her core, "out of her poverty, has given all that she has to God."

His words hung in Sarah's thoughts. Your whole heart, your whole soul, your whole mind, and all of your strength. She watched the woman walk out of the courtyard unaware she had caught anyone's attention, and wondered, how do you give God everything?

Jesus straightened to speak to all those spread on the floor before him and perched on rooftops above him. "The Scribes and Pharisees sit on Moses' seat, so respect their authority to teach. Practice and observe all they tell you but not all they do. For they preach but do not practice. They bind heavy burdens, hard to bear, and lay them on people's shoulders, yet they themselves do nothing to help these people walk under those burdens."

Sarah sighed with disappointment. She had hoped he was done with his tirade, that the woman had distracted him and everyone would leave, maybe let the situation calm enough that they could get out of the city.

"These leaders" he said, nodding toward the gathering cloud of religious leaders that once again darkened the entryway, "do all their deeds for others to see, not for God. They enlarge their phylacteries and lengthen their fringes, and they love the best seats in the synagogues, salutations in the marketplaces, and being called rabbi."

He stood and looked at the men. "Whoever exalts himself will be humbled. And whoever humbles himself will be exalted." With his gaze still fixed on those standing in the entrance, he stepped forward into the crowd. "Woe to you, Scribes and Pharisees. You shut the kingdom of heaven against men, for you neither enter yourselves nor allow others to enter who would have gone in. You hypocrites." He pointed to the treasury. "You fulfill your lawful obligation and tithe, yet you neglect the weightier matters of the law – justice, mercy, faith."

He turned and walked back to the bench, then faced them again. "You blind guides. Straining out a gnat and swallowing a camel."

The men didn't move. Not one searched for a stone or lunged into the crowd toward him. They just watched and listened, their faces no longer angry but determined.

"You cleanse the outside of the cup and plate," he said, "but inside they are full of extortion and greed. You blind men. You are like whitewashed sepulchers. Beautiful outside, but dead inside. Full of dead men's bones and all uncleanness.

"You build tombs for the Prophets and adorn monuments for those Prophets who were murdered for their faith, and say, 'If we had been alive then, we would never have killed these men.' You are sons of those who murdered them. So go ahead, finish the work of your fathers, you serpents. You brood of vipers. How will you escape being sentenced to hell?"

The men turned as one body and left, but the air hung heavy with vengeance.

Chapter 35

Morning dew sparkled on the hillside. Sarah sat on a rock near Salome, Joanna, and several other women and tried to hold polite conversation while gnawing on stale, dry, unleavened bread. Her back and neck ached from yet another night spent on the ground, but at least they were no longer in the city. Below them, the road looked almost snow-covered as shepherds guided their lambs through the gates for the Passover sacrifice.

Judas, the Iscariot, climbed up the path, his head down as if consumed by his thoughts, and she wondered where'd he gone so early in the day.

In the midst of a grove, she saw Jesus standing alone, looking down at Jerusalem. The rising sun, blocked by its walls, cast long shadows into its streets, darkening the city rather than giving it light.

Philip called to Jesus, "Where should we go to prepare for the Passover?"

Not Bethany, not Bethany, not Bethany, Sarah thought, as if she could convey her wish to Jesus.

He turned to Simon and John. "Go into the city."

The city. She hadn't even considered that a possibility, certain his words to the religious leaders the day before had been a final, farewell volley.

"A man carrying a jar of water will meet you there," he said. "Follow him, and whatever house he enters, tell the master of the house, 'The Teacher says, my time is at hand. Where is the room where you entertain guests?' Tell him I will keep the Passover at his house with my disciples. He will then show you a small, furnished upper room."

251

Sarah's head spun with the bizarre scene his words painted. She couldn't latch onto any one thought long enough to process it, except for the understanding that he was sending Simon on this mission.

Her husband stood, eager to go, John at his side. Without even a glance her way, he started down the hillside. She ran to catch up, but when she did, he seemed not to notice. The two men talked only of Jesus and seemed unaware of anything else as she walked with them down the mountain and into the city.

They strolled past shopkeepers setting out their wares, preparing for more than just another day as hordes of shoppers rushed to get to the stalls to fill their holiday needs. Shepherds herded lambs around them on their way to the Temple, and Sarah cast a grateful glance to heaven as it became apparent that, without Jesus, the three of them were irrelevant.

A man walked around the corner, a water jar balanced on his shoulder. He nodded a polite, impersonal greeting toward them, and Simon rushed to catch up to him.

"What are you doing?" she said, hurrying to keep pace with her husband.

"That's him."

"Who?"

'The man with the water. That's the man Jesus said would meet us."

"He didn't 'meet us,' Simon. He's just some servant heading back from the well. Look around you. There are people everywhere doing the same thing."

"Didn't you see him nod at us?" Simon said.

"I saw him being civil. His eyes happened to meet yours, and he nodded. That doesn't mean he expects you to follow him home like some lost puppy."

The man turned down a side street, and Simon and John turned with him. Sarah broke into a trot, trying to keep up with them. He walked into a house at the far end of the street, a house that looked no different from the dozens of other houses hugging the edge of the road. Without hesitation, Simon and John followed him through the door. Sarah stood in the middle of the street, unsure what to do. She couldn't go in there but then, neither could Simon. What was he thinking? Another man stopped him in the entryway as the servant continued deeper into the house.

She cringed and waited for her husband to come flying out of the house, tossed into the street with John right behind him, angry words chasing them all out of town. Instead, the man reached out and warmly embraced Simon. Then, taking him by the shoulder, he led him through another door toward the gated courtyard. Simon looked over his shoulder and made a motion for Sarah to hurry up and join them.

Unsure what to do, she stepped gingerly into the house and glanced from side to side. The servant walked out from the back of the house and into another room, smiling at her as he passed. She moved into the courtyard and saw Simon and the others walking up the stairs. Hesitant, she climbed up behind them. When they came to the top, the man unlocked a door and welcomed them into a guest room. A large, low table filled the center, surrounded by mats and cushions. Rays of sunlight streamed in through the small windows, illuminating freshly swept floors. Sideboards and cupboards stood bare and clean, ready to be heaped with food. Firewood lay stacked, prepared to bring warmth into the room.

Simon beamed at Sarah, his faith rewarded, his joy unbridled.

* * *

As the late afternoon sun slipped toward the west, Jesus led the small group into Jerusalem, walking sure and confident, as if he knew exactly where to go. Along the way, they stopped at crowded booths and gathered what they needed for the evening's meal.

Sarah thought he would surely stroll past the side street, one of many that shot off the main road, but he turned onto it with the same assuredness and took them straight to the door of the house she, Simon, and John had visited earlier that day.

When they entered, a servant welcomed them and pointed them to a small alcove off the entryway. Another servant awaited, cloth in hand, a water jar on the floor beside him. He knelt on the hard stone floor and one by one, removed the sandals of the visitors, exposing feet blackened by the dust of fields, roads, and city streets. The men chatted and laughed with one another as they took turns lifting their feet over a clay basin while the servant poured a small amount of water over each dangling foot and wiped it clean with the cloth.

Sarah watched the man as he focused on his work, not looking into the faces of those he served, disappearing into the water and cloth, anonymous.

The men followed one another into the courtyard and up the stairs to the guest room while the women waited. Salome and the others paused, unwilling to let a man, even if he was a servant, touch them. After a few moments, a slender girl walked in and knelt next to him. One by one, the women genteelly lifted their feet for the man to pour water over them while the girl cleaned them with the cloth. Within moments, they returned to their conversations, paying no more attention to the servants wiping the filth of their journey from their soles.

When the last woman slipped her foot back into her sandal, the man glanced over to Sarah. She met his eyes, and a sadness ached in her heart.

He was meant for more.

She unfastened the straps, took off her shoe, and held her foot over the basin. As the chill water washed over her foot, she looked up and into the eyes of Jesus, watching her from the doorway through which the others had already passed.

The man arose, signaling that they were done, picked up the jar and the basin full of muddy water, and left the room. Sarah watched him carry the bowl to the courtyard. She followed him past Jesus and turned toward the stairs, glancing off to the side to see the servant pour the dirt from their feet into the soil around a jujube tree.

Gazing up into its branches, thick with thorns, she wondered how a tree so beautiful in bloom, with fruit so appealing, could hide such ugliness beneath its leaves.

Chapter 36

The dimming light of early dusk cast shadows on the stairway as Sarah climbed to the upper room. Harsh, smoky scents of a cooking fire rose up from the yard below.

Simon and the others stood awkwardly inside the doorway, as if unsure where to go, worried maybe Jesus wasn't joining them. Mary, the mother of the younger James, worked her way around the men as she searched nearby chests and cabinets for utensils. Salome and several other women bustled around the sideboard and shelves, arranging food on platters while Joanna lit lanterns in preparation for the approaching darkness.

Sarah studied Joanna a moment, curious and uncomfortable that she would be with them tonight, a night when it would seem she should be with her husband, in Herod's house. Then, feeling a need to make herself useful, she picked up a nearby water jar and looked for something to fill.

Jesus came into the room and dropped down onto a mat at the table. The men scrambled to grab cushions and mats close to him, grumbling under their breath when they had to settle for something more removed.

Before they could fully recline, he said, "Let the greatest among you become as the least." He glanced at Sarah. "For who is greater, the one who sits at the table or the one who serves them?"

"Here," Salome said, as she handed Sarah a bowl. "See if you can find more of these and fill them so the men can wash their hands."

Sarah walked toward the cabinet, water jar and bowl in hand, unsure where to begin looking for more. Sensing that someone was nearby, she turned to see Jesus at her side. He took the vessels from her and placed them on the table. After pulling his shawl from around his shoulders, he laid it on his mat and removed his tunic. Then he hiked up his garment and girded it around his waist like some kind of servant.

The other women stopped their work and watched, unable to imagine what he might be doing. He took a cloth from Salome, glanced again at Sarah, then picked up the water jar and bowl and knelt down before Thomas.

While Jesus removed his sandal and poured water over his foot, Thomas looked around the table, as bewildered as everyone else.

"What are you doing?" he said.

Without response, Jesus wiped his foot dry.

"The man downstairs just washed my feet," Thomas said, as Jesus removed his other sandal and poured water on his foot. "They're not dirty. I couldn't have walked twenty steps through the courtyard."

Jesus dried his foot, picked up the jar and bowl, and stood. The once clear water sloshed in the bowl, murky, clouded, darkened. How could it be that even a little dirt could muddy the waters nearly as much as all the dirt they had brought into the house?

He knelt before Simon and reached out to remove his sandal.

"What do you think you're doing?" Simon said, drawing his foot away.

Jesus looked up, and said, "What I am doing you can't understand now. But later, you will."

"I would never let you wash my feet," Simon said.

"If I don't wash you, then you will have no part with me."

Simon's eyes widened as an appreciation of what these words meant sank into his consciousness. "Master, then don't wash only my feet, wash my hands, my head."

Jesus smiled. "If you've bathed, you need only your feet washed to be clean throughout." He bent and poured sparkling water over Simon's foot. "And you are clean." He dried Simon's foot and stood, saying, "But not all of you are clean," and moved on to Philip, then Nathaniel, Judas the Iscariot, John, James, and the others.

While Jesus worked, Simon looked over at Sarah. She shrugged, as puzzled as he. Silence hung heavy in the air, broken only by the occasional sound of leather being unstrapped and water splashing into the clay bowl.

After he had washed the feet of every man in the room, Jesus stood, ungirded his garment, and slipped on his tunic and shawl. He carried the bowl to a corner and handed the jar to Sarah. As he did, he looked into her eyes, and she felt he could see into her very heart.

He moved aside to allow Salome to squeeze between him and a wall. As she headed down the stairs, he sat again on his mat and glanced around the table. "Do you understand what I've done here?"

No one answered.

"You call me Teacher and Master, don't you? If I then, your Master and Teacher, have stooped to wash your feet, you ought to do the same to one another. I have given you an example so that you, too, will do to others as I have done to you and be a servant. No servant is greater than his master, and you are blessed if you do these things I do."

His eyes lit with a tender sadness. "I know those I've chosen and the choices they'll make. And I know the prophecy will be fulfilled, *He who ate my bread has lifted his heel against me.*"

Men young and old studied the table, embarrassed to look him in the face, no doubt remembering their anger at not getting the best seat in the house.

Sarah noticed his gaze seemed to linger on Judas, the Iscariot. She studied the slouch of the man's shoulders, the tilt of his head, the steady expression as he listened to Jesus. After all this time together, she still felt she didn't really know Judas.

The sound of crackling flames filled the silence. Flickers from lanterns brought a false and ever-changing light into the space, illuminating the sadness in Jesus' eyes.

Joanna reached past him to set a plate of bread amid scattered dipping bowls, and the men reached in, eager to take advantage of the distraction.

As they ate and chatted, Jesus said, "Truly, truly I tell you, one of you will betray me."

Immersed in conversation, few seemed to hear him, but Sarah saw Simon glance across the table toward John, who was dipping bread into a nearby bowl. He nodded at the younger man, encouraging him to ask the obvious question.

When he didn't, Simon said, "Who are you talking about?"

John turned to Jesus. "Who would betray you?"

Jesus tore off a bit of unleavened bread just as Judas, the Iscariot reached across the table to dip a piece. He immersed his bread in the olive oil and handed it to the Iscariot.

The room darkened as the sun neared its final descent. Salome carried in the heavy stew pot, and James hurried to help her. As she set it on the table, Jesus smiled at her, a smile so gentle and loving, an earnest smile, a smile that broke Sarah's heart.

Although she too had work to do, she didn't move. Instead, she stayed where she stood, across the room from him, and clutched the water jar closer to her chest.

"I have deeply desired to eat this Passover with you before I suffer," he said, as he watched those around the table reach past to dip their bread into the steaming pot.

In the midst of their reaches, he suddenly stood and held his bread out to thank God for the gift. The others rushed to stand along with him. Sarah bent her head and closed her eyes, and in her heart, she knelt before God as he said the blessing.

Jesus broke the bread, looked at those gathered in the room, and handed it to the two men nearest him, saying, "Take this and eat. This is my body, which is given up for you. Do this in remembrance of me."

They took pieces from it, and he nodded for them to pass it to the others. As they did, everyone exchanged uncertain glances. Philip took the bread and turned to pass it on to Sarah. She set the jar on the sideboard, pulled off a small bit, and ate it, not fully processing the words about his body. Then she picked up her jar again and held it close.

Before they could sit, Jesus lifted his cup of wine and gave thanks for it. He then handed it to John, saying "Take this and drink. This is the cup of my blood, the blood of the new covenant, which is poured out for many for the forgiveness of sins."

As John took it, Jesus looked out to the others, and said, "I will not drink of the fruit of the vine again until I drink it new with you in my Father's kingdom."

John hesitantly sipped from the cup, then passed it to Nathaniel. They again exchanged confused glances before Nathaniel, too, sipped from it and passed it on to Levi. As the cup circulated around the table, Sarah tried to make sense of his words. What new covenant?

Simon took the cup from Levi and, to Sarah's surprise, drank from it, sharing in the "covenant." Drinking Jesus' "blood" as if it might give them some kind of pagan power. Had they all gone mad?

He gave the cup to Philip, who took his sip and passed it to her. Sarah hesitated, unsure how to refuse, unwilling to follow the crowd into heresy. She looked at the deep ruby wine glistening in the cup, and the pungent bouquet awakened her senses even without her drinking from it.

Despite her desire to resist, she found herself setting her jar on the floor and accepting the cup. She sipped from it and felt the wine flow through her veins, reaching to the depths of her being, filling her with a fiery comfort and a feeling of new life, renewed strength, the sense that a power beyond her own now pulsed through her very heart, as if even her blood was no longer her own.

She looked over the edge of the cup to Jesus, his long ago words echoing through her thoughts, words that had turned thousands away from him, words that had been so impossible to believe, impossible to accept. *Unless you eat my body and drink my blood, you cannot have life within you.*

He returned her gaze, and she knew he had just made the impossible possible.

The men sat down again in silence, each trying to make sense of what had happened. Their expressions ranged from bewilderment to surprise to uneasiness. She was disturbed by her own feelings of awe at something she didn't really understand, something she shouldn't have accepted, but something that seemed more true than her own existence.

She noticed Jesus and was struck again by his demeanor. Here she was feeling some kind of joy, some kind of hope, some kind of peace because of what he'd done, and there he was looking somber and troubled, even heartbroken.

She leaned in to clear the bowl in front of him. As she picked it up, he said to no one in particular, "The one who dipped his hand into the bowl with me will betray me."

He grew still, and she straightened, wondering what he meant and if she was supposed to have some kind of response.

Before she walked away, she heard him say, "The Son of Man goes as it is written of him, but woe to that man by whom he is betrayed. It would have been better for that man if he had not been born."

The others kept chatting, apparently oblivious, but Judas, the Iscariot, sat opposite him and heard. "Do you mean me?" he said.

"You have said so," Jesus said.

261

Judas' face grew dark with rage, a rage Sarah wasn't sure anyone else noticed as Jesus quietly said, "What you do, do quickly."

Furious, Judas stood and left the room, and conversation ceased. The sound of his footsteps as he descended the stairs into the courtyard below resonated through the silence. No one spoke until they heard the distant sound of the closing gate as he went out into the night.

"Where did he go?" Simon asked.

"I don't know, but he took the money bag," John said. He turned to Jesus. "Did you send him out?"

Jesus didn't respond.

"It's the Passover," Levi said, as he reached for some grapes. "He must have sent him to give something to the poor."

The others nodded and resumed their discussions until Jesus leaned forward with his arms on the table and said, "I'll be with you for only a little while more."

"You're leaving, too?" Simon said. "Where are you going?"

"Where I go, you cannot come. So I give you a new commandment." He looked intently at those gathered around him. "Love one another."

He let the words hang in the air a moment, then said, "After I am risen, I will go before you into Galilee, but where I am going now, you cannot follow. At least, not yet." He glanced toward Simon. "But someday you will."

Simon jumped to his feet. "Why can't I follow you now?" He looked around as if the answer lay somewhere in the room, then said, "I'd go anywhere with you. I'd lay down my life for you."

"Will you lay down your life for me?" Jesus said. "Truly, I tell you the cock will not crow before you have denied me three times."

"If I must die with you, I will not deny you," Simon said.

The room erupted with similar calls and shouts as Sarah withdrew into herself, hearing only her husband's words, *if I must die…*

"It's okay, Master," John shouted, as he and James leapt up from their mats. Both held their fishing knives high in the air. Lantern light glinted off the short blades.

"We have these two swords," James said, slicing through the air as Simon's hand rushed to his own scabbard.

Jesus watched them a moment before saying, "That's enough. Don't let your hearts be troubled."

The men sheathed their knives and dropped back onto their mats, and Sarah sighed with relief that the moment had passed, that Jesus had calmed this storm.

"You believe in God?" he said. "Believe also in me. In my Father's house there are many dwelling places. And when I go and prepare a place for you, I'll come again, and I will take you to myself, so that where I am, you may also be. You know the way."

"We don't even know where you're going," Thomas said. "How can we know the way?"

"I am the way," Jesus said, "and the truth, and the life. No one comes to the Father except through me."

He glanced around the table, with an earnest intensity. "If you'd known me, you would have known the Father. From here on out, you will know him. You have seen him."

"Master," Philip said, "show us the Father, and we'll be satisfied."

"Philip, have I been with you so long, and yet you don't know me?" Jesus said. "Those who have seen me have seen the Father."

Sarah shut her eyes to close out the world and let his words and the jumble of thoughts racing through her mind settle into some form she could understand. He couldn't be saying what she'd struggled to accept for so long, could he?

Could he?

She opened her eyes and saw him looking at her.

Then he leaned forward on the table toward Philip. "How can you say, 'show us the Father'? Don't you believe that the Father and I are one?"

He glanced again at Sarah, and her heart pounded hard within her. She wanted to sit a moment, but every seat, cushion, and mat was taken.

"Believe me, that I am in the Father, and the Father is in me," he said, looking at each person in the room, some stunned, some uncertain, some utterly confused.

He reached toward the windows and the world outside. "At least believe me for all the works I've done. Truly, I tell you, anyone who believes in me will do the works I do and even greater works than these. If you ask anything in my name, I will do it so that the glory of the Father might be made known in the Son.

No one responded as they tried to process his words.

"If you love me," he said, "you will keep my commandments. And I will ask, and the Father will give you an Advocate, a Helper, who will be with you forever. My very Spirit. The Spirit of Truth."

He gazed out the window into the darkness. "The world isn't open to him because it neither sees him nor knows him," then turned his attention again to those in the room, "but you know him for he dwells with you even now."

Sarah struggled to follow him. His spirit? His very breath, the source of his being? What does that have to do with truth?

"I will not leave you orphans," he said. "I will come to you. In just a little while, the world will see me no more. But you will see me. And because I live, you will live, too. In that day, you will know that I am in the Father, and you are in me. And I am in you."

John suddenly sat up straighter and listened with an intensity that made her wonder if he actually understood what Jesus was talking about.

"Anyone who keeps my commandments loves me," Jesus said. "And if he loves me, he will be loved by my Father, and I will love him and make myself known to him."

Judas Thaddeus said, "Master, how will you make yourself known to us and not to the world?"

"I will make myself known if a person loves me and keeps my word. And my Father will love him."

The continual thread of love wove through Sarah's thoughts, stringing them together, forming them into an understanding not yet clear.

"I have told you all this now, while I'm still with you," he said, "but the Advocate, the One the Father will give you in my name, he will teach you all things, bringing to your memory all that I have said to you."

He looked at the befuddled faces staring back at him, the love he spoke of shining bright in his eyes. "Peace I leave with you. My peace I give to you, not a peace the world gives. Don't let your hearts be troubled, and do not be afraid. The ruler of the world is coming, but he has no power over me. I do as the Father has commanded me so that the world may know that I love the Father.

"So, arise. Let us go forth."

Chapter 37

The small group left the house and stepped into the damp chill of night. The quiet of the streets spoke of thousands safely ensconced in their homes for the evening. Sarah trailed the others, struggling to make sense of all that had happened and all Jesus had said in the short time they had been in that upper guest room.

As they walked, he quietly sang the familiar words of a Passover hymn, *"O, give thanks to the Lord, for he is good; his steadfast love endures forever. They surrounded me, surrounded me on every side. I was pushed hard so that I was falling, but the Lord helped me."*

Others joined him. *"The Lord is my strength and my song; he has become my salvation. The right hand of the Lord is exalted. I shall not die, but I shall live. This is the Lord's doing; it is marvelous in our eyes."*

Sarah's heart usually surged with joy and gratitude whenever she heard these words. The Hallel had been one of her favorites as a child, but tonight she thought of her own children, hearing the hymn without her.

The night closed in, oppressive and thick. No hint of starlight or moonlight pierced the darkness. They left the city and climbed the Mount of Olives, walking deeper into the shadows. Jesus stopped, and people found places to sit on the ground.

"Love one another as I love you," he said, as he watched them help each other find a smooth spot, a level spot, a rock, a fallen log. "By this will everyone know that you are my disciples, if you love one another as I have loved you. A man has no greater love than this," his words caught in his throat, "that he lay down his life for his friends." He looked beyond them, beyond, it seemed, anything they could see. "And you are my friends, if you love one another. If the world hates you, know that it has hated me first."

No one responded, and the silence became as oppressive as the night.

"If you were of the world," he said, turning his attention back to them, "the world would love its own, but because you are not of the world, for I chose you out of the world, the world hates you. Remember what I told you. The servant is not greater than his Master. If they persecuted me, they'll persecute you."

He walked a few steps from them and gazed out at the flickering lights beyond. Ever-changing shadows crawled along the walls of the Temple.

"If I had not come and spoken to them, if I had not done the works I did among them, works no one else has done, they would have no sin. But now, they have no excuse. They have seen these works and hated both me and my Father, fulfilling the word that is written in their law, *They have hated me without cause.*"

Some near Sarah shifted on their rocks and stumps, uncomfortable with the truth he spoke even though they'd been witnesses to the hate.

After a few moments, he turned back to them. "But when the Advocate comes, whom I will send to you from the Father, the Spirit of Truth who proceeds from the Father will bear witness in your hearts." He sat on the ground among them. " And you, too, are witnesses because you have been with me from the beginning. I've said all this to keep you from falling away when they put you out of the synagogues. For indeed, the hour is coming when those who kill you will think they are offering service to God."

Sarah's heart tightened at his words.

"I am telling you these things," he said, "so that when your hour comes, you will remember that I told you. In a little while, you will see me no more, but then in a little while, you will see me."

Nathaniel leaned past Sarah and said to Philip, "We won't see him, then we will? What's he mean?"

Philip shook his head with no response.

"This doesn't make sense?" Jesus said. "Truly, I tell you, you will weep, and the world will rejoice. You will be sorrowful, but your sorrow will turn to joy. Yet, the hour is coming, and now is here, when you will be scattered, every man to his home, and I will be alone." His voice dropped, as if he were talking to himself. "Yet I am not alone, for the Father is with me."

Simon protested. "I would never leave you alone."

Jesus looked at him with quiet intent, as if no one else was anywhere near. "I have said this so that, in me, you will have peace. In the world, you have tribulation, but take heart. I have overcome the world."

He stood and, with a slight nod, signaled to Simon, James, and John to join him, then climbed farther up the mountain, around a bend, and out of sight of the rest of the group. Sarah glanced around at those who remained as they lit fires and spread out cloaks and mats, preparing for yet another night under the gnarled trunks of olive trees. Quiet conversations gradually wound down into the sounds of sleep.

When it became apparent Simon and the others weren't coming back any time soon, she walked the twisting, rock-strewn path they had traveled. As she stumbled along the way, she glanced into the sky, wishing for the light of even one star. Ahead, the path snaked through a grove of trees. Their leafy, arcing branches hung heavy above her, casting the night into even deeper darkness.

Rounding a curve, she almost tripped over her husband, lying near James and John, all three nested among ancient, protruding roots, sleeping as soundly as those she'd left behind. Jesus was nowhere in sight. She heard twigs snap from somewhere beyond the grove and slipped behind the massive trunk of the tree under which Simon slept.

A man moved toward them in the shadows, stooped and staggering as if he bore a weight so heavy he could barely walk. He came closer, and she drew in a quick breath at the realization that this weak and weary man was Jesus. He leaned against a twisted tree and looked at the sleeping men, his hair plastered against his forehead, sweat beaded on his face, blotted on his tunic.

"Are you still sleeping?" he said, his voice a choked whisper. He looked up to the darkened heavens and shut his eyes.

Then he glanced down the mountainside. "The hour is at hand."

From behind the tree, Sarah followed his gaze and saw torches held high above a mob moving steadily toward them. She stepped out from her hiding place, unsure what to do, and Jesus looked her way.

As if gaining some kind of strength from her steadfast perseverance, he stood straighter and in a stronger voice spoke to the sleeping men at his feet. "The hour has come. The Son of Man is betrayed into the hands of sinners."

Simon and the others stirred and lifted their heads, groggily trying to focus on him.

"Arise," Jesus said, a calm resolve seeming to come over him. "Let us go forth. My betrayer is at hand."

The sound of angry shouts caught their ear, and they turned to see the approaching torches. Drawn swords reflected the burning fires. Those without swords swung thick wooden clubs in the air. Sarah searched for escape, but the threat came from every direction, closing in from all sides.

Simon and the others leapt to their feet, suddenly wide awake. As the horde drew closer, Sarah recognized the

269

uniforms of the Temple guard and to her horror, Roman soldiers. Among them mixed the prayer shawls and robes of the chief priests, Scribes, and elders. And ahead of them all, she saw Judas, the Iscariot.

He walked with purpose to Jesus and greeted him, saying, "Master!" Then he embraced him and kissed him on the cheek.

Profound sadness darkened Jesus' eyes. "With a kiss, Judas?"

A Temple official next to the Iscariot signaled to those close by, and they lunged toward Jesus. Chaos erupted as John and James shoved some to the side while the mob surged forward, eager to get their hands on Jesus. Swords clashed, and clubs flung madly around Sarah. As she ran into the brush, she saw her husband draw his fishing knife from his side. Before she could even shout to him, he sliced blindly into the night.

As the official grabbed his head, blood spurted through his fingers and into the air. He pulled his hand away in shock, revealing a gaping gash where his ear had been. Sarah felt her knees give way, and she fell against a tree, struggling to stay upright, unable even to find breath to gasp.

Jesus reached past those dragging him by the arms and waist and touched the official's wound. As they pulled him away from the man, Sarah saw an ear, healthy and pink even in the flickering light of the torches. The man reached up to touch it and looked her way, her own surprise reflected in his face. Still the mob roared and slashed and dragged Jesus down the mountainside.

Had they all become so oblivious to the miracles he worked that they didn't even notice he had put an ear where there was no ear?

Chapter 38

Simon followed the mob down the mountain, leaving Sarah no choice but to do the same. The roar of hate and venomous rage filled the air, crowding out any thoughts she tried to string together to make sense of the scene around her. As some dragged Jesus over the protruding roots and stones, others wrestled his wrists together and tied them with rope.

They passed the spot where only a short time earlier his followers had bedded down for the night. Abandoned mats and cloaks lay scattered along the hillside. Among them stood Salome with the younger James' mother, Joanna, and a handful of other women, lone figures of familiarity amid the chaos. Sarah struggled with whether to run to them or stay with Simon, but she knew she couldn't leave her husband. She moved farther away from them, shock, confusion, and fear freezing them in place.

The guards dragged Jesus to the bottom of the mountain and into the city, followed by the raging mob. As they clamored down the road, past closed stalls and shops and the massive, looming walls of the Temple, people emerged from their houses and observed from the shadows. Few spoke. None wanted to draw attention.

On the edge of Jerusalem stood the home of the high priest, Caiaphas, and it became increasingly clear that this was their destination.

As others realized this, some peeled off one by one and disappeared into the night until only Simon, John, the religious leaders, and those in control of Jesus remained. The bronze doors of the residence opened to admit them. A tall, solid woman stood next to the guards, carefully watching the

271

procession enter. John never slowed as he followed Jesus into the courtyard beyond, but Simon paused at the foot of the steps, hesitant, and looked around as if unsure what to do.

Sarah hurried toward him to pull him in the direction he needed to go, any direction as long as it was away from the high priest's house and out of the city.

Glancing over his shoulder, John saw Simon. He walked back to the woman at the entrance and said, "This man is with the group that just came in."

She glanced at Simon and nodded for him to enter. To Sarah's horror, he did.

Rushing to follow him, Sarah slipped past the woman and the guards, unworthy of their notice, just as the woman said to Simon, "Wait. Aren't you one of that man's disciples?"

Sarah's heart clutched with fear as her husband stopped, staring straight ahead, unwilling or unable to turn and face the woman.

"No," he said.

He continued moving deeper into the courtyard. Looking for a way to dissolve into the fabric of the scene around him, he joined some servants and court guards at a fire. Men and women hovered close to the flames in their efforts to warm themselves in the growing chill of night. Sarah slipped between them to stand beside her husband, seeing no other choice in the moment.

As those around the fire watched the determined gang of religious leaders and guards force Jesus across the polished stones toward a row of doors, some told the others who the man in ropes was. Still more men, members of the Sanhedrin, filed past the fire to join the officials and high priest, their faces solemn and decisive.

They surrounded Jesus, with John close behind as they entered one of the doorways and stopped near the threshold.

"Why would John go in there?" Sarah whispered. "What could he possibly be thinking?"

"I don't know," Simon said, staring blankly at the doorway, rubbing his hands over the heat as if it helped.

Terse words drifted out of the room and into the courtyard as Caiaphas stood in the shadows and demanded that those gathered make their charges against Jesus. Angry voices shouted out accusations, arguing with one another over what they had heard him teach, each trying to appear greater in the eyes of the high priest.

"The man's possessed," one said.

"He's convinced people he's the Messiah," another said.

"He's trying to start a rebellion," said yet another. "Stirs up trouble everywhere he goes. Promises the people they can have everything they've ever dreamed of having."

Finally, one man spoke, his voice rising above the others. "I'll tell you what he said. He said he would destroy the very Temple of God and build it up again in three days."

Simon glanced at Sarah, and she shut her eyes in a silent prayer.

"What do you have to say about that?" Caiaphas asked Jesus.

Sarah heard no reply. She peered into the lantern-lit room and saw Jesus standing in the midst of the mob, silent and straight, his hands still bound.

"I command you by the living God to tell us if you are the Christ, the Messiah, the son of God." The high priest's words twisted with sarcasm.

"You have said it yourself," Jesus answered, not denying the assertion even though he'd been commanded to speak under oath to God. "And moreover, you will see the Son of Man sitting at the right hand of power, and coming in the clouds of heaven."

Caiaphas reached up to his own collar and ripped it from around his neck, rending it, separating himself from the sacrilege, and condemning Jesus for his blasphemy. Sarah gasped before quickly turning her attention to the fire. When

273

shouts erupted from across the courtyard, she glanced up again to see others in the mob spit in Jesus' face and slap him again and again, so hard his head snapped back.

As the anger within the distant room intensified, those around the fire studied Simon more closely.

A man beside Sarah leaned past her and said, "You're one of them, aren't you?"

"No," Simon said, "I'm not."

"Sure he is," another man said. "Listen to him. He's a Galilean. I'd know that accent anywhere."

"I don't know what you're talking about," Simon shouted. "I don't know him."

As a rooster crowed somewhere in the distance, Jesus turned and looked into the courtyard, his face bruised and bleeding, his eyes the saddest Sarah had ever seen. Simon followed her gaze. When he saw Jesus looking at him, he ran from the house.

Although every instinct told her to run with her husband, Sarah stayed, unwilling to turn so quickly and leave Jesus there alone. Those surrounding him dragged him deeper into the darkness of the house, and unsure where else to go, she quietly walked out the doors and into the world beyond.

***

It seemed everyone in Jerusalem had awakened to the news that Jesus had been arrested and taken to the high priest. Streets, empty only a short time earlier, now swelled with a growing sea of people gathering outside Caiaphas' home. Rays of early dawn slashed across the roads as Sarah stood on a step, searching in vain for some sign of Simon.

The doors of the house opened behind her, and she hurried to the road, hoping to become hidden in the crowd. Those who'd arrested Jesus pulled him out and dragged him down the steps, accompanied by officers of the high priest, and the horde surged toward him. Armed guards shoved people out of the way, shouting for them to move back.

Angry voices and flailing arms filled the air around her as Sarah searched for a way out. In the midst of the chaos, she felt the presence of someone beside her and turned, relieved to see it was John. Without a word, he took her by the hand and steered her through the crowd, struggling to keep pace with the high priest's men as they made their way down the road with Jesus.

All around, stalls and booths fell and merchandise scattered. Still, John wove through the mob, guiding Sarah across the city and through the crush of people.

At the end of the road, the men dragged Jesus up the broad steps of a palace and across the wide portico. The sentry posted at the entrance stopped them, and they demanded that they be allowed to see the Roman governor, Pontius Pilate.

John ran up the steps behind them, Sarah in tow, and followed them into the expansive courtyard lined with marble statues of pagan gods, the ground tiled in mosaics, opulent residences at either end. Soldiers, swords at their sides, spears in hand, stood at attention, awaiting any signal to attack, blocking every exit.

A small man clad in a Roman robe of authority walked out from a distant door. Behind him, steps rose up to the imposing, dominating seat of judgment. He gazed at the religious leaders, who had stopped short of the judgment hall for fear of becoming unclean and unable to participate in the day's coming Passover feast.

They threw Jesus onto the tiles before Pilate, as one of the chief priests said, "We found this man perverting our nation with heresies."

The governor adjusted the drape of his toga and waited for something more interesting.

"And he told the people not to pay taxes to Caesar," another priest said.

Pilate glanced at the man without response.

"And," said yet another priest, "he has declared himself the Christ. A king."

Pilate turned to Jesus. "Are you the king of the Jews?"

Jesus struggled to stand up before him, unable to lift himself on his bound hands. Pilate nodded toward a soldier, who pulled him to his feet.

Standing before the governor, his face bruised and swollen, his knees split and bleeding, Jesus said, "You have said so."

The governor studied him a moment before walking toward a nearby door. As he left, he said to no one in particular, "I find no crime in this man."

"But," said the first priest, "he's been stirring up rebellion with his teachings all over Judea, from Galilee to Jerusalem."

Pilate stopped and turned toward them. "The man's a Galilean?"

"Yes," the priest answered, thrilled that he finally had the Roman's attention.

"Then take him to Herod." Pilate looked at one of the officials at his side. "He's in the city, isn't he? Surely he's here. I think they're all here for their celebration." He turned back to the religious leaders. "Take the man to him."

And he left.

The priests looked at one another, unsure what to do. Roman soldiers moved in toward them, giving them no choice but to leave. They yanked Jesus to Herod's residence on the other side of the vast courtyard. Their anger burned even more intensely in response to the difficulties they were having getting this man executed.

John led Sarah close behind them. No one seemed aware of their presence as all eyes focused on the small mob of men clothed in the garb of priests, Scribes, and Pharisees, dragging a bleeding, bound man across the courtyard, from one end of the palace to the other. They followed as the men marched

Jesus past towering columns to Herod's residence, the religious leaders' fury increasing with every step.

Herod stood on a portico and awaited them, greeting them with an odd enthusiasm. "So, this is Jesus," he said. "I've heard so much about you."

Nausea rose in Sarah as she realized he'd likely heard much from the Baptist, before he ordered his beheading.

His receding hairline revealed a heavy brow and a forehead red with excitement. "They say you're healing left and right, casting out demons, raising the dead. Of course, there's that problem of working miracles on the Sabbath, but still, raising the dead?" He looked around at the band of irate religious leaders and Roman guards. "Surely someone here must have something he can heal."

The men surrounding Jesus looked at the king in bewilderment.

"He's claiming to be the Messiah," one of them said. "And the King of the Jews."

"King of the Jews?" Herod said, with delight. He stepped down to Jesus and walked around him slowly, taking in his bound hands, shackled feet, and bloody, bruised face. "You're the King of the Jews?

"Oh, great King," he bowed and retreated a few steps in mock homage.

Then he swung the robe off his own shoulders and tossed it to one of the soldiers, who draped the purple silk around Jesus. Other guards dropped to their knees before him, laughing so hard they struggled to get up again. Jesus watched without response.

"Send this king back to Pilate," Herod said, no longer amused. "Tell him the man's stirring up the people and sedition. We don't have the authority to handle a 'royal' predicament like this."

The religious leaders turned to make their way back again across the courtyard to the governor's residence, their faces tight with rage and impatience. They dragged Jesus with such force, he stumbled and fell to the mosaic floor and still they dragged him. John stepped forward to help him, but Sarah grabbed his arm and pulled him back before anyone noticed.

When they pulled Jesus up again, shredded skin hung from his knees and shins, and blood streaked down his legs.

Word apparently had made it to Pilate before they did. He waited, arms crossed, standing in front of the judgment seat on the platform above them. The religious leaders stayed back while the soldiers dragged Jesus forward.

As they drew near, Pilate spied the royal robe draped around his shoulders and smiled. "So, you really are King of the Jews?"

Jesus looked steadily at the governor. "Is this your accusation, or are you basing it on the word of others?"

"Am I a Jew?" Pilate snapped. He pointed to the mob of priests, Scribes, and Pharisees. "Your own nation and chief priests have handed you over to me, accusing you of treason."

He descended a step closer. "What have you done?"

"My kingdom is not of this world," Jesus said. "If it were, my servants would fight for me, but my kingdom is not of this world."

Pilate stepped back to the judgment seat. "So, you are a king?"

"You say that I am. I will tell you," Jesus raised his bound hands, "it is for this that I was born, and for this that I have come into the world. To bear witness to the truth. Everyone who is of the truth hears my voice."

Pilate raised a dismissive hand into the air. "What is truth?"

As he sat on the judgment seat and studied Jesus, a centurion climbed the steps, leaned close, and said something to him. Pilate looked up at the man and then out across the courtyard to a distant door. Sarah followed his gaze and saw a woman dressed in Roman finery standing in the doorway. She slowly nodded at him.

278

He turned his attention to the religious leaders. "I find no crime in this man."

They erupted in cries of disbelief. Angry voices restated their claims against him.

Understanding their need to save face, he said, "You people have a custom that I should release a prisoner for your holiday. I'll release this King of the Jews."

"No," they said, horrified that they had come so close only to now see it all fall apart.

Someone in their midst yelled, "Not Jesus. Give us Barabbas." And they all shouted their agreement.

Barabbas? A vicious, murdering thief? A man so barbaric everyone in Jerusalem knew his name? Sarah looked at Jesus, standing still before them, and her heart broke with sorrow.

Pilate considered the men, weighing his decision. Then he turned to the soldiers on either side of Jesus, said "Take him and have him scourged," left the courtyard, and disappeared into the palace.

Out of the corner of her eye, Sarah noticed the woman in the doorway drop her head, turn, and walk away.

While the religious leaders congratulated one another, the soldiers led Jesus off through another door. Sarah lost sight of him as he vanished into the dark depths.

As word got out of the Sanhedrin's victory, others trickled into the area, at first tentative, but soon the courtyard around her filled with people. Empowered, they no longer hesitated to walk through the praetorium gates. Men, women, and children surrounded her, many of them the same men, women, and children she had seen reaching out to Jesus in the streets of Jerusalem only days earlier. Nowhere did she see the confusion, the fear, the horror she felt. Instead, the air filled with a perverted jubilation.

John shifted uncomfortably beside her, but neither said a word. Her throat tightened with sadness and terror until she could barely breathe. The sun crept higher into the early morning sky but did little to warm the chill of shock that froze her blood.

A soldier ran out into the courtyard, drawing his sword, and the celebration erupted into cries of alarm. The crowd surged back to the edges of the open space as those near him scattered. Ignoring them, he sliced off some low-hanging, dead branches of a jujube tree and gingerly gathered them together, trying to avoid the stab of their two-inch thorns. When he disappeared again into the palace, the crowd returned to its triumphant mood.

A short time later, a distant door opened. The mob grew still as Pilate walked out onto the platform above them and stood again beneath the judgment seat.

He looked down into the crowd, and said, "I am bringing him out to you. I find no crime in him."

The celebration grew quiet, and the religious leaders stiffened at the announcement that this man might yet go free.

As soldiers pulled someone onto the platform, Sarah stifled a cry. Before her stood Jesus, beaten and barely recognizable. The thorned branches had been twisted into a ring and plunged onto his head. Blood streaked down his face, his hair. Beneath the purple robe, his garment was soaked in blood. Gaping rips and wounds covered his bound arms and shackled legs.

"Look at this man," Pilate said, as if giving them one last chance to come to their senses.

The religious leaders said, "Crucify him," and immediately, the mob took up the chant.

As their call grew to a roar, Pilate coldly gazed out at them. "Take him yourself and crucify him. I find no crime in him."

One of the Scribes said, "We don't have the authority to impose death. But we have a law, and by that law he should die."

"For what?" Pilate said.

"He has proclaimed himself the son of God. Not a son of God, but the son of God."

Pilate turned in alarm to Jesus. "Where are you from?"

Jesus looked him steadily in the eye, blood running down from his brow, but said nothing.

"Answer me." Pilate moved toward him. "Do you not know that I have the power to release you and the power to crucify you?"

"You have no power over me unless it's been given to you from above."

Pilate turned to the angry men standing just beyond the court of judgment. "Let me release him."

"No," they shouted.

"If you release this man," a priest said, his voice rising above the clamor, "you are not a friend of Caesar." He pointed to Jesus. "Every man who makes himself a king sets himself against Caesar."

Pilate let the words weigh down upon him. Then he turned from Jesus, climbed the steps, and sat on the judgment seat.

"Bring him here," he said, with a curt gesture.

The soldiers yanked Jesus closer to the Roman governor, who signaled with a swirl of his hand that they should face him toward the crowd.

As they did, Pilate looked out over the mob. "Here is your king."

"Crucify him," a voice shouted, and the air filled again with the chant.

"Shall I crucify your king?"

The chief priests answered, their voices strong with authority and devotion. "We have no king but Caesar."

Pilate glanced toward the empty doorway where the woman had been, then walked to a low table, poured water into a bowl, and dipped his hands into it. "I wash my hands of this whole matter." He turned to the religious leaders. "His blood is on your hands."

"Let his blood be upon us and upon our children," they said with deep solemnity as the praetorium erupted in cheers of celebration.

Sarah watched in disbelief as Pilate nodded to the soldiers to take Jesus out and crucify him.

Chapter 39

Soldiers ripped the royal robe from Jesus, then shoved him down the judgment seat steps and through the crowd. As he passed, people mocked him and spat at him. John and Sarah ran along the back wall to a door where a mob awaited in the streets. Everyone stretched and craned, hoping to catch a glimpse of Jesus, and no one noticed them as they stopped at the bottom of the steps, melting into the background.

When the soldiers dragged him out of the palace and onto the road, some gasped at the beaten man they saw, but most shouted taunts and jeers. Two centurions emerged from the shadows carrying a wooden cross, roughly chopped and splintered. A soldier unshackled Jesus' legs and unbound his hands. Moments later, the centurions thrust the cross at him, knocking him off-balance as it fell heavily onto his shoulder. He stumbled into the crowd, scattering those nearby, and fell.

No one moved to help him.

A soldier pulled the cross off him and let him stand again before shoving it back into his arms. Then, with a kick, he prodded Jesus forward.

John led Sarah through the crowd as he tried to keep Jesus in his sight. All they could see was the tip of the cross moving slowly through the packed streets. When it would slow and stop, the snap of a whip cracked in the air, and the cross would resume moving. At one point it vanished, and Sarah knew he had fallen again. A few moments later, it rose above the crowd and resumed moving forward with painful slowness.

As the road turned a corner, she followed John between people, then stopped short when they came up against a wall of Roman soldiers holding back the crowd. Jesus struggled past them, sweat dripping from his bloodied brow. He looked ahead to some distant, unseeable goal even as he bent under the weight of his cross.

Farther down the other side of the road, Sarah saw Salome and Joanne sobbing into their veils along with the younger James' mother. They held on to one another for support while the crowd jostled against them.

As Jesus staggered past, he noticed them and said something she couldn't hear.

The jeers grew louder, drowning out the tears and any comfort the women may have given him.

A cobbled stone tripped him, and he dropped to the ground. Sarah grabbed John's arm to keep him from rushing into the street. Soldiers angrily ordered Jesus to get up, but she could see he had no more strength. He lifted his head and weakly pushed up on his hands.

A centurion reached under his arm and jerked him up, then, spotting a man on the edge of the crowd, said, "You. Pick up his cross."

The man looked at the soldier in surprise and pointed to himself. "Me?"

"Get over here, and pick it up."

Two young boys clutched the man's hands to try to hold him back. Turning to them, he said something, and they reluctantly let him go. He stepped warily into the street, still looking back at the boys he'd left behind, while another centurion lifted the heavy cross from the ground and shoved it at him.

As the first soldier led Jesus forward, the man tried to keep pace, dragging the wood along the uneven stones of the road. The crowd closed in behind. A sea of people seemed to stretch to the farthest walls of the city, most taunting while others wept and lamented.

John turned away from the road and pushed through the crowd, clearing a path for Sarah. They walked, pressed against the walls of shops and houses, peering over the heads of the mob, following the tilted arm of the cross along its path. High above loomed the gates that opened to the place outside Jerusalem where the Romans executed with abandon.

Golgotha.

Sarah wanted to leave, to find a place to crawl away from what was happening and shut her eyes. Maybe if she slept, she'd find this was all just a terrible dream.

As the cross moved through the gates out of Jerusalem, the crowd slowed. Some followed while others dropped off to the side, no longer sure they wanted to see anymore. It was enough to know the religious leaders had been victorious.

John and Sarah walked through the gates to where the rocky overhangs of a mountainside cast deep shadows on the ground below. A centurion handed Jesus a cup of the myrrh-laced vinegar wine the Romans pretended would dull the pain, but Jesus shook his head, refusing what the man offered. After tossing the bitter wine into the dirt, the soldier stripped off Jesus' tunic and threw it to the ground. He ripped off his loincloth and shoved him into the barren dust. Another took the cross from the man who had been conscripted from the crowd, dismissing him with a terse nod.

The man looked around, trying to make sense of where he was and what he was seeing. He spied his children in the crowd and pushed his way through to rejoin them, catching them up in a tearful embrace before rushing to get them back inside the city walls.

The soldier dropped the cross onto the rocky ground while another stooped and grabbed Jesus under his arm, rolling him heavily onto the splintered wood. Jesus cried out as his head fell against the cross, shoving thorns deep into his skin. Fresh blood poured down from his hair and puddled in the dirt.

A hand grabbed Sarah's. She turned to find Lazarus' sister, Mary, at her side, her eyes red and filled with tears. Although she clung to Sarah, she stared straight ahead at Jesus.

"I heard," she said, "but I didn't believe. I had to see for myself. How could they do this to him?"

The sight of a hammer being raised high into the air caught Sarah's attention. She turned to see it slam down onto a spike, driving it into Jesus' hand, nailing it to the wood below. He screamed out in agony even as another soldier held his other hand in place. The centurion with the hammer crossed over Jesus, knelt beside him, and slammed another spike into that hand. The entire universe seemed to reverberate with Jesus' screams of pain.

Still another soldier held his feet in place. The man armed with a hammer walked over, straddled Jesus, dropped again to his knees, and with one blow, drove a spike through his feet, into the wood. Finally, a soldier handed him a board carved with letters telling the world the charge against Jesus, and he nailed it above Jesus' head.

The wood groaned and split as other soldiers pulled on ropes tied to the crossbar. The cross, heavy with the weight it bore, slowly lifted into the sky. Jesus' body shifted and slipped along the splintered timbers as they hoisted the cross and slid it forward into a well in the dirt. It dropped into place so hard, the ground shook. Other soldiers rolled stones to the base to keep it upright.

No one spoke. Even those in support of his execution needed time to absorb the gruesome scene. Jesus hung above them, looking down at them, unable to do otherwise without the thorns piercing his scalp. The skin ripped away from the spikes in his hands and feet as his body slid into a final position. Although stripped of his clothes, Sarah didn't even see his nakedness. The sight of his body torn and bruised, shredded and scourged, blinded her to anything else.

Without moving his head, he looked up to the skies and spoke, his words little more than a groan, "Father, forgive them. They do not know what they are doing."

Mary clutched Sarah's hand tighter and sobbed, while Sarah prayed that this might all just end, that someone might run in and say there's been a terrible mistake.

As she stood hopeless, unable to take in what she was seeing, John grabbed her arm and pointed to the dirt where several centurions cast lots, gambling for Jesus' tunic. "Look," he said, "he's still fulfilling prophecies."

Sarah and Mary stared at him, bewildered.

"The words of the Prophet. *They divided my garments among them, and for my raiment they cast lots.*" Even in his sorrow, excitement radiated from John. "Don't you understand? He could have fulfilled all kinds of prophecies and still be a fake. I mean, he could have orchestrated everything all these years. But this," he gazed at the man hanging helpless, nailed to a cross, struggling even to catch his breath, then pointed again to the soldiers in the dust, "he can't fake this."

Sarah's heart ached at the memory of the rest of the Prophet's words. *Trouble is near, and there is none to help. They have pierced my hands and feet. I can count all my bones. They stare, and gloat at me.*

Dozens of people standing before him, and no one reached out to the man who never hesitated to reach out to everyone.

Several soldiers dragged two more crosses and tossed them onto the ground, one on either side of Jesus, while others led two men to the site. They hurled the men onto the unforgiving wood, then proceeded to crucify them as well. Once they were hoisted into place, they faced one another, with Jesus hanging between them, so they could each watch the other slowly die. One of the men glanced at the board above Jesus' head listing the charge against him: The King of the Jews.

"King of the Jews," he said, "What kind of king is this?"

His bitter words caught the attention of others in the crowd.

"King of the Jews," a woman shouted. "The man who would destroy the Temple and rebuild it in three days. Look at you now." She kicked dirt toward Jesus.

"Hail the king," a man said. "Save yourself, almighty king."

"Not only king of the Jews but son of God, right? Isn't that what he said?" another shouted. "If you're the son of God, come down from that cross."

The Scribes, Pharisees, and priests, who had been standing at the perimeter, wanting to ensure he died but not wanting to risk becoming unclean, joined in. "He saved others, but he can't seem to save himself... He's the king of Israel. Let him come down from the cross so we can believe in him... He trusts God. Let God deliver him now... If God wants to save him."

People laughed, their howls and sneers a cacophony of pandemonium in Sarah's head.

The soldiers looked up from their gambling and joined in, mocking the Jewish king.

A centurion, standing next to the cross, dipped a hyssop-covered spear into a bucket of the vinegar wine and held it up to Jesus. "Here, king of the Jews, maybe this will give you the power to save yourself."

All around Sarah, men and women shouted and shoved, closing in on Jesus, their faces contorted with anger as they spewed words at him. The soldiers kept them from rushing the cross even as they were entertained by the scorn.

Dizzy with the chaos swirling around her, Sarah felt she had been sucked into hell itself. She looked at Jesus, the crown digging into his head, and the last words of King David rose up before her: *Godless men are like thorns.*

Several women moved through the crowd and stopped near Sarah. She turned to see Salome fall sobbing into John's arms. Beside her stood the younger James' mother and Mary, the mother of Jesus.

Sarah's breath caught in her throat. A mother should never see something like this. But the small woman stood strong and still, looking up at her dying son, offering him strength through her loving gaze. Her eyes revealed a broken heart, a soul pierced with love for her son, yet even in her sadness, she exuded a confidence beyond any Sarah could ever imagine.

Then, Sarah realized the woman had always known this moment would come.

She knew the words of the Prophets as well as anyone, and she clearly believed her son was the Messiah, destined to fulfill their prophecies. And still, she hadn't hesitated on that long ago day in Cana to get him started on his journey to this hour and this place.

Heavy clouds gathered as a damp chill filled the air. Sarah drew her cloak close, then glanced up at Jesus, hanging with nothing to protect him.

He tried to look to the heavens, but the thorns drove deep into his skin. Dropping his head again, he said, "My God, my God, why have you forsaken me?"

One of the crucified men said, "The Christ," and spit at him with what little breath he had. "If you're the Christ, save yourself and us."

The other man hanging across from him said, "Have you no fear of God? You're dying yourself. We're both dying for crimes we committed. But this man," he looked at Jesus, "has done nothing wrong."

Jesus lifted his head just enough to meet his eyes.

"Jesus," the condemned man said, "remember me when you come into your kingdom."

"Truly," Jesus struggled for breath to speak to the dying man, "I tell you, you will be with me today in Paradise."

The centurion who had offered him vinegar looked up at him in surprise. Sarah struggled to comprehend that Jesus would use what little life he had left to give another man hope.

As those listening continued to mock him, Jesus gazed out to his mother. "Woman, behold your son."

Sarah's heart broke for the woman who couldn't miss the unbearable sight, who surely couldn't see anything else in that moment.

Then, he said to John, "Son, behold your mother."

As if he understood exactly what Jesus meant, John put a protective arm around Mary's shoulder and drew her near to his side.

With blood running down his face, Jesus glanced out from under the thorns at those who had scorned him, who still taunted and sneered, and said in a hoarse, weak voice, "I thirst."

The centurion seemed caught off-guard. He dipped the hyssop into the myrrh mixture, no longer with an air of mocking but with caring concern.

As the soldier lifted the wine to him, Jesus looked at the man, accepted what he offered, then in little more than a whisper, said, "It is consummated."

His eyes lingered on the centurion a moment before he turned his gaze heavenward, and said softly, "Father, into your hands I commend my Spirit," and his head dropped onto his chest.

The clouds that had been mounting rolled over the sun, leaving the day dark as night. The ground beneath trembled, and people screamed and grabbed onto one another. Boulders rolled down from cliffs, and stones fell from graves carved into the mountain's walls.

Grief anchored Sarah and the others in place, leaving them numb to fear while those around them ran. As soldiers hesitantly stood their ground, she saw the centurion drop into the dirt before Jesus and say something to the man hanging dead on the cross.

The quaking ceased, but the dark remained. After a few moments, a shaken commander gave an order. A soldier walked to one of the men hanging beside Jesus and swung a heavy iron club into his legs. The man screamed out in agony as the last of his blood seeped from the shattered bones. The soldier walked to Jesus, glanced at his fellow centurion still kneeling in the dirt, then studied Jesus a moment. Unsure whether he might already be dead, he took the kneeling guard's spear from the ground and shoved it into Jesus' side. Blood and water poured out, but Jesus never moved. Convinced he was indeed dead, the soldier moved on to the last man and smashed the club into his legs.

Lazarus' sister, still clutching her hand, leaned her head on Sarah's shoulder and quietly wept. Sarah struggled not to collapse into a sobbing heap.

Even in her darkest fears, she never imagined it would end like this.

She looked up at Jesus, hanging limp and lifeless, and knew she could never go back to life as usual again – a life surreal, empty, dead compared to the reality and vibrancy of the last few months.

She had known when Jesus was present even when she didn't see him and had felt his absence even when it had been her choice. But now, he was gone forever.

Chapter 40

The darkness deepened as night approached. Still, Sarah and the others hadn't returned to the city. How could they leave him?

Dust swirled in the gloom. The chill wind blew their veils and cloaks as they stood in the desolate chasm beneath the cliffs in a landscape forever changed.

Several centurions prepared for the end of their day's work. Two rolled rocks away from the cross of one of the men who had hung next to Jesus, letting the wooden structure and the body fall heavily backward to the ground. They discussed their plans for the evening while slashing the ropes that bound the dead man's hands to his cross, oblivious to the skin their knives ripped through. Together they tossed him into a cart. Leaning on the wooden wheels, they chatted and waited while other soldiers rolled the stones from around the second man's cross. From time to time, they swatted at the growing swarm of flies.

A soldier approached from the city, walking into the scene without so much as a glance at the grief and suffering around him. He said something to the centurion standing at Jesus' feet, then looked up at the gaping gash in his side, and left.

After the soldiers tossed the second man into the cart, the two who had been waiting tugged it up the hillside and out of site. A short time later, they returned, the wagon empty, and waited for Jesus to be loaded. Centurions rolled the rocks from the foot of his cross and stepped back as it fell with a force strong enough to send a tremor through the ground beneath their feet. While they tore the spikes out of his hands and feet, the small group of followers waited, huddled together, unable to move, with nowhere to go.

Beyond the soldiers, two men walked out from the city toward the grisly scene.

Pharisees.

Sarah started to turn from them, not out of fear but out of revulsion, when she noticed one was Nicodemus. He struggled to carry a heavy alabaster jar. As he drew closer, she saw the horror in his tear-filled eyes. Soldiers stepped back and drew their swords, but he walked past them without hesitation. The other Pharisee said something to them, and they nodded to the men by the cart, dismissing them.

While Nicodemus walked straight to Jesus, the other man, holding a wooden box, stopped to talk to John. "Have you heard? The earth quaked earlier. Did you feel it here?"

John nodded.

"It shook the Temple so hard, the veil of the Temple tore in half. Ripped to the very ground." He looked at Jesus. "What have we done?"

John shook his head, no words to express what had been done.

Nicodemus approached Jesus and gazed at the bloody, bruised, torn body lying on the splintered remains of a cross. Then, dropping to his knees, he set the jar on the ground, gently lifted Jesus' head, and eased the thorny crown from his brow, throwing it into the dirt of the desolate hillside beyond. He pulled the stopper from the jar, and the bitter aroma of myrrh rose into the air, melding with the stench of death. He soaked the edge of his prayer shawl and gently rubbed the oil into Jesus' skin, cleansing and salving the battered body of a man who could no longer do anything for him. As he cradled Jesus' head to wipe the blood from his hair, the other Pharisee walked over to him. Kneeling, he opened the box he'd been holding and handed him fresh linen burial cloths.

Jesus' mother joined the men as they lovingly wrapped the cloths around her son while the others kept their distance, unwilling to risk being so close to Rome's soldiers.

When they finished preparing Jesus' body for burial, Nicodemus and the other Pharisee carried him up into the hillside to a tomb recently excavated out of the limestone. Without a word, Lazarus' sister left Sarah and followed them. She sat on a rock opposite the tomb while the men disappeared with Jesus into the darkness of its depths, then reappeared without him, somber, silent.

As they stood in prayer before the opening, a commanding soldier said something to two centurions. They climbed to the tomb, set down their spears, and heaved a massive, rounded stone that had been propped against the mountain wall. Bracing themselves, they rolled it into the opening. Another soldier carried rope to the tomb, set it in clay at one end of the opening, stretched it across the stone, and set it in clay on the other side. He shoved a ring into the clay, sealing the tomb with an impression of the power and authority of Rome.

Chapter 41

Lazarus' sister clutched Sarah's hand the entire walk through the quiet streets of Jerusalem. Vendors' carts lined the road as merchants emptied their booths, the last to go home for the holiday. When she stopped at a spice stall, the man kept his back to her, unwilling to serve a customer so late in the day, in the shadow of the looming Sabbath.

"Sir, please," Mary said, "would you help me? I just want some myrrh and aloes."

He turned his head toward her, then, struck by the sorrow in the woman's eyes, gave her his full attention. With a nod, he packaged the salves and oils, accepted her money, and resumed shutting down his booth.

The small group headed to the house with the upper guest room where they assumed the others had gone. John pushed the door to the house, but it wouldn't open.

"It's locked," he said.

He knocked once. Twice. Then a hard third time. Sarah saw someone peer through an opening between the closed shutters of a window. They heard something slide across the floor, and the door eased open just a crack. The man who owned the house looked out, saw that he recognized everyone on his stoop, then opened the door and ushered them in quickly. A servant helped him move a heavy trunk back into place in front of the door. Then they lifted a second one onto the first.

Only a few lantern lights burned within, as if no one could bear anything more than gloom. Another servant rounded a corner and picked up his towel and jar of water, but the group silently shook him off. The sadness in his face told them he understood.

The homeowner led Mary, the mother of Jesus, into a side room along with Joanna and the mother of the younger James. He looked over his shoulder at the others, nodded toward the courtyard, and said, "They're upstairs."

When they tried to open the door to the upper room, they found it too was locked.

John impatiently knocked, saying, "It's me."

The sound of rushing footsteps approached from the other side, and the door opened. James greeted his mother and brother with a silent hug as the group stepped into the dim space. The remnants of the Twelve stood and sat apart from one another. Simon slumped on a stool and stared into the fire, his shame even more apparent than his grief.

When he turned to see who had entered, he leapt up, hurried to Sarah, and held her close, his tears dampening her hair. "Where were you? I stopped outside Caiaphas' house, but you were gone. I looked all over for you, then figured you must have come here. When you weren't here, I couldn't imagine where you'd gone."

"I couldn't leave him."

Simon pulled away and stared at her. "You stayed? You were there? The whole time?" He glanced at John, and his voice grew hoarse. "To the end?"

"To the very end," John said.

Simon stumbled back to his stool and collapsed, sobbing, while the other men gazed down at the table or out at the walls. John led his mother to a cushion by the fire while Lazarus' sister quietly pulled a bowl out of a cabinet. The bitter scent of myrrh and sweet aloe stung Sarah's eyes as Mary hurried to finish her work before the sun made its final descent into the Passover Sabbath. Philip and Nathaniel offered the women wine and unleavened bread, but they had no desire to eat. Food could do nothing to fill their emptiness.

***

No one slept that night, and when the Sabbath dawn broke, the light that filtered into the closed room felt cold and glaring, an intrusion into their sorrow. Sarah lay by the fire and watched Simon pacing before a shuttered window. She couldn't imagine he would ever again be the husband she once knew.

She left her mat and walked over to him, and he let her hold him. Others slowly gathered around the table, no one speaking, no one ready to look another in the eye, everyone unable to bear the heartbreak they would see.

But as the streaks of light rose higher on the walls, a renewed life began to fill some.

"I can't stop thinking of the Prophet's words," John said. *"As a shepherd seeks out his flock when they have been scattered, so I will seek out my sheep, and I will rescue them on a day of clouds and thick darkness."*

"How could something so horrific rescue anyone?" Levi asked.

John shook his head. "I don't know, but he fulfilled the prophecies again and again."

"Sure," Thomas said. "We all saw that. But this…"

"No, I mean hanging there on the cross, when he couldn't control anything, still he fulfilled prophecy after prophecy, again and again." He turned to Mary. "You saw it. *When they look on him whom they have pierced, they shall mourn for him as one mourns for an only child and weep bitterly as one weeps for a first-born.* They pierced his side to be sure he was dead rather than breaking his legs to finish him off."

"They didn't break his legs?" Nathaniel said. "I thought they always did that. You know…just to be sure…"

"No." John's excitement grew. "Again, fulfilling the prophecy. *He kept all his bones. Not one of them was broken.* As terrible as yesterday was, all I could see was how he kept fulfilling prophecies."

He turned to Sarah. "You saw it, remember? Those soldiers gambling for his tunic?"

"They cast lots for his clothes?" James said, suddenly interested in what his brother had to say.

"Yes. There he was, nailed to the cross, hanging above them, helpless, and there they were in the dirt, gambling just like the Prophet said they would do."

John sat on a stool and studied the wood planks beneath his feet. "All day, the words of Isaiah ran through my head. *He was despised and rejected by men. He was wounded for our transgressions, he was bruised for our iniquities, like a lamb that is led to the slaughter. By oppression and judgment he was taken away and cut off out of the land of the living. And they made his grave with the wicked.*"

Sarah thought of the horrendous scene on that hillside, and the rest of Isaiah's words broke her heart. *He poured out his soul to death.*

There was no better way to describe what she had witnessed. Not just yesterday, but for the last three years.

***

As the sun slid beyond the horizon, marking the end of the Sabbath, Sarah and Salome rose and gathered stale unleavened bread and dried fruits onto platters, no energy to do more. Mary sat on a mat near the fire, her shawl slipping down from her shoulders. She gazed at the stones of the hearth beside a fire that could offer no warmth. Ash filtered through the air, falling to the ground before her.

Sarah poured wine into cups for those at the table, but she kept her eye on Simon, sitting on a stool across from Mary. He'd stared into those flames the entire day as if they could burn the haunting thoughts of his betrayal from his mind.

She set the jar of wine on a bench and knelt on the floor beside him. "It's all right, Simon."

298

Without turning from the fire, he said, "It's not all right, Sarah. It will never be all right. I abandoned him." He shut his eyes against the memory. "And he knew I would. He said someone in that room the other night would betray him. He even told me I would. But did I believe him? No. Like some cocky, invincible kid, I told him I'd never leave him. I'd face death itself rather than abandon him." His words trailed off into the smoke rising up into the air. "But he knew."

She took his hand. "Maybe he did know, but he didn't stop caring about you. He didn't order you out of the house or refuse to talk to you, did he?"

Simon shook his head. "But if you'd seen his face when he heard me deny him, Sarah."

"I did see it."

He turned to her, remembering he'd abandoned her in that moment too.

"He forgave you, Simon," she said, with a tenderness that conveyed her own forgiveness.

The sorrow in his eyes touched her heart, and she knew the one who would never forgive Simon was Simon.

"How could he?" he said. "Look what happened. I should have stopped them. I should have done something to get him out of that place and away from them. How could he possibly forgive me?"

"Even as he was hanging there on that cross," she said, "he forgave the people who were mocking him, the soldiers who were killing him."

"How can you know that, Sarah?"

"He said so."

John leaned in. "I heard it, too. He wasn't angry and vengeful. He didn't pray that he'd survive or that they'd burn in hell. He was dying, with barely any breath left in him, and yet he prayed that God would forgive them. Out loud. As if he wanted them to know they were forgiven."

A flicker of hope illuminated Simon's eyes.

"So you have to forgive yourself," Sarah said. "If you don't, how can you accept that he's forgiven you?"

"I hear you, Sarah," he said, "but still, I'm as guilty as the men who killed him. No," he slammed his hand against the stone of the fireplace, "more guilty. They didn't even know him. He was an anonymous stranger, and they were just doing their sick, sick job. But me? I was his friend." He hung his head and ran his fingers through his hair. "His friend."

"It wasn't your fault," John said. "It was almost as though he allowed them to kill him." He looked at Sarah. "You were there at his judgment. Did you hear him say one word to convince them not to kill him?"

"No."

"No, not one word, even though Pilate asked him again and again to defend himself. The only thing he said was something about having the power to lay down his own life."

"What kind of power is that?" Simon said.

John paced in thought as he said, "Do you remember that time when he said, 'If you don't believe me, then believe my works, and you'll understand that the Father is in me and I am in the Father?' I couldn't figure out what he meant. How did the works he did mean God was in him and he was in God? What could God have that could be in him, and what did he have that could be in God? " He stopped pacing and turned to them. "It only made sense if he meant the power of God was in him. So then, I started paying attention to what he was doing, trying to figure out the source of his works, his power. Everything he did, everyone he healed, all the miracles he worked, where did they come from?"

Several of the men drifted closer, drawn in by the question.

"He never called on God to do anything. Did you notice that?" John looked at the others, who silently shook their heads. "Every work he did, he did through his own power. Other people, whether they're fakes or prophets,s call on God

300

to heal someone or work whatever other miracle they do. But he never did."

Simon glanced toward Sarah, and she knew he was thinking about her words when Jesus raised Lazarus from the dead.

"I kept asking myself, where did he get his power? I mean, could it have been some kind of evil? Was he possessed like the Pharisees said? He wasn't calling on God. He wasn't calling on anyone. And yet, he obviously had some kind of amazing power. So, what was it?"

Blank faces looked back at him.

"I'll tell you what it was. Love. His power was love."

John walked into the middle of the room. "You all saw how he looked at those people. Love generated everything he did. Love is what is in God and in him. And that was the power he used to lay down his life. He died out of love."

The room grew still as they tried to comprehend what John said. No one argued or challenged or offered a different perspective.

Sarah thought about Jesus, about the man she'd come to know, a man who enjoyed life, who enjoyed good times and good friends, a man who got hungry and weary and lonely, a man she knew didn't want to die. But he did. He understood the danger. He could have backed down anytime, but he didn't.

"Why though?" she said. "What did he accomplish by dying? He could have done so much more if he'd fought to stay alive. Or if he'd just stopped saying and doing things to stir up trouble."

How many times had she prayed that he would stop?

"I don't know, Sarah," John said. "I keep asking myself the same thing."

"He told us why," Philip said. "That night he was arrested, remember? He said something about the greatest love a man can have is to lay down his life for another."

Sarah thought of him hanging there, dead on that cross, no longer able to help himself, no longer able to do anything for anyone, stripped of all power.

John was right. The only power they couldn't strip from him was love.

Yet, she still didn't understand. Had he feared the mob would have killed them all if he hadn't gone along with them? Had he really suffered all that he'd suffered and died that horrible death out of love for them?

Out of love for her?

Why? Was there no better way to show how much he loved them?

Her heart ached deep within her as she realized how much she loved him. Not the way she loved her husband or her children or anyone else. A different love. The purest, most chaste, most perfect love imaginable. With her whole heart. With her whole soul. With her whole mind. With her entire being. She loved him. And he was gone.

Chapter 42

A knock at the door startled everyone. James looked across the room at Simon, then opened it just enough to peer out, bracing it against himself as he pulled. He relaxed with relief and stepped aside to make way for two men who had long followed Jesus. They nodded a grim, silent greeting to the others while Salome showed them to some cushions at the table.

As she set cups before them, the taller of the two, Cleopas, said, "Sure was the quietest Passover I've seen. Nothing felt right about it. Even the smell of roasted lamb was nauseating. The streets seemed so still, so empty," he turned to his companion, "eerie even, wouldn't you say?"

The man nodded.

"And you heard about Judas?" Cleopas said.

"No," Nathaniel said. "Have you seen him? We wondered where he went."

"He's dead."

"Dead?" Philip said, looked around at the others with alarm. "Who killed him?"

"No one killed him. He killed himself."

While gasps broke out around her, Sarah watched Simon, praying the news wouldn't push him into similar despair.

"Why?" Philip said. "Why would he do something so drastic? Why didn't he just back here with us?"

"You don't know?" the man said.

"Know what?"

"He sold Jesus to the Sanhedrin," Cleopas said. "For thirty pieces of silver."

Icy silence filled the room as the impact of his words descended on everyone.

"Sold him?" James said. He turned to the others. "That's why he was with that mob. He wasn't trying to stop them. He was there to show them which of us was Jesus. And he showed them with a kiss." He tossed a stool into a corner. "A kiss."

"He apparently had second thoughts," Cleopas said, "but it was too late. After he found out they'd condemned Jesus to death, he went to the Temple to give them back their money, but they hid in the Holy of Holies to get away from him. So he threw the silver in after them, ran out of the city, and hanged himself."

"Hanged himself?" Philip said.

"Hanged himself. With the strap of his money bag."

"But why would he do that to Jesus?"

"None of this makes any sense," Thomas said.

As the room erupted in theories, anger, and condemnation of Judas, Simon stood and looked at Sarah with renewed hope. He hadn't been the one Jesus was talking about when he said someone would betray him.

***

Sarah lay on her mat and gazed at the morning star through the slit in the shutter, watching as it faintly gave the fading night its light. A shadow moved across the room, followed by another. She turned to see Lazarus' sister and Salome walk over sleeping men toward the door. When they unlatched it, she sat up, surprised that anyone would leave the room, especially when it was still dark.

Salome motioned to her to join them. Sarah glanced at Simon, grateful he had finally found peace enough to sleep. Wrapping her cloak around her, she followed them down the stairs and into the courtyard where Joanna and Mary, the mother of James, waited for them. The chill air closed around them as they hurried toward the gate.

304

White starry jujube blossoms brightened the gray of pre-dawn, but Sarah's heart broke at the pain they hid beneath their petals.

Mary handed Salome a small jar and slid the brace from the gate. With no time to think and not yet fully awake, Sarah followed them into the silent streets. Too early for vendors, too early for shoppers, too early even for birds.

Leaning over the top of the gate, Mary let the brace drop down again into its supports, beyond any man's reach. Salome gave her the jar, and she led them forward along the road.

"Where are we going?" Sarah asked.

"To the tomb," Salome said.

Sarah stopped in mid-stride. "Jesus' tomb?"

"Yes," Mary said, without slowing her pace, even as her voice broke. "Jesus' tomb."

Instinct told Sarah to turn around, but where would she go? The house was locked, the gate was braced, everyone was asleep. She couldn't stand in the middle of the street, shouting Simon's name into the night, and she didn't want to be anywhere alone. Left with no choice, she went with them, praying they could get this over with and get back to the house before daylight.

They left the city and walked past Golgotha. Even though predawn darkness shrouded the scene, a chill raced through her at the echoes of suffering those rocks had witnessed.

As they climbed the path to the tomb, Sarah caught sight of metal blades reflecting the dimmest light of early dawn and ducked under the cover of a twisted bush. "They've posted guards," she said, afraid to raise her voice much louder than a breath.

Salome turned to leave, but Mary grabbed her arm.

"We can't go there with guards around," Salome whispered, as she pulled the others off the path to join Sarah in the shadows of the shrub. "Besides, now that I think of it, who's going to roll the stone from the tomb so we can anoint him? We'll come back later with the boys."

Mary looked through the branches at the tomb, and as she did, the ground trembled. The women grabbed onto trunks, shrubs, and one another to support themselves as rocks crashed down the hillside past them. The soldiers fell to the ground, then crawled back away from the grave. When the ground stilled, Sarah could see the rock had rolled from Jesus' grave, the sealed rope of Roman authority left broken and dangling.

As the guards struggled to move the stone back into place, Mary smoothed her cloak and resumed her ascent with Salome, Joanna, and the other Mary close behind. Unwilling to be seen by Roman soldiers but even more unwilling to be alone amid the stench of death rising up from Golgotha, Sarah followed

At the sound of their approach, the guards drew their swords and spun around, only to relax at the sight of five women.

Lazarus' sister led the small group forward along the path. As they drew near the tomb, the sun seemed to suddenly rise from above it. White light bathed the air, brilliant light surrounding a man who stood before it, a man no one would mistake for a Roman soldier, an ethereal man who was there but not there.

The guards dropped their swords and froze in fear as the man said to the women, "Do not be afraid. I know you're seeking Jesus, but he's not here."

"Not here?" Mary said. "He has to be here. I saw them put him in this tomb myself."

"Come," he said, "and see where he was laid."

She took a step closer, and the man and the light vanished. Mary looked at Sarah, and Sarah looked at Salome, each wondering if the others had seen what they'd seen, heard what

306

they'd heard. The guards backed away from the tomb, then left and hurried down the mountainside to the city.

Sarah stayed where she was and watched from behind while Mary walked to the open grave and peered into the darkness. The same light began to shine from within, illuminating two other men with a glow so radiant they seemed translucent.

"Why do you seek the living among the dead?" one of the men asked. "He's not here."

Mary looked to the others before turning again to the men. "Then, where is he?"

"He is risen."

Chapter 43

Rays of dawn lit the sky as Sarah and the others stumbled down the hillside and into Jerusalem. The city stirred with awakening. Women and servants carried water jars to the well as birds called to one another from rooftops and trees.

Mary took Salome by the hand and led the group through the streets to the house where they'd left the others sleeping. She knocked, and a servant peeked out through the closed shutter. They heard him slide the trunks out of the way before he opened the door.

"What are you doing out there?" he said.

They ran past him through the courtyard and hurried up the stairs. She knocked again, and James let them in.

"Where have you been?" he said, while the other men scrambled to meet them. "We figured you were downstairs, but I just came back from there, and they said they hadn't seen you."

"The tomb's empty," Mary said, grabbing James by the arm. "He's not in there."

"You went to the tomb? Are you crazy?" He shut the door tight behind them.

She turned to the other men. "We went to anoint him, and he was gone. The angels said he wasn't there."

"Angels?" Andrew said.

"They had to be angels," she said.

"You're imagining things," Thomas said.

"The stone was rolled away, wasn't it?" She glanced toward the other women for support. "After the earthquake. And the tomb was empty. I walked up to it and looked in, and he's not there."

Thomas turned to John. "You saw them put him in there, right?"

"Yes," John answered.

"Don't you understand?" Mary said. "They've taken him somewhere else."

Simon looked at Sarah, and she nodded. He pushed Levi aside and tripped over a stool as he ran out of the room with John close behind him. Mary hurried after them, still clutching the jar against her chest, and Sarah struggled to keep up as they hurried through the city to the tomb.

No one noticed as they ran through the streets. Sarah huffed to catch her breath and slowed to a jog outside the city gates. She tried to avoid looking at the place where the cross had been and instead kept her eye on Simon as he climbed the path ahead of her. When they got to the tomb, they found John peering into the opening, no guards in sight, the stone still off to the side where it had rolled.

Sarah stayed near a rock as Simon rushed into the tomb and disappeared into its depths. John followed him, and a few moments later they both walked out, glancing around as if they might find Jesus' body somewhere in the brush.

"No guard, no body," John said. "They've done something with him."

"But what? Isn't it enough that they killed him?" Simon said, as the two men headed down the mountain, looking for any sign of Jesus.

Mary didn't follow them. She stayed behind, staring into the empty grave. The jar of ointments slipped from her hands, shattering on the rocky ground as she leaned against the stone entryway and wept.

Sarah watched Simon and John descend toward the city, then looked back at Lazarus' sister. Before she could make a move to comfort her, a light pierced forth out of the tomb. She looked past Mary and saw the two ethereal men clothed in brilliant light sitting on the low rock shelf where Jesus' body should have been.

"Woman, why are you crying?" one of the men asked Mary.

She reached out, pointing to the world around her. "Because they've taken away my Master, and I don't know where they've taken him."

Before she could say more, the light and the men vanished, and the tomb was once again dark.

She turned from the grave, and a man stood right in front of her, a solid man in a solid tunic, a man Sarah hadn't noticed, hadn't heard walk past her.

"Woman," the man said to Mary, "why are you crying? Who are you looking for?"

"Sir," she said, clutching at her chest with longing, "if you've moved him, tell me where you've laid him. I'll take him somewhere else and bury him."

"Mary," the man said. A word so personal, so intimate, so loving.

A word that opened Sarah to the unimaginable truth.

Joy filled Mary's voice as she said, "Master," and reached to embrace him.

He stepped back beyond her grasp. "Don't hold me. I haven't yet ascended to the Father."

Mary turned to look for the others, then turned back again to him, but he was gone. She ran to Sarah, grabbed her by both arms, shouted "He's alive!" and hurried down the mountainside to the city below.

Chapter 44

Sarah didn't know what to do. She saw it, but what did she see? As soon as he'd called Mary by name, she knew the man was Jesus. Alive. Alive, strong, healthy. Not even a little weak.

But how could that be?

The day brightened around her as she walked along the path and back into Jerusalem. The city might have been noisy, people might have been in her way, but she didn't notice.

He was alive.

She knocked, and the door quickly opened. With little more than a glance and a smile at the servant, she hurried through the courtyard, up the stairs, and into the room.

Mary must have arrived only moments ahead of her because she was still explaining what had happened. "But he's alive. I saw him. I talked to him."

"That's impossible," Thomas said. He turned to Simon. "You were there. What did she see?"

"I don't know. The tomb was empty. No one was around but us."

"Right after you left, the angels came," Mary said.

"More angels?" Thomas said.

John moved toward her. "I think maybe you need to rest a while, Mary. We'll find out where they took him."

"They didn't take him anywhere. He's alive."

"Then where is he?" James said. "If he's alive, why didn't he come back here with you?"

"I don't know. I looked for you," she pointed to Simon and John, "and when I turned back, he was gone."

"He's not alive," Thomas said.

"Still," Andrew said, "he's not in the grave, so what do we do? Should we go out and look for him?"

"We can't go out there," Nathaniel said, walking to the door and locking it. "If something's happened to his body, if someone's done something to the guard and taken him, Jerusalem's going to be crawling with soldiers."

"His body isn't gone," Mary said.

"But the tomb is empty, right?" Nathaniel turned to John. "Right?"

"It's empty," he said.

Simon gently pulled Sarah into a corner near a cabinet. "Did you see anything?"

She nodded.

"What?"

"A man."

"Jesus?"

"It didn't look like him," she said, "but as soon as he spoke, I knew."

"What did you know?"

She couldn't answer, and he knew.

**

As evening approached, Sarah helped Salome lift a pot of lentil stew from the hearth while Joanna searched for meats or fish.

"I couldn't find much. Just those few broiled fish," Salome said.

"They have plenty downstairs," Joanna said. She turned to Thomas. "Go down and get some for us, would you?"

While the mood had lightened, the fear had not. James unlocked the door, said "Knock when you get back," and locked it again behind Thomas.

Moments later, Jesus walked into the room.

No one responded at first. No one even moved, each afraid no one else saw what they saw, but Sarah's heart believed what her eyes couldn't.

"Shalom," he said, looking around the room. "Peace be with you."

John and Andrew rushed to his side, while the others crowded around him.

Simon alone stood back.

"Is it you?" Nathaniel said. "Is it really you?"

Jesus held out his hands. Holes pierced through the pink, healthy flesh, but there was no wound. James grabbed his hand and gazed into it, while others looked down at Jesus' feet, some dropping to the floor to see them. Shouts of joy erupted even as they struggled to believe what they saw.

"Do you have anything to eat?" he asked.

Andrew grabbed the plate of fish from the sideboard and handed it to him. As Jesus ate, they watched in hushed astonishment.

"Peace be with you," he said again, looking across the room, beyond the ecstatic swarm around him, to Simon.

Then he turned his attention back to the others. "As the Father has sent me, I send you." With a breath that seemed to fill the entire room, he said, "Receive the Holy Spirit. If you forgive the sins of any, they are forgiven. If you retain the sins of any, they are retained."

He looked again to Simon.

Simon slowly walked over to him and gazed not into his hands but into his eyes, and Sarah could see the whole world lift off his shoulders. And again she knew Jesus worked no miracle greater or more healing than forgiveness.

313

Chapter 45

A knock at the door drew their attention, and when they turned back, Jesus was gone. While the others looked around the room, trying to figure out where he was, James unlocked the latch. Thomas stepped in, his arms filled with provisions.

"Did he pass you?" Judas Thaddeus asked, looking past Thomas and down the stairs.

"Who?"

"Jesus."

Thomas set the baskets and jars onto the table. "What?"

"Did Jesus pass you?"

"What are you talking about?"

"He was here," the younger James said.

"Who was here?"

"Jesus."

Thomas picked up a peach and bit into it. "That's impossible. You're all imagining things." He pointed to Mary. "She's got you all worked up."

"He was here, Thomas," Simon said. "We all saw him. He talked with us. He showed us the holes in his hands and feet."

Andrew held out the empty plate. "He even ate some fish."

"How did he get in here?" Thomas said. "No one came through the house while I was down there, and there's a servant in the courtyard. He never said anything about seeing him. You'd think he'd mention it, don't you?"

"He came in right after you left," Simon said. "You had to have passed him on the stairs."

"I didn't pass anyone going down or coming up."

Simon looked at the others. "Did someone open the door for him?"

"No," James said. He looked at Thomas. "I'd just locked it behind you. I was still standing there when Jesus walked in."

"So you unlocked it for him," Simon said.

"No, I didn't know he was there until he was here."

"Well, he got in somehow," Andrew said. "He couldn't just walk in through a locked door."

"See," Thomas said, dropping down onto a cushion. "You all imagined it."

As they protested, he said, "Look, I wish what you said was true. There's nothing I want more. But unless I see him myself – no, not just see some imagined vision, but touch the holes in his hands, put my hand in the hole in his side – nothing will convince me that Jesus is alive."

***

Sarah helped the other women clear the morning meal only to stop in mid-motion when someone knocked on the door. James ran to unlock it, hesitant but expectant. The rest of the previous day and all through the night, they had tossed around theories and possibilities, trying to make sense of what they'd seen. But nothing made sense.

Still, they awaited Jesus' return, certain he must return, with no idea what to do, how to move forward, if he didn't return. With the knocking on the door, they felt their wait was over.

When, instead, Cleopas and his friend walked in, everyone sighed with disappointment.

Without even stopping to offer a greeting, the two men set their satchels on the floor and flung their cloaks over a bench, as Cleopas said, "We saw him. We saw Jesus."

"Where?" John said, as everyone in the room perked up.

"Heading into Emmaus. We were walking along, talking about things, you know, his death and everything. And this

315

man walks up beside us, overhears us, and asks what we're talking about."

"We looked at him like he was crazy," the other man said. "How could he not know what we were talking about? How could anyone within a day's walk of Jerusalem not know what happened here?"

"So, I told him," Cleopas said. "I went through the whole thing, the arrest, the crucifixion, the whole thing."

"And we told him that you," the other man looked at Mary, "went to the grave yesterday, and it was empty, and that you saw Jesus. Alive. At least, that's what we heard. We ran into one of the servants in the marketplace."

Mary nodded.

"The man called us foolish," Cleopas said. "Told us we were slow to understand everything the Prophets said."

"Can you believe it?" the other man looked around at those encircling him. "I thought, who does this guy think he is?"

Cleopas nodded. "But then, the man started talking. And beginning with Moses and going through all the Prophets, he explained how Jesus fulfilled the law and prophecies in ways I never imagined. But when he said it, it suddenly seemed so clear."

"I know," the other man said. "It was like, how did we not see it before?"

Sarah glanced across the room at John, who returned her gaze.

"I mean, as he explained it," the other man said, "my heart was on fire."

"Mine, too," Cleopas said. "Burning to know the law and the Prophets better. Burning to know Jesus better. Sorry that I'd missed so much when he was alive."

He grew quiet a moment, then said, "Anyway, when we finally got to Emmaus and turned into town, this man kept going, even though it was getting dark. So I told him to stay with us for the night." He turned to James. "We stayed at that inn just inside town. You know the one? Anyway, he agreed, and while we were eating, this man took the bread and blessed it. Then he broke it and gave it to us." Cleopas paused and looked at his friend. "As soon as he broke that bread and handed it to me, I recognized him."

His friend nodded. "But before we could say anything, he disappeared. Just like that. Vanished. We're sitting there holding this bread, and Jesus is gone."

Chapter 46

Eight days had passed since they'd seen Jesus. The air in the closed upper room hung heavy with cooking odors, body odors, and a desperate need to be refreshed. Sarah longed to fling the shuttered windows open and let the daylight in, but she didn't dare. The sound of Roman armor still passed the house from time to time and paused, leaving none of them feeling safe.

She uncovered a jar and considered how to stretch the little bit of flour that remained. As she reached for a bowl, a knock sounded at the door. Everyone tensed, no longer expectant but still afraid as they waited to see who would enter.

James opened the door, and they relaxed at the sight of a servant from the house below. He laid a cloth sack on the table, pears and apricots rolling out. Flour puffed from a clay jar as he set it down.

"Have things quieted in the city?" James said.

"A little," the man said. "The holiday crowd has emptied out, and I think Rome's easing back a bit."

"Have they found Jesus' body?" Thomas asked.

The servant hesitated and gave him a curious look.

"He doesn't believe we saw him," James said.

"Well," the servant said, "it doesn't sound like they've found any sign of him. Word has it the guards are saying you all went out to the tomb in the middle of the night while they were sleeping and stole it."

"Us?" John said. "We haven't left this room except that morning when he was already gone."

"That's what my master told the soldiers who came here. I don't know if they believed it or not, or if it's just not all that important to them, but we haven't seen much of them since."

When the servant left, James locked the door and turned back to the others, then gasped. Sarah followed his gaze to find Jesus standing among them. Thomas jumped up from his cushion at the sight of the man he knew was dead.

"Peace be with you," Jesus said, looking around the room at each of them. "Don't be afraid. Go, and tell your brothers in Galilee that there they will see me."

He walked over to Thomas, who stood speechless, his mouth open, his eyes wide.

Holding out his hand, he said, "Put your finger here, and see my hands." When the stunned man didn't move, he pulled the tunic open at his waist, revealing a healed but gaping wound pierced beneath his ribs. "Place your hand in my side. And believe. "

Thomas dropped to his knees. "My Lord and my God."

Sarah sucked in her breath at his proclamation. She looked at the man standing before them, smiling, saying nothing to counter Thomas' words, and she knew she'd been right. He hadn't just claimed to be God.

He was God.

Chapter 47

Everyone turned to Sarah at her sudden inhalation, and when they looked back, Jesus was gone.

"I've been telling you that he said over and over he was God," she said to Simon.

"He can't be God, Sarah," he said, gazing at the closed, locked door.

"Then who is he? And where did he go?"

"I don't know, but the very thought is blasphemy."

"What are you talking about?" Nathaniel asked.

She looked to Thomas. "You know, don't you? You just called him God, and he didn't deny it or stop you or say anything to try to set you straight, did he?"

"Who else can he be?" Thomas said. "Look at what he's done. No one works miracles like that. Not even Elijah." He clutched the fringe of his prayer shawl and gazed down at the floor, deep in thought even as he spoke. "He healed everyone. Everyone. Everywhere we went. He fed thousands of people with nothing, not once, but twice. He walked on water. He calmed storms. He raised people from the dead." He looked up at Sarah. "Only God has that kind of power over his creation."

"He even raised himself from the dead," John said.

"He couldn't have raised himself from the dead," Nathaniel said. "He was dead. How can a dead man do anything?"

"Then, who raised him?" John's voice broke with excitement. "Don't you remember that day when he said 'Destroy this temple, and in three days I will raise it up'? That's what he meant. The Temple of his body. They destroyed it, tortured it, beat it, buried it, sealed it in a tomb, and he raised it up again "

Salome dropped down onto a stool while others silently tried to comprehend the impossible.

"But how could he raise himself? By what power?" James said.

"By his own power." Sarah said. "Just like you said John. His power is love." She could almost see the pieces fall into place before her. "His love was beyond any I've ever known. Who else reaches out to everyone spontaneously the way he did?"

She looked around at the others, some eager to hear more, some trying to comprehend, and some…Simon…struggling with the very notion. "Can you think of a single time when he hesitated to reach out or thought of himself instead of someone else. "

"That makes him a nice guy," Nathaniel said, "but it doesn't make him God."

"But what if he really is?" John said. "What if Jesus is somehow the embodiment of God's very nature? God in the flesh?" He turned to Sarah. "You were there. When Caiaphas confronted him and asked him under oath if he was the son of God, he didn't deny it, did he? Maybe that's what it means to be the son of God, that he's God himself."

"That's not what it means," Simon said. You're just trying to make his words fit your ideas. None of this makes sense. God doesn't have flesh. He doesn't die. Jesus died. And not after some fierce battle with other gods but at the hands of men. More than that, I prayed for him. We all prayed for him. What kind of God needs us to pray for him? What kind of God can man kill?"

"They killed his body," Sarah said, "but they couldn't kill his spirit. His love."

James paced the perimeter of the room. "Let's just say, for the sake of argument, that he is…God." He struggled even to speak something so heretical. "What's the point?"

"I don't know," Sarah said. "And I admit, at first, I wanted to cover my ears and pretend I wasn't hearing what he was saying, because it was so wrong. But then," she turned to Simon, "after you told me about that time on the mountain when you saw the light and heard God's voice, I started wondering, what if?"

"We did hear the voice," John said, while James continued to pace. "And what did he say? *This is my beloved son.*"

James nodded, but Simon refused to look up from the planks of the floor.

"We didn't even question it," John said, "but God can't have a son. Not like the Romans claim their gods do. Sons that are gods. There's only one God. The one, true God. So," he glanced at Sarah, "maybe this is what it means to be the son of God. To be the humanity, the flesh of God himself. Maybe this is God's way of showing us who he is. His way of showing us that he…," he paused and then breathed out the word as if a prayer, "…God…by his very nature, is everything Jesus is. Kind, loving, forgiving."

The room grew still until the only sound was the crackling of the fire in the hearth.

After a few moments, John said, "Think about it. Maybe Jesus has shown us that God isn't up there somewhere judging us and condemning us. Instead, he showed us that God knows what it's like to be us." He grabbed his brother by the arm. "Can you imagine? God. The almighty, the all powerful God, knows what it's like to be us. To be tired, to be hungry. To go through all our struggles. And he doesn't only know. He cares."

He gazed at the door between them and the outside world. "If Jesus is the embodiment of God, then love isn't just God's power. It's his nature. His essence. His being. God is love itself."

Chapter 48

"You know, I'm still not convinced about the whole God thing," Simon said, as he sat with Sarah amid the budding irises and daisies of the courtyard. "I admit, something remarkable is going on, and I still can't understand how he could be alive. I know he's Messiah, but he can't be God. It's heresy to even think something like that. There's only one God, and he is not a man."

"I understand," she said. "I'm not going to try to prove it to you."

They sat together in silence for a few moments and absorbed the beauty of spring. The sunlight clear and warm. The birds calling out in celebration of new life. The blossoms sending forth gentle, sweet scents. Even the mud had the fragrance of hope.

"Don't you think it's time to go home?" Sarah said.

James descended the steps to join them. "Home? We can't go home."

"Why not?" she said. "Jesus told us to go tell the people in Galilee. And it's safer now. Even the servants say no one's interested in us anymore."

"I'm not worried about safety. What if Jesus comes back?"

"He can 'come back' anywhere, not just here," Sarah said. "Mary saw him at the tomb. Cleopas saw him in Emmaus." She paused a moment, not wanting to say the unthinkable even though it had to be said. "And what if he never comes back? We can't stay here forever."

"She's right," Simon said, standing, his voice strong with resolve. "It's time to head home. I'll tell the others, and we can leave first thing in the morning."

***

Home. The sight filled Sarah's heart with gratitude. They'd received word that everyone was safe in Capernaum, but still, it felt so good to see it for herself.

When she opened the door, Hannah screeched with delight while Abi and Micah ran into her arms, nearly knocking her to the dirt floor. As she regained her balance, the children hurried out to greet their father. She saw her own mother hunched near the hearth, looking older than when they'd left her.

Leilah straightened and took in the sight of her daughter. "You're okay?"

"We're good, Mother."

"I heard about it," she said, as she limped closer for an embrace. "Terrible, terrible. And someone said you were there the whole time?"

Sarah nodded, unwilling to discuss or relive the horror of those hours.

"They say Simon and the others stole his body," Leilah said.

"That's not true. No one stole Jesus' body, Mother. He's alive."

Leilah looked up sharply at her daughter. "He's not alive, Sarah. He's dead. Died a dreadful, horrible death."

"I know," she took her mother's hands in her, "but he's alive. We saw him."

As Simon and his brother walked in with the children, Leilah shot him a worried glance.

"Tell her," Sarah said. "Jesus is alive."

"He's alive," he said. "We saw him ourselves, didn't we, Andrew?"

"We did. Still not sure how he got in and out of the room, but there he was. In fact," he looked around the room, "we thought he might be here waiting for us."

Leilah's face clouded with disbelief and concern. She turned back to the hearth and stooped to stir a pot suspended over the fire. "Well, anyway, I'm glad to have you back."

***

Dawn spread through the night sky with faint hints of crimson. The familiar smell of the sea and vineyards brought Sarah peace as she stood in her courtyard and watched the shadowy image of Simon sailing toward shore after fishing with Andrew, John, James, and some of the others. Maybe life could get back to normal at last.

Yet she never again wanted normal.

She should be happy to be home, but even as she immersed herself anew in her children's lives, busy once again with routine and responsibilities, her existence felt hollow. Every moment of every day, her heart sought something more.

Despite what Jesus had said, he hadn't appeared anywhere in Galilee, at least not that they'd heard. They had all stopped looking with hope at passing strangers. They'd even stopped talking about him. She knew Simon and the others had gone fishing in the middle of the night because, without Jesus to lead them, they didn't know what else to do with themselves.

She walked to the beach to await the boat and noticed another person standing at the shore, a silhouette in the fading night, with a fire burning in the sand at his feet.

"Have you caught any fish?" he called out to the approaching boat.

"Not a single one," Simon said.

"Cast your net to the right side, and you'll find them."

Even though they were several lengths from shore and the light was dim, Sarah recognized the rebellious straightening of her husband's shoulders, irritated that anyone, especially a stranger, would tell him how to fish. Andrew picked up a corner of the net, handed it to him, and said something. Simon shrugged and tossed the net over the side.

Almost immediately, she heard shouts of surprise and delight as the men all shifted to one side and struggled to haul the filled net out of the water.

John grabbed Simon's arm, pulling him upright, and pointed to shore. "It's the Master," he shouted, so loud, Sarah could hear.

Simon looked to the shore and then dove into the sea while the others rowed the boat in, dragging the heavy net along with them.

Joy swept through Sarah as she hurried to the beach, stopping under the low arcing branch of a palm, unsure whether to rush out to greet Jesus herself even though she wanted nothing more. The men drifted the boat onto the sand and jumped out to surround him while Simon splashed through the surf and ran to his side.

Early daylight illuminated Jesus, fish grilling on the fire, a basket of bread nearby. Despite her certainty that this man was Jesus, she struggled with the something that was different about him, even unknowable.

"Bring some of the fish you caught," he said to Simon, and his voice, friendly and familiar, resonated within her heart.

Simon ran to the boat and with one heave pulled the overflowing net onto the beach. As he rushed back with a fistful of fish, he said, "You guys won't believe it. A haul that big and not one hole in the net. Nothing to mend at all."

"Come and eat," Jesus said.

He put Simon's fish on the fire, adding their catch to what he'd provided. Then he sat in the sand, and they all settled in around the crackling flames that warmed the morning sea air. He took bread from the basket, gave it to them, and handed them some of the fish he'd been cooking.

After they ate, he leaned back on one elbow, and said, "Simon, son of Jonah, do you love me more than you love these others?"

Simon stretched his legs out before him and relaxed, letting his tunic dry in the rising sun. "Of course, I do. You know that I love you."

"Feed my lambs," Jesus said.

Sarah gazed out from the early morning shadows, wondering what he meant but grateful he had given Simon a chance to tell him he cares. She knew her husband still spent sleepless nights wrestling with his denial on that dark, terrible night, struggling to accept the forgiveness Jesus had offered, struggling to forgive himself.

Jesus said again, "Simon, son of Jonah, do you love me?"

Simon looked confused. "Yes, Master. I love you."

"Tend my sheep."

The memory of the shepherd on that mountain and the words of the Prophet came back to her. She thought of Jesus telling the crowd, 'I am the good shepherd,' and wondered why he would ask Simon to tend his flock when he could do it himself now that he was back?

Jesus sat straighter, leaning close to her husband. "Simon, son of Jonah, do you truly love me?"

"You know everything," Simon said, becoming agitated, running his hand through his hair with frustration. "You know that I truly love you."

"Feed my sheep."

Jesus stood, and the others scrambled to their feet.

He put his arm around her husband's shoulders, and said, "When you were young, you girded yourself and walked where you wished. But when you are old, you will stretch out your hands, and another will gird you and carry you where you do not wish to go." He focused hard on Simon. "Follow me."

Sarah's breath caught in her throat as she recalled the rest of what Jesus had said on that long ago day, 'and the good shepherd lays down his life for his flock.'

Jesus glanced her way, his gaze uniting with her very heart, giving her the strength to release the branch to which she clung and trust him. When he led the men to the road, she stepped out from the shadows and joined them with no fear, no hesitation, joyful just to be with him.

As they turned away from her house to walk down the road toward town, Sarah noticed her mother on the courtyard bench talking to the children, watching the group. Simon ran from Jesus' side and said something to Leilah. She looked surprised, then leaned forward to better see who was leading them. With a cry, she hurried out of the courtyard to greet Jesus as Simon followed with their children.

The village had awakened. Some they passed clutched their mouths in surprise. Some shouted and pointed at Jesus with joyful recognition and turned from wherever they'd been heading to run to him. Others hurried to share the news with those still at home.

Jesus welcomed each person and led the growing crowd to the mountain on the edge of town. As he climbed to the peak, people continued to stream in from beyond the village and blanketed the hillside, settling in as if he had never been gone at all.

He looked down at the crowd covering the grass and sand beyond, then sat among the eleven men whom he had chosen on that same mountaintop so long ago, and said, "We're heading back to Jerusalem in a few days, where you'll stay to wait for what the Father promises to give you."

Sarah's joy clouded at the thought of returning to the city. So far, no one had come to their house, demanding that Simon turn over Jesus' body. She'd convinced herself that everyone had forgotten about them, that they were safe tucked out of sight in Capernaum. But the Romans must still be looking for the body their guards lost, and the Sanhedrin would no doubt be less than thrilled to see the man they'd executed walking the streets of their city.

"John baptized with water," Jesus said, his words breaking into her thoughts, "but soon you'll be baptized with the Holy Spirit. Go, then, into all the world, and make disciples of all nations, baptizing them in the name of the Father and of the Son and of the Holy Spirit. Teach them to observe all that I have commanded you." He gazed intently at those gathered close around him. "And know that I am with you always. To the consummation of the world."

With that, he stood and led them back down the mountain and into the crowd of people.

Chapter 49

The sweet scent of lilies filled the fields as Jesus walked with the group along the familiar road to Jerusalem. Overhead, birds called out and swooped along the path before them, delighting in the late spring day.

Sarah traveled alongside Salome and Lazarus' sister. The thought of returning to the city didn't thrill her. The crowds in Capernaum hadn't followed them, weary of traveling, wary of the Romans. They had no doubt Jesus was going there to drive out Rome and reestablish the kingdom. Better to let him do it and then join him.

She had suggested to Simon they do the same, but he wouldn't even consider the possibility, and in her heart, she knew she too didn't want to let Jesus go without them.

As they approached the city gates, a feeling of dread passed through her. Then, to her relief, rather than turn into Jerusalem, he headed up into the Mount of Olives. When they neared the place where she'd been on that terrible night of his arrest, she almost couldn't breathe. Memories of abandoned cloaks scattered amid the trees, of angry hate-filled faces choked her, haunted her, but Jesus didn't stop there. He led them farther up to the top of the mount, out of the shadows and into the brilliant light of an open pasture, where he stopped.

"So," James said, gazing back at the city, "is it finally time to restore the kingdom?"

"It's not for you to know the time or the season," Jesus said. "The Father has fixed these by his own authority. But stay in Jerusalem, and you will receive power when the Holy Spirit comes upon you. Then you shall be my witnesses in

Jerusalem, in all Judea and Samaria, and to the very ends of the earth."

As he finished speaking, even as they started to ask him what he meant, he appeared to rise up above the earth. A cloud blew down from the heavens and slid beneath his feet before lifting him high into the sky and out of their sight.

While they were still staring into space, trying to make sense of what they'd just seen, they heard someone speak. "Why are you here, looking into heaven?"

They turned away from the sky to find two men in radiant white robes standing with them, ethereal men, there but not there, gazing not at the clouds but at them.

One of the men said, "Jesus was taken up from you into heaven and is seated at the right hand of the Father. He will come again someday in the same way as you saw him ascend."

Before anyone could respond, both men vanished, leaving behind bewilderment. No one spoke as the group stood still, waiting for Jesus to suddenly step into their midst or walk out from behind a tree. But nothing happened. The soft breeze continued to blow the aroma of lilies into the air, and birds continued to sing and call. Nothing more.

After several minutes, John said, "What was that all about? Where did he go?"

"Maybe into the city," Nathaniel said.

"But the man said he's in heaven," Levi said. "Right? You heard him speak, didn't you?" He looked around at the others. "Did Jesus die? Has he been dead all along, and we were just seeing apparitions of him? Or imagining it all?" His words trailed off.

"We didn't imagine anything," John said. "He was here. Real, solid, alive. He ate with us. He was with us in the city. He was with us in Capernaum. And he was here."

"Then where did he go?" Andrew said. "Is he coming back here? Or is he meeting us in the city?"

Simon stood beside Sarah and gazed up into the clouds as if he might see far enough that he could find Jesus.

"He's not coming back, " Sarah said, with a conviction that surprised even her. "At least, not any time soon."

"How can you know that?" Thomas asked.

"The man said Jesus was seated at the right hand of God, didn't he?" she said. "So, that means his work here is done."

The others looked at her in confusion.

"She's right," John said. "*And on the seventh day he rested.* Every time God sits or rests in the Scriptures, his work is done."

"But that's God," Thomas said. "What's that have to do with Jesus?"

Sarah exchanged glances with John while the others looked again to the skies.

"So that's it?" Andrew said. "He's gone forever?"

"Then why did he come back at all?" Philip said. "It was hard enough to lose him once. Now we have to go through it all again?"

James swept his hand out to the city. "And what about the kingdom? Why would he go without establishing the kingdom?"

"He's not gone," Sarah said.

"You just said he was."

"No," she said, "he's not here, but he's not gone."

Simon looked at his wife with concern.

"Don't you understand?" she said, as the incomprehensible revealed itself to her with clarity, a most profound truth spoken to her very soul. "He came back. He walked with us, he talked with us, he ate with us to show us he isn't dead. He's alive. And to show us he still cares about each one of us." She turned to Lazarus' sister. "You know that, Mary, don't you?" The bewildered woman nodded as Sarah looked back to the others. "He wanted us to know that none of that

333

has changed. But he couldn't stay here with us, bound to a time and a place. Not if he's God."

Taking Mary by both hands, she said, "That's what he meant when he told you not to hold him down. He has to be more to us than a man. He wanted you to understand that the relationship you had with him is a relationship with God. As much as Jesus loves you, that's how much God loves you."

"That's what he just showed us," Sarah said to the others as she walked to the edge of the ridge. "He's not where God is. He is God. He didn't go up because God is up there somewhere in the heavens above, far from us. He went up to show us he has the perspective of God, a perspective not limited by time or space. The highest, farthest perspective. A boundless, eternal perspective."

She gazed down at the city and then to the desert stretching beyond it, fading into the horizon. "Those men said he's at God's right hand," she said, speaking as much to herself as to the those around her. "But God doesn't have a hand. He has a reach. They were telling us that Jesus has that same reach."

Turning back to the others, wanting nothing more that they understand what now seemed so clear to her, she said "Before, when he walked these streets and lived in our homes, he could only reach out to the people he met. But now, he's shown us he can reach out to everyone, everywhere, forever. Because he's God."

John nodded in eager agreement while the others listened with varying degrees of acceptance or at least consideration. Simon alone stared off into the sky in search of an answer that wasn't heresy.

***

The warmth of day turned chill with the setting of the sun as Simon led the group down to the city, finally conceding that Jesus wasn't coming back to the mountaintop anytime soon.

They walked through the streets, past merchants loading their wares into carts amid shuttered shops and stalls. As they made their way to the house at the far end of the side street, no one seemed to recognize them without Jesus.

Simon knocked, and the familiar servant greeted them. With a nod, he directed them through the courtyard to the upper room. As soon as she stepped in, Sarah noticed it no longer felt claustrophobic. The fresh air coming through the open windows seemed to blow away the memory of long days spent closed up in the space, locked away from the world.

She watched her husband pick through a basket of fruit on the sideboard, knowing he didn't really see the apricots and pears, knowing he still wrestled with the impossible possibility that the man he'd come to know so well and love so much could be God.

**

As the week passed in quiet routine, Sarah relaxed, increasingly convinced Rome and Jerusalem had forgotten about Jesus. Even those with her seemed to be adjusting to life without him, accepting that he was not going to walk back into their lives again, that this time he really was gone.

With the sun descending on yet another day, she bent her head along with the other men and women gathered in the upper room as Simon led the small group in prayer, asking God to give them some sense of what to do now that they no longer had Jesus to lead them.

Her husband started every morning and ended every night with the same prayer, and she knew the plea to God stayed heavy on his heart.

The small group spent their time in Jerusalem in lengthy discussions of the law and the Prophets as they awaited some sign of what they were to do, where they were to go. For Sarah, each new understanding of the Word of God shared by

335

one of them opened her to ever-deeper recognition of the ways Jesus had embodied those words. Every passage became more meaningful, more life-giving as she began to see God in the light in which Jesus had presented him – someone who knows her, cares about her, loves her, and forgives her. The same God who knew and cared about Abraham and Jacob knows and cares about her.

While she always believed that God loved his people, she never thought he really cared about her. Not on a personal level. He had bigger concerns. All of creation to tend to. Wars and famines and floods. Even though she prayed to him and told him how to handle every situation in her life, she didn't really think he cared all that much. She'd figured she was just a small, small part of that creation, no more significant than a leaf falling to the ground.

But she isn't insignificant. She isn't hidden. She isn't invisible. He knows her. And he loves her.

She had no doubt Jesus cared about her. But the realization that his love for her was God's love for her left her breathless.

Even when she hadn't wanted him in her house, he loved her. Even when she tried again and again to deny him, he loved her.

Her heart swelled and broke when she recalled her endless denials and his endless patience.

Simon concluded the prayer, and before the others could lift their heads, a breeze blew through the window, extinguishing a candle on the table. Sarah stuck a piece of straw into a burning lantern and leaned between Philip and Nathaniel to relight the wick. As she tossed the straw into the fireplace, she noticed her husband gazing past the newly lit flame to the mat where the Iscariot used to sit, a mat everyone avoided.

Without looking away from the empty place, Simon said, "I've been thinking, Jesus knew Judas would betray him. He knew the words of the Prophets, *Even my bosom friend in whom I trusted, who ate of my bread, has lifted his heel*

336

against me. It is not an enemy who taunts me. That I could bear. It is not an adversary, but you, my companion, my friend." His voice broke, and Sarah knew his heartache was not for Judas' betrayal.

He silently studied the table a moment before continuing. "He knew those words had to be fulfilled, yet still he chose Judas, numbered him among us as one who would take on a part of the work, one who would share with others what he shared with us. One of the Twelve." His shawl slipped off his shoulder as he leaned forward, still deep in thought. "We can't sit here, closed off from the rest of the world forever. That work needs to be done, and Jesus intended for twelve of us to do it, twelve of us to reach every single child of the twelve tribes of Israel. He chose us even as he knew Judas would not be one of those twelve, even as he knew the prophecy, *Let his days be few and another take his place of leadership.*

"So," Simon looked at each of the remaining Eleven, "it seems we need to pick someone to take his place."

"I don't think that's our responsibility," Thomas said. "I mean, if Jesus wanted to replace Judas, he could have chosen the person himself. He never once mentioned it in the days he was with us."

"I've thought about that," Simon said, "and I've decided that he knew we'd eventually realize he intended for us to be twelve, and he left it for us to handle, to get us moving forward without him. That seems to be the most obvious starting place, don't you think? He started by bringing us together, so we need to start by filling the place that needs filled."

"But with who?" James asked.

"Someone who's been with us from the beginning," Simon said. "Someone who has stayed with us through it all."

The men considered the notion and tossed out names of some of the one-hundred or so people scattered throughout

Jerusalem that night, people who fit that description, people who had walked the endless roads with Jesus through desert heat and winter chill, people who had listened and questioned and followed with relentless persistence.

"What about Barsabbas?" Levi said.

"Barsabbas Justus?" Nathaniel said, as others around him nodded their agreement. "Maybe. But what do you think of Matthias?"

"Both good men," Simon said, "and both good choices."

"I can't think of anyone better," James said.

"But how are we supposed to decide between them?" Nathaniel asked. "We didn't choose each other. Jesus chose us. How can we possibly know who Jesus would choose now?"

Simon stood, walked to the window, and peered into the night. Then he looked intently at Sarah before returning to the table.

"I think we need to let him make the decision for us." He turned to Andrew. "Go down in the courtyard and get a stone."

Andrew hurried out the door and reappeared with a small, flat stone.

He handed it to Simon, who scraped a mark on one side with his fishing knife, and said, "This is for Matthias." Then he scratched a different mark on the other side. "This is for Barsabbas."

He looked again for a long moment at Sarah. She nodded in quiet affirmation. Then he gazed up to the ceiling and did something she knew would have been heresy, blasphemy, criminal to him even a day earlier.

He prayed to Jesus.

"Lord, you know the hearts of men. Show us which of these two you choose to take Judas' place in your ministry and apostleship."

With a flip of his hand, he tossed the stone in the air. It spun and landed on the table in the midst of those gathered in the room.

"Matthias," he said.

Chapter 50

The sun shone bright in a cloudless sky on the feast of the spring harvest. Music, singing, and sounds of celebration echoed through the streets. The day always filled Sarah with gratitude and joy. Although they'd spent the entire night in the traditional discussion and reflection on the writings of Moses, still she felt wide awake and ready for the day.

Her heart beat with a gentle calm as she sat in the courtyard on the side street in Jerusalem and watched men and women pass on their way to the Temple, laden with baskets full of their offerings of first-fruits and loaves of bread. Several turned in at the courtyard gate, people she recognized as some of the most faithful followers of Jesus, and she greeted them with warm words of welcome.

Still more came behind them and headed to the upper room. A few moments later, others walked in, greeted her, and walked up the stairs. Soon those on the steps ceased moving forward, the upper room too full to hold another person. And still they entered the gate, packing into the yard around her until the crowd overflowed into the street beyond.

She heard the sound of people shuffling on the steps and looked up to see them sidling aside to make way for Simon. He squeezed past them, took her hand, and led her up to the room.

Every corner was filled. People perched on ledges and trunks and stood and sat on every floorboard. They leaned left and right to make a path as Simon led her to the table where Levi stood and offered her his cushion beside Jesus' mother. Salome beamed at her from across the table, seated with her sons on either side of her.

"We're ready to read from the scroll of Ruth," Simon said.

"Aren't you going to the Temple for that?" Sarah asked.

"Not now. Later. For now, we're just going to celebrate here together with those who have followed Jesus all these years. Being together makes it feel like, in some way, he's still with us, teaching us, praying with us, you know?" He looked through the room at the gathering of men and women, young and old, people who seemed to share a common serenity, a unity of peace.

Sarah knew that same peace, a peace that once would have been unimaginable in a world that demanded her time and attention. But here, apart from that world, her spirit rested, finding its quiet in the memories it held of Jesus. She understood why all these people wanted to begin their celebration of thanksgiving to God by first coming together here.

She thought of Isaiah's words, *To us a son is given. The governing of the world shall be upon his shoulder, and he shall be called Wonderful Counselor, Mighty God, Eternal Father, the Prince of Peace.*

Prince of Peace. If only the world knew such peace.

She gazed at the men and women around her, one-time strangers, each with his own plans and goals, frustrations and worries, now bound together by their relationship with Jesus.

And she realized he had founded his kingdom.

Not a kingdom of tyranny, violence, and war. His kingdom was peace.

Shutters suddenly slammed against the walls as a powerful wind blew in from the calm day and swept through the room. An explosion of brilliant white light flashed from above, bathing every person in illumination.

They all began to proclaim the wonders of God, truths none had known but truths so obvious. Truths of the love God is, of the good God does.

Sarah's heart swelled within her, overflowing with uncontainable joy. Even though Jesus was nowhere to be seen, she'd never felt closer to him. His very essence seemed to surround her and fill her being.

The room emptied as she followed the others down the stairs and out into the world, all still proclaiming the magnificence of God. People from throughout the region packed the streets on their way to celebrate the holy day at the Temple. They stopped, bewildered by the outpouring from the house, of everyday men and women extolling aloud the wonders of God.

"What language are they speaking?" a man near her asked. "They look like Galileans, but I think they're speaking Parthinian."

"No, they're speaking Median," another man said.

"You're both wrong," a third man said. "They're clearly speaking Cretan. Listen to them."

"They're drunk," yet another man said.

"How does that explain what we're hearing?" a woman asked.

"Then you're drunk," he said.

"Don't you hear them?"

"Of course, I hear them. They're filling the street all around me, shouting."

"In what language?" the woman said.

"Mine."

"And you are?"

"Egyptian." The man looked at those praising God in his native tongue and grew still.

Sarah saw realization dawn on him. This disparate, uneducated mob couldn't possibly all know his country's language. And she rejoiced. Their words didn't matter. Their joy spoke to every heart.

Simon walked up beside her and stood near the courtyard gate. She looked out at the mass of people in wonder that, despite the crowds and such exuberant jubilation in the midst of the city, she felt no fear of the Romans or the Sanhedrin. No fear of anything.

"Everyone, listen to me," Simon said, his words rising above the excitement in the streets, stilling the commotion. "These people aren't drunk. What you're hearing fulfills the words of the Prophet. *God declares in the last days I will pour out my Spirit upon all flesh, and they shall prophesy. And it shall be that everyone will be saved who calls on the name of the Lord.* Jesus."

"Yeah, right," a man shouted from somewhere in the crowd. "Look what happened to him. Dead and gone."

"Jesus isn't dead," Simon said.

"What do you mean?" a woman said, as a toddler wrestled to be free of her grip. "Of course, he died. I saw it myself." She turned to those around her. "Hanging there, dead. Worse thing I ever saw."

"You're right," Simon said. "He died. And just like you, we thought when he died he was gone forever, but he isn't dead. He's raised up again. We are all witnesses." He pointed to those in the courtyard and out to the crowd spread before him, including some who had been with Jesus on the mountainside in Capernaum only days earlier.

"Then where is he?" another man said.

"He's here now. Within us. Among us. He received what the Father promised, this Spirit that you see and hear in us. His Spirit, poured out on us. He told us he wouldn't leave us orphans, and he hasn't. He hasn't abandoned us, even though we betrayed him…" his words trailed off.

Throughout the crowd, sobs broke out. People looked down at the ground and up at the sky, anywhere but into the eyes of others who, like them, had done nothing to stop that brutal execution, some who may even have encouraged it.

He turned to Sarah, and she moved closer, praying he could finally, and forever, trust Jesus' mercy. In his tear-filled eyes, she saw a brightening light of conviction before he turned back to the crowd.

"Even though we betrayed him," his voice strengthened, "he forgives us. There is nothing we can do that he doesn't forgive." He glanced again to Sarah. "Nothing."

"But we thought he was the Messiah," a young man said. "We thought he was here to save us."

"He has saved you," Simon said. "He laid down his very life for you. He rose again for you. And he's here now, for you, in this Spirit you see and hear."

"But nothing's changed," the young man said, as the group of friends that surrounded him nodded in agreement. "Life's no different than it was."

"You have to change," Simon said. "Be baptized in his name and die to your old ways, to this corrupt world, this corrupt life, and you will receive his Spirit. Then you can let him guide you in his way, a way that leads to peace, the way of love, of forgiveness, of salvation."

He looked out to the throng, now filling the road to the very heart of the city, and pointed to the young man. "I'm not just talking to him. God's promise of salvation, the salvation Jesus offers, is for all those he calls, those near and those far, far from him. Hear his call. Be open to him. He's calling you."

The crowd swelled toward the gate, everyone shouting their desire to know this Jesus, to embrace his Spirit and live the life he came to give them. A life of joy. A life of love. A life of peace.

Sarah never imagined it would end like this. She took her husband's hand and held it close.

"Amen, Peter," she said. "Amen."

The Disciple's Wife follows the Gospel of Matthew as a general timeline, interspersing other Gospel accounts into the story. Below is a list of Scripture references found in the book, in order of appearance in the book[1]:

Jesus Calls His First Disciples – Matthew 4:18-22
The Rejection of Jesus at Nazareth – Luke 4:16-30
The Call of Philip and Nathaniel – John 1:43-51
Baptism of Jesus – Matthew 3:16-17
The Marriage Feast at Cana – John 2:1-12
Jesus Expels a Demon – Mark 1:21-28
Peter's Mother-in-Law – Mark 1:29-32
Jesus as the Bridegroom – John 1:26-27, 3:30
Crowds Grow and Follow Throughout Galilee – Matthew 4:23-25
The Sermon on the Mount – Matthew 5, 6, 7
Healing of the Leper – Matthew 8:1-4
Jesus Calms a Storm – Matthew 8:23-27; Luke 8:22-25
The Man Possessed in Graveyard – Matthew 8:28-34; Mark 5:1-20
Raising of the Widow's Son – Luke 7:11-17
Healing of the Paralytic – Matthew 9:1-8
Against You Only Have I Sinned, O Lord – Psalm 51:4
Jairus' Daughter, The Hemorrhaging Woman – Matthew 9:18-22; Luke 8:40-56
Jesus Takes Apostles to Preach Elsewhere – Matthew 11:1
The Call of Matthew – Matthew 9:9
Eating with Sinners – Matthew 9:10-13
The Choosing of the Twelve – Matthew 9:36-38, 10:1-42
John Sends Disciples – Matthew 11:1-4; Luke 7:20-27
A Reed in the Wind – Matthew 11:7-17
Prophecy of Isaiah: I the Lord Will Come – Isaiah 35:4-19

---

[1] Scripture passages, characters, and timeline based on The Holy Bible, Douay-Rheims American Edition of 1899, translated from the Vulgate, Public Domain

The Man with the Withered Hand – Matthew 12:9-14
A House Divided – Matthew 12: 22-32; Mark 3:19-34
Mary Seeks Jesus – Matthew 12:45-48
Nicodemus – John 3:1-21
Jesus Sits by the Shore – Matthew 13:1
Sowing Good Seed/Pearl of Great Treasure – Matthew 13:36-51
Wisdom – Proverbs 2:4-6, 3:15-17
The Death of John the Baptist – Matthew 14:1-12
Feeding the 5,000 – Mark 6:30; Matthew 14:13-33, Luke 6:1-13
Jesus Walks on Water – Matthew 14:22-33
Unless You Eat My Body and Drink My Blood – John 6:11-7:9
Festival of Tabernacles – John 7:10-7:36
Teaching in Temple – John 7:37-44
People Go to Their Houses – John 7:53, 8:1
Woman Caught in Adultery – John 8:2-11
Both man and woman caught in adultery must die – Deuteronomy 22:22; Leviticus 20:10
Unclean Hands – Matthew 15:1-20
Martha and Mary – Luke 10:38-42
Jesus Drives Seven Demons from Mary Magdalen – Mark 16:9
Martha and Mary – Luke 10:38-42
Pagan Woman – Matthew 15:21-28, Mark 7:24-30
King's Highway – Numbers 20:17
Deaf and Mute Man – Mark 7:31-37
Jesus Feeds the 4,000 – Matthew 15:29-39
Leaders Demand a Sign – Matthew 16:1-4; Mark 8:11-13
We Have No Bread – Matthew 16:5-12, Mark 8:14-21
You are Peter – Matthew 16:13-20
Get Behind Me, Satan – Matthew 16:21-28; Mark 8:31-9:1
Transfiguration /Man With Son – Matthew 17:1-20, Mark 9:22-27

Who is Greatest in Kingdom – Matthew 18:1-4, 10-22; Mark 9:31-37

Rich Young Man/Eye of Camel – Mark 10:17-31

Prediction of Passion – Luke 18:31-34

Grant Us Seats in Your Kingdom – Matthew 20:21-28; Mark 10:35-45

The Ten Lepers – Luke 17:11-19

Blind Beggar – Luke 18:35-43

Zacchaeus – Luke 19:1-10

The Good Shepherd – Ezekiel 34:11-12, 15-16

To Those Who Have, More will Be Given – Luke 19:11-27

Jesus and Abraham – John 8:31-59

Man Born Blind – John 9:1-31

Raising of Lazarus – John 11:1-44

Jesus Rides Triumphantly into Jerusalem – Matthew 21:1-11; Luke 19:28-47, Mark 11:1-11

Prophecy of Messiah's Entrance into Jerusalem –Zechariah 9:9

Hosanna – Psalm 118:26-28

Den of Thieves – Matthew 21:12-17; Mark 11:15-19

Destruction of temple foretold – Mark 13:1-4

Woman with Alabaster Jar – Luke 7:36-50, John 12:1-11

Fig Tree – Matthew 21:18-20

Prophecy of Den of Thieves/Withered Fruit – Jeremiah 7:11, 20

Confrontation with religious leaders – Matthew 21:23-27

Sadducees Question Resurrection – Matthew 22: 1-14

Great Commandment – Matthew 22:36-40; Mark 12:18-33, John 13:34

Denunciation of the Scribes – Mark 12:38-40

Widow's Mite – Mark 12:41-44

The Upper Room – Matthew 26:17-26; Luke 22:7-13

Foot Washing – John 13:1-11

Last Supper, Prediction of Judas' Betrayal – Matthew 26:26-29, Mark 17:25, Luke 22:14-23, John 13:31-26

Through bread and wine, he makes the impossible possible –
This understanding is not a Scripture passage but a teaching
of St Cyril of Alexandria

New Commandment – John 13:31-35, 15:12-13-17

Peter's Denial Predicted – John 13: 36-38

Two Swords – Luke 22:38

Advocate – John 14:1-31

Singing Hymn (Psalm) – Matthew 26:30

Give Thanks to the Lord – Psalm 118

Love One Another – John 15-16

Gethsemane – Matthew 26:36-46, Mark 14:43-50, Luke
22:39-44

Arrest, Healing of Ear – Matthew 26:47-56, Mark 14:43-51,
Luke 22:47-53, John 18:1-11

Passion and Judgment – Matthew 26:57-27:31, Mark 14:53-
15:20, Luke 22:54-23:25, John 18:28-19:16

Jesus Before Herod – Luke 8-12

What Is Truth? – John 18:33-39

Pilate's Wife – Matthew 27:18

Crucifixion and Death of Jesus – Matthew 27:32-56, Mark
15:21-40, Luke 23:26-49, John 19

Prophecy: Casting Lots – Psalm 22:18

Burial of Jesus – Matthew 27:57-61, Mark 15:42-47, Luke
23:50-55

Death of Judas – Matthew 27:3-6

God Is Love – 1 John 4:16

Resurrection – Matthew 28:1-10, Mark 16:1-11, Luke 24:1-
12, John 20:1-18

Jesus Appears to Disciples – Luke 24:36-49, John 20:19-23

Emmaus – Luke 24:13-35

Jesus Appears to Thomas – John 20:24-28

Accusation Against Disciples – Matthew 28:11-14

Return to Galilee – Matthew 28:10; John 21

Feed My Sheep – John 21: 1-19

Appearance to Many – 1 Corinthians 15:6

Ascension – Matthew 28:16-20; Mark 16:19-20, Luke 24:50-52, Acts of the Apostles 1:6-11

Choosing of Matthias – Acts of the Apostles 1:12-14

Pentecost/The Holy Spirit – Acts of the Apostles 2:1-41

Questions? Thoughts? Feel free to contact me at
thatyoumayproclaim@gmail.com

Made in the USA
Columbia, SC
25 March 2018